I0662645

Que Será Serees

What Will Be, Serees?

CJ Carter

Dedicated to…

Everyone willing to stand in the way of the tanks
wielded by the arrogantly powerful.
You are, always have been, and always will be
the true heroes.

Into the Breach

Secretary General Alberto Mitchell leaned against a wall in the automated communications bay. He stared at the well-defended alien device the Sereesians called "Seetun". The charcoal-gray box, about the size of one of his wife's dachshunds, sat in its custom alcove. No lights. No sound. No indicators. Just two finger-thick cables magnetically attached on one end. According to the Chamber of Ministers, that small piece of technology was a Damoclean sword hovering over Earth's prosperity. He had to believe that…right?

"Excuse me, Mister Secretary,"a female voice said.

"Hmm?"

Miko Chopratama, the tiny and seemingly ageless Minister of Extra-solar affairs, stepped into the room, attracting the attention of one of the automated weapons that framed the Seetun. "I hoped I could talk to you about Project Alcatraz."

"What more is there to be said?" Though the minister looked to be in her 30s, her scolding eyes showed every one of her ninety-two years. The secretary general straightened from his leaning and tugged at the hem of his jacket to remove some bunching. "I think I made a mistake."

Minister Chopratama didn't expect to hear that. This new secretary general might not be quite the waste the past two had been. "Sir?"

"I've been thinking through all the steps we…" Mitchell stopped, closed his eyes, and sighed. "Naveen played me."

"Yes sir. He did. Tereshkov, too, from what I saw."

While Mitchell hated hearing that about his long-time chief of staff, he couldn't deny that there had to be some complicity. "Well, mistake or not, we're committed."

"Yes sir. We are."

"While we wait for confirmation, Javrurhal," Verina said, "I should mention that your aide impressed me earlier."

"How so?" the large hairy alien said to his blue-skinned host.

"He asked, very diplomatically, which pronouns to use when addressing my people. I appreciated his audacity. It's rare to find a willingness to speak up like that from someone so early in their career."

Javrurhal's large, cylindrical body quivered subtly and slowly —one of the Quinkst's forms of expressing appreciation. He remembered when he first dealt with Verina's uni-gendered species. Though just as curious as his aide had been, he simply followed the lead of the then-ambassador, never questioning if it was correct. "Vaiyarhures has a boldness that I also find refreshing. What was your answer?"

"I explained that even on Serees most species have two distinct genders, and our pronoun set for them is essentially the same as yours. I told him that amongst ourselves we have another pronoun category where ey, em, and eir roughly correspond to she, her, and his; or he, him, and her. I did make it clear that we really have no preference and that he should use the standard of the Quinkst."

The alien flattened his one-and-a-half meter tall, matted orange-hair covered, sea cucumber-like body. Adding a respectful crossing of his tri-pincer posterior claws, Javrurhal said, "You've certainly earned your First Negotiator title, my friend. You honor us by teaching when others might scold. Your example will make Vaiyarhures more able as he matures."

Verina bowed slightly, in one of the accepted interplanetary modes. Ey was the youngest First Negotiator in 126 years and was eager to validate the faith eir superiors placed in em. Ey said with eir upper mouth, "I'm the one who is honored by such comments from a Holder of the Red-claw, Javrurhal. Thank you."

Javrurhal again flattened and crossed his claws. Like many Quinkst, he liked the Serees—their label for the Ligrosian species to which Verina belonged. Although they felt bipedal tetrapod bodies were aesthetically inelegant, the success of both the Serees and the Humans spoke to the soundness of the design. They especially liked their turquoise skin, which varied individually from a sea-green to a sky blue. The red "fringe"—running from the top of their heads, down their backs, and tracing down the dorsal line of their limbs—was considered to be a particularly attractive attribute.

The melody of the Serees languages only added to their appeal for the Quinkst. Verina's people had three specialized mouths which gave them the ability to voice the largest catalog of sounds of any known species. They could, and sometimes did, speak in three different languages at once—often sounding something like an *a cappella* trio or a music-backed duet. This evolutionary quirk made them masters of multiplexed communication and contributed to their unquestioned skill with negotiations and diplomacy. It gave them an advantage with all the other species, whose languages were less complex.

Verina was equally as appreciative of the Quinkst. Though bulky at two-and-a-half meters long, they moved with a quiet elegance as the cilia on their underside allowed them to glide as if on a frictionless table. Ey even appreciated their natural aroma—which most found disturbingly similar to decaying flesh. As one of the oldest known species, they were secure in their place in the universe. Verina considered them to be good company.

The Infolux on the table beeped. Verina glanced at it and said, "The contract has been received in full by both our governments." Verina powered down eir Infolux and said, "Javrurhal, I believe that covers everything."

"That pleases me."

"And me. I can't remember having such a smooth negotiation."

"You owe much of that to yourselves. The Serees have always treated us fairly. You've earned your reputation. Though your price is high and your license strict, you never allow the spirit of the matter to be violated due to unexpected technicalities."

"That was an amazing compliment, Javrurhal of the Quinkst," Verina said, reverting to the official form of diplomatic address. "On behalf of my government and my people, I thank you very much."

"More personally, Verina, First Negotiator, I am hoping I can share something with you that I have told your maetor, though in more detail with her than I will with you."

"I give my word it will not leave this room."

"No. No, I can't accept that. You may need more…freedom than that. All I ask is that you don't implicate your source."

"Of course not."

"My government has noted that the Earth people have moved parts of their military fleet in what could become a threatening posture against Serees."

"Why?"

"There is a rumor that your government will enact the Seetun bandwidth limitation clause all of your licensees agree to. Your maetor did not confirm that for me. It's much too early for my government to say with accuracy where all of this is headed. We fear that the signs don't bode well for Serees. I'm not warning you about anything specific; however, I suggest you pay attention to the signs around you. A person of your status will come into information that the general public won't."

Verina paused for a moment, trying to absorb this very disturbing information. The Quinkst were cautious by nature and tended not to share their worries. Perhaps, with Quinkst being less than eight days away from Serees, they felt a greater urgency. "I still don't understand. We aren't a threat."

"Have you negotiated with Earth?"

"Not personally."

Javrurhal's pincers slowly tapped anxiously. "I have. While the reasons are undoubtedly intricate, I believe it comes down to this: they fundamentally fear what they cannot control. Serees is the only source of a device that provides faster-than-light communication. They don't trust you."

"But we gave up space flight to reassure the other species. We are mutually dependent."

"That happened long before Earth became interesting or had influence. They don't yet respect the history the various civilizations have shared."

Verina understood what eir Quinkst friend was saying. This situation had happened before with tragic results. "Thank you, Javrurhal. I suspect you've just done me a great favor. I hope, one day, I'll have the opportunity to pay you back in kind."

"I accept your offer, but I expect no payback. That is not necessary among friends."

Verina stood and casually bowed eir head, "No, it isn't." Ey moved toward the door but paused. "Since we have finished a few days sooner than scheduled, is there anything I can do or arrange for you to make the rest of your time here more pleasant?"

The Ambassador glided silently toward the door, following Verina. "That's very kind, but I've been away from Quinkst for nearly a year on various business. I'm eager to return home. Hopefully, my surviving children will recognize me."

"How many do you have now?"

"Twenty-four that are from my previous broods, and three from the most recent. The youngest are almost two years old, now."

"Twenty-seven? That's amazing."

"That would be thirty-three in your system—you shouldn't have to do the conversion now that negotiations are over."

Verina smiled. "I appreciate that. But thirty-three is…I can't even imagine having that many. We average about one each." Verina was now at the door. "Since I treasure my own family, I won't be the cause of any further delays keeping you from yours. Javrurhal, Holder of the Red-claw, thank you for your visit. I wish you a safe journey and happy return to your home."

The large hairy alien paused, saying, "Verina, First Negotiator of the Serees, I am happy to have worked with you again and look forward to our next meeting. Be well."

Javrurhal slid out into the empty corridor, leaving Verina to worry about the Ambassador's warning. Ey walked back to eir seat and sat on eir heels, resting eir knees on the chair's padded panel. The small, empty room now seemed to engulf em. The specter of an Earth invasion was something ey never considered. After several minutes, Verina roused emself from eir unproductive brooding by remembering one of the proverbs ey learned in school: "Action solves problems, worry does not."

Verina pulled a telestick from eir jacket and said, "Akehru."

Several seconds passed without an answer. "Leave message," Verina said. "Aki, I'm leaving work in a few minutes. Let me know if you want me to pick up something for dinner. See you at home."

Verina tucked the telestick back into its pocket, grabbed eir Infolux, and headed for eir office two floors up. After getting off the elevator and making it halfway down the corridor, ey heard, "Excuse me, First Negotiator." Verina turned to see a young Ligrosian dressed in the brown hues favored by the intelligence division, who said, "You need to come with me, please." Verina's heart beat faster. Could they know what Javrurhal told em? The room was supposed to be secure.

As Verina followed, ey noticed how immaculately-kempt eir escort was. The jacket was smartly tailored and eir pareu—the wrap-around, ankle-length skirt worn by most on Serees—betrayed no wrinkles. Verina was happy the negotiator office didn't require that degree of discipline. After several minutes going farther into the bowels of the building than Verina's security level permitted, the young aide prompted the First Negotiator to enter an office. Verina stepped across the threshold, not expecting to recognize the person behind the desk: "Nancimare."

"Verina. I'm happy you got here so quickly. Sit."

Verina noticed that eir nervousness had evaporated. Though ey had only met Nancimare on a couple of occasions incidental to work, Verina enjoyed eir company. If not for the restrictions their high-responsibility jobs imposed, Verina might have considered a more intimately personal relationship.

Nancimare's office featured the same academic disarray as the apartment Verina's pame, or birth parent, lived in. Reports overflowed their allotted storage units and were laid very orderly all around the floor. Nancimare sat behind eir plain government-issue desk while Verina sat in the only one of the three chairs not covered with stacks of material. The intelligence official reached into the keyboard box under eir desk; the office door automatically closed, leaving the aide outside. With another short, typed sequence the locks engaged. Nancimare said, "OK. We are now isolated. I'm advising the maetor, and I need your opinion. This is off the record. I don't want to draw attention to you at this point, since we're…not exactly friends, but certainly friendly. What you and I say here is between us."

"OK."

"From your download, it appears you've just finished negotiations with the Quinkst. So, it's correct to assume you're up-to-date on the standard license, right?"

Verina nodded.

"I need to know: is there any option, no matter how technical or not-quite-in-the-spirit of the contract, that could be used to either sever a licensee's bandwidth or, alternatively, circumvent the mandatory restrictions and sanctions that are in place which would otherwise force us to enact them?"

Verina considered mentioning eir concerns about Earth, but dismissed it because Nancimare might infer that the information came from Javrurhal. "No," Verina said. "Not only are the requirements clear, but there are also cross-requirements with other planets. Our contracts force us to be morally scrupulous. The entanglements are there to assure our licensees. It's a safeguard we put in place for our own security. If we ever allow the more belligerent worlds to question our integrity, then we're nothing more than a target." Pointedly, ey added, "We honor our contracts."

Nancimare sat straighter in eir chair. "That is at the heart of it, isn't it? The mantra."

"It has to be."

"What about Seetun? What if there's a breach?"

That's what this is about, Verina thought. "We are very clear that if any attempt is made to learn the secrets of the Seetun device, we will be immediately informed of the attempt before the self-destruction of the box internals. Restrictions and sanctions automatically come into force based upon the circumstances of the security breach—whether it was by accident or design. The contracts unambiguously list the conditions and our responses. There hasn't been a violation in one hundred twenty-seven years."

Nancimare considered Verina's words, absently bending eir fingers to eir forepalm and then to eir backpalm. After a minute, Verina commented, "I do that, too."

Nancimare followed Verina's gaze to eir hands. "Oh. Bad habit." After another few moments, ey said, "I'm not going to say that this information isn't a little disappointing, but it's what I expected. Thank you for your time."

As Nancimare keyed in a code to unlock the room, Verina asked, "That's it?"

"That's it."

Verina felt there was more to say but wasn't sure what. "See you sometime?"

A flash of sorrow quickly crossed Nancimare's face before it was masked by socially polite pleasantness. "Probably. Czep-tan isn't that big of a city."

Verina nodded and said, "Yeah, I guess not."

After Verina stepped out of the room, the door closed automatically behind em. As the young aide escorted the First Negotiator from the high-security area, Verina couldn't help thinking about what ey'd learned. Did Earth try to uncover the secrets of their faster-than-light communications device? That would be bad. Bad for Earth and—if Earth treated Serees like it did Lrat—bad for Serees. Very bad.

2

Crashdown

Verina's skin glistened with oily perspiration. Ey started learning the martial art of jujibtanibarre three years before to relieve stress and to stay in good shape. The discipline was difficult, having grown from an ancient rite of passage. The modern version consisted of complex routines whose quick, dance-like movements allowed the practitioner to evade projectiles being shot at them. In the first months of training, the projectiles were soft balls made of a natural rubber. Once second-degree skill was reached, the balls were upgraded to composite darts with sharpened four-bladed tips. It was from this point onward that injuries were inevitable. Fatalities weren't common, but neither were they rare. Verina's body earned its share of fine scars over the years—a result of testing emself and not quite measuring up to that standard.

The best practitioners of jujibtanibarre could dodge one hundred fifty shots a minute for twenty-four minutes. For someone with only three years experience, Verina was doing well in eir current session. Eir precise movements ensured that the darts fired at em missed their target. In an extended round, ey lasted seven minutes before fatigue, and eir mind wandering back to the Earth problem, let a projectile leave a hair-thin line of blood over Verina's lowest rib. "Enough!" ey shouted to the automated system before falling to the ground, gasping for air. Jujibtanibarre practice was not the time to lose focus; the blood now on eir fingers from touching the fresh cut made that clear.

After a quick shower, Verina felt better—even Javrurhal's week-old warning couldn't break eir good mood. As ey walked through the central plaza on this warm, sunny afternoon, ey thought about worlds such as Quinkst which endured extremes of weather. Javrurhal described seasonal extremes ranging from frigid to withering in addition to the always blowing high winds. Verina much preferred the constancy of Serees. One single continent ringing the equator of a planet with negligible tilt in relation to its star. The temperature was even. While it rained often, it wasn't excessive. The end result was a lush landscape almost everywhere except for the newly forming land in the Divergent Zone.

The Ligrosian negotiator wended eir way through the bustling plaza that beckoned the majority of businesses and vendors of the city to set up shop. Busy marketways divided the boulevards which, in turn, divided the area into sections of storefronts. The open-air vendors created an exciting air of chaos that added vibrancy to a metropolis that could, at times, seem a bit staid in comparison to Serees' other major and tier cities.

Verina headed straight to an unadorned, long-established food market set at one of the angled corners in the middle of the plaza. Its interior was almost entirely white. Four long, white counters were each manned by an attendant dressed in a white jacket and ankle-length pareu. Two customers at the counters, and the two customers waiting in an alcove near the display window, were dressed in much more vibrant colors. A slightly heavy but muscular, white-clad attendant called, "Verina! Hi!"

Verina smiled. This was one of the reasons ey liked this store. "Hi, Elekin."

Elekin touched some controls at eir station. "You didn't call in your order?"

Leaning in so only Elekin could hear clearly, Verina said, "You know I like to go in the back."

Elekin's lower, membrane-covered mouth clicked a quiet worry as ey said single-voiced, "You know Vintiny doesn't like that."

"Is Vintiny here?"

"That's beside the point."

"You know, the sooner you let me back there, the sooner your fringe will be free of me," Verina said—all three mouths smiling and with a twinkle in eir eyes. Elekin returned the smiles, stepped back, and allowed Verina to lead the way into the back room.

An explosion of colors and smells inundated Verina's senses. The storage and processing room contrasted so much from the clean anteroom of the store that it seemed like a different world. Immediately ey savored an aroma from the hundreds wafting about. "Oh my word. Is that fresh yanekt-a-toush?"

Verina rushed to a phalanx of barrels filled with soft yellow bricks. Ey waved eir hand over the barrel, guiding the odor to eir face, and basked in the aroma. "Three years. I haven't had any yanekt-a-toush in three years."

"You want a taste?"

Verina's pupils widened. Elekin nodded to the supplier to cut off a sample. Verina put it in eir middle mouth and paused to savor. Ey cooed from eir bottom maw as ey said with eir top, "I could cry, that's so good."

"I can see that, you're starting to redden," Elekin said, pointing to the involuntary, color-shifting patches around eir friend's eyes. Verina looked away. Elekin continued, "Can I box some up for you?"

Verina looked at the price. "Oh, I wish. But I can't."

"But you're a First Negotiator!"

"And I have to look and act the part. I've got less money now than before the promotion."

"I can get you a discount," Elekin pressed. "Come on, you don't hardly go out any more. You need to enjoy life. Remember the *Ip Et-ris*? 'The burdens of the day can best be managed when the spirit is light.'"

"I know. I can't." Verina's eyes showed that ey dearly wanted to. "What kind of fish do you have?"

Elekin led Verina halfway across the storeroom to the trays of just-arrived seafood. "There you go. Whatever you want."

Jokingly, Verina said, "Shmuptl?"

Elekin double grinned and quietly said "I've got some stored away…"

With an air of suspense, Elekin casually led Verina over to a hidden collection of trays. Certain there were no prying eyes, Elekin uncovered a quintet of torso-sized animals, roughly fish-shaped, but with a body made up of a jellyfish-like gelatin. The clear skin allowed Verina to see that they were *extremely* fresh. Ey said, "Where…how did you get living Shmuptl?"

Elekin quickly shushed em and said, "Quiet. Vintiny would kill me if ey knew I had these and wasn't offering them for sale."

"But how…?"

"Every now and then a good friend of mine—"

"Haipuxan?" Verina interrupted.

"Of course. She gives me some when she has some extra from the harvest."

Verina couldn't quite hide eir wanton awe. "That's some friend. But if I'm not getting any yanekt-a-toush, you *know* I'm not getting live shmuptl. Besides, Aki and I are going out of town in the morning. There just isn't time."

Elekin looked disappointed. "But next time?"

"Maybe."

Covering up the shmuptl, Elekin said, "Yeah, maybe. What else do you need?"

After twenty minutes Verina and Elekin were back at the front of the store. With everything now paid for, Elekin handed Verina back eir public access crystal. The wrapped groceries rested on a push-plate—a levitating platter with a small control box gripping the edge. "When are you going to come out and join your friends?" Elekin asked. "Let everyone know you're still alive?"

Verina had to admire Elekin's tenacity. Ey was a good friend. Over a year ago they'd spent a couple of evenings getting to know each other better. They knew the difference in their positions and work schedules barred anything long-term. All they'd ever have was friendship. "Maybe when I get back." With a smile ey added, "I'd like to remember what life was like before work got crazy."

Elekin put one last item on the pile sitting on the push-plate. Verina asked, "What's that?"

"A little yanekt-a-toush." Before Verina could object, Elekin added, "Just a gift to a…to a good customer."

Ordinarily, Verina would refuse the present even though ey craved it. People often offered em gifts. Verina knew it was because ey was widely considered to be attractive—even by many alien species. Ey didn't see it emself. Still, ey constantly dealt with the consequences and expectations of accepting gifts. With Elekin it was different; didn't friendship change the rules? "Thanks," Verina said, adding a three-note tone indicating sincerity. "I'll make sure I hide it from my sib when I get home."

"I know you'll enjoy it," Elekin said with a slight lowest mouth hum indicating eir own pleasure with the giving.

Verina touched eir access crystal on the port of the push-plate and pressed the green button for homing. The laden disk now floated behind em as ey left the store for eir apartment. Elekin shouted out, "Enjoy your trip."

The next morning, a Basic transport sped through the rain, down the coastal transway from Czep-tan. The thick shelf of clouds muted the beauty of both Consetru, the northern ocean to the right, and the undulating wilderness to the left. It matched Verina's own gray mood. Akehru instead sat back and drank in everything: ocean, woods, and even the rain. When the sun finally appeared, Akehru said, "The rain's stopping. Maybe we can go swimming as soon as we get there."

"Maybe," Verina said with enough fake enthusiasm to placate eir sib.

The high status of both Verina and eir pame—Verina and Akehru's birth parent, Ceyelna—gave the family liberal use of any of several holaxex when they were available. A few days following her negotiations with the Quinkst, Verina reserved one of these getaway homes as a personal reward.

When the transport cleared the last thicket of woods, a familiar red house popped into view amid a botanical island of dagger-leaves and flowers. The two-level house was small but colorfully stood out from the yellows, blues, and greens of the surrounding meadowland. Akehru, a pair of grins on eir face, looked over to Verina. "Hey, you."

"Hmm?"

"Look at all of this. Smile. Just one. Just a little one."

Verina could never resist eir sibling's prodding and surrendered a smile. Akehru said, "That's better. No more glum face for the rest of the time we're out here, understand? We're going to have fun."

"Okay," Verina said without enough enthusiasm.

"We're. Going. To. Have. Fun. Even if it kills you. We never spend time together."

"We live together, Aki."

"I mean going out and having fun together. The last six vacations, it's been all three of us. Don't get me wrong, I love Pame as much as you do, but sometimes I just want to have fun with my little sib. So, you're going to have fun."

Verina's defenses finally lowered. Ever since their sire left when Verina was a child, Akehru had been big sib, best friend, confidant, and second parent all rolled into one. Ey adored em. So, with two very big grins on eir face, Verina said, "Do you want to unload the transport first or go swimming?"

Akehru good-naturedly punched eir sibling in the ribs. "Phoog."

The vehicle pulled up to the front door of the holaxex. The transport's wind cover retracted and Akehru immediately jumped from eir seat and stripped off eir jacket and pareu. Verina headed, instead, for the transport's cargo platform. Akehru yelled, "What are you doing?"

"I have to let Xadow out."

Following a quick flick of the carrier door's lock, Verina's two-legged, blue-gray ball of fur burst for freedom. Looking something like a flat-faced walking tail: thick and oval at the front, tapering to a near-point at the rear; Verina's pet haiwa was a loving companion—except when there was a new space to explore. Xadow didn't even pause to let Verina stroke his fur—not when there was important haiwa work to be done. Akehru said, "Okay. He's out. Will you come on?!"

Verina's wrap-around skirt and jacket joined eir sibling's. Ey then followed Akeru as they both sprinted across the water-smoothed decline of sandy regolith toward the warm tropical waters of Consetru. Though the Ligrosian species evolved for life on land, their evolutionary ancestors came from the oceans blanketing eighty percent of the planet. They never lost their love of the sea and still retained many of the adaptations of their predecessors: the semi-permeable, capillary-rich membrane of the lower mouth that allowed them to breathe, the useful sonar ability, the omni-flexible joints that aided swimming, the shades of turquoise skin which were effective aquatic camouflage, and the oily sweat that shed heat in air but was a slippery protective film in the water. "Aki, wait," Verina called.

"What?"

"I've got to catch my breath."

Verina stopped and breathed heavily as Akehru jogged back. Akehru said, "You're kidding me, right?"

"Was the beach always this wide?"

"You've got to get out from behind that desk more."

"I know. I thought jujibtanibarre would help."

"Running would help. And now that you mentioned it…are you sure being a target in a gym is such a good idea?"

Verina straightened. "Now don't you start."

Akehru looked contrite. "Sorry. It's just that Pame said…"

Verina interrupted, "…Pame said that jujibtanibarre isn't a sport that—" Verina's eyes locked onto something in the sky. "Look!" Verina said while pointing at a shining point in the western sky a few fingers up from the horizon. "Do you see that?"

A smoke or water vapor trail traced the object's route. Xadow bounded up to the pair, making a sound somewhere between a siren and a seal's bark. Akehru said, "I think it's getting bigger."

Tens of seconds passed as the meteor, or whatever it was, grew brighter and larger. The two siblings realized they were standing on the bull's-eye. Without consciously exchanging any signal, both Ligrosians dashed for the ocean. Seconds before impact, the object veered down and inland. A blinding light flashed the moment the object slammed into Serees, forcing Akehru and Verina to shield their eyes even though the light was behind them. Except for some morops taking to the air, and the cresting waves, there was no sound—not yet.

Verina and Akehru jumped into the body of an eight-meter wave that had crested not far from shore. A fraction of a second later, they found themselves tossed about as the wave's momentum changed unnaturally. They were disoriented by dizzying currents, swirls of bubbles, and warming water. A very low rumble filled the turbulence with the unmistakable tone of a close call.

As the undercurrents subsided, both Akehru and Verina sonared locating calls to each other. Upon hearing the hoped for replies, they surfaced and reunited a hundred fifty meters from shore. Akehru said, "You OK?"

"Yeah."

"It's lucky we were on the beach. That shock wave could have killed us."

Their eyes met, triggering a mutual spasm of fear-releasing laughter. Every time they thought they were regaining control, they again looked at each other and a new round of laughter began. Finally, looking back to the beach, Verina said, "It doesn't look like the holaxex is too damaged."

"Yeah. Just a little bit of the roof, I think."

"Why didn't the explosion flatten the house? I thought we were dead for sure."

Akehru scanned the landscape and said, "Look over there, in the direction of the smoke. See where the woods break? It's off to the side of the holaxex. It might have shaped the blast wave— saving the house but putting us in its path. And look: Xadow didn't even get thrown into the water."

The pair swam quickly back to shore. Walking out of the ocean, Verina said, "It doesn't look like the whatever-it-was landed too far away."

"What are you suggesting?"

"You know what I'm suggesting. We have to help. It's the law."

Akehru's scientific detachment melted into self-preserving reticence, "I know, I know."

Verina and Akehru discovered that the blast wave threw the transport into the holaxex. Though the vehicle still worked, the storage bay had burst open causing the siblings' belongings to be blown about over hundreds of meters. They grabbed the nearest jackets and pareus to put on, ignoring the rest for now. "Xadow! Come here!" Verina commanded.

While Akehru double-checked the status of the transport, Xadow returned to Verina's side, seeking comfort by pressing against his owner's leg. Ey picked him up and loaded him back into the carrier, which was still firmly attached to it's platform. "We should lock him in the house," Akehru said.

Verina motioned no. "We might need him. He's smaller than we are."

Since it really didn't matter, Akehru let it drop. Once Verina secured emself in eir seat, they set off and quickly covered the kilometer to the crash terminus. The path from there wasn't difficult to follow as singed and fallen trees clearly marked a direct route. Akehru said, "It wasn't a meteor. There isn't enough damage."

"You're kidding."

"No. It looks more like an explosion, but definitely bigger than I've seen before."

When they reached the impact site, the space vehicle in front of them immediately provided the answer. The modestly-sized ship hadn't landed so much as crashed—but it had been a controlled crash. Although its nose disappeared into the newly-formed crater, there was little obvious external damage from the collision itself.

The tangled remains of what looked like the engine's destruction hinted at why the ship arrived on Serees with little control. That wasn't Verina and Akehru's concern. Their responsibility was to find any survivors and give whatever aid and assistance they could.

"What do you think?" Akehru asked.

"It's an Earth ship. I can tell from the writing on the hull." Ey followed the text with eir finger and read each word, struggling with the translation. "Diplomatic. Ministry. Of. Earth."

"That can't be good."

"It doesn't matter," Verina said. "We need to get inside."

The two Ligrosians surveyed the outside of the ship, which the surrounding debris and still-burning roots made difficult. They stopped near the nose on the starboard side and stared at the secured hatch. Akehru said, "Any suggestions?"

"Why are you asking me? You're the engineer."

"Of Serees technology, little sib. I don't know much about what these aliens use. You've at least seen them before. Right?"

That much was true. Five years ago, Verina *had* seen some Humans from a distance. Ey wasn't directly involved with them, so how could that help? Ey quickly rummaged through eir memories and decided that ey didn't have an answer. Feeling foolish just standing there, ey figured that, like in a negotiation, it was better to act like you knew what to do when no one else was any wiser. Ey walked up to the hatch and pounded on the door. In the smattering of Human-speak ey knew, ey said, "To be emergency. Open. We to be help."

Nothing.

Akehru said, "You know, I don't know their language at all, but even I could guess that was pretty bad."

"They have seventy primary languages."

"You're kidding."

"All of them are used in diplomatic documents. I know that they do have some preferences, but I don't know any of them well. Not that it probably matters. The controls, whatever they are, might not be voice-responsive."

"I don't know anything else we could try. There was talk that some Earth ships are artificially sentient. If this is a government ship…"

"It's alive?"

"I don't know. It probably thinks it is; if those types of ships exist and this happens to be one of them."

Verina glared at eir sibling. "This isn't helping."

"Hey, I don't know, Verni. I'm trying."

Verina cooed a mild apologetic tone and then stepped up to the hatch. "Please. Me to offer you harm, negate. Me to offer you help. Open door."

The very feminine voice of Ship said, in Haipo, the formal spoken Ligrosian language, "Please stand away from the hatch."

Verina and Akehru startled and moved several steps away from the ship—many more than necessary. Small clicks emanated from the mechanical seals as they released. The hatch moved inward several centimeters before hinging up and positioning itself horizontally, stopping at the top of the hatchway. Akehru turned to Verina, "Wait. I understood that."

Verina nodded, "Yeah."

The pair slowly approached the ship again. When nothing unexpected happened, Verina called out, also in Haipo, "May we enter?"

Ship answered, "Yes."

Verina stepped inside and immediately gave a surprised, "Ack!" combined with a reflexive low-volume warning tone.

"What's wrong?!" Akehru double-voiced.

"Nothing," Verina said, sheepishly. "I lost my balance. Be careful. There's artificial gravity here, but the ship's tilted from level, so it's a change once you board."

Thankful that it didn't seem to be anything dangerous, Akehru took a calming breath and stepped through the doorway. "Whoa!"

"See?"

The airlock opened into the middle of the starboard passageway. With the aft door of the corridor closed and the front open, it was clear where to go first. Verina led the way into the cockpit.

Consoles and displays dominated the room. The arc of controls in the middle of the space obviously represented the primary control station. A human body lay in view at the front of this main console, halfway between it and the forward displays. Verina rushed to him. The pool of what appeared to be blood nauseated em, but now was not the time for distraction, so ey ignored it. "It's breathing."

Akehru clasped eir hands and bowed eir head. "Bailera is merciful."

Verina said, "Computer, are there any other survivors?"

Ship answered, "Internal sensors not functioning."

"Sprag," Verina said quietly.

"There's no need for that kind of language," Ship chided.

"My apologies," Verina said, seeing Akehru trying hard not to laugh. "How many passengers, including this Human, are on board?"

"Four."

"May we have access to the others?"

Non-directional sounds echoed through the hull. The Ligrosians couldn't tell if the computer was opening hatches or closing them but assumed it was probably some combination of the two. The sounds stopped and the hatch at the opposite end of the passageway opened. Akehru said, "I guess it's my turn."

"Be careful."

Akehru quickly disappeared into the core of the ship, much of eir initial fear having calmed. Verina turned eir attention back to the alien. "Computer, can you diagnose this Human's injuries?"

"Internal sensors not functioning."

Verina's frustration grew. Ey didn't know anything practical about Humans. Ey could easily kill him with ignorance. Wait…"Computer, can you give me a list of chemical compounds suitable to use as medicine for this species?"

"Specify, please."

"Painkillers, antiseptics, strengtheners or correctives for organ injuries, replacement fluids, and anything else in your database that could be useful. Understand that I am not trained in medicine."

"Understood. Downloading now."

An Infolux on the floor and off to the side lit up. *Did everyone use these?* Verina thought. The Ligrosian retrieved it, relieved that the information was being downloaded in Lipo, the primary common language that Verina had been speaking since entering the ship. Verina said, "Computer, is there a portable translation device this Human and I can use if it awakens and you are not available?"

"I will download appropriate translation matrices to the same Infolux as the medical information. A portable translator is also available in—"

"Verni, get up here!!!" triple-voiced Akehru.

Verina dashed down the passage, through the hatch, and up the half-flight of stairs to a sectioned-off open area containing the unmistakable odor of recent death. Off to the side lay a Human, somewhat longer than the first, its neck bent at a very awkward angle. "Aki?"

"In here."

Verina moved quickly to the rear section of the space, finding eir sibling standing outside what seemed to be an open conference room. "Watch out for the vomit," Akehru said.

Verina side-stepped the moist patch on the deck and peered inside the room through the transparent airlock. Two reddish dead aliens stood behind a table that was still anchored to the deck. The beings were impaled to the wall by a large display screen that had broken loose from its moorings on the opposite side of the room. Below the table, two large chunky puddles of slowly congealing red ooze emanated from each of the bodies. "Verni?"

Verina said, "They are," eir lowest mouth trilled C one octave above middle C, the true pronunciation of the Antyerian species' name. "I always thought they looked like giant blood-blisters with legs. By the looks of things, I wasn't too far off the mark."

"I've got to get out of here," Akehru said, rushing away from the gory display.

Verina followed. Finding Akehru bent over, ey stroked eir sibling's back. "You alright?"

Akehru turned eir face to Verina. Ey wasn't alright. If anything, shock was starting to set in. Verina said, "Aki, we have one survivor. We have to…Aki! Stay with me. We have one survivor. We need to take it back to the house."

Wanting not to be weaker than eir younger sibling, Akehru said, "I can do that."

"Okay. Don't scare me like that. I depend on you."

The pair returned to the cockpit. Verina said, "Computer, please repeat and complete what you were saying before I was called away."

Ship replied, "I will download appropriate translation matrices to the same Infolux as the medical information. A portable translator is also available in the primary first-aid kit located beside the hatch to the aft cargo bay."

"What does this first-aid kit look like?" Verina asked.

"It is a transportable box. Using standard units, it measures approximately one hundred dis, by—"

"Computer," Verina interrupted. "Please convert from do'octal to octal." Turning to Akehru, ey added, "Better it do the conversion than me."

"Using Serees numbering, the box measures approximately one-hundred-forty-four dis by two-hundred-twenty-six dis by one-hundred-forty-four dis. The base color is white. It is marked with three red symbols: a crescent, an equilateral cross, and a solid circle."

With the thirty-by-forty-five-by-thirty centimeter box being small enough to carry, Verina resolved to take it with them. But first, "Aki, help me get this… Computer, what is the gender of this Human?"

"He is male."

Verina continued, "Okay. Aki, help me get him onto the transport. You get its…his legs."

Akehru lifted Li's legs at the knee while Verina picked the man up from under his arms—which wouldn't have been a bad idea except for his shoulder injury. The man moaned loudly and contracted into himself.

With surprise replacing some of Akehru's shock, ey said, "I don't think you should do that."

"He must have injuries there. I can't see how I can pick him up anyplace else."

Using eir engineering mind, Akehru said, "Drag him?"

Verina smiled; Aki was back. "Go ahead. He's not that heavy."

Akehru dragged the Human to the hatch feet first. He moaned slightly, but there was less obvious discomfort than the lifting attempt had caused. At the hatch, Akehru jumped out and fell to the ground, forgetting about the difference in gravitational orientations between planet and ship. "Ow!"

"You OK?"

"Yeah," Akehru said sheepishly; though it was a small enough price to pay to be out of that alien ship.

Akehru positioned the transport next to the hatch. After ey repositioned Xadow's carrier, it was a simple matter to roll the Human onto the cargo platform. While Akehru secured him for the trip, Verina re-boarded the ship to collect the Infolux and the first-aid kit. Before leaving, ey said, "Computer, three of your passengers are dead. We are moving the survivor to a place where he can be treated. Should we return to deal with the remains of the other three?"

"Internal sensors not functioning. Cannot properly assess the situation. I will adjust life support to preserve the deceased until further analysis is possible."

"Good enough. You can close the door now. We're leaving."

"Thank you," Ship said, genuinely impressed with how these aliens, that one in particular, had conducted themselves.

Verina walked off the ship directly onto the waiting transport. Akehru guided it away from the *Mir 4 Arms* without delay, not noticing the hatch closing and locking behind them.

"Are we going back to the city?" Verina asked.

"We didn't dock the transport into a station when we stopped. We have to take the Human to the holaxex and treat it there."

"The computer said he was male, remember? You shouldn't say, 'It.'"

"Does it matter?"

"Probably does to him."

The journey back seemed longer than the rushed trip out. When they arrived at the red house, Verina hopped out of the transport and rushed inside. Akehru called, "Verni!"

Getting no response, Akehru properly docked the transport into its recharging station so that they wouldn't be caught unprepared again. Not knowing what to do next, Akehru unlocked the haiwa carrier, letting Xadow bound out again. Verina emerged from the holaxex with an eighty-centimeter disk following em. "I could only find one push-plate."

"Why don't we just carry him?"

"How, without hurting him?"

Akehru gazed pointedly at the push plate. "That'll never hold his mass."

Verina stopped at Li's side, and said, "My thought was that it doesn't have to. If it supports as much mass as possible at his head and shoulders, we can carry the rest of him. He's not heavy, just injured."

"OK. That sounds good. You should have gone to an engineering academy."

"Math," Verina said with disgust.

Verina positioned the push-plate under the human's shoulders. The siblings then carefully moved him off the transport and guided their unlikely conveyance into the building.

Like most holaxex, the house was sparsely accoutered. On one side was an open kitchen with an extended preparation area that doubled for a table. In the rest of the downstairs area, sleeping pallets and cushioned chairs folded neatly into the walls and floor. They extended one pallet and rested the alien onto it.

"I'll be back," Verina said.

The negotiator rushed outside and soon returned with the Infolux and the first-aid kit. "I had the ship's computer download medical information onto this. I'm hoping that most of the items we'll need to help him are in this kit."

Akehru popped open the first-aid kit's lid. The contents consisted of several bags of cloth and five different boxes. "The computer said there was a portable translator in the kit," Verina said.

The older Ligrosian looked at the gadgets, but nothing stood out as a translator. "And it looks like…?"

Verina swallowed down a moment of uncertainty and loudly said, "Medical kit, we need instructions for use."

A small blue light activated on a twenty-five-centimeter-long flattened cylinder. In clear Haipo, the device replied, "Please state the nature of help needed."

Akehru and Verina looked at each other, a little surprised that it would be that easy. Verina said, "We have an injured Human male. We suspect he was hurt in a high-speed impact. One shoulder is damaged, but we don't know if that is the only problem. We also don't know the purpose of the materials and devices in this first-aid kit."

"Understood. Please remove the largest of the devices."

Akehru cleared out the loose bags filling much of the container, revealing a device on the bottom taking up nearly a fourth of the kit's volume. Ey grabbed the box, feeling some electromagnetic resistance which quickly disappeared. The translator said, "Place this device on the patient so that it is stable and cannot be dislodged."

"Does it matter how I orient it?" Akehru asked.

"No."

Akehru placed the gadget on Li's abdomen. A second later, various indicators lit on the device's exterior. Verina was about to ask about what was happening when the translator said, "Diagnostic probing in progress. Please stand by."

While they waited, Xadow ran into the house and started exploring. Verina quickly assessed the surroundings and determined that he wasn't going to hurt anything. Haiwas were great pets —very loving. Their only annoying trait was their penchant for exploring every nook and cranny in their environment over and over again. Verina was so engrossed with watching Xadow that ey was startled when the translator said, "Diagnosis complete. Please remove the diagnostic tool from the patient and orient it so that you can see the report."

Akehru removed the box from the Human. The top of the box displayed an upside-down image of an idealized Human male. Akehru turned the device so the image was right-side-up. Patches of blue highlighted numerous areas of the body schematic. As the translator spoke of each injury, the appropriate spot on the display changed from blue to red. "In decreasing order of seriousness, the basic medical conditions are as follows: fluid loss due to dehydra-tion and blood loss; a concussion to the head resulting in mild intra-cranial swelling; three broken ribs on the right side; right shoulder separation; a ruptured vertebral disk; torn ligaments in the neck; contusions to both knees; a laceration to the skull; minor bruising on torso and legs. End of summary. Treatment directions to follow."

The siblings followed the translator's instructions for half-an-hour. The Human was first stripped of his clothes. The gray-black cloth pieces in the first-aid kit were wrapped around the man's body and head forming a kind of body suit with an attached skullcap. Verina was amazed how the material stuck together without any apparent fasteners; Akehru suspected nano-scale tech-nology. With the suit assembled, Verina placed another box on the injured man's chest. This device sent hair-thin tendrils into the fabric. Soon, the suit adjusted itself to snugly fit the Human's contours. It then began carefully moving the encased patient into various poses. Upon questioning, the translator informed them that the fabric was, indeed, constructed of various nano-scale technolo-gies. In conjunction with the micro-pharmaceutical constructor currently resting on the man, the suit and devices would realign his skeletal structure and encourage repair to the other injuries while also delivering the medicines and nutrients he needed for the fastest and most complete recovery.

Verina stood in awe of the sophistication of the technology. Akehru studied the devices and queried the translator for details. Ligrosians and other aliens alike thought of Earth as being parasitic: a technology exploiter more than a developer. It was easy to overlook that even an exploiter had to have a significant amount of expertise. They concluded that it wasn't surprising something as advanced as a portable medical center would be invented by these people. After all, they were rather militaristic, and that tended to lead to battlefield injuries. *Of course* this planet would develop efficient and portable medical treatments.

With the alien cocooned in his one-man emergency room, there was little for the siblings to do. Watching him lay there quickly became boring. Verina said, "I guess we should check the house for damage and repair what we can."

"Yeah."

Night fell before Verina and Akehru took time out from their tasks to eat. They'd brought several day's worth of prefabricated meals, so the menu was quickly assembled. Xadow, as usual, begged for scraps, but both Ligrosians were too tired and hungry to want to give up any of their hard-earned food. With dinner finished, Verina got up to check on their patient while Akehru took care of the meal's cleanup.

The Human looked essentially the same as when the siblings began working on the house. The medical devices seemed to perform well. His shoulder appeared to be in a more natural position, and his reclining posture seemed straighter.

Verina noticed movement out the woods-side window. "Looks like some transports are coming our way," ey called out to Akehru.

"That will probably be the security force."

"Right. Half the planet probably saw that fireball."

"And I called them."

Verina looked surprised. Akehru responded, "First you must render assistance, then when conditions warrant, officials must be notified. I know the law, too, Verni."

Verina looked back out the window. The transports were getting closer.

3

Escalation

"Pame, it's me," Verina announced. "I'm just returning Xadow."

Inside eir birth parent's apartment, Verina opened the carrier. Xadow bounded out and started assessing the space, taking a mental inventory of what had changed in the days he was away. Verina hated that Xadow had to stay here instead of with em, but eir building was very strict about pets. Ceyelna rushed out from one of the back rooms. "Verina. Sorry. I was in the wasteroom. I don't know what it was—the bakeron or maybe the boiled xip I had for lunch, but I've been so gassy."

"More than I need to know, Pame."

Ceyelna was essentially the only parent Verina had known. Verina and Akehru's sire left after discovering ey was carrying the couple's third child, eir first. Verina had just turned five. After-wards, Verina's pame created a loving, if somewhat disheveled home. Since Ceyelna also occupied a seat as senior instructor at the university—specializing in alien cultures—upper-level govern-ment officials often courted eir opinion in interstellar relations. A side-effect of this was that Ceyelna's papers, books, and 'luxes usually covered table tops, crowded into the spaces under every piece of furniture, and filled closets. When it overflowed, after about a year, ten-to-fifteen days of culling and editing resulted in a dramatic reduction of material. It now looked like it had been cleaned out not too long before; chairs and tables were plainly visible. It actually looked no messier than how Akehru left their apartment most days. "So, how did you and Aki like your holiday?"

"Fine. It was fine."

"Really? I thought it would be pretty memorable, what with finding that Human and all."

Verina felt caught in a lie, even if only one of omission. "You know about that? No, of course you do. Who else would they call if a Human happened to drop out of the sky?"

Ceyelna disappeared into the kitchen. Verina followed in time to see eir pame drinking, or rather, swallowing, something thick, white, and apparently unpleasant. A loud belch quickly resulted. "Ugh," Ceyelna complained as ey rubbed eir abdomen. "They brought him to the medical sciences center two days ago. He was wrapped in some sort of dark cloth."

"That was first-aid material from a kit we took from his ship. He had a lot of injuries."

"Whatever it was, it seemed to help. Unfortunately, the drugs it's been administering have kept him unconscious." Ceyelna sighed. "Not that it matters. We've sent Earth a message that we judged them in violation of contract and that we'll impose sanctions in ten days."

Verina suddenly didn't feel well. "Oh."

"You know what that means? They are certain to attack. You don't seem surprised."

"Um…I'd heard rumors."

Ceyelna could tell Verina was holding something back. "Just

about the only questions that remain circle around this Human."

"What do you mean?"

"Why is he here? Was he spying? Can we use him as a bargaining tool? Things like—"

"Pame," Verina interrupted, "I know who he is."

Ceyelna couldn't remember the last time ey was so surprised. "He spoke to you?"

"Not exactly."

Verina peeled off eir day-pack. Ey didn't normally carry one, and Ceyelna's stomach was causing enough distress that ey hadn't noticed it. "I took an Infolux from his ship," Verina said, pulling the portable device out of the bag. "The ship's computer downloaded medical information and translation matrices for us to use. I didn't tell the security team that I had it when they arrived. Turns out that there's a lot more information on this than what I had downloaded."

Ceyelna motioned Verina to sit. They both rested away from the food-prep area, sitting on their heels on padded chairs. "His name is Li Jefferson Rinaldi. He is a high-ranking military negotiator for Earth, specifically regarding armaments."

"I think I've heard of him."

"I definitely have—just casual talk from some of the other aliens that have had lengthy dealings with Earth. He's feared just like all of their negotiators, but he's also respected. He tries to understand more than his own narrow point of view…or Earth's."

"So, was he sent here to—"

"No," Verina interrupted. "He wasn't sent. I scanned his log. He was on his way back from a lengthy holiday. I don't know why he's here, but I don't think it was intentional on his part."

Ceyelna reached over and touched the alien's Infolux. "May I read this?"

Verina handed the 'lux to Ceyelna, who got up and disappeared with it into a back room, the one Verina remembered eir parent always went to whenever ey had to concentrate on some convoluted research.

Verina settled into one of the viewing stations and activated the screen. A quick sampling of the news told about the recently announced cutback in Earth's bandwidth as well as a lot of analysis of the just-released-to-the-public information that Earth's forces were on their celestial doorstep.

Bored with this "news" that ey had known about for days, Verina flipped to one of the felony court channels. The case on-air concerned an illegal trespass of a pleasure boat beyond the continental shelf. From the little ey heard, if Verina was in this particular jury pool, ey would vote for punishment and reparations. Eir mind wandered, thinking about how tough it must be on this crop of jurors. With the news about Earth's forces, there must be a great temptation to watch the news instead of the trial.

"Wake up, Verni," Ceyelna said.

"Hmmm?" Verina mumbled, fighting back from mid-doze.

"We have to talk."

Verina struggled to wake up. The stress of finding the Human, of knowing of the impending invasion, and maintaining a pretense for Akehru's sake had finally caught up to em. Four hours of sleep would have been welcome. A glance at a timer showed that ey'd only dropped off for four minutes. Slowly, the fuzziness in eir mind cleared. "Okay. I'm awake."

"We have to free this Human."

Verina was now very much awake. "I must still be asleep."

"No. You heard me right."

"But…why? That doesn't make any sense."

"It makes sense on so many levels. Come. I'll make us some chofey."

Reluctantly, Verina followed eir parent back to the kitchen. Ey sat back on eir heels at the nearest stool. Eir mind might have woken up, but eir body definitely hadn't. Ceyelna busied emself creating a Ligrosian comfort drink. "We have to free him," Ceyelna said as ey began concocting eir brew, "if, for no other reason, to keep both of us out of prison."

"Prison?!"

"Willfully withholding information, for you. And we've deliberately read the materials on the 'lux. We are both guilty of a lot. You know that as well as I do."

Verina simply nodded eir head and slumped further down in eir seat. Ceyelna continued, "So we can't turn it in. Regardless of what happens officially to Rinaldi, the fact is, based on what I know of Earth, they'll assume that we have done everything possible to acquire information from him and his ship's computer. That's their nature. Even if their government doesn't think it's true, they will do what they can to make their forces believe it. The end result, for our planet, will be more-or-less the same."

Verina said, "How will freeing him help?"

"It takes our government off the hook. Mostly. It enables them to blame a small group of radicals seeking to destabilize the situation." Ceyelna used a hand-flourer to pulverize six spices into a very fine powder while the weight of eir last statement was fully understood.

Finally, Verina said, "No! Forgive me, Pame, but…no! This is insane! I'll just hide—or destroy the information. I don't want the Earthers here any more than you do, but I'm not going to become some sort of vigilante just because you're not willing to adapt to the inevitable."

"Humans. Not Earthers."

Verina glared. Ceyelna said, "I made some calls. Preparations have been made to—"

Verina made a three-voice sound that was very much like nails scraped on a piece of slate. What was eir parent mixed up in? This was not normal, but then what was? Ceyelna knew more about these Humans than just about anyone else on Serees, so maybe... No. This was crazy. "I'm getting out of here."

Verina rushed from the kitchen, found the troublesome Infolux, jammed it into eir bag, and dashed out of the apartment. Ceyelna continued the chofey process as if nothing had happened.

The seat of Earth's government, the *Terra Animo*, was stationed at the locus between Sol and three other systems. Hours after Secretary General Mitchell called for an emergency meeting of the Presidium, sixty-three of the sixty-eight ministers on-board were gathered and waiting in the Speaker's Hall. Within the blond wood room, the ministers buzzed with speculation of what could warrant the urgency of a special session when the body regularly met twice-weekly. The five permanent members from the Chamber of Ministers didn't need to speculate, as they'd had a hand in forming the events leading to this session. The room was sealed once Secretary General Mitchell entered.

Mitchell stood at the dais as the ministers got seated. He didn't want to be here. Politically, he had no choice as events had spun out of control much faster than he'd expected. His job now was to project a strong and righteous Earth. He noticed how quiet the chamber had gotten. Only mild creaks and squeaks from wooden chars trying to accommodate too much girth or too little good posture breached the silence. The Secretary General's eyes met those of Minister Chopratama. She wasn't happy. Worse, Mitchell knew she was probably right—but they were on the wrong side of a hawk-led power play. *Might as well get it done,* he thought. "Thank you, ladies and gentlemen of the Presidium. There is a situation the Chamber of Ministers and I have been monitoring for some time. Up until a few hours ago, we hoped that it could be taken care of with a minimum of fuss. Unfortunately, this is not something that is expected to go away.

"As you well know, our ability to communicate over the distances necessary to ensure our security is dependent on a license we've obtained from the Sereesian government for the use of their Seetun technology. Due to an unexpected accident involving one of our ships, the Sereesians believe that we violated the conditions of our agreement. While we would never do anything to damage relations with a long-time provider, they refuse to believe any of the clear and incontrovertible evidence we provided that would absolve us of any misconduct. This is hardly surprising, as we've all long known that they have given safe haven, and aid and comfort, to a number of species that are known to harbor ill will toward Earth and its allies.

"My office has just received a communique that the Sereesians have made a final ruling accusing us of violating our license. Consequently, they say they will reduce our total allowed band-width using their system to forty-seven-point-five percent."

The room erupted in an incomprehensible cacophony of concern and protest. Slowly at first, and then very quickly, the room quieted. Mitchell continued, "As we currently use ninety-five percent of our available capacity, this cuts our allotment exactly in half. This restriction is scheduled to remain in place for no less than five years.

"We have ten standard days to file a protest, which of course we will, but unless they stop listening to the lies told to them by others, there is really no hope of changing their minds.

"Ten days, ladies and gentlemen. Ten days before we are again attacked by a hostile government. No, not with weapons as we have known them in the past, but with one more insidious. They will take away our voice. Think about it. Think about how many lives we save every year because we can easily and effectively communicate with each other over the vast distances of space. I can guarantee you that many of those lives—Human lives—will be lost because we won't hear their call; or if we do, we won't be able to send our rescuers quickly enough for them to be of any help.

"Consider, too, this, our seat of government. You can communicate with Earth, our colonies, our representatives, and a myriad of others. In ten days, much of that is going to disappear. We will all be here, alone in the night.

"The reason I stand in this chamber today is not only to inform you of this infamous action by the Sereesians, but to ask you for the authority to reverse it. In ten days we will be under attack. I don't think that this council wants to go down in history as the one that looked the other way while the life that Earth's citizens enjoy is lowered because another government—an alien government— doesn't like our values and thus unilaterally declares war upon us. *I* can't let that happen. *YOU* can't let that happen.

"Time is running out. Today the Sereesians threaten to muzzle our voices, but how long before they decide to try to silence us completely? If we don't act quickly and decisively, we might as well paint our skins blue and pray to that second planet of theirs. I think our destiny is greater than that. We cannot allow another government to use terror methods to cause us to doubt that our faiths, which have always supported us, are less than theirs.

"We should all now gather together and pray for the strength and guidance we need to defeat this enemy of freedom. Minister Diford, if you would, please."

Throughout the chamber, ministers clasped hands with each other and bowed their heads in prayer. For the next hour, Minister of the Faiths Diford invoked the three tenets so that all would have guidance in the decisions soon to be voted on.

Li was a butterfly stuck halfway out of its chrysalis. All around him, the world moved and changed, but not him and his lepidopteran home. Then, in a flash of insight, Li realized that this was not reality. Grasping that tiny detail, Li mentally crawled his way back toward consciousness. "Ship?" he rasped. Not noticing whether he heard anything, he repeated, "Ship?"

Certain that there was no reply, Li forced himself to open his eyes.

The lights were low and nothing looked familiar. Adrenaline shot through his body. His pulse increased, his breathing quickened, and he became hyper-alert. Li's eyes focused, quickly adjusting to the darkened surroundings. He lay on something soft that was more-or-less a bed. The furnishings were sparse: no recognizable chairs, though there seemed to be several footstools scattered along the walls. The scant lighting was indirect ambient with a hidden source. If he had to make a guess, it would be that this was a hospital room—or maybe a hotel bedroom.

Li rolled to his side, swung his legs over the edge of his bed, and sat up. The lights brightened. It wasn't unexpected. Li lived his life in an automated environment. If the lights hadn't come up he might have noticed.

The first-aid pack pulled at his chest but stayed connected to the trauma cloth covering him. He disconnected the medical box, remembering how much pain he had been in. He'd slammed hard into the ship's console. Twice. Now he felt pretty good. Rested, in fact. Li scanned the box for the list of injuries that had been treated. He slipped off the large swatches of cloth that covered him. While he liked their warmth, they itched like crazy. He'd rather face a chill but found he didn't have to. The room was much warmer than he expected.

The brighter light didn't help Li gain any more information about the room, although it did let the dull yellow walls and the red floor and footstools show their colors to best effect. It looked like a low-rent hotel room.

A faint sliding sound brought Li's attention to the opening door. A bluish alien walked in carrying a tray of instruments. It was a Sereesian. He'd never dealt with them directly, but given that Ship had been plummeting toward Serees after the engine was destroyed, it didn't take a genius to put the pieces together.

Since Sereesians were the only other known sentient humanoid species, Li thought the similarities would be closer. Even ignoring the turquoise skin, there would be no mistaking Sereesians and Humans. The alien's face was substantially flatter. The lack of a nose wasn't as off-putting as the lack of ears. The large network of crevices framing the face looked sort of like ears, but without standing apart from the skull. The almond-shaped eyes were placed wide and higher than on a human. They had blue irises surrounding horizontal pupils, with the outer portion of the eye having a kind of iridescent sheen. Then there were the three mouths, which simply looked wrong.

On the whole, the Sereesian body was sleeker than Humans, which was likely due to an aquatic ancestry. The four-fingered hands were odd. Like the other knobby major joints on this body, all of the finger joints were ball-and-socket, enabling the fingers to bend into inhumanly disjoint positions. Body details were hard to discern as the Sereesian wore a kind of sleeveless sports coat topping a kind of skirt. At first, he thought the alien wore shin protectors, but soon ascertained that it was an anatomical trait. Then there were the feet: no toes and eerily flipper-like despite being about the same size and shape as a Human's.

The academic cataloging of the alien stopped when two others entered. Li could tell immediately that he had no chance of understanding what the aliens were saying. The language was mostly spoken, but what came out of one mouth wasn't always what came out of another. Then there were the clicks, tones, and other assorted sound effects coming from, apparently, another one of the mouths. There was no way a Human could mimic this without a tech assist.

The smallest of the three aliens approached Li. "Who are you?" it said, in Quinkst, with a thick accent reminiscent of a dancer Li once spent a weekend with in Cairo.

"Abraham Yorkton," he said, also in Quinkst, using one of his government-assigned aliases. "Where am I? Where are my passengers? Where's my ship?"

The small one talked to the other two. While that conversation continued, the small one used its middle mouth to say, "In the interest of expediency, we will help you with the information you seek. We will expect similar consideration. You are on the planet of Serees. Your ship did a high-speed minimally-controlled landing, leaving you as the only survivor. Two citizens, with the help of your technology, tended to your injuries. You have since been brought here to Complex Number Two for your safety…and for ours. Your ship has been moved to a storage facility. More than that, I'm not authorized to volunteer."

It was actually more than Li expected. The small Sereesian continued, "What were you doing in our space?"

"I didn't intend to be," Li said. "I was en route from Harper to Antyera to drop off two of my passengers when my ship collided with something. After that, I was mostly unconscious, but I do know we were out of control. Frankly, I'm amazed that I'm still in one piece."

Following more gibberish between the aliens, the small one said, "We find your answer disingenuous. No matter the supposed cause, you were near enough to our space for our planet to be an obstacle. I'm sure you'll agree that in times like this, a Human in our space, in an Earth-licensed government ship, is cause for suspicion."

"'Times like this?' What do you mean, 'Times like this?' What's going on?"

The medium-sized Sereesian picked up something that looked like a silver button from the tray and approached. The aliens no longer seemed quite so benign.

When Verina entered eir apartment, Akehru called out, "Thanks for making me unload the transport. I enjoyed it." Eir remarks were punctuated with strong high clicks indicating eir annoyance.

"Sorry. Sorry. I was waiting for Pame to finish reading something in the back room and I fell asleep. I didn't mean to take so long."

Ey joined eir sibling in the media room. Akehru pointed to the news image. "I suppose you knew about this invasion, too? That's why you were so weird at the beach?"

Caught. "Yeah, more-or-less. For a while."

Both siblings sat quietly. Verina wanted Akehru to calm down. Akehru needed time to absorb these new events. As the reporting began to recycle earlier reports, Akehru said, "Well, at least we have that alien. Maybe we can use it to bargain with."

"Aki! That's a terrible thing to say."

"That doesn't mean it's a bad idea. Look at the opinion numbers. Seven out of ten agree with me. One more point and it would be unanimous."

"And that makes it right? I mean, Earth is going to invade no matter what we do. You know that, right?" Akehru didn't reply. "We could have their leader and they'd still invade. If Lrat taught us anything, it was how ruthless they are. In fact, trying to use the

Human might make things worse. Then again, if just giving him up means that there's no one to…but if he…"

"What?"

Verina got up and rushed to the door with Akehru yelling after em, "What?! Where are you going?!"

Verina was already gone.

Five minutes later, Verina stood outside eir parent's door. When it opened, Verina said, "We have to get him out of there."

"Come on in."

4

Eve

Fleet Marshal Pervikh arrived at the Fleet-class warship *Housatonic* two days late. Only one day remained before the threatened bandwidth restrictions would come into effect. It left little time to finalize the planned course of battle. Pervikh went directly from the docking bay to his command center for a meeting with his Strategy Council.

The lozenge-shaped command center was larger than the current four member command staff needed, but it was the most secured facility for tens of light years. One wall, three meters high and nine meters long, served as the main 2d/3d display with a resolution density greater than the human eye. A three-dimensional view of Serees went from floor to ceiling.

Pervikh stared at the globe. It was a brilliant blue-and-white ball of water with a continuous belt of land around the equator separating the two hemispheric oceans. While not quite as visually diverse as Earth's patchwork of land and sea, it was just as beautiful to his aged eyes, nonetheless. After two or three deep space missions, a soldier learned to appreciate every single jewel of habitability there was. "Have we confirmed their defenses?" Pervikh asked the group who had been at attention since the general arrived.

"Yes sir," replied the one-star, General Chavez. "It's as intelligence outlined, nothing more than an array of various beam weapons." Pervikh finally turned and motioned for his officers to sit. Chavez, still standing, said, "Their space-based projectors are all plotted. It's a straightforward automatic defense grid. Breaking it won't be difficult."

Pervikh considered Chavez as the report continued. William Chavez wasn't the general's first choice to be on his staff, but he was the Regional Commander before Pervikh's recall to duty and Minister of Military Affairs Naveen's rising star. The general didn't doubt Chavez's expertise. On several occasions the one-star had managed impressive results with not-enough ships. For anything other than an invasion, Chavez would be a prime choice. But Chavez hailed from a militaristic state with dubious morals. The years he and his family endured subjugation might cause him to favor the point of view of the ones they were here to suppress.

"There are suspected sites on the ground," Chavez continued, "but we can't reliably confirm their location or type without hard intelligence. Given the Sereesian's lack of significant military-industrialism, it's not likely they are anything more than higher-power versions of their space-based weapons. We should be able to take out any projectors on the ground and all those in space fairly quickly. Even so, it's likely we'll take our share of hits."

"Casualty estimate?"

"Five to ten percent of personnel will be affected by the energy discharges, though fatalities should be negligible. One or two ships will likely suffer enough damage to need a repair station, though this is dependent on the Sereesians concentrating their firepower on only a few well-chosen targets. The Fleet- and Carrier-class ships shouldn't be severely damaged in any event."

General Pervikh nodded with satisfaction, "Good. Colonel Bryce, what about the planet-side population?"

Colonel Rachael Bryce rose from her chair, her two-point-two meters of height tagging her as space-born. Using the image of Serees as a visual aid, she said, "The population solely inhabits this equatorial land mass. While there are scattered islands in both oceans, none hosts anything other than plants and wildlife. As General Chavez mentioned, they have no military to speak of, just local security forces armed with nothing more powerful than laser point-cutters and a kind of stun gun. Their significant arms are outgrowths of their tools, and seem to be restricted to beam weapons. Sereesian culture is neither overwhelmingly passive nor aggressive. While there might be some reticence in accepting our presence by some pockets of individuals, it is extremely unlikely that they will present us with any resistance that we haven't dealt with before.

"There are eight major cities, four on each coast. Several of these cities have smaller sister cities nearby. Their society is tightly bound together by the communications technologies which are nearly identical to the ones they export.

"Though the land mass has only slightly less area than Earth's, the total population is small, hovering at just over two hundred million. More than fifty-percent of the available land is undeveloped. They have underutilized agricultural areas that are insufficient to support their population; they therefore garner most of their food stuffs from the sea. However, as they appear to stay close to shore and don't have anything like a navy or merchant fleet, we have no idea how they are harvesting as much from the oceans as they consume."

"So," Pervikh said, "basically, while they might grumble a little, they'll pretty much just bow down to us."

"Um. Yes sir. It rather lacks some of the finesse I was trying to get at, but—"

"Rachael," he interrupted, looking at her like a commanding father figure, "you're my best psyops commander, but you have a tendency to be a little long-winded."

"Yes sir," she said, moving back to her seat.

"You should work on that."

"Yes sir."

Six hours of capability assessments later, General Pervikh said, "It's late. No matter how pessimistic we try to be, the fact is this isn't a formidable enemy. Once we've taken out the defense shield there isn't likely to be any opposition at all. Agreed?"

The other officers nodded their assent. Pervikh continued, "Our forces should concentrate, then, on removing the defense shield. After that, I'm thinking that we simply land our forces at the prime locations Colonel Bryce outlined—that way we don't have to worry about coordinating a blitzkrieg action."

"Sir?" asked three-star General Bhoutto.

"Yes, General?"

"Playing devil's advocate while I still have the chance…what if they actually have stronger forces or resistance than we've been talking about? What if our intelligence is consummately wrong?"

"Fair question. That is why we have much more force available than, in my opinion, is necessary for a population of a few billion, much less the 200 million that are here. We're still going to get bitten on the ass by something. Even if everything happens as expected, some of our planning is going to SNAFU."

"Yes sir."

"We just have to be ready to improvise."

"Yes sir."

Pervikh pushed back from the conference table. "I suggest that you all return to your commands and then get some sack time. If we do have to improvise, I think we should be awake."

Verina emerged from behind a thick growth of shrub-like sawrexu hoping no one noticed em vomiting. Ey resumed eir mission to Complex Number Two. No matter what happened after ey entered the building, this would end eir career. Hours earlier, when Ceyelna pointed out that the invasion would end eir career in any case, Verina wasn't comforted at all. Ey pulled out eir telestick. "Two six one one Pame," ey said as ey held the fifteen-centimeter stick to eir face. The speaker end sounded, "Verni?"

"I don't have a good feeling about this."

"I found out some good news. It appears that Earth doesn't know he's here. The Advisors and Responsiblars have been waiting until the last minute to tell Earth that he's in custody."

"So this actually has a chance of working?" Verina said with no conviction.

With a lilt in eir voice, Ceyelna said, "I didn't say that."

"You're not helping," Verina complained. "Endco."

Verina stuffed the stick back into its pocket on eir pareu. Ey said to emself, "I've got to be out of my mind."

Getting into the building posed no problems—Verina had more than enough official permissions. The question was: how close to the Human would eir permissions take em?

It didn't take long for Verina to conclude that Earth's fleet would have no trouble at all in conquering eir world. Even the threat of invasion didn't impede eir attempts to access information about the captured alien. Ey not only found the floor and room where he was being held, but also his feeding schedule, the interrogation methods used, and when officials were scheduled to meet with him. It was easy.

Was that the point—that it was too easy? The information had to be a deception. Not even a temporary janitor was this careless with information in her department. Once again, ey called Ceyelna. "This isn't going to work."

"It'll work. Room ten-seventy-one."

"No. That's what the information here says, too. But it's too easy. There's no way he's going to be there, but I know who will: security."

"Don't over-think this," Ceyelna said calmly. "The Humans certainly will. Trust me. He's there."

Sighing, Verina said, "Promise you'll visit me in prison?"

"Visit? We'll probably be sharing a cell."

"You're very bad at this confidence-building thing, Pame. Endco."

Steeling emself for eir inevitable arrest, Verina walked down the hall to room ten-seventy-one. The veins on eir hands visibly pulsed, which confirmed the internal pounding ey felt. Ey slipped eir government access crystal into the lock. The door slid away. Ey stepped inside. There was Li, looking much better than the last time ey saw him. Taking a small device from a jacket pocket, ey did a quick scan of the alien. Good. No indications of any Ligrosian or Haipuxan technology. "Come. We go," ey said in the language ey knew the Human understood.

"Where?"

"No time. We go," Verina insisted.

Not knowing the rules on this crazy planet, Li figured that his best course in the short term was compliance. He got up and followed Verina down the hall to an elevator. Once inside, ey inserted eir crystal and said, "Security lock. Transport level."

The elevator replied, "Lock enabled."

The uninterrupted ride took the pair to an enclosed garage. Verina led Li to a nearby vehicle, a twin of the one used to move the injured Li from his ship to the holaxex following his spectacular arrival. Verina opened the cargo bay and motioned, "Inside."

Li broke out in a sweat. He was either being kidnapped or he was about to be executed. Even Verina could tell that the alien was anxious. If he ran, or otherwise attracted too much attention, then there would be no chance of escape. Ey unpocketed eir telestick and pointed it at Li's chest, hoping he wouldn't call eir bluff. "Inside now." Then, remembering a subtlety from eir language lessons, ey added, "Please."

Valor was a marvelous thing, especially if you were a soldier. Li was a diplomat with few valorous illusions. He climbed into the trunk. Verina closed the lid, locking him inside. Ey got in the vehicle and headed out of the building and away from the city as fast as ey could.

Czep-tan was soon far behind. Verina couldn't believe security forces weren't tailing em. The only part of this escape that wasn't traceable to em was this transport. Ey looked at the timer on the dash: forty minutes. Too long for em not to have been discovered and caught. How bad were their security forces, anyway? When the transport slowed as programmed, Verina scanned the transway ahead looking for... There. Another transport parked by the side of the road with several bags sitting behind it.

Verina pulled up and stopped behind the parked transport. Ey got out, removed an Infolux from one of the waiting bags, and then opened the cargo bay. As Li's eyes adjusted to suddenly being in the bright equatorial sun, he noticed the Sereesian activating the Infolux, which then translated as the alien spoke. "Hello, Li Rinaldi. My name is Verina. I am the one who rescued you from your crash and tended to you before the security forces took you. I have taken a great risk to once again rescue you in the hope that we might be able to save my world from yours. I need you to get out of the transport."

Li's head filled with so many questions that even he felt let down when he asked, "How long have we been traveling?"

Li stepped out from the transport while the Infolux converted Verina's answer to Human conventions: "About two hours, forty-two minutes."

Which left Li very unsatisfied. He didn't doubt the answer, it felt like he'd be locked up for at least a couple of hours, but didn't know of what use it was now that he knew. Verina returned with a question that seemed equally useless, "What is your mass?"

"Mass? Uh-eighty-three kilos."

Verina went to one of the roadside bags and activated the push-plate it sat on. The plate stayed planet-bound. Verina keyed in a number and then removed sand from the bag until the push-plate lifted. Ey then moved the floating disk to the cargo area and pushed the bag of sand inside before closing the bay's lid. Verina put a second bag of sand, already pre-measured, into the driver's seat. Ey reached over and activated the on-board navigation system. As ey took a step back, the transport moved forward, avoiding the parked vehicle blocking it. It quickly accelerated down the road.

Verina went to the second transport, already sporting extra weight in the driver's seat. Ey once again activated the automatic system. The second vehicle followed the route of the first for nearly a kilometer before it veered onto a road to the left. Verina put the still-active Infolux into a semi-rigid day-pack and slipped the carrier onto eir back. "We're going to the ocean," ey said.

Following closely, Li thanked God that he'd just spent over five months with a vigorous child—his until-recently estranged seven-year-old daughter. He'd been worked into shape by an expert. Low grass-like plants quickly gave way to a thickly wooded wilderness with no trail. With the changing terrain, Li was grateful for every bit of endurance he'd gained. "Why would Earth attack your planet? What's going on?"

Verina filled Li in on the political mess. "It's our hope that if you can return to Earth's sphere of influence on your own, then they will have—"

Li stopped. "Do they know I'm here, now?"

"The last I heard, no."

"Then we should keep it that way. As long as they don't know I'm here, they won't increase their attack."

"I don't understand. Won't they want to get you back?"

Li followed after Verina, who had not paused eir walking, "What you describe is considered by my government as, 'A fomenting situation.' Any ranking Earth citizen detained by a foreign power for any significant length of time is considered to be compromised. They become expendable and their captors become excision targets."

"They'd be killed."

"More. It's not unusual for a large number of family and friends to go missing as well."

Verina stopped and stared at Li for a few moments. "What kind of monsters are you?"

Li ran his fingers through his hair. How do you apologize for an entire species, especially if you've been a party to their acts? Verina continued walking. Li followed, saying, "It's policy. It's to ensure others will fear our wrath if we are wronged."

"And where does being a seller of weapons fit into this?"

Li's mouth dropped. His interrogators seemed clueless about him. He figured he was anonymous on this world. Even Verina calling him by name didn't strongly register. Clearly, the jig was up with this Sereesian. She knew. "I'm as guilty as any. I was good at my job. And honestly, I enjoyed it most of the time."

Li thought about adding that he was leaving his post, but he couldn't think of a way that didn't sound like a lie. "So, why were you planning on quitting?" Verina asked.

Damn. How much did this alien know about him? "My daughter."

"Susan."

"Yesss," Li said through his teeth, increasingly annoyed and defensive.

"Excuse me," Verina said as ey pulled eir telestick from its sleeve. "Yes?"

Ceyelna's voice replied, "I thought you'd want to know that there's a planet-wide search for you and the Human. You are the most wanted person on Serees."

"Great."

"Don't use this phone again. Destroy it and trash it as soon as you can so that it can't be traced to you. I'm using a disposable stick now. I included four in your bag."

"How will I get in touch with you?"

"You don't. Not for a while."

"Pame…"

"Security forces are certain to detain me for questioning very soon, probably your sibling as well, since ey had contact with the Human. Don't worry about us. You're in more danger…at least until the invasion starts. After that, I don't think it's going to matter one way or another."

"So, I'll just follow our plan, then?" Verina asked, trying to muster up enough conviction to actually continue with the mission.

"That's the only way. I love you, Little One."

"I love you, Pame."

The line went dead. Verina couldn't remember ever feeling so alone. But…eir freedom was in danger and now was not the time to wallow. Ey scanned the ground for rocks, but the undergrowth effectively hid anything so inert. Unexpectedly, Li presented em with a pair of five-kilo specimens. "Wha—?" Verina questioned.

"I'm sorry. I overheard," Li offered.

Verina had tuned out the on-going translation from the Infolux. Of course he overheard. Ey would have to be more careful, but it was too late now. Verina took one of the offered rocks and motioned for Li to place the other on the ground. Putting eir 'stick on that second rock, Verina slammed the other onto the device. Seeing little apparent damage, ey did it again. And again. On the fourth try, the case cracked and a bright flash momentarily blinded both travelers. The telestick was dead.

"Come on," Verina said, "we have to keep moving."

Fifty minutes later, the woods thinned and merged with the blue-gray regolith of the seashore. Li paused to catch his breath upon seeing the size of the waves. "Can you swim?" Verina asked.

"Uh, yeah. A little," Li replied, not at all certain he was going to like the next stage of his "rescue".

"Good. How fast?"

"How fast? I don't know. How far do I have to go?"

Verina thought about it for a moment. When Li heard, "About twenty kilometers," coming from the Infolux, his eyes opened wide. This was crazy. He said, "I'm not a great swimmer, and I'm not in great shape. Days, maybe."

The estimate disappointed Verina. Ey had expected better. "How long can you stay underwater?"

Li definitely didn't like the direction this was going. "I don't know. A minute, maybe."

Verina double-checked the conversion in eir head, and then said, "Okay. It will be hard, but I think this will work."

"What will work?"

Verina removed eir pack and rearranged the various straps. Ey said, "We have to escape via the sea. I'll have to tie you to my back so you can breathe. I guess I'll be doing all of the swimming myself. I think I can make it, carrying you."

Li backed up a couple of steps. "Now wait a minute. I'm not going out in that!" he shouted as a tsunami-worthy wave crashed down.

"The waves are not going to be a problem. You said you can be underwater for one of your minutes. That's more than enough time to get to the shelf."

Verina removed eir jacket and pareu then packed them into the day pack. "Unless your clothes are unharmed by sea water, I suggest you take them off."

Li looked at Verina's naked body—there were some pretty impressive scars. He also noticed that she was taller than he was by a few centimeters. He'd probably lose if he had to fight. Seeing the alien this way made him wonder if "she" was the proper pronoun. Moving that debate for a later time, Li decided that living with wet, salt-encrusted clothes was worse than going native. After all, that was an alien in front of him. What did it matter?

Once the pack was sealed, Verina placed it not on eir back but in front. Ey said, "Stand with your back against mine."

The Human didn't move. Verina realized eir mistake. Ey opened the pack, adjusted the volume on the Infolux, and sealed the pack again. "Stand with your back against mine."

Li understood the louder, muffled translation. He went back-to-back with Verina. Eir arms danced around attaching straps in a makeshift five-point configuration. It wasn't much different than being strapped in an acceleration chair, except Li found watching the Sereesian's fingers bend in totally inhuman ways a little unsettling. "Hold on," Verina said as ey bent forward.

Li's feet left the ground, and he instinctively reached to keep from falling. Verina took a few steps before lowering Li back to his feet. "Ungh! You're heavier than I remembered," ey said.

"Can I do anything to help?"

"We'll walk together to the waterline. Then I'll carry you into the ocean. I will count from three to zero. By the time I reach zero, we will be underwater, so prepare yourself."

Li wanted to have a case of the screamy-meamies but kept his head. He could panic later—when it was safer. For now, he'd have to put his trust in a naked, blue-skinned alien.

Together they walked to the waterline. Li heard the thunderous crash of a wave and the low-frequency build-up of another coming to take its place. Again, his feet left the ground. Looking up, he saw the crest of the approaching wave. When Verina started running, Li closed his eyes—it was easier not to be sick that way. Too soon he heard, "Three…two…one…ze—"

The last number was cut off by the immediate completeness of wet. Eddies and currents swirled around Li, but at no point did he feel out of control. Riding the waves with Susan four months ago was scarier, and those waves were only a meter high. Li relaxed and concentrated on holding his breath. Before he knew it, he lay face-up on the surface of the ocean. He looked back to land and saw that, in just this brief span of time, Verina had taken him a least a hundred meters off-shore. He wanted to ask questions, but Verina was completely submerged and taking them out to sea at a remarkable rate. When the shore disappeared from view, Li figured they must be at least a couple of kilometers out. Verina made a sharp turn and headed back in the direction of the city they just escaped from. With nothing else to do, Li settled back to enjoy riding on the back of what he could easily imagine as a dolphin on a more familiar world.

After nearly twenty minutes of continuous swimming, Verina tilted back to tread water and get some air. "No wonder we left the sea," ey said, panting. "This is hard."

With the Infolux now underwater, Li understood nothing of what Verina said—not that it mattered. Li knew there was nothing he could contribute other than not interfering with the alien's movements.

Li estimated they stayed in the treading water position for something like five minutes before Verina once again went horizontal and swam on. This pattern persisted until after sunset. Li saw the position of the stars change; they were heading back to shore. The roar of the monstrous surf grew. Verina stopped again. While one mouth gasped for breath, another said in Li's language, "We go under water soon. Not under wave. Into cave. Protect head. Again count. Three…two…one…zero. Understand?"

"I understand."

They bobbed in the swells until Verina's breathing became less labored but far from rested. "Make ready for under water. Ready?"

"Ready."

"Three…two…one…zero."

As quickly as before, the Human felt water surrounding him. The difference this time was the disorienting blackness. Li was certain they now moved faster than at any other point during the day. He also heard what sounded like dolphin clicks. Just as his lungs started suggesting to his brain that he breathe, Li felt he was inside something. The water seemed different. Cooler. Calmer. Or maybe it was the difference in pressure. *Something* was around him—the scraping of his knee confirmed that. Fighting against the water rushing past, Li covered his head and face with his hands. His lungs were now no longer suggesting—they demanded attention. Li needed to take a breath soon. He just hoped it would be in —

Air!

Verina treaded water and lit the emergency beacon on eir day pack. Even with light, the shadowy walls of the small cave didn't improve much on the suffocating darkness. Li unexpectedly felt himself sink. Verina had quick-released the straps tying the Human to em, leaving him to find shore on his own. The Ligrosian, still tied to the pack on eir belly, struggled to climb onto the floor of the cave. When ey was safe, ey collapsed in exhaustion; eir breathing so heavy that it seemed ey would suck all the air from this confined space.

Recovered from the surprise of being freed, Li followed Verina's example and climbed out of the pool. Sitting on the opposite side of the small cave, he waited. Naked. At least there was light, which gave Li some primal reassurance that he wasn't dead. At least, not yet.

Verina unfastened the pack and slowly rolled to a kneeling position. Ey opened the pack and removed Li's clothes. "You might need these to stay warm," ey said via the now unfettered translator as ey tossed the garments to the Human.

Li noticed that he was actually rather comfortable. If anything, the warm and humid conditions of the cave could have used a fan. Even so, given the mores he'd been raised with, Li much preferred cloth to skin. As he dressed, Verina said, "I'll be back soon," and then disappeared through an opening Li hadn't noticed until now.

With Verina's steps having faded, Li crawled over and reached into the pack for the Infolux. Li's excitement at the prospect of learning new intelligence about his host quickly disappeared when he noted the ID on the corner of the case. This was the data pad *he* used the most. No wonder she knew so much about him. He did a quick scan to see if anything had been deleted and was relieved that no information had been lost. In fact, there was added data: the translation matrices as well as a significant amount of medical reference. Why? Was she an agent? That would explain the scars. Was it to be torture? Was that why she needed medical data on Humans?

He heard Verina returning. Not wanting to be seen as a threat, at least not at the moment, he put the Infolux back into the pack and quickly returned to his place. Verina arrived with two more very full day packs. "Supplies."

Verina put down the bags and noticed that eir clothes weren't as neatly folded as before. Ey said as lightly as possible, "As you've discovered, the Infolux is from your ship. I needed to take it with me to help treat your injuries. You're lucky the security forces didn't find it when they took you into custody."

Li thanked God for the low light hiding his red cheeks, not that Verina would have divined his embarrassment from them. Ey opened one of the new packs and withdrew a bottle and a sealed container. Bringing them to Li, ey said, "Here's food and water. I don't know if it will be to your liking, but according to the data I got from your ship, it will nourish you."

"Thanks," Li said, accepting the offering.

Verina returned to the packs and pulled out a container of food for emself. It seemed to Li as if the alien simply inhaled the contents, as quickly as they disappeared. Ey grabbed another container and wolfed the contents down almost as fast. Noticing Li staring, ey said sheepishly, "I never eat like this. I used a lot of energy today."

Li diplomatically said, "I understand. I'm amazed you lasted that long."

Verina nodded eir head in an interstellar norm of affirmation. Ey took a third container and ate it with proper decorum. Ey said, "I should probably be rationing this, but I figured I might as well tend to the immediate need. Better to regain my strength than to get sick."

"Makes sense," Li said.

Touching his forehead with his right hand, and then touching his heart, followed by his left then right shoulder, Li whispered a simple prayer, "Thank you, Lord, for this gift of food. Please continue to help me with your merciful guidance. Let it be so."

Though ey didn't hear the prayer, Verina assumed its purpose and noted it for the future. Ey watched as Li opened his container. He picked up what looked like a cut piece of fruit. He bit into it cautiously—years in the diplomatic core taught him that form and flavor only occasionally coincided. The morsel crunched easily between his teeth. It tasted something like a cross between an apple and a parsnip. Not great, but certainly far from indigestible. The next item looked like sashimi. It tasted like sashimi. Li hated sashimi. Intellectually, though, he knew that this was very likely to be his primary source of protein as all indications were that these Sereesians lived off the sea. He might as well get used to it. The last item was so bitter-tasting that Li removed it from his mouth the second it touched his tongue. "Radock is an acquired taste," Verina offered, the corners of one of eir mouths oddly pinched into a smile.

"Honestly, I don't think I can eat it. It's too bitter."

Verina motioned for him to give it to em. In exchange, ey gave him a reddish piece of fruit, different from the first he'd tried. "You liked the ha'poehn, so I think you'll like this better. It's sweeter. It's called kashta."

Still remembering his experience with the radock, Li sampled this new item more carefully. At the first bite his expression changed from trepidation to happiness. "This is wonderful!" he said.

Verina smiled. "It's a favorite everywhere."

"It's like the sweetest kiwi fruit I ever had, except more sugar-ier."

Though the Infolux failed to translate the last word, Verina felt happy that Li was pleased. Maybe these Humans had some redeeming aspects to them after all. Ey popped the radock taken from Li into eir mouth, savoring the taste. Li picked up a second piece of the sashimi thing and asked, "What's this called?"

"Vahr," ey said, simultaneously adding a sort of clucking sound with eir bottom mouth.

"I can do the 'vahr' part, but the rest of it…"

"Yes. Our ways of communicating are difficult for many aliens. We use one, two, or three voices where most species only have the ability to produce or comprehend one at a time. Sometimes it's a problem in negotiations."

Li perked up. "You're a negotiator?"

Verina nodded. "I negotiate licenses between my world and others for our technology."

Li nodded as well. "I do the same."

"No," Verina said with some disgust. "It's not the same. *You* sell weapons."

Li looked down into his food container. He didn't want to start this again, but damn it, why did he have to keep apologizing? "Look," he said defiantly, "we couldn't sell weapons if others didn't want them. You might think that you're living in a warm and fuzzy part of the universe, but it's the weak versus the strong. It always has been, and it always will be. To think anything else is naive and unrealistic."

Li's sudden defense of his people took Verina off guard. Ey had thought maybe this Human had some morality. He seemed sincere when talking of his daughter. Maybe it was just an act to gain eir sympathy. If that was how it was to be, ey could play that game, too. Verina closed the pack filled with food. Ey then sealed up the pack ey had carried through their journey and put it on. "No. Stay there. Stay sitting." Turning out the light on the pack and plunging the cave into total darkness, ey said, "Understand this, Li Rinaldi: even without a weapon, *here* I am the strong and you are the weak."

The high rate of clicking and the footsteps both faded into a non-directional, echoing quiet. The silence, as profound as the darkness, brought home to Li how dependent he was on his—

whatever she was. This felt different from when she retrieved supplies. Li wasn't certain if Verina would return. Now wasn't the time for pride. "Don't go!" he shouted. "I apologize!"

Nothing. The cave's sensory deprivation skewed his perceptions, and Li quickly lost track of how long Verina was gone. The Human rubbed the rough and slightly damp walls in an attempt to stay rooted to this reality. Li didn't hear Verina return. He only noticed when the pack beacon slowly raised in brightness. Li said, "I don't mean to be ungrateful. I'm a patriot, just as you probably are. You struck a nerve."

Verina put the packs down, then sat on her heels. Ey said, "I need to pray."

Li sat quietly—waiting for the fight to begin.

5

Battle Fog

Fleet Marshal General Pervikh looked through the latest batch of communiques which included a mention of a missing arms negotiator. Nothing important enough to distract from the task at hand: starting a war. He just needed the provocation to make it legal.

Serees and its neighboring space dominated the wall-sized display. Pervikh focused on an overlay graphic showing Earth's Seetun bandwidth capacity. If the Sereesians were as good as their word, then the number would change…now.

It held…

…and held…

…and…it changed. A moment later, it went back to the previous figure. Was that the moment? Was something wrong? Then the graphic changed again, to approximately half its original value and didn't waver. "Computer," Pervikh said, "initiate battle sequence Buster."

"Initiating battle sequence Buster, aye," the youthful AI male voice answered.

Intelligence Advisor Kridrent walked into the maetor's large but thinly-populated office. "Maetor, Serees is under attack by Earth," ey said in the prescribed manner.

Maetor Retahlik tapped a few command buttons on eir Infolux. Ey stood and faced Kridrent and Nancimare—both dressed in their standard brown and beige, Ceyelna, the Advisor for Ligrosian Affairs, and the Liaison to the Haipuxans. "I have activated the invasion clause. Earth's bandwidth is now cut an additional third from their sanctioned bandwidth. I have also activated security protocol seventeen.

Kridrent explained, "Except for one standard line and a backup, normal modes of communication around Serees have been severed. There's also the emergency very-low-bandwidth network for planetary security—if anyone is able to use it after the aliens settle in."

The Haipuxan Liaison left the room to forward the information to the older species. The remaining five stood quietly, every face showing sadness and anxiety. "I'm sorry," Retahlik said. Ey then voiced the tune of a hymn usually reserved for a dying loved one. Ey said over the tune, "Let's join in asking Bailera to guide and comfort our fellow Serees who will survive—both Ligrosian and Haipuxan. Let them look up in the sky and see that our world's sibling has not forgotten them."

The other Ligrosians joined in musical chorus of the hymn while each also whispered their own private prayers for their loved ones, for their way of life, and the hope that one day their planet would be rid of these invaders.

The fleet marshal watched dots of light move against the black background on his display as all twenty-eight Earth warships fired precision missiles at the space-based weapons platforms. Flashes

of detonations were quickly enveloped by clouds of debris sparkling in the sunlight. The sky was dotted with explosive displays as
weapons on both sides destroyed one another. General Pervikh
thought that battles always seemed so anticlimactic when beam
weapons were used as they were invisible without enhancement.
"Computer," Pervikh said, "replay attack. Use overlay filter."

The computer repeated the instruction in proper military fashion and then replayed the attack as ordered. The missile dots
moved as before, but now streaks crossed the field of view, showing the paths of the previously unseen beams. As each weapon
found its target—poof—a debris cloud. Pervikh now clearly saw
the nature of the Sereesian's defensive strategy. General Chavez's
assessment was turning out to be very accurate. "Computer, initiate battle sequence Go Dark."

"Initiating battle sequence Go Dark, aye."

"Computer, return to real-time display, maintaining filter."

The screen lit up with activity as projectiles and multiple waves
of missiles launched from their ships. Lines crisscrossed the
enhanced display as both sides unleashed the fury of their lasers
and other beam weapons. It all looked like an over-budget public
sim. Off to the side, Pervikh saw a large gas out-burn on the
Trenton. Though impressive, it wasn't a ship-threatening breach.
Fewer beams now crossed the screen. Most were concentrated on
the *Kursk*, more than a hundred thousand kilometers away from
Pervikh's flagship. "Computer, subscreen the *Kursk*."

A smaller display opened up that covered most of the view of
Serees. Scores of beams blasted away at the Marauder-class ship.
Hull breaches mottled the hull, with out-gassing and burn-throughs
very apparent.

Then the beams were gone.

"Computer, close subscreen."

The view returned to the black battlefield. The streaks that had filled the screen minutes before were gone. What remained were the sparkles of destroyed weapons and the small moving dots of missiles still seeking targets. A deep voice announced over the comm, "Message from General Chavez, sir."

"Put it through," Pervikh said. "Computer, subscreen incoming."

The image of General Chavez floated above the blue planet. "Sir, I'm pleased to inform you that we can detect no functional weapons to impede our advance."

"Very good, General. I suppose you want to send in the *Golden Eagle* to verify?"

"Yes sir."

"Very well. Stay on the line. Computer, move message to the side and create subscreen focused on the *Golden Eagle*."

The engines of the Carrier-class vessel, *Golden Eagle*, the third largest in this armada, glowed with life. Fighting inertia all the way, the ship moved closer to the planet. A bright flash overwhelmed the display, briefly blinding the general. As his vision cleared, Pervikh glanced at the subscreen on his display; it seemed that Chavez experienced the same event. Looking back at the main display, the *Golden Eagle* was still visible but dark. The glow of the engines was gone. Chavez said, "General, we've lost contact with the *Golden Eagle*. Computer, scan for a reason we've lost contact."

Pervikh waited as Chavez received the data. The fleet marshal promted,"General?" Impatient for a response, Pervikh said more clearly, "General Chavez, what does your intelligence say? Was it an EMP, or something more—"

In the conference room of the *Manila Bay*, Chavez's connection with General Pervikh suddenly went dead. That was supposed to be impossible. The five fleet-command ships in the armada boasted the most robust and secure communications Earth's technology could provide. Even a total power failure to any of those ships would have no effect on the comm systems. Chavez's eyes darted around all the data on his display. Downing the *Golden Eagle* was one thing, but silencing the more powerful *Housatonic*...

"Computer," the general said, "is the loss of communications to the *Housatonic* related to the loss from the *Golden Eagle*?"

"Unknown. The *Golden Eagle* no longer registers on sensors."

"What do you mean? I can see it on my screen. It has to register."

"At the last known position of the *Golden Eagle* there is a dense cloud of ions and monatomic particles which are currently diffusing."

Chavez's heart beat faster and stronger. "Scan the *Housatonic*. Do the same conditions exist?"

"At the last known position of the *Housatonic* there is a dense cloud of ions and monatomic particles which are currently diffusing in a manner similar to the previous query."

"Computer, emergency staff conference, now."

The images of General Bhoutto, Colonel Smythe, and Colonel Bryce appeared in subscreens on his display. Chavez said, "You've seen what's happened. Our top priority is finding that weapon's origin and blasting it into soup before we're nothing but clouds. Agreed?"

As the computer announced lost contact with the *Baghdad*, the three other commanders said, "Agreed," and muted their own screens as they worked on finding the source of that deadly light.

Moments seemed like hours. The unexpected events were replayed from every available source. Sims were ordered to confirm possible targets. The *Tochtepec* disappeared. Escape wasn't an option, Chavez knew. Earth's forces were being hit too fast. Ships depended on their speed of— "Found it," Colonel Smythe said. "I've just lost it over the horizon. I'm sending coordinates."

Chavez watched his tactical display of Serees as the targeting grid appeared. "I'm closest," he said. "Computer, launch our Carbon-fourth at the coordinates just received. Colonel," he said pointedly to Colonel Bryce, "launch yours as well."

Bryce hesitated for a moment. "I…yes, sir. Computer, launch Carbon-fourth at the targeting coordinates just received."

Verina slumped from eir straight-backed praying posture. The solitude provided by the cave made eir sense of time as unreliable as Li's had been. The anticipation of…what? Bombs dropping? Ey wasn't sure what ey expected, but quiet definitely wasn't it. The Ligrosian reached into a pack for a timer to confirm if the attack should have started by now.

The ground jerked. Both Li and Verina lost their balance even though they sat on the cave's floor. Water sloshed up in peaks from the pool. Then another strong jolt, as bad as the first.

The subsonic rumbling faded, leaving only the sounds of water smoothing out the lingering oscillations. Both Li and Verina calmed their breathing. Verina quietly said, "It's started."

Two more temblors disturbed the cave again but much less severely. Li said, "Uh oh."

"What does that mean?"

Li looked at Verina trying to figure out a way to tell the alien what the shaking meant. Verina said, "We expected this. The bombing of our cities."

"That's not what that was. At least, that's not what…"

Verina inched closer and unintentionally became more threatening. "What was it?"

Li closed his eyes and considered his words. "When we…when Earth…invades a planet, we take out targets—strategic targets—

that might help the enemy. We use lasers, and bombs, and anything else we need. For a variety of reasons, our choice is precision munitions. They are quite destructive, don't doubt that, but unless they were dropped right on top of this cave, even a full-on attack wouldn't feel like that."

After a quick sip of water, Li continued, "You are aware, I'm sure, that we maintain in our arsenal a number of weapons that most…wait…" *Mustn't say too much*, Li thought. "Some of our ships carry a bomb that doesn't fall into the precision category. It's a nuclear device whose core can fuse carbon atoms. Its power is something like slamming a modest asteroid into a planet, but with more controlled devastation. Its effective yield is in the neighborhood of forty exajoules."

Li waited for the Infolux to convert the number and saw the change in Verina's expression as the alien confirmed the calculation in her head before he continued, "We call it the 'planet shaker.' I'm fairly certain that your world was hit by more than one. I'm guessing on the opposite side of the planet given the character of the seismic waves. The impact had to—"

"Shut up," Verina said in a near whisper before turning off the light.

"Computer, replay again," General Chavez said.

The wall display of Serees reset. In the southern ocean, between the land belt and the south pole, a bright light flashed. Clouds pushed away at hypersonic speed. As a ring of water rippled out from the now-dimming flash point, another flash brightened the area. Cloud patterns around the globe were affected as the blast waves washed around the planet. A second ring of water followed after the first. "Computer, real-time display."

The picture jumped. The two rings of water were barely visible and far from the initial flash point. Thousands of kilometers of coast had been washed over and were currently underwater. It would take hours, more than a day in some places, for the floods to roll back to the ocean. "Computer, reconvene staff meeting."

Three subscreens zoomed back into position and un-muted. Chavez waited until everyone's attention turned back to him. "It seems the attack has stopped, General," Colonel Smythe said.

"We're fortunate that nobody ever makes more than one or two doomsday weapons," Chavez said.

"Except us," Colonel Bryce offered.

"Am I hearing a lack of enthusiasm for the measures I took to save the fleet, Colonel?"

"No sir, General. I just wish something less...profound...could have been used." Then, before Chavez could comment, she added, "But the safety of the fleet is paramount, of course. Survival comes first."

Chavez looked critically at the images in front of him. The outspoken colonel didn't seem as committed to decisive victory as the others on the staff. He'd keep an eye on her. "I, too, wish we could have used less force. I've never seen anything like that weapon."

General Bhoutto offered, "It would have made a fine addition to our arsenal."

"No arguments here, General," Chavez said. "You should all know that I've dispatched a message to Minister Naveen informing him of our loses. I've also informed the Minister that I've assumed command of the fleet until we receive new orders."

The others looked a little surprised at Chavez's power play. General Bhoutto could have challenged on the grounds of rank, but he had little political clout in either the Presidium or the Chamber. There was no dissent. Chavez smiled inwardly. It wasn't the way he'd imagined ascending to a fleet command, but in a pinch it would do. Colonel Smythe said, "Shouldn't we be testing to see if the area is, indeed, safe?"

"My thoughts exactly, Colonel. Since they didn't fire on our smaller ships, I think we're going to have to risk another carrier… unless one of you would be willing—"

Colonel Bryce spoke up, "I'll volunteer the *Spitfire* to assume strategic orbit."

"That's very brave of you, Colonel."

"I think it's my duty to be no less afraid to face the enemy in battle than the corps under our command. Wouldn't you agree?"

Chavez bristled at Bryce's implication. Keeping his emotions in check, he said, "Absolutely Colonel. Godspeed to you and your crew."

The subscreen with Colonel Bryce flickered off. Chavez's tactical display showed the small blob representing the *Spitfire* moving closer to Serees. On the other side of the planet, another dot moved closer. And off to the side, closer to Chavez, another. Moving a battle group wasn't what the general had in mind. Minutes passed as each of the ships moved into a medium orbit around Serees. No more beams crossed the screen. The theater display showed nothing but two planet-sized worlds and two dozen very formidable fighting vessels.

Verina and Li sat, waited, and stared. Quiet permeated the cave. *This isn't our usual M.O.*, Li thought. "Don't you have a radio or something in that thing? Something untraceable that can tell us what's going on?"

Honestly surprised, Verina said, "I forgot!"

Verina rummaged around the contents of the third pack. Ey returned with a disk three centimeters high and ten centimeters in diameter. Though silvery gray, it didn't seem to Li to be either a metal or a synthetic. Verina placed the device between them and pressed the center of the flat top. A bluish Ligrosian head appeared, in an immaculate three-dimensional rendering. Unfortunately for Li, it spoke with all three voices, each in a different language. It was too much for the Infolux to process and translate. The head said in one voice, "Only just now getting fractured reports from Yavent." While a second voice said, "I…it seems… no, that can't be right." And the third suggested that the island of Gopro might be the source of the waves.

The severity of the news grabbed Verina's complete attention. The head described a massive wave demolishing up to a third of the southern coast. The grand city of Yavent, the oldest and most revered of Serees' four major cities, had been shattered. Twelve of the fourteen magnificent buildings by the sea were now missing— the original treasures they contained now lost.

There was scant mention of casualties. Given the circumstances, and considering Ligrosian physiology, drowning and surviving at sea weren't concerns. Had the disaster been anything other than sea-borne, there might have been more emotion. For now, people assumed the survivors swept out to sea would turn up on shore sometime in the next several days—that is, if they had the courage to return at all.

The reports from Yavent consumed much of the news but by no means all. Cities and towns on the same coast, to either side of the once grand metropolis, were also badly destroyed or wiped from the map. While there was a reluctant admission that the planetary defenses had been taken out by Earth Fleet in a matter of minutes, there was no mention of direct attacks on the land band or of Earth ships entering the atmosphere. This wasn't going at all how Verina had expected.

Once the information started repeating what ey already knew, Verina turned off the device. Li let Verina be contemplative for a while before asking, "What's going on?"

Verina spent the next few minutes filling the Human in on what had happened. Li wasn't surprised by the run of events. "Now that you know, what's your plan?" he asked.

"The plan has always been to stay here, outside the city, for ten-to-fourteen days. Then I'd assess the situation and—"

"That won't work," Li interrupted.

Verina didn't like the attitude of this Human all of a sudden. Who was he to tell em what would and wouldn't work on eir planet? Verina took a breath. Calmer, eir negotiator's training kicked in. He might have a better insight into his own people than eir parent did. "Why?" ey asked.

"Staying here will just ensure our capture. One of the first things the military does when securing a world is to set up a detection-and-capture infrastructure. It starts at the occupied zones and gradually expands outward and along paths of travel. If we stay here for an extended period of time, given how close I think we are to the city, it's entirely likely we'll be unable to move more than two feet outside this cave without the land forces knowing."

"So you think it's better if we move now?"

"No. I think it's imperative. We need to move away from the city into the country. Then we need to try to contact, or set up, some sort of resistance. I can help with that."

Verina's absentmindedly flexed eir right hand fingers from forepalm to backpalm and back. This alien—this Human—who only a day before was being interrogated by Serees security, was now willing to help em fight his own people? Suspicious didn't even start to describe eir feelings about the situation. Still, there was an element of truth to his story. If he did plan to get em captured, and maybe some of eir confederates as well, he would want to first gain eir confidence. To that end, at least in the short term, he might give em more information about Earth tactics than ey could get on eir own. If this detection grid was any indication, he already had. Li asked, "You're wondering why I'm doing this, aren't you?"

"Just a little bit, yes," ey replied.

"You've read my 'lux. I'm done. I just want to be with my daughter on some pleasant enough world or station that will leave us be."

"And that's enough for you to betray your planet," Verina said without masking any of eir sarcasm.

"What have you got to lose? I get the feeling you aren't trained in military tactics. I'm not a strategic expert, but I did my service. Plus, I'm a weapons merchant. Might be helpful."

Verina knew when ey was being handled, and this Human's weak arguments were hardly compelling. It simply didn't make any sense. Betrayal was a certainty, but when? As long as ey knew the trap was coming, maybe he could be of enough help to tip the scales in eir favor. "I'm not binding to anything. We'll see how this develops," ey said.

"Fair enough."

Verina stopped fidgeting. "What's our first move?"

"We need to get inland; better yet, to the other coast."

"Why?"

"The survivors will have more reason to want to fight back. With your defenses down, the cities up here won't face anything like the same level of destruction. If you want to start an effective resistance, you have to recruit the ones who don't have to be sold on the idea. Also, the ruins of the cities will be more time-consuming to grid, so you'll probably have an easier time finding shelter."

"You want to travel to the other side of Serees?"

"I'm not trying to get you caught," Li said, his voice colored by an anxiety that went undetected by the bluish alien. "I think it's our best chance. The real invasion is going to start soon; the farther away we are from civilization when that happens, the better."

Verina stared at Li, trying to find some hint of dissemblance in that alien face. "Okay. We'll go." Verina packed the broadcast disk away. Once all three packs were sealed, ey handed Li one containing consumables. "Here. You carry this."

Li took the container and noted the similarity between this and a Human backpack. Though proportioned for a different species, Li adjusted it so that it wasn't too uncomfortable despite it being much heavier than he expected. The Sereesian was obviously stronger than she looked. Verina slung the remaining packs, including the one with the Infolux, on either shoulder and led the way out of the cave.

Despite the relatively straightforward path through the winding tunnel, it took some time to reach the exit. Li struggled to breathe —a side-effect of a bureaucratic life. Even after spending nearly half-a-year with an energetic little girl, he was not conditioned for this kind of exertion on a higher-than-he-was-used-to gravity well. The fresh air revived him when the emerged from the tunnels.

Verina looked around. The reflected light of the sister planet gave form to the shadowy wilderness in front of them. While darkness protected them, the glow on the horizon said that dawn was not far away. Verina wished ey had a plan. The one formulated with Ceyelna was not going to work. Yavent's destruction took away the personnel and equipment that ey'd been counting on. Maybe the Human was right. But how was ey supposed to get halfway around the world and not be seen? Verina stopped. Li's breathing was already labored. Ey said, "We can't walk to the other coast."

"We need to get…one of those cars of yours…before the invasion…gets too far along," Li said.

"Won't your people trace us?"

"Probably. Do you have a quicker way to travel large distances?"

Verina readjusted the packs on eir back. "This way," ey said, guiding them from the cave.

Through the pre-dawn and dawn, Verina led Li through the woodland path that wasn't a path. Given the undergrowth, it was barely a suggestion of a path. After half an hour, Li relinquished his pack in order to keep up.

Verina knew species differed dramatically in their levels of strength and stamina, but ey couldn't believe how weak these Humans were. Was that why they were so warlike, so others wouldn't realize how vulnerable they really were? As tantalizing a topic as that would make at an evening meal with Ceyelna, the fact remained that Verina now carried all three packs. Their weight was taxing enough, but trying to manage the third pack made traveling all the more difficult.

Fueled by fugitive determination, the travelers reached a transway by mid-morning. "Here," Verina said, shoving the third pack back to Li, "we have to follow the road until we find a transport station."

Li got lucky: it was only a three kilometer hike. A four-seat Group Transport arrived within minutes. Verina opened the cargo area, intending to stow eir packs. Li said, "We should probably keep these with us. If we have to run, we might not have time to take these out of the trunk."

It made sense enough. Verina went along with the suggestion. Verina and eir packs occupied the forward passenger section while Li and his pack sat in the rear. Verina punched in a destination for the transport. The vehicle quickly accelerated to maximum speed as it headed away from Czep-tan to the interior of the land band.

Li pointed out a collection of pollen-sized dots high in the sky.

Following standard procedure, the flotilla of troop vehicles first descended on industrial cities and cities serving as infrastructure hubs. Even though Czep-tan was the seat of government, it only had secondary strategic importance. That respite was short-lived. Six battalions, needing thirty troop transports, landed around the outskirts of the city. Each battalion supplied eight hundred ground troops plus sixty special operations fighters armed with "high-effectiveness" tactical weapons and vehicles. The capital was now under siege, awaiting occupation.

Maetor Retahlik's image appeared on displays throughout the planet. Though not intentionally reclusive, the nature of the office kept em from public view. Many viewers noted that Retahlik looked tired from eir five years of service as eir people's leader. Even eir skin, once a lively green, now looked drab and sapped of vibrancy. Ey stood with great dignity in front of the oldest copy of Ligrosian law: a carved stone hundreds of thousands of years old —written in an all-but-forgotten language—that spoke of the agreement between Ligrosians and Haipuxans to live in peaceful cooperation. Ey said, "As many of you are aware, forces from Earth are landing and occupying Serees. I ask that you, the public, don't needlessly antagonize these invaders. They are too strong; that is an unassailable fact. However, that does not mean that I encourage you to collaborate with or comfort them. Preserve our way. Retain our knowledge. Hold on to our character. Keep to your souls that which is ours alone. It has always been thus, and so it will be now.

"Like the fury of the haverta storm, we will endure these aliens, not embrace them. If we give them no cause to do otherwise, they will likely allow us to live in peace. This is my command as law. I will not issue another binding one until the invaders leave our world. I will not step down to have another give commands in my place. I will remain strong for the sake of all of us who live on

Serees, and I ask all of you to do the same."

The broadcast from the maetor ended and normal broadcasts continued.

In less than fifteen Human minutes, Earth's ground forces had control of Czep-tan.

6

Rebel

Li's bladder reached its limit. "We have to stop."

"What? Why?" Verina asked via the Infolux.

"I…my body…I have to relieve myself. It will only take a minute."

Verina clicked an epithet then ordered the transport to stop. Li hopped out, turned his back to the alien, and let nature flow. He'd have preferred a tree, but the landscape had flattened considerably —resembling the Kansas Local more than the Black Forest Preserve. Finished, he turned to Verina. "I though you said we'd be taking a break every seventy-five minutes."

Confused, Verina countered, "We've only been traveling twenty-three!"

Now Li was confused. Then it hit him. He'd forgotten to do the local conversion. "Flg-chith Gr'p!"

Verina said, in Quinkst, "You speak Quinkst!" Li looked back at Verina, surprised to hear something familiar. Verina continued, "Of course you speak Quinkst. You're a negotiator. Sprag, I'm so stupid."

Li's face broke into a grin before he started laughing. It hadn't occurred to him either that with Quinkst being the interstellar *lingua franca* of commerce and diplomacy they had a common language. When he settled down enough to talk, Li said, also in Quinkst, "If *you're* stupid, then I'm an idiot."

The Human climbed back into the transport as Verina shut off the no-longer-needed-for-translation Infolux. Ey said, "So, why were you cursing?"

"Huh? Oh. I forgot that after you reset the Infolux it defaulted to local measures."

"Ah. Yes. I sometimes have the same problem during negotiations. I hate do'octal," saying the last word in eir own language.

"Do…? Oh. Decimal. So what do you use? Octal?"

Verina held up eir knobby four-fingered hands. "Of course."

Li wasn't relishing doing the math. It wasn't difficult, just tedious. "Fair enough. Your planet, your measures."

The pair returned to their road trip. Midway through their first scheduled break Verina said, "We have a problem. A big problem."

The hair on Li's neck rose. Verina turned to Li and said, "I figured our travel time based on not having to stop for anything other than our breaks."

"Yeah. So?"

"It's not like before. I can't just call up a replacement transport or plug into a station to recharge. We're going to have to rely on solar regeneration. That means traveling only in daylight and stopping around noon for a deep charge. At most, we'll get about three hours of travel a day. Sprag!"

That *was* going to be a problem. They were going to be out in the open, alone, on an occupied planet, for an uncomfortably long time. Li said, "Do we have any other options?"

"Not really. So, that's our answer," Verina said.

Except for the threat of imminent capture, Li enjoyed the trip.

Serees was an attractive planet with more wilderness than most. Verina was as intelligent a person as he'd met in years, so the company was good. Though distracted by the circumstance of war, Verina felt that her enemy alien companion was also acceptable company.

Late on the second day, after they'd turned south, the transition from the open agricultural flats to the sheltering woodlands of the Family Lakes area made Verina feel a little more protected. The transport sat in the open to gather solar energy while ey and Li enjoyed the cover of old-growth trees. Li commented, "You have a lot of undeveloped areas on your world."

Verina nodded. "That is intentional. Most other worlds reach a point where they can only survive using artificial additions. When that eventually fails, they leave their home to populate others. We've decided to take from Serees only what Serees can provide on its own."

Li smiled. "How did your people get so smart?"

"It's important to know what is important," Verina quoted from the *Ip Et-ris*.

The next day left Li breathless. The Family Lakes bettered any remaining on his own planet. Scattered through the woodlands were large glassy planes of water purer than any open expanse of water Earth had seen in centuries. Bird-like animals populated many areas, though most stayed near shore. Large, iridescent tongostam swam in unison over deep water, submerging as one for seconds at a time in their quest for food.

Li's appreciation of this world grew with every new vista. The journey through the Family Lakes impressed him beyond expectation—this world was too beautiful to trust to humanity. Still, he knew that this idyllic aspect wasn't all there was to this planet. His time with their interrogators taught him that. These Sereesians were no paragons, regardless of how well they tended their home.

Verina avoided cities like Fan-tan and Miklao-tan. Ey directed the transport to go through, not around, the river- and canyon-filled western mountain region. Li imagined the mythic heroes Lewis, Clark, Audubon, and Chapman found their unspoiled North American state to be as wondrous as Li did Serees. The increasing altitude even made the equatorial weather more tolerable. It made it easy to forget the warships patrolling the vacuum above them.

Li awoke on the eighth night when a light poked through the forest canopy. At first, he thought they'd been discovered. He quickly realized it was nothing more than planet-shine from the gibbous sister world. Seeing the vague outline of Verina by the transport, he got up and joined em. "Couldn't sleep?" ey asked.

"The light woke me up."

"Bailera is burning bright these days," Verina agreed. "We should be celebrating her return. But that's not going to happen, now."

"Return? It isn't always like that?"

Verina couldn't help a smirk in the dark. "No. Serees and Bailera share nearly the same orbit, but different enough that they exchange positions when they approach closely enough."

"How often does that happen?"

"A Baileriat occurs every three-hundred-one-and-a-half years, a complete Bailerion cycle in double that. Our tradition is that the outer planet is always the one contacting the inner. With Bailera the outer this time, we think of her as checking to see if we are doing well. It's all myth, of course." Verina leaned on the transport. "But it helps bind my people together. We still maintain some of the ancient traditions, especially during a Baileriat. Mostly, we just enjoy and welcome the return of our sibling. It's comforting to know we aren't alone. Serees has eir sibling, and we have each other."

Li nodded. "Your faith grew out of superstitions about

Bailera?"

"I'm not sure 'faith' is the right word. Maybe it is. In any case, our 'faith' grew out of fear. Some of our most revered books tell of the ancients, terrified that gods from the sky were descending on Serees to seek vengeance for our sins. They performed rituals. Eventually, Bailera retreated back to the heavens. It took thousands of years before we learned about orbital mechanics. The fear was replaced by...I guess you'd call it 'relieved wonder.'"

Li looked back up in the sky, unexpectedly comforted now that he knew the big piece of shining rock was simply checking up on them.

On day thirteen, Li saw the largest fresh-water inland sea he'd ever seen. In fact, he'd have sworn it was an ocean. Margran-ip was nestled between young mountain ranges to the east and the growing towers far to the west. This made a perfect valley for rain-water to collect. With it raining seemingly every other day, there was no lack of water to fill something so massive.

Two days later, Li saw mountains taller than the Himalayas growing in their path. "Wow."

Verina's attention was instead on the map ey'd unfolded across the front compartment of the transport. "You'll learn to hate them."

"Why?"

"Only fools and adventurers venture into the subduction zone. The mountains are a side effect."

"I don't understand."

Verina half-turned in eir seat to face Li. "This is where the land band starts and ends. Our side dives under the edge, raising these mountains. New land forms on the other side. That means land-quakes, lava, impassible roads." Li sat back in his seat. Verina added, "At least I know we won't be followed."

Four tense days later, the fugitives gratefully found themselves driving their now-battered transport through a calm, verdant land-scape. With danger behind them, they slept well. Starting in the morning, just before dawn, Verina set the transport to its highest possible speed. In the early afternoon, Verina pulled the transport over. Ey said, "We're getting out, now."

Li exited the vehicle, taking his pack. Verina unloaded eir packs and punched in the commands to send the transport on its way. "It's on a random path until it runs out of energy," ey said. "We'll camp here until dark."

"We're traveling at night?"

"And the morning. Don't worry—once she rises, Bailera provides more than enough light."

Verina busied emself with setting up a bivouac for them to wait out the heat of the day. After positioning the lean-to frame they had used throughout their trip, Verina unwrapped a new cloth to cover it. "Now that we're close to a city, we're going to have to use this. It isn't as durable as what we've been using, but it's 'stealthy' to Human technology since you can't detect anything in Fa'run space."

"Fa'run?"

Whoops. Verina hadn't intended to mention that. The lengthy time with Li had made em too casual. Ey would have to watch that. "Most species can detect and use Fa'run space. As I under-stand it, your people can only detect it indirectly via mathematics and the side effects Fa'run space has on ordinary space. It's no secret that the reason you enslaved the Gelrahtem was to force them to use their skill with Fa'run materials to make your engines. What do you call them—'TVerse?'"

Li nodded. "So, Fa'run space is like hyperspace or dark-phys-ics?"

"I don't understand those terms. It's really fairly complex, my sibling could explain it." Verina paused and thought back to when ey was in school. "Let me try a very simple construct. Within all the universe, there are naturally imposed limits to perception forced on every species. Some can hear a broad range of frequencies. Some can see a large segment of the electromagnetic spectrum; some, much less. The limit for a few species, including yours, is what you call the visible spectrum. You've created instruments to see more, but they don't see everything. Your perception is limited by this and so is your ability to reason something beyond it. Most species can see more than you, mine included. It's our reality. If we were to look out onto our world with your eyes, it would be as if some of the colors of the spectrum had been taken away. We could infer the presence of the missing colors, but we couldn't actually know what they looked like."

"So, you just see more than we do?"

Verina shook eir head. "No. I told you, it is very complex. There are differences between perceiving and interacting. Not all species who can directly perceive Fa'run space can manipulate it. It requires more than sensing. It requires a certain amount of a species' makeup to be *of* Fa'run space, although, in a sense, we are all of Fa'run space. And I really can't explain it any more. I'm not a science specialist, and I don't have enough knowledge of your science to make good analogies. All that really matters is that your people are essentially incapable of detecting anything under this cloth unless they happen to walk up to us."

Li felt confused and relieved at the same time. For many years he struggled with the knowledge that some aliens had access to materials that Earth didn't know about. Apparently, there were materials that Humans *couldn't* know about. It seemed so simple. In a universe full of color, Humans were colorblind. "Thank you," he said. "I can't say that I fully understand your explanation, but what you told me makes a great deal of sense."

Verina pulled out the map ey had been using for the past twenty days. Ey folded the long strip of reinforced paper to the panel centered at one-twenty secir south: Foer-tan. Ey pointed to a spot northeast of a symbol on the map and showed Li. "This is where we are now. We're about sixty-two feo from Foer-tan, one of our tier cities."

Though still struggling with the conversions, Li estimated the distance at somewhere around fourteen or fifteen kilometers. "What's your plan?" he asked.

"Foer-tan. It was hit by the giant waves, but it's not too damaged. I hope there might be, as you suggested, people wanting to fight back."

"Okay. So, then what are we likely to find in Foer-tan?"

Verina hesitated before answering, "I'm not sure. I've never had to know that. I think the major export is energy converters, but I might be thinking of Fan-tan. In any case, we still have to get there. We'll leave when Bailera rises."

The Ligrosian lay back under the lean-to, closed eir eyes, and went to sleep. Li sat and fidgeted. It was too warm, the gravity a little heavy, and that blasted sun was too bright. Mix that in with Li's difficulties of sleeping during the day even in the best of circumstances and it was certain that nap time wasn't in the cards. The lean-to did offer shade and shelter from the rain that looked to be coming their way. He settled back and worried. He didn't notice that he'd dropped off until Verina nudged him. "Wake up," ey said. "We need to start moving."

Li thought he was still on his ship and was having an incredibly real dream. One more nudge from Verina cured him of that illusion. Yawning deeply, Li took a few steps away from camp while Verina packed up the lean-to. When he returned, Verina sported eir pair of packs, obviously eager to move. Li donned his pack and followed the alien down a narrow trail.

The light from Bailera, though enough to see by, didn't provide

Verina much more light than ey needed to avoid obstacles. At least there were established trails here, unlike the area near Czep-tan. Ey often felt Li placing his hands on eir packs so as to not lose his way. Dawn neared and Bailera reached its zenith. Verina stopped. The silhouette of Foer-tan was visible below them. The outskirts of the sprawling, park-encrusted city looked to be about a kilometer away. Verina pointed to the south. "We'll camp over there for the day, away from these paths. Assess the situation."

Finding a well-secluded spot not far from a creek, Verina again set up their small camp. Li took the last of the rations from his pack and laid out the preserved food. Verina savored the meal. Though ey still carried six or seven more days of food in one of eir packs, the prospect of re-provisioning occupied eir mind. As noon approached, ey settled back for a nap.

Evening arrived. Verina rose from the shelter to find a place to relieve emself. Ey moved less than five meters from the lean-to when a loud rustling to eir left caused em to back into a craftentz tree. Ey tried to make emself as invisible as possible. "You!" ey heard a voice say in the Human language. "What are you doing outside of the—?"

The voice didn't get the chance to finish. Verina's jujibtanibarre training kicked in. With practiced ease, ey dropped to a knee and then upended the potential threat. Though shorter than Verina, this being was noticeably bulkier from the many levels of equipment and armor it wore. Even so, the person inside was clearly more massive than Li. Had it not been for surprise, Verina wasn't sure ey would have been able to send eir victim to the ground. But now what? There was so much armor it didn't seem possible to actually hurt it. Li quietly said, "Hold his arms down! Open his hands if you can."

Inherent Ligrosian flexibility became an immediate asset as Verina stretched eir arms and legs wide, pinning the person's arms down with eir feet and putting enough pressure on the alien's fingers to keep them stretched out. "Wow," Li said before kneeling down beside the soldier.

Li released the micro-med-kit on the soldier's leg, removed a red and yellow striped tube, and plunged the socket end of the tube into a small receptacle in the neck of the body armor. Seconds later, the soldier relaxed. "You can let him go," Li said, "He's unconscious."

"What did you do?"

"I gave him an anesthetic-paralytic mix. Usually the automatic med-kit tends to field injuries, but all military personnel have these manual drugs available in the event the automatics fail."

Verina relaxed. "Why did you make me hold him that way?"

"A soldier controls the communications in this suit via an embedded keypad in the palm. It interfaces with a data gateway implanted under the rib cage."

"Wait. Let me understand this. You insert machines into your soldiers to make them deadlier?"

"We like to win. Look," Li said holding out his hand, "you can still see the scar from when they removed mine."

Verina shook eir head and frowned. "So, what now? You probably want me to kill him."

"No! No, you don't want to do that. When they find him—if he's still alive—they won't try so hard to track us down. You hit us, we get annoyed; you kill us, we get pissed."

"How long do we have?"

"A few hours, maybe. I can give him another shot, but he'll have been missed by then in any case. I don't think it will help."

Verina sat on eir heels and thought about the situation for a moment. "Can you disrupt his communications system? Maybe make it look like there's some sort of malfunction?"

A smile spread across Li's face, "I like da way you tink,

sistah," he said in a bad Hawai'ian accent, dropping out of speaking Quinkst.

"I don't understand," Verina said.

"Never mind."

Li pushed the soldier over slightly to access a panel on the grunt's back pack. He opened it and used the soldier's own multitool to cut a trace that connected the processing crystal to the data bus. "There," Li said. "If I did it right, it should look like his comm system is on the fritz. Nothing out of the ordinary. By the time he wakes up and wanders back to base, we should be far enough away not to have to worry."

"Then let's go," Verina said with some impatience.

"Wait," Li said. He again bent over the downed form. "Here." Li efficiently handed Verina various items off of the soldier, which ey divided between Li's empty pack and one of eir own: energy packs, meal packs, the multi-tool, grenades, and a "double-beamer" that could be used both as a small cutting laser and as an ionic digging tool. When Li got up he said, "Never leave behind supplies if you don't have to."

The pair set out toward the park-like city surround. While they didn't see any signs of others nearby, neither Verina or Li could shake the feeling that eyes were on them.

The Serees sun, Maygola, hugged the horizon. Verina and Li stood just inside the edge of the woods. About a hundred meters away, eight Human guards stood watch outside the newly constructed city gateway. Seeing alien soldiers outside Foer-tan with eir own eyes galvanized Verina's resolve. This was no longer a plan concocted by em and eir pame. This was real. Very, very real. "You said that killing them was a bad idea?"

"Yeah...at least not until you have something more than a one-person backup."

Verina's mind raced. If only every Ligrosian simply attacked at once, the Humans would be quickly defeated. Yes, there would be tragic losses, but survival was at stake. Unfortunately, the maetor's speech all but guaranteed that wasn't going to happen. "I heard a word your people use…sabotage?"

Li smiled. "That's what we call it. I think you're right. That might be the safest course for us, at least for now."

Verina looked pointedly at Li. "There is no 'us'. I don't trust you. You are Human, and you are a government official. Our motives are definitely not the same."

Li nodded.

Verina's posture relaxed. "And you're a problem. I don't trust you to join me. I imagine I'll have to exit quickly so you have to be able to follow."

"I'll be here when you get back."

"If you aren't, the next time I see you I'll kill you." Li was certain this diplomat had never killed anyone before, but he sensed that this wasn't an idle threat. Verina continued, "You say that you are a moral person. You're going to have to show me."

"All I can say is that I'll do my best not to let you down. Swear to God."

Verina nodded. "Fine. What happens happens. I won't mention it again." Verina turned back to the gate. "Do you think I could disable those vehicles over there, by the fence?"

"It won't make much impact. In fact, they probably won't even notice."

"No. Probably not. I've never done this before. I've never been a…a…"

"Freedom fighter?"

"Yes. I like that. Freedom fighter. I've never been a freedom fighter before. After all, you don't catch shmuptl when you first learn to fish."

Understanding the context, Li said, "Then your best bet will probably be to drain the hydraulic lines. The fluid we use is pretty volatile and should evaporate fast enough that the guards won't detect it before you can get away."

"Sounds easy enough."

"If you aren't spotted. I can't even tell you how to do it. Shoot, I can only do repairs on my ship because she tells me what she needs me to do. I don't work with ground vehicles."

"I guess I'll just have to find out on my own."

Verina unlocked eir pack. Ey removed the laser and the stolen multi-tool. After a long drink of water, ey worked eir way over to the vehicles. With every step, Verina thought both *What am I doing?* and *If not me, then who?* Ey wanted to run into Foer-tan, hide out in a nice and safe house, and hope the Humans didn't bother em too much. But then, who would help save em? Ceyelna instilled a great sense of duty—which Verina channeled into being someone respected and trusted in the government. With most of the government killed or imprisoned by now, how could ey let them down?

In the growing darkness, Verina moved slowly and quietly through the detritus at the edge of the woods. Once ey reached the cleared area, Verina saw with eir peripheral vision another barrier to be overcome: the thin streaks in the air suggesting a laser fence. Since details of the beams faded when ey looked too directly, ey relied on the edges of eir vision. It seemed like there was enough room to slip between the gossamer detectors without interrupting any of them, but it was hard to be sure. Ey would just have to estimate their height and then dive into the parking area.

Verina removed eir jacket and pareu and waited for a moment of opportunity. The delay gave em too much time to think. What was ey doing? Ey didn't sneak around places like some common thief. Or, at least ey didn't until ey broke that Human out of detention. Was this eir true nature? It went against the sacred learnings.

No. No, this *was* moral. Eir world had been attacked. Ey had to defend it vigorously. There was no other way.

A flight of morops made a terrible racket as they nested in the forest near the gate, distracting the guards. The naked Ligrosian dashed toward the parking area, making a risky, laser-evading, one-and-a-half-meter-high jump three meters away from the closest vehicle. Ey rolled when ey hit the ground. The nearby vehicle blocked Verina from being seen by the guards. Ey took a moment to catch eir breath and steady eir hands. Verina felt alive in a very primal way.

This first vehicle wasn't much larger than the four-person transport ey and Li used in their flight from Czep-tan. Verina took eir time examining the machine. It stood one meter high and had no roof. The undercarriage hugged the ground. The body was so smooth it almost felt oily. The cockpit was filled with metal components. Verina had never seen such a conspicuous use of these alloys anywhere on Serees. Well, maybe that one experimental piece of artwork at the now-destroyed grand museum in Yavent, but that was the only example ey could think of.

Verina worked eir way around the vehicle, looking for some way to access those hydraulics Li suggested. After completely circling the car, Verina thought a couple of large panels might be hatches. Ey re-examined the cockpit. Much of it appeared automated, like the transports on Serees, but there were also many individual controls with symbols suggesting function. Figuring it wouldn't hurt to try, Verina pressed a button with the pictogram that looked like an opening hatch. Ey heard a latch release and saw the panel on the top of one end of the car rise up slightly. Moving to the front, constantly checking that ey wasn't being watched, ey raised the hood a few centimeters. Setting the laser on wide-diffuse-low, ey spied a tangle of cables. If there were any hydraulics to be found, this was a good place to look.

Forgetting about the unfamiliar multi-tool, Verina used eir focused laser to randomly cut through the spaghetti-like web of cables. Since the vehicle was not powered up, this had no perceivable effect. When ey severed one finger-thick line, Verina's foray into civil destruction turned chaotic. A pressurized, silvery fluid gushered from the severed tube. Amazingly, little of it hit the Ligrosian. While trying to contain the situation, Verina neglected to turn off eir laser. The focused beam ignited a small puddle growing on top of one of the fuel cells. Seeing this, Verina ran for the woods—not forgetting to jump through the gap in the laser barrier. Ey almost reached the safety of the forest.

Pain filled Verina's consciousness as ey woke. The entire back of eir head and torso felt like thousands of red-hot drills were being pressed into eir skin and slowly twisted. Ey opened eir eyes and saw a few candle flames providing a weak and patchy light. It didn't feel like ey was still outside, but eir disorientation removed eir ability to be sure. "What in Traxaguese did you think you were doing?" an unknown voice said in a southern dialect of Limto.

"What—?" Verina murmured, still trying to get a handle on reality.

"The maetor commanded us not to antagonize these people. Then you create a conflagration that kills eleven of them—and nearly yourself as well. I ask again, what were you thinking?"

Whoever spoke hit an emotional nerve. Forgetting eir pain, Verina said forcefully, "Invaders…not people. It's our duty to save our world; to make them leave before they've taken everything worthwhile from us."

"And I—"

"They aren't welcome here," Verina interrupted.

"And I suppose you are an expert on what these Solari are

like?" came the sarcastic reply.

Verina didn't want to play anymore. Eir previous outburst drained em. "I hold my own," ey said, gathering enough strength to add, "I'm a First Negotiator."

Verina waited for another goading response. Instead, ey got a lengthy silence. For that, ey was thankful. It gave em a chance to let eir brain clear. Ey heard the familiar clicks and slides of a locally made, hand-entry terminal. A few moments later the voice said, "There's a reward out for you."

Verina felt less secure. "A big one?"

"Not really. There's the one our government issued, and then there's one from the Solari. Oh! For both you *and* the Solari you kidnapped. We captured him, too."

That actually eased Verina's mind, though ey didn't know it had been a concern. "May I ask who you are? Or where we are?"

"We're nobody. Some of us got washed away when the waves hit the cities. Some of us just fled. Either way, we don't much want to be under the thumb of the Solari."

"Humans," Verina corrected. "They call themselves, 'Humans.'"

"Like that makes a difference."

"It's only a matter of time before they start looking for you. With what I did, I think that's a certainty."

"You *have* limited our choices," the voice agreed.

There's my opening. "Then why don't we work in a common cause? To really irritate these invaders?"

"Because we'll lose, and you can't."

"What do you mean I—ahhhowWWW!" Verina triple-voiced when ey absently tried lifting emself up from being belly-down on a cushioned table.

Verina gasped from a pain like ey had never imagined. Ey might even have lost consciousness for several moments—ey

wasn't sure. Once it leveled off, ey said, "Can I get some paink-
iller?"

"You're at maximum non-lethal dose now. The explosion tore
off a great deal of skin from your back and almost all of your
fringe. You also have seven broken ribs. We can keep you alive,
but there's only so much that we can do. I'm sorry."

Even though ey understood what was being said and unsaid,
Verina didn't feel a moment of vanity. If anything, ey was proud of
emself for not caring that she'd be so badly scarred. Instead, ey
said, "When you found out who caused the waves, and then saw
them land and imprison our people, didn't you want to fight
back?"

"I have to admit that—the textors of Gav-toh forgive my weakness—I wanted them all dead."

There it was. The critical moment in any negotiation. The
matter was already decided, the owner of the voice just had to
have time to reach the inevitable conclusion. "My name is Verina,
as you already know from the database. May I please know
yours?"

"Thothwai."

"Thank you, Thothwai."

The episode took its toll. Verina relaxed slightly and sleep
consumed em immediately.

When Verina woke, the scene was just as ey remembered,
except Thothwai wasn't hovering over em. Nearby, however, Li
sat beside the foot of the table. "Hi," Verina greeted him in
Quinkst.

Li moved closer. "How are you feeling?"

"Stupid question."

"Maybe. You look awful. There's this dark purple gunk all over
the back of your body and head."

"Bet it feels worse than it looks. But that's OK."

"OK."

"For future reference," Verina added with a pause to let a stab of pain lessen, "when cutting hydraulics, don't use a laser."

Li couldn't help laughing. Worse, he couldn't stop. Finally some of the stress and anxiety found a release. "I wondered what you could have done to…BOOM!" He chuckled again, but not quite as heartily. "That would do it."

"You could have warned me."

"I didn't know I needed to. I'll do better next time."

"Yeah. Me too." Verina paused as another assault of pain consumed all eir focus for a good Serees minute. When it subsided ey said, "How are you doing? I can't imagine a Human is too popular around here."

"I'm not. You aren't either."

"I figured that."

Li leaned in close and spoke softer, "I've managed to learn a few things while you were out." Off Verina's expression, Li continued, "These people are more than simply homeless refugees. They've got some pretty impressive surveillance systems in place."

"We *are* noted for our communications, you know," Verina remarked.

"Yes. Well, it seems that soon after the attack started, your leader ordered almost all of the local Seetun access cut. Apparently there was already a workaround in place, but it isn't as secure. The Sereesians here—"

"Serees. We're called Serees."

"The Serees here have tapped into it. I haven't heard much, but I think your planet is in serious risk. Fleet Commander Pervikh was killed during the initial attack. He would have set up a more-or-less peaceful occupation. His replacement, General Chavez…he has ties to ministers who have strong Earth-first points of view.

I've also heard some things about his character. Nothing solid, but I think he's going to make your people suffer. I don't believe any level of diplomacy will work for long with him. He's already implemented a stage two martial law order. It's probably only a matter of time before that elevates to oppression and then subjugation. You have to fight. And I think you have to do it qui—what are you doing?"

Verina's eyes were closed. With great effort, ey pushed and slid emself off the table. As much as the broken ribs hurt and restricted movement, it was the fiery stabs caused by the huge amount of missing skin that made eir eye-mask patches turn a bright red and eir healthy skin to glow in an oily sweat. Li was amazed that ey managed to stand on eir own two feet—although calling it standing was a very generous description. Verina's feet rested on the floor, but ey was bent low with most of eir weight resting on eir hands, which tightly clutched the table. Eir eyes stayed closed. Eir breathing was very deep and very deliberate.

Li said, casually, "That must hurt."

A small unintelligible sound escaped Verina's mouths, and then ey said, "Don't make me laugh. Please." After a couple of breaths ey added, "And yeah, it hurts."

With heroic effort, Verina straightened up. Though it was obvious ey wanted to take a step, eir body refused. Placing eir right hand on Li's left shoulder—as well as, the Human noted, a great deal of eir weight—Verina took two very small shuffling steps. Thothwai walked in and yelled, "What do you think you're doing?!"

Verina clucked and said, "You keep asking me that."

"You are confined to that bed for at least five days."

"After you fill me in on all your intelligence to this point," Verina said in Limto and Quinkst, with more of a commanding tone than even ey expected. "And before you object to the

Human…for the time being he is to be considered an ally." Verina looked at Li. "Not a trusted ally—at least, not yet—but an ally just the same."

Thothwai resented this treatment. Though there had been no official vote, ey had been the one the others here came to for direction. "What gives you—?!"

Verina interrupted, "This isn't a debate. I'm the highest ranked person here. I'm trained to deal with aliens, and I have an informed ally willing to help."

Li felt Verina pressing down on him to stand straighter, but it was definitely he who bore most of the weight. Verina added, "Understand?"

Verina hated to pull rank like that. Ey had only done it once before to a Second negotiator who didn't know eir place at a delicate stage of talks with the Tariri. Thothwai was obviously very proud of what ey had accomplished, and it was sad to see that resolve melt, no matter how subtly. "Please, lie back down," Thothwai said. "I'll bring you the information."

Verina nodded. Thothwai and Li helped Verina back onto the table, after which Thothwai quickly left. Verina was exhausted. Not enough to keep from feeling the pain, but it was enough to let em fall asleep.

7

Resistance

On the twelfth day after arriving at the refugee camp, Verina walked around without obvious limitations. Eir body had healed enough that ey wouldn't do any additional harm. Breathing came easier once eir ribs partially healed. More troublesome was the skin the explosion had flayed from em. A new membrane, a few cells thick, had regrown on eir back, neck, and patches of eir head. It was enough to prevent infection, but it did nothing to alleviate the soul-crushing pain. If anything, it made the pain worse. Any pressure, sometimes from the breeze of a person walking nearby, sent tendrils of fire through eir nerves. When roaming about, ey wore a loose wrap of the lightest fabric available—one that gave more protection than irritation. The chronic pain ensured the patches around eir eyes stayed red. Pain killers didn't help much. Not wanting to use more than eir fair share, Verina lessened eir reliance on them—opting to use them only for sleep.

The abandoned mine about three-hundred feo from Foer-tan served as an ideal base. Three main tunnels formed the compound's backbone. They were as wide as a four-lane transway and two stories tall. More modest corridor-sized tunnels capillaried out into a web of narrowing passages—some barely wide enough for a single person. The walls, laser-fired for strength and water-fastness, had an even, mildly textured finish. Thick ribs corseted the tunnels, reinforcing their designed-in stability. Though the mine had been abandoned generations ago, only one minor side tunnel had experienced a structural failure. Some weeds had managed to infiltrate the cracks in the floor and walls until the refugees reclaimed the space.

The mine provided shelter and a surprisingly large cache of fresh water that filtered in through some cracks. Unfortunately, it lacked good access to food and energy. The lack of power affected every aspect of the community. Strategically, it made intelligence gathering and analysis difficult. The energy packs and devices that were taken from Verina and Li's packs when they were brought in had doubled the available capacity.

Even though communications were rationed, information still made its way to Verina. The most encouraging, and depressing, information coming in from around the planet was about the easy compliance of the general populace. This left the large cities as little more than guarded camps. The occupying force no longer expected significant resistance.

It was the disappearances that made Verina anxious. During the time when ey and Li were on the road, important people—most in or connected to the government—could no longer be accounted for. The occasional information gleaned from attempts to intercept Earth's communications seldom gave details about individuals, but news of the maetor's summary execution when Czep-tan was captured had leaked to the refugees in the mine. Earth Fleet had not officially reported this to the populace…probably waiting until it could be psychologically advantageous to do so. As far as the Ligrosian public knew, the maetor was living in "protective custody."

Using the codes assigned to em when ey was promoted, Verina accessed the low-bandwidth network activated by the maetor before Serees fell. While there was little doubt that the officials who knew about it had long since been captured or killed, the network wasn't silent. Verina learned of at least two other enclaves of displaced Ligrosians in this hemisphere with rumors of others to the west. They weren't doing anything other than laying low and surviving outside of Human control, but that they existed at all was a good sign. It wasn't much, but it was enough to raise Verina's hope that maybe they would have enough to fight the invaders.

Verina wended eir way through the ant-colony of tunnels to reach Thothwai's chamber. Like most of the living spaces, the only bow to privacy was the curtain covering the door. "It's Verina," ey announced.

Thothwai pushed the curtain aside, "Come in."

Verina had visited the former leader's chamber the day ey was first able to walk. Because of the uninterrupted dose of strong pain medication ey took at the time, Verina's memory of the event lacked the details she now saw. The three-meter-cube was efficient and relatively comfortable. To the side of a makeshift table was an actual mattress that had been rescued from the flotsam caused by the Invasion Wave, as it was being called. The most impressive touch was the half-completed mural on the back wall. It spoke of Ligrosians spending quiet time in the park promenade of Foer-tan. Verina briefly imagined hearing the quiet sounds of wildlife lingering at the fringes of the oasis. "Are you ready?" Verina asked.

"I wish I weren't," Thothwai said, sitting on a chair and motioning Verina to do likewise. "I know it makes me sound like a coward, and vain, and so many other bad things, but I don't want to end up with half my skin torn off."

"Like me."

Thothwai lowered eir head in acknowledgment. "But I'm not backing out. From what we've learned, and from what you've told us of Lrat, I don't think I have much choice." Ey got up and stood beside the mural. "I make art," ey protested.

Verina stood and with quiet sadness said, "I know." Verina moved to leave but turned when ey pushed the curtain away. "Sundown. Make sure everyone knows."

Thothwai nodded, "I will."

Verina fought eir growing anxiety. Ey, too, was afraid to die. Admitting it didn't help the feeling pass. The dark blue skin on eir back with the honeycomb of red blood vessels served as a constant reminder of how breakable ey was. Even more, ey feared for the poorly trained, badly supplied refugees about to risk their lives— not just tonight but quite possibly for many nights to come. How many would be killed? How many maimed? The faith taught that every individual carried the responsibility of their actions. All the Ligrosians on this mission were volunteers; they each knew the responsibility was ultimately eirs. For Verina, the reality was more intense. Ey was their leader. It was eir plan. If ey was wrong, then…*No*, ey thought. *No more negative thinking.* Ey had been devil's advocate enough during the planning; now was the time for optimism.

Ey literally ran into Li, who strode out of a side passageway without slowing. Verina clutched at the wall for stability as eir knees buckled from the traumatic electric fire shooting through eir body. Slowly, deliberately, ey straightened—hand still on the wall —and focused on Li. Eir eye patches shown bright red even in the poor light. Verina didn't notice the constant stream of "I'm sorry," spoken by the Human during the time when ey made no sound at all. With great control, the Ligrosian said, "It's OK. See?" Verina pushed away from the wall to stand on eir own, "All better."

Li nodded. "I've been going over our supplies. I wish we had more…well, more of everything."

"I know. We are not ready. Unfortunately, we can't wait, either. The Humans are becoming too entrenched. We have to attack now while their detection grid around the city continues to be unreliable."

"I still don't like it."

Verina stopped. "You don't have to like it. *I* don't like it. I'd like to be living in my apartment or be running in the park. I'd like to be able to move without feeling like half my nerves were exploding. But I can't. I can't because *your people* don't know anything but deception and conquest. *Your people* can only talk with the end of a gun. So I have to fight an army using scared refugees armed only with rocks and sticks. I don't give a yav-ti kur what *you* like."

Verina stormed down the passageway leaving a stunned Li with three equally stunned Ligrosians who saw but didn't understand the exchange except for the curse at the end. Verina never lost control like that. It was fairly common knowledge that when the medics scraped off the scabs from eir back in order to minimize scarring, ey stayed calm and measured. That's what made this loss of control so remarkable.

Li tried wrapping his mind around the outburst. He had been chewed out before, but never so completely. Verina's voice didn't quite rise to the volume of a yell, and yet his ears still rang from the memory of it. But she was right. This wasn't his fight. Why was he doing this? Li's mind flashed to the one time he visited Lrat. There wasn't even the pretense of Earth having "advisors" to ensure orderly manufacture. It was a planet-wide slave camp regardless of what euphemisms the Chamber of Ministers chose to employ. His dissatisfaction with Earth started there. It wasn't until now that he fully realized it. He wanted a divorce from Earth. Was that why he bonded so quickly to a daughter he hadn't known? No. This was different.

Verina reached eir cavernous *sanctum sanctorum* with eir hackles still raised. The flood of emotions against the Humans caught em totally off-guard. Ey hated them. Having never felt honest and complete hate before, Verina was unprepared for how it manifested itself. Li didn't deserve to be the target of eir vitriol. He'd been nothing but helpful, but ey had trouble getting past the fact that he was part of the same species that stole eir life away. Ey would have to work on that. But for now, he was a constant reminder of the world ey'd lost. Verina knew ey could never let any of the others see em like that again. One outburst might be excused but a second would show weakness of character. The sociology of it transcended worlds. A successful mission tonight would erase the slip, but a significant failure would crumble the rebellion before it started.

The Ligrosian stared at the various maps and intelligence reports the refugees were able to generate in a remarkably short time. *So much could go wrong.* No. Ey had decided no more negative thoughts. Verina walked around the massive table and sat on a backless chair. Closing eir eyes, ey visualized the mission step-by-step, trying to account for all the variables from as many ways as possible.

A filled glass placed on the table in front of em nudged Verina back to reality. Li said, "It's nearly time to suit up. There's some water."

Verina nodded. "I'm not apologizing for what I said. I do, however, apologize for how and where I said it."

Li paused. His lips pursed, like he wanted to say something. He finally settled on, "Thank you."

Verina stood, taking the glass in eir hand. "You do realize that we've reached a point of no return, you and me."

Li looked puzzled. Verina sipped eir water and then continued, "You are a valuable asset. You also know too much about what my people are doing and what I plan to do."

"So, I'm a prisoner."

"Not exactly, but close enough. We can't…*I* can't let you have your freedom. Not until my people and I have ours. I'm sorry. That wasn't my intent when I rescued you."

"I had my opportunities to leave," Li said. "I didn't have to stay. You'd be foolish to simply believe me, and I know you don't, but we're on the same side. Maybe for different reasons, and certainly not to the same extent, but I want Earth put in its place, too. "

Verina downed the last of the water. "Well. I guess I have an appointment."

The Ligrosian walked out of the chamber. Li wondered if he'd ever see her again.

Using the only seven working push-plates they had as makeshift transports, it took four trips and two hours for Verina'a assault teams to reach their positions around Foer-tan. The plan needed to start soon, before Bailera-rise, at maximum darkness.

Gamat squad moved first. The four Ligrosians emerged from the sea, carefully avoiding the extensive but well-mapped field of explosives and traps the Humans had installed at the shore. Once clear, they headed to the communications center the Humans set up in what had been a school building before the invasion. Three clusters of fist-sized antennae sprang gargoyle-like from each of the edges of the roof. A larger antenna array couldn't be seen from street level. Though Gamat squad hugged buildings and clung to shadows, it was extremely difficult to remain undetected.

Bharta and Junije squads infiltrated from the west. Using portable trampolines, Bharta squad vaulted over a newly installed laser fence that bisected Foer-tan's historic arboretum. Guarding against the possibility of audio sensors in the trees, the six members shared a sound-nullifier as each jumped the fence and positioned themselves in the branches before moving toward the city. Junije's six-member squad stayed on the ground outside the laser-fence perimeter.

A storage farm sat about one feo away—or about three hundred meters as the Humans measured it. These large units held most of the materials to be used in the nearby factories. Intelligence reports suggested that three of the house-sized holding tanks should still contain important volatiles. The expanse between the rebels and the strategically important tanks was patrolled regularly by the modest military security force. Since the wide, open area surrounding the farm was ringed by a heavy blast-redirecting wall, the Humans figured they didn't need to heavily fortify this area as the natives had done it themselves in the name of safety.

At the northeast part of the city, near the main gate where Verina attacked weeks earlier, Mazet squad joined up with Verina's own Gopro squad. Both five-member squads easily bypassed the laser and hardware security fences. Their inexperience ensured that no one noticed Earth's security was tailored to prevent escape, not entry.

Mazet and Gopro moved into Foer-tan. The Invasion Waves hadn't been able to reach this far inland. The buildings stood as if nothing had happened—blending into the carefully tended land-scape. The local armory occupied a small cluster of "re-purposed" warehouses close to the city limits. Though there was a visible guard presence throughout, the reports Verina saw indicated only the four largest of the seven buildings were being used. Upon reaching the high ground, the two groups split up. Mazet moved farther in while Gopro held.

Verina looked at the timer strapped to eir forearm and then carefully adjusted eir clothes. Even with pain-killers and an anesthetic foam coating eir injuries, the pressure of the fabric itched and burned so strongly that Verina thought ey would go insane if it went on for too long. After doing the best ey could with the uniform, ey sat and scanned the city. Gahleh, the most athletic member of Gopro, sat next to Verina. After several minutes, Gahleh quietly said, "If the Humans hadn't invaded, what would you be doing now?"

Verina paused. Though a chat seemed inappropriate, ey felt a little relief that someone was actually willing to talk to em about anything other than this plan. Turning eir attention back to the city, ey said, "I don't know. Maybe watching an entnews program to find out if Yallew had given birth yet."

"I loved *In the Nest, In the Sea.*"

"I know," Verina said with a smile. "Don't you think that was eir best work?"

"I don't know. *The Dark House*—"

"You're right. You're right. No, you're wrong. *In the Nest...* was more entertaining. At least I thought so. Especially with the kulp and—"

Verina interrupted emself. The few lights in the southern part of the city just went dark. Verina stood. "Show's on."

On the ocean side of the city, a trio of Earth Fleet soldiers had walked to the communications center and convinced the two guards closest to the building's entrance to go off with them. Taking advantage of the opening, Gamat squad rushed to the building—starting their attack two minutes earlier than planned. One member worked on the lock, two climbed an access ladder to the roof, and the fourth kept watch.

The recently installed door locks from Earth easily succumbed to run-of-the-mill Ligrosian decryption tools. Leaving no trace of the break-in, the Gamat locksmith and the guard entered the building. The well-lit interior still bore clues of it having been a school: announcements clung to community boards, storage bins lined the halls, and decorations hung from the ceiling. A quick reconnoiter revealed three communications rooms that were each manned by two operators each, five unguarded systems closets filled with processing equipment and supplies, and tightly-packed systems closets on the second floor. The compact layout made it easy to plant explosives for maximum effectiveness.

On the roof, the other pair of rebels used lasers to fatally neutralize two Human guards. They then set charges on each of the small clusters attached to the roof's edge. The bulk of their munitions were attached to the flattened-pyramid antenna array that took up a third of the roof's area. With the explosives set and armed, they left the roof via the same access ladder they used earlier.

The squad rendezvoused a block away, around the corner of a market building. Once gathered, the squad leader triggered the weapons. The explosives on the roof made a very crisp and loud low-frequency BOOM, which soon showered fragments of metal and synthetics over a three block area. The sound of the bombs inside the building were considerably muffled but no less effective as all the lights in this section of the city went out. The mission was to disrupt Human communications locally in order to hide the larger attack. Unfortunately, the destruction of the alien technology caused an unintended local power overload. The blackout effectively painted a target on the source. Gamat rushed from the area, hoping to make it back home safely.

Thothwai saw the lights go out on the south side. The Human, through Verina, warned that events never go as planned and leaders needed to adapt to changing conditions. Thothwai wasn't convinced this was one of those situations. Ey wanted to hold to the schedule. The plan called for em to wait two more minutes. Thothwai saw Human soldiers, not far out from the storage tanks, react to the unexpected outage. Ey couldn't wait; the Humans would be sending out patrols. Thothwai pointed eir unfocused laser at the barrier wall at a point between eir squad and Junije: two flashes followed by one flash.

Both Bharta and Junije fired on their targets: the volatile-liquid holding tanks at either end of the farm cluster. Every member of each squad focused their "mine cutter" lasers on the tough storage shells. The night was clear without a hint of fog, allowing the laser beams to remain invisible and focused. After a few minutes of continuous fire, the smooth skin of the tanks flaked off where the concentrated beams ablated the surface. The roughened surface sped the process causing material to flake and vaporize at an increasing rate. The tank Thothwai's Bharta squad fired on started venting through a small puncture. As the puncture widened, two more nearby holes began out-gassing. Soon, the venting transitioned to actual leaking. Judging the damage to be adequate, Thothwai said, "Hold."

Junije wasn't having the same success. Nothing came from a large hole made a third of the way up their tank. It had been drained since the last report. The squad leader flashed two quick and one slow spots on the wall, telling Thothwai of the empty tank. Thothwai ordered the squads to pull back while ey stayed behind.

When the squads found cover, Thothwai reset eir laser to a needle-thin high-intensity beam sufficient to encourage ignition—which wasn't going to be easy at this distance. Starting near the leak, the Ligrosian coursed the beam to various areas, lingering on promising surfaces. Nothing. Then ey noticed it: the two-meter square Earth machine not far away from the tank. Ey aimed at the device. The pulsing beam of cutting light caused only minor sparking, but it was enough to ignite the growing cloud of nearly invisible vapor.

The night lit up to midday brightness as a million liters of volatile liquid exploded. Close to the fireball, all the oxygen was sucked from the air for a moment. Thothwai's shield—the massive blast wall—did its job as designed, directing the entirety of the blast upwards. It also withstood the second explosion when a neighboring, filled-to-capacity tank was breached by the first blast. The thunderous shock wave was noticeably stronger.

Though the wall worked as designed, Foer-tan wasn't untouched. The set of blast waves shattered most of the city's windows while the locally moderate landquake broke the glass that remained. Scattered showers of fiery debris rained across the area, though the damage was minimal due to the heat-resistant ceramic structures and generally damp climate.

When the debris bomblets subsided and the bright glow from the still-raging inferno inside the barrier lessened, the two squads joined back up with Thothwai and started their trip back home. Verina had gotten eir diversion, now it was up to em to fulfill the mission's primary objective.

Verina and Gahleh sprang into action when they saw and felt the explosive results of Bharta and Junije's mission. Verina thanked now-rising Bailera that things were going more-or-less as expected. Taking advantage of the confusion certain to be growing in the city, Verina and Gahleh raided a market for the fifty large push-plates they needed to meet their objectives. The pair left the market with their bulky cache of secured, stolen plates and headed east to rejoin the rest of their squads—currently engaged in their own battle near the armory. Two blocks from the market, the bindings on Verina's half of the push-plates came undone. Ey stopped. When Gahleh moved to help em, ey said, "Go. I'll handle this. Get in position. If I'm not there in two minutes, go ahead without me.

GO!"

Gahleh moved on, quickly disappearing around a group of buildings. Verina hurriedly worked to arrange the plates back into a compact and transportable configuration. From the corner of eir eye, ey saw a young Ligrosian—not a child, but clearly not yet an adult—lying in the shadow of the media store three buildings down. Understanding it might be a tactical mistake, Verina stopped what ey was doing and went over to check on the young one.

The adolescent Ligrosian lay on eir side, a small pool of blood under eir torso. When Verina touched the youth's jacket, it felt sticky-damp. A deep cut ran from the top of the victim's head and down the side of eir face until it reached eir torso. Blood pumped from the wound; this was clearly the worst of the injuries. "Oh Gods," Verina said. Looking skyward, she added, "Bailera, help me."

The rebel debrided the cuts as quickly as ey could, feeling guilty that eir spectacular diversion was the cause. Ey used wound adhesives from eir small first-aid kit for the obvious body lacerations and chose tape for the head wound as it would be easier to remove. A quick spray of hema-hibit slowed the bleeding. "Hey," Verina said to the semi-conscious form. "Hey, where do you live? What's your dom-locale?"

Barely audible, the young one mumbled what sounded like, "Six-haf-East, Widek, Foer-tan."

Verina retrieved one of eir cached push-plates and put the adolescent on it. Ey programmed the understood address and activated the plate, hoping ey would be cared for at the destination. Verina quickly bundled eir goods and followed after Gahleh.

By the time the rebel leader arrived at the warehouse section of the city, Gahleh was already moving from the staging area to the armory. At a dead run, Verina caught up to em. Gahleh noticed the large amount of blood staining the late arrival's clothes as well as eir labored breathing. "Bailera's soul," ey said. "Are you alright?"

"I'm fine." Verina gently massaged eir healing ribs. "I had to help someone. What's the situation here?"

"Most of the guards from warehouses one and two are dead. Mazet took them completely by surprise. Our people are holding their own, but I think we better hurry."

Verina blasted open the armory's personnel entrance's lock with a small charge. Once inside, ey half-raised the main loading door. Gahleh guided in the two bundles of push-plates and unbound them. Verina said, "As fast as you can."

Each rebel took a plate and headed to various pieces of ordnance on their shopping lists. They filled push-plate after push-plate to capacity with weapons of war and tied them down for traveling. For each loaded push-plate a pre-programmed flight plan was slipped into the destination receptacle and a small timed charge was placed on the controller, ready to destroy all record of the plate's route should the rebels not recover it in time. As each round pallet was ready, it was sent on its way. In twenty minutes, all of the plates were gone.

Verina and Gahleh rounded two warehouses to join up with their small force. Verina saw that the Humans would soon be in position to neutralize both eir squads. With no time to lose, ey shouted, "Brights and bombs!"

Every Ligrosian tossed a jacks-ball-sized sphere toward the soldiers. As each projectile landed, it emitted a full-spectrum light that effectively blinded the Humans despite their cyber-vision additions. The effect only lasted seconds, but it was enough for the Ligrosians to wind up and throw their antipersonnel grenades: 100-gram high-explosive charges that had been laced with sharp fragments. Eight charges, eight blasts, and the Human squad was rendered inoperable. Two Mazet members looked ready to cheer, but Verina stopped it cold with, "Quiet everyone. Let's get out of here."

As the squad filed past Verina, ey counted seven. "Wait," ey said, "We're two short."

"Uytil and Roshil were killed after the guards regrouped," said Tamira, one of the Mazet fighters.

Verina nodded. "Keep moving."

As quietly as when they entered the city, the ten-person double-squad worked its way to the main gate. Verina took point for this stage of the egress. The two deaths nagged at em. Being Ligrosian, ey accepted that loss of life was inevitable. The annoyance was the weakening of numbers. Ey didn't have the manpower to spare. How many from the other three squads died? How many Humans did they kill? Verina's plan provided no quarter for mercy or pris-oners. Death was not something to fear, but ordering the killing of others, alien or not, was crushing. Verina knew ey would have to pay that price someday. *Look at what they've made of me*, ey thought.

The need to escape the city forced Verina to focus eir attention away from philosophy and morality and back to the immediate problem of survival. The squads rounded the last buildings and trees. They could now see the main gate. Gahleh said, "Six guards. Two inside, four outside."

"Lasers," Verina said.

Ten invisible beams focused on the heads of the armored figures standing guard. It took several disciplined seconds, but the beams soon did their job and pierced the hard shell of the helmets, permitting the collimated light to wreak catastrophic damage to the organic material within.

Though Verina escaped the city, the mission wasn't over. The refugee members not involved in the fighting had designated areas to go to. They waited to retrieve the push-plates before the plates dumped their cargo and the timed charges destroyed their controls.

The rebels deactivated the charges on the loaded push-plates, re-commanded the disks to follow, and lead them back to base. Li had suggested the complicated logistics as a necessary step until reliable intelligence on Earth Fleet's installed tracking tech had been gathered. The materials were too necessary to lose to incautious planning.

In the last hour before dawn, the collection teams began arriving at the mine. Their cargo was quickly inventoried and stored. Fifty drops had been planned. Getting everyone back to base before sunup had always been a tricky proposition. Li bit his nails waiting for this fractured caravan to end. Blood already leaked from the exposed quick of his right ring finger when Verina entered the artificial caverns. Like many of the last returning squad, ey looked like they had been in a fight. Their clothes and skin were stained with dirt and grime. Wait... Verina had a great deal of blood on em. Ey didn't look hurt, but the uncertainty doomed another millimeter of Li's fourth nail.

Verina immediately asked the supply leader, "Squad counts?"

Without missing a beat, the answer came, "Two missing and known dead from the attack squads. All drop bearers accounted for."

"How many drops?"

"Forty-seven."

Verina allowed emself to relax. Ey and Gahleh had taken fifty push-plates. Subtracting the one Verina used for eir errand of mercy, then all the drops were accounted for. Ey couldn't quite believe it...the plan worked. Yes, two new comrades died, but they had expected at least five to fall in the various assaults. It was a good first step. They now had weapons—true weapons. Eir small group could show eir fellow Ligrosians that surrender wasn't inevitable. They could fight. If they wanted their freedom as a people, they *had to* fight.

8

Terrorist Acts

"I will not tolerate terrorists on my planet!" General Chavez shouted at Colonel Bryce. "Do you hear me, Colonel? I'm sure God will damn them all to Hell for the six hundred forty-two lives they've taken, but I'm not going to wait that long."

"No sir," the colonel said.

"Actually, Colonel, *you* aren't going to make me wait that long."

A flash of confusion followed by loathing flickered across Bryce's face. It wasn't much, but it was enough to egg on the general who had been working on finding a crack in the façade of the "Ice Colonel". The general smirked. "Yes," he said, "that's right. I'm putting you in charge of stopping this rash of terrorism —by any and all means necessary."

"Yes sir."

"I mean it, Bryce. By any and *all* means. Do you understand me?"

"I believe so, sir," Bryce answered with more obvious control than she'd wanted.

Calmer, Chavez said, "I don't want there to be any misunderstandings between us. All information filters through fleet command—through this headquarters. We'll sanitize any compromising information. You'll have no reason not to use quick and effective means."

Colonel Bryce stayed at attention, focusing on not giving the general the satisfaction of seeing any emotion. Ironically, it was this facade of non-emotion that informed Chavez of how effective he'd been. He said, "Computer. Announce to Lieutenant Potaryanii that I want to see her here ASAP." The general slowly padded in front of Bryce like a cat. "Now, Colonel, I don't expect you to dirty your hands with pissant intel, but I do insist that you interview the high-priority detainees yourself."

A loud knock from the door prompted Chavez's, "Enter."

Lieutenant Potaryanii, a mousy and weathered woman, unexpectedly mature for her low rank, stood at attention beside Colonel Bryce, the top of her head not quite reaching to the senior officer's shoulders. "Lieutenant Potaryanii reporting as ordered, sir."

Chavez smiled. He liked this officer. She'd taken several court-martialed demotions as a result of following his orders. How he rewarded her steadfast loyalty was one of the tightest secrets in his command, but she never complained about being ill-used. "Lieutenant, you'll be assigned to Colonel Bryce, planetside. You will be managing and filtering the initial interviews with the locals to determine those worthy of the colonel's attention."

Potaryanii struggled to contain her smile. "Yes sir."

Chavez smiled in reply. Turning back to Bryce, he said, "Remember Colonel, I'm expecting this little insurrection to be nothing more than a short footnote, so end it. End it with lies, end it with privation, or end it with blood. I don't give a shit. Am I being clear, Colonel?"

"Yes sir."

After moments that seemed like hours, Chavez finally said, "Dismissed."

Both subordinate officers about-faced. Potaryanii lead the way to the door. Chavez said, "Just a minute, Colonel, there's one more thing."

Bryce stopped, composed herself, and executed a textbook about-face. "Sir."

Chavez waited for Potaryanii to close the hatch. He then said, "I want you to coordinate with Bhoutto. He's executing the Presidium's disinformation plan. This will include decoy attacks scripted by us that will turn the populace against these insurrectionists. Don't step on his toes."

"No sir."

Tired of goading, Chavez said, "Dismissed."

"Yes sir," Bryce said before quickly about-facing and exiting.

Although Rachael was now away from Chavez, she couldn't let her guard down. The comm center outside the office was filled with junior officers known to be more than eager to report any perceived disloyalty. She had intended to simply march through the hive but saw a familiar face. Smiling, she said, "Lieutenant Evelyn!"

The junior officer started to stand, but the colonel motioned him to remain seated. "Colonel?"

"How's your wife? Has she had the baby yet?"

The lieutenant's smile was colored with concern. "I haven't heard anything, ma'am. She was due four days ago."

"Send a message to my office when you find out. And if you get a picture, send a copy of that, too."

Smiling broadly, pride overcoming concern, the lieutenant said, "Yes sir. Thank you, ma'am."

"Captain," the colonel said to the duty officer, "please inform my shuttle crew to prepare for immediate departure."

"Yes sir."

The colonel exited the command deck and was met in the passageway by Lieutenant Potaryanii. "Colonel."

Bryce rolled her eyes. She didn't want to deal with Chavez's spy right at this moment. "Lieutenant. I'm sure there will be plenty of time for us to get acquainted. For now, you need to stow your gear on my shuttle, we're leaving immediately."

"Yes sir."

The colonel's eyes quickly glanced over to the officer's head. "I'll be with you shortly."

"Yes sir. I'll make sure they don't leave without you," the diminutive officer said with a smile and a nod.

Bryce entered the head. A quick survey showed it to be vacant. She leaned on the counter and stared at herself in the mirror. Anger and hate contorted her face. Quietly, with control, she said, "Son of a bitch," with the degree of venom only the females of this particular species could muster.

On General Chavez's command display, an overhead view of this scene showed in a subscreen on the display. "That I am, Colonel," the general said with a smile.

Verina's resistance pod was on the move. They traveled on foot and modified push-plates—which they now called personnel-plates—away from their Foer-tan base to a rendezvous with a squad sent out six days earlier, led by Gahleh. The pod's seventy-two Ligrosians plus one Human intended to join up with a barely-active cell of rebels holed up in the canyons south of Fan-tan. In the twenty-four days since their attack on Foer-tan, Verina's fighters moved east and attacked targets of opportunity. During this period, Verina also coordinated a handful of "nuisance" attacks using other resistance enclaves around Serees. Although these raids didn't achieve anything significant, they diverted attention from the skirmishes Verina's fighters engaged in.

Having crossed the subduction zone, the resistance pod neared one of the villages dotting the shores of Margan-ip. Verina, Li, and Thothwai had the point position—leading the troops as well as staying out of earshot. Verina said in Limto and Quinkst, "We need to start planning something big."

"Like what?" Li asked, with Verina providing simultaneous translation for Thothwai.

"I don't know yet. It needs to be a crippling blow."

Thothwai moved closer and spoke quietly. "Why now? Don't we need to get good at this, first?"

Verina clicked an almost-tune of agreement and negation. "We're going to get killed if we prolong this. The more time the Humans have to figure us out, the more chances they have to crush us. We've got to make them reconsider being here before they get entrenched."

Li said, "You don't have the manpower to do something like that. All you have are a few cells, only two of which we know who are worth a damn in a fight."

"And we need to change that soon." Verina said. "There need to be cells and pods within striking distance of all the major and tier cities. The leaders of the squads we formed will teach the others. We don't have the luxury of letting this build slowly. We need to have as our goal an army sufficient to hurt the Humans and take back a city while also having enough in reserve to continue the fight on other fronts."

Thothwai said, "Forgive me, but these Humans have trained for war. They have equipment that we don't have. They—"

"This isn't their home," Verina interrupted.

Li and Thothwai walked quietly for a while, letting the emotional peel of Verina's statement ring out. Li asked, "What do you have in mind?"

Verina smirked. "I honestly don't know. Think about it a little. We'll talk later."

The column continued moving, a few pockets of chatter in the ranks breaking the silence but nothing that would disrupt the emerging discipline. When Bailera touched the horizon, Verina ordered a meal break. Pod members found spots between the road and the woods. Many spied Thothwai helping Verina off with eir jacket. Whenever anyone saw their leader's dark blue skin with red spider veins, not to mention the loss of so much fringe, any resentment for Verina not carrying anything other than the burden of command disappeared. Ey rarely took medication for eir injuries, saying it should be saved for those who could benefit from it. That only helped eir stature grow. If *ey* was still fighting, how could they expect less of themselves?

From the rear came the tonal alerts of a threat approaching. The rebels quickly melted into the woods. A small convoy of transports carrying Human troops drove by, passing the rebels in less than a minute. Verina turned to Thothwai, "How many is that?"

"Seven. Two more convoys to go."

"Good. Spread the word: we'll wait here. We could use the break."

At Guard Station Bravo Ninety, the first lights of the last expected convoy rounded a curve two hundred meters down the road. Except it wasn't the convoy. It was a single Command Coach ATV closing quickly. It braked hard but overshot the designated halt-point. Six guards, all with high-powered weapons pointed at the single occupant, approached the vehicle. The skin of the coach bore laser scoring from a firefight. The rider, a staff sergeant in full armor, stirred. The inter-squad comm system crackled, "Name and rank!"

"Staff Sergeant Neligong, squad six leader, logistics cavalry unit, sir."

The station's sergeant approached the driver. "Visor."

Pressing a button on his uniform's gauntlet, the driver's optical shield slid into his helmet, revealing two very Human eyes. When the guard lowered his weapon, the others at the station relaxed as well. The driver re-activated the visor and said, "My convoy is under attack by terrorists. Comm out. We need immediate backup."

Though there was no obvious communication transmitted, a score of various armored vehicles appeared from behind the guard station and proceeded at high speed back down the road from where the convoy ATV came. "Thank you, Sergeant," a raspy female voice said over the inter-squad band. "We've been waiting for this."

"Permission to travel with you, sir. That's my unit back there."

"Granted."

Wasting no time, the small vehicle turned around and joined up with the end of the speeding armored column. The guards at the station walked back to their post with some bounce in their steps.

Several minutes later, the special forces vehicles approached the convoy's coordinates. The raspy voice asked, "Where's the firefight, Sergeant?"

"Just ahead…around the bend, Captain."

"Flying wedge alpha."

Five of the armored carriers formed into a tight, elongated wedge that presented maximum firepower while showing a minimum profile. Not that it mattered. When the vehicles rounded the curve, they found nothing but open road; there wasn't even the suggestion of a fight. The rest of the vehicles closed ranks, stopped, and disgorged their lethal passengers. The Sergeant's vehicle pulled alongside the Captain, who shouted, "Where the hell is the fight, Sergeant?"

Calmly, as he removed his helmet, Li said, "I told you, Captain. Right here."

Soldiers fell in their tracks as lasers caused havoc within their helmets. The ones better protected from the invisible beams succumbed to the high-volume resonant sounds Verina's rebels broadcast through the Human comm systems. In less than two Serees minutes, all of the Humans assigned to the armored column were dead.

Verina's pod emerged from the woods. Most of the force placed nondescript cases onto the chassis of each of the large, heavily-armed vehicles. Other fighters scrambled to place small boxes all over the road. With all the devices in place and the force joined up behind Verina, ey commanded, "Lift them."

Remotes activated the devices. The cases attached to the vehicles burst open and large heavy-lift balloons quickly inflated. Once half the vehicles were airborne, and the others in the process of joining them, Verina called out, "Decoys."

The devices placed on the road, and many others scattered around the countryside during their trek, began spewing forth a multitude of electromagnetic noise using both electronic and pyrotechnic means. The secondary devices attached to the vehicles now fired their rocket packs, propelling the captured supplies to predetermined spots over the ocean. Once there, the balloons partially deflated, allowing their cargo to submerge but not sink. Underwater squads of Ligrosians would guide the spoils toward their final destinations along the coast.

In an afternoon, Verina's forces had captured both a convoy and an armored column. Amazingly, the Ligrosians suffered no casualties. Li remarked to Verina, "You do more with the smallest number of people than anyone I've seen. You're very good at this."

"Thanks," Verina said, not quite sure if eir skill was really such a good thing. "Everyone! Very good work today, as always. I want each squad to head to their staging areas. We'll regroup according to the schedules already delivered to those bases, minus two days."

Colonel Bryce stared out her office window. The three long weeks since General Chavez tasked her to stop the terrorism hadn't gone well. Eight separate incidents. They began with the lost convoy and missing armored company, and led to the latest raids targeting industrial machine stockpiles, materials, and energy components in three different cities on the same night. The attacks exhibited no obvious pattern. Even so, the larger, successful missions had a certain "flavor", as if they were all the result of a central command. The galling thing was that while Bryce felt certain she knew who was behind this insurrection, she couldn't confirm it.

Sitting on her desk was a file with everything known about a Sereesian named Verina Some-terribly-long-last-name. She had been one of the planet's top negotiators. A prodigy. And a kidnapper—the last item in the jacket listed the security tracks of her taking Li Rinaldi from the Sereesian government just before Earth liberated the planet. She hadn't been seen since—nor had Li.

A week into her posting to Czep-tan, Colonel Bryce had received a "most secret" study that she assumed came from Chavez via his little spy, Potaryanii. In dispassionate detail, every page described various methods to induce pain in a Sereesian, the degree of pain, estimated amounts of short-term physical and mental damage, and suspected long-term damage. It sickened Bryce to learn that "research" of this sort still went on. Also sitting on her desk, with a note from General Chavez, was a copy of *Unknown Intelligence*—a centuries-old black-ops military manual.

It described the most effective methods of obtaining information from individuals—as it euphemistically phrased it—"under duress". Knowing that Potaryanii sent frequent reports to the general, Bryce felt backed into a corner. She needed to interrogate prime suspects, and the general all but insisted on "pressure" being applied during all of these procedures. Bryce hoped that her level of "duress" would be less than anyone else Chavez would send.

Three days later, Bryce sat in her protected chamber in a dimly-lit empty room. A pair of guards brought in a terrorist. The green-tinged Sereesian, legs and arms shackled with teftanium bands, was positioned in the center of the room. Magnetic locks engaged, holding the prisoner in place. The armored soldiers moved to either side of the room's now-sealed door. To Bryce, the alien looked like just about every other alien on this planet, the only striking difference was the oily slick covering its body. She'd learned it was essentially a form of sweat—but that didn't make it any more palatable. Bryce calmly said, via the built-in translation matrix, "You have just endured three rather unpleasant days. I'm sorry. I didn't want to expose you to that, but your lack of friendly cooperation forced me to authorize that step. You don't have to go through that again, you know. You have the choice.

"I'm going to ask you a few simple questions. If you help us—help me—stop the random violence that threatens your people and your family, then you'll be able to survive in relative comfort. I'm sorry I don't have the power to give you your freedom. Not any more. Not since you've been less than forthright. But I can guarantee that your life won't be in tiny locked rooms. And you won't go hungry.

"On the other hand, you do realize that you are causing me to spend more resources on you than I'd like while receiving nothing in return. That makes me...um...what's the word? It doesn't matter. It'll come to...cranky! It will make me cranky. What that means for you is more discomfort. It will be increasingly profound and intense. I don't want to do this to you, but I assure you that there are many here that enjoy making our guests…uncomfortable. You'll want to die, but we won't let you. Every day will be worse than the one before. And I don't have to watch any of it. No. I'll be in another location entirely, eating my meals, enjoying some entertainment. I don't have to watch what our experts do to you. I don't have to *know* what they do to you. They'll simply do it and then deliver you here to me. And then we'll do this all again. It's only a matter of time, in fact a short time, but you will answer my questions. You have to ask yourself: will all the pain you have to endure be worth it, and will the reward you receive when you finally tell me be anywhere near as generous as what I'm offering you now?

"So, let's begin. What is your name?"

She stared at the oily alien, waiting for a response. Bryce frowned, unhappy with herself. How easy it was for her to casually threaten the poor figure standing in front of her. It hadn't been badly abused at this point. If it didn't answer, that was going to change.

The alien stood up straighter and said, "My name is George Washington," while also baring its central-mouth plates, the equivalent of teeth.

Bryce couldn't tell if this was a smile or a challenge. She nodded slightly, admiring the defiance. "Guards."

The colonel wrote on a small Infolux: *Very likely that Li Rinaldi is collaborating.*

A second terrorist was brought in with nearly identical results. The only difference being that the name given was, "Thsphuk kra-Ta'Yavuk"—a historical leader on Lrat from centuries past. When the lone civilian was brought in, she almost didn't let the colonel finish her speech when she said, "I'll tell you anything I know.

Please…"

Colonel Bryce leaned forward. She asked, "What is your name?"

Potaryanii slowly circled the restrained Ligrosian. A dim overhead light illuminated little but the prisoner. "Since you couldn't know the name 'George Washington' unless you were part of the uprising, that tells me that you are a patriot. I respect that. Fighting for your home is noble—when there is some hope of winning. It's happened on my world many times. Of course, much more often than not, the rebellion was crushed and the fighters killed, imprisoned, or enslaved.

"The colonel was telling you the truth, you know. She just wanted answers. Nothing more." The lieutenant stopped circling. "Now you are my problem. I can do with you whatever I want until the colonel calls you back. I'll tell you upfront, my plans for you are very different than hers. I'm not going to be offering you luxury or the guarantee of a full belly. Not even close."

At the rebel stronghold in the Ira-mo canyon, the infirmary was nestled under an overhang with rocky bulwarks. Because it was safely hidden within a harsh landscape, the infirmary had the luxury to become the most hospital-like of the rebel/refugee medical facilities on Serees. When Verina walked inside, a field medic immediately attended em. "Hai-Verina, welcome. We heard you were in the area. Is there something you need? Treatment?"

"Not right now, thank you," ey said, with forced patience. "I'm looking for Gahleh?"

Before the medic answered, Li rounded one of the curtain partitions. Though Li's face was now commonly known; some couldn't quite mask their loathing of one of *his* species—despite his status with Verina. "Yes. Last I remember, ey was in bed twenty-seven."

"Thank you…uh?"

"Yaqlith'o."

"Yaqlith'o. Thank you."

Verina walked down the partitioned beds reserved for those needing constant monitoring, Li followed close on eir heels. Verina was happy that Gahleh had been near this facility—it was probably the only one that could have saved eir life.

When Li and Verina reached Gahleh's bed, Li recoiled from the sight of eir injuries. Almost a week before, by his reckoning, Gahleh led a mission to take some power generators from a supply dump near Fan-tan. Gahleh stayed to the rear to ensure the rest of eir platoon escaped. The blast door ey stood under unexpectedly crashed down, crushing eir head and an arm. Two of eir team used lasers to cut em free and bring em back. Now Gahleh lay in front of eir leader with half of eir head missing—ey lost an eye and almost half of eir auditory canal system to the accident—as well as eir left arm to just below the shoulder. It was the semi-head that made Li's stomach flip-flop. While he understood, intellectually, that eir brain case was positioned somewhere in the middle of eir pelvis and that the head was mostly just an input-output stalk, a lifetime of body assumptions made the head injury seem much more dire than it actually was.

"You did a good job," Verina said. "How long are you going to bask in your victory and lie in bed? We need you."

Gahleh sat up a little straighter. "Doctors say I'll be able to do non-strenuous activity in seven-to-eleven days."

"Good. I'm going to want you to help me plan something big. I need every experienced mind I've got if we're going to pull this off."

"Just say the word, and I'll be there. You know that."

Verina placed eir hand on Gahleh's right hand. "I know. Seriously. Get better. I really do need you." Verina's eyes suddenly brightened. "Oh, I almost forgot. Yallew gave birth two days late."

It took a moment for Gahleh to switch gears, but ey responded with a smile, "What's the baby's name?"

"Radock."

Gahleh made a face. As Li received a note from a guard, Verina said, "I know. Why didn't ey name it Ha'poehn, or Kashta, or Shmuptl for that matter?"

"Heh. Ow. Oh, don't make me laugh." Gahleh settled down but couldn't stop smiling. "I know what you mean. It's going to be tough growing up named after food."

"What can you do? It takes a certain weirdness to willingly be in the public eye like that."

"Do you think maybe it was the birthing drugs? Maybe they asked, 'What do you want to call it?' and ey thought they were talking about some radock on eir table or something?"

Li stepped forward, "I hate to interrupt this little gossip-fest…"

Li handed Verina the just-delivered message. Ey quickly read the short note and again projected the aura of command. "Gahleh, I'm sorry. I have to leave. I want to see you back at command as soon as you're cleared. Understood?"

"I'll be there. Go. Be safe. And watch out for closing doors."

Verina grimly smiled in reply as ey and Li exited the infirmary. Referring to the note, ey said, "I don't remember sending a team out there. Do we have a ready-team that far out?"

"It's not ours."

"I don't—"

"I think—" Li stopped and quickly surveyed the area. Seeing no unambiguously secure spot, he guided Verina outside. They walked toward some noisy whitewater. When the din was sufficient, he continued, "I think Earth Fleet did it."

"Why?"

"It's old. I didn't think of it because it's historic. Basically, you attack your own forces but ensure a lot of the innocent civilians your forces are 'protecting' get killed or injured. Then you blame it all on the terrorists. Us." Verina scowled. Li continued, "They're laying the groundwork to have the population see us as a general threat—not only to Earth, but to everyone on Serees. We'll just be these crazy terrorists out for blood and power, and the Humans will be the protectors keen on keeping the civil population safe, even if they are actually killing hundreds or thousands of them."

Verina shook eir head in disbelief. "I'll never understand your kind."

Li wanted to both defend his race and apologize for it. He had happily sold Earth's weapons and bullied those who weren't enthusiastic about it. Some of what was happening here was his fault. Seeing it through the eyes of its victims, he felt more astonished and ashamed than he'd ever expected.

Verina's frustrated, inarticulate, very loud, three-voiced scream interrupted Li's self pity. Ey said, "We were right to fight. If I have to lose my head and both arms to drive your people off my world, I will."

Verina gazed daggers at Li, who raised his hands and backed-up a step. "I'm not arguing," he insisted. "I chose my side."

"We aren't ready to stage anything major. But I think I— I think *we* can send a message to both our people. What was that word you used? Prop…?"

"Propaganda."

"Propaganda. We'll just have to make our point without ambiguity."

Verina's malicious tone worried Li. It sounded like ey was making this personal. From his experience in and around the military, he knew that that was a very dangerous course—but he wasn't in a position to argue. He hoped the rebel leader wouldn't lose eir righteous focus. Everyone needed to keep their mind on the bigger picture: freedom. And, while walking with em on this path, he hadn't noticed that he no longer thought of Verina as "she".

In under three minutes, hundreds of mortar-fired bomblets rained down on the barracks of sleeping troops from Earth Fleet. Two-thirds of the buildings soon collapsed from the sustained damage. Only a few dozen soldiers emerged without serious injury; most were so disoriented from the concussions of the blasts they couldn't put up a fight. Over seven hundred casualties awaited processing.

"There's no doubt you'll be the most hunted person on the planet," Li said, standing with Verina on a hill, observing the carnage.

"We've already killed at least as many since the war started as we hurt here tonight."

"This is different. Before, the deaths were a consequence of the plan, not the sole intent. This was simply murder."

"A point has to be made: we don't hurt our own. We aren't going to harm any of the Humans still alive, if that's what's worry-ing you."

"It's not." Li stepped in front of Verina, to face em. "You may have lost your soul today. You've certainly lost some of my respect."

Verina angrily grabbed two handfuls of Li's shirt. Ey stared him in the eyes. Li wanted to run, but his body refused to move. The Ligrosian's self-control took over. Ey relaxed and let go of the shirt. Ey calmly said, "I may have."

Verina walked away. Though standing as straight and tall as

ever, ey looked smaller…weighed down as eir decisions and their consequences piled on eir shoulders.

9

Leadership

The sun rose in Vehnyo-tan, Halvek-aziq, Esri-tan, and Czep-tan. Outside both commercial and residential buildings lay bodies. Human bodies. Most were alive. Many missed limbs. Some were dead. All had a note attached: "We only hurt Humans. Anything else is a lie. Freedom!"

Colonel Bryce was not happy. The heavy-lidded major standing before her seemed even less so. "And would you care to guess what I saw when I left my quarters, Major?" Bryce said softly enough for the hairs on the major's neck to rise.

The major kept a prudent silence. "Major!" The colonel exclaimed before resuming her calculated tone. "When I ask a question, I expect an answer."

"Yes sir," the anxious man said crisply. "From the colonel's tone, I imagine she found bodies—"

"Bodies! Of *my* troops!" Bryce volumed again before moving face-to-face with the officer. "But I'm not mad about this, Major. I already knew the terrorists had attacked the barracks. Would you like to tell me why I'm upset?"

"Sir. I would think the colonel is upset because the bodies were —"

"The bodies were laid out in not one but four cities—delivered there by our own stolen vehicles. I'm upset because not one of my garrison saw a *GODDAMN THING*!" Bryce immediately crossed herself, looked up and whispered, "Please forgive me my blasphemy." Turning back to the major, she continued, "None of my troops saw five hundred mostly-wounded soldiers being carried and placed in public areas by who knows how many of the enemy. Tell me, Major, how can that be?"

"Sir, these terrorists surely know the ins and outs of these cities better than we do. So far."

"You think so?" she said without bothering to hide her sarcasm.

Colonel Bryce walked around the room and settled by the window that overlooked an aesthetic garden filled with plants and artwork. "Major... Get the hell out of my office."

Snapping a crisp salute, the junior officer about-faced and made a hasty and welcome exit.

Bryce stared out at the garden. After a few moments, she calmed her mind. Now she could *see* the garden. None of the plants were capable of flowering, but their inherent color was used very skillfully. She appreciated subtle acts of creativity. "Sir," Lieutenant Potaryanii said, announcing herself.

Bryce turned and answered the salute but did not put the lieutenant at ease. The colonel said, "There seems to be a lack of information about access into and out of the cities that the Sereesians know about and we don't. You've been interviewing them for weeks, and we were still infiltrated as easily as if we invited them in. I'd appreciate some insight as to why."

"Sir, if I may say, the answers you receive are only as useful as the areas I'm directed to question. My team's focus has been to find the rebel leadership, not for this sort of intel."

Bryce turned, happy to have the upper hand with Chavez's minion. "And how is that area of directed questioning coming along?"

For a moment, Potaryanii actually looked uncomfortable. "As you know, ma'am, these aliens are annoyingly difficult to break. Those few rebels we've captured simply aren't high enough up the chain of command to yield anything useful."

An amplified male voice announced, "General Bhoutto returning your alert, Colonel."

"On the main display. Dismissed, Lieutenant."

While Potaryanii exited, Bryce absentmindedly checked her own uniform as she walked to the half-wall-sized display. General Bhoutto's image appeared in a large subscreen. "Colonel. I hear you've been having a little bit of rebel trouble."

"Yes sir. I'm sure you already know the important details, so I won't waste your time with a briefing. Suffice it to say, it looks bad.

"Suffice it to say."

"How do we turn it to our advantage?"

Bhoutto smiled a grim smile. "I just finished an emergency call with Minister Psiharis about this very problem. A detailed tac-rec will reach you soon, but the short of it is that we more-or-less pretend that the bodies were Sereesian. We'll talk about the terrorist butchers and how they don't represent the ideals of moral, law-abiding Sereesians. That sort of thing. We'll combine this with our continuing disinformation strategies so that the general population will turn against these madmen."

"If we keep them from getting more aid and recruits, then we can win by attrition."

"If necessary. It's easier if we simply chop off the serpent's head before it goes much further. The longer it continues, the more trouble we'll have maintaining control during the transition."

"Yes sir. I understand completely."

"Is there anything else, Colonel?"

"No sir."

"I'll send you a copy of the tac-rec by eleven-hundred."

"Yes sir. Thank you, sir."

Bhoutto's subscreen disappeared. Colonel Bryce mulled the current situation. It might not be as bad as it first seemed. Security holes were being evaluated, she'd lit a fire on that annoying Potaryanii, and an Earth-approved propaganda strategy was coming on-line soon. General Chavez might even have to let-up on her for a while so the strategies would have time to take root.

That hope turned out to be wrong. In the weeks immediately following the doorway "messages", General Chavez made Bryce justify every decision that was more important than cream-or-sugar.

Colonel Bryce joined the campaign to win hearts and minds by using some of the more cooperative "interviewees" as whisperers of dissent. Nothing overt. They simply interjected the fact that it was the Sereesians that littered their streets with bodies, not the Humans. They also mentioned how it was against ig'itwa-toh—roughly meaning "all the faith"—to wage war. The dozen or so other messages in their rehearsed repertoire echoed the same sorts of interpreted truth. After training the whisperers so they wouldn't comment more than once or twice a day, they were released to the various large cities around the planet. This seemingly benign force, combined with the news reports that broadcast Earth-approved stories on the conflicts, started affecting public opinion. The shift wasn't profound, but the psych-op teams tracking public mood reported confidence that the shift was happening—just not in the four cities where the bodies had been dumped.

Bryce's on-going headache was keeping the residents in the cities Verina delivered her "message" off-balance enough so they couldn't form a consensus. Since they saw the bodies and read the notes, Bryce had to concede that the rebel's morning surprise was amazingly effective. Not only did it harden local opinion among the Sereesians, but it sowed enough nervousness through the stationed ground troops that they required rotation to less strategic locations. To further improve morale, and at General Chavez's insistence, the regs regarding harassment of the locals were relaxed. Nothing blatantly abusive was tolerated, but slowly, with the perceived ability to strike back, even in a token way, the mood of the soldiers improved considerably.

The most worrisome aftereffect of the body incident came from the sudden absence of terrorist acts planet-wide. Something was definitely in the works, but the colonel's inability to obtain information about it continued. The leader, presumably Verina, professionally compartmentalized her organization. No matter how much pressure was applied on the few terrorists Earth Fleet captured, no compromising information was revealed. And always on Bryce's mind was the general's order to stop the terrorism quickly. "Quickly" had long since passed.

Potaryanii's world became more difficult. Chavez pushed her no less than Colonel Bryce. Also, the climate around "Minneapolis" and the surrounding cities had markedly changed. Damn the rebellion.

When the lieutenant walked through the streets, the litter of bodies still flashed in her mind. Though it was only whispered about far from Human ears, Potaryanii's sources told her that public opinion was swaying. It was obviously more pro-rebellion and anti-Human than it had been. The off-book network she was building suffered a hit from this shift in patriotism. The junior officer hoped that after this initial flush of public emotion, she might be able to do as General Chavez had told her so many times when plans inevitably went askew: "Make lemonade."

Verina sat in the early morning drizzle, eir exposed back massaged by the gentle mist. After sixteen days of steady progress westward, ey allowed eir pod a day's rest at Artef-ip, the largest of the Foot-step Lakes. Jestartam, a fit and road-weary squad leader who had been with Verina since the first assault on Foer-tan, walked up to the rebel commander. "Excuse me."

"Sit. Relax a while."

Jestartam sat on the damp ground, facing Verina. "All major fighting cells have acknowledged receipt of the code system."

"Mmhmm…" Verina acknowledged. "Tell me, Jesi…be honest. Do you think we can win this fight?"

The older, but junior, Ligrosian thought seriously. "I hope so."

Verina's eyes became alert and stared at Jestartam. "Do *you* think we can win?"

Reluctantly, Jestartam said, "No."

Verina nodded. "Then why do you fight? Following me, you'll probably end up dead; orphan your children…and all for a lost cause."

"That doesn't matter. This is *our* world. If we don't try to protect it, then who are we? I think we have to do whatever it takes to get our home back."

While the answer dripped of passion, it also echoed Verina's own rhetoric. It worried em. Was ey creating a cult of fanatics, willing to walk into fire simply because ey led them? That was no reason to fight. "If one of your teachers asked you that question back when you were in school, hypothetically of course, and you tried to imagine yourself in this situation, what would you have said back then?"

Jestartam said, "I actually *was* asked that. We were studying modern interstellar history, and that came up when we talked about Lrat. We didn't know then what I've learned in the past few months, but I thought that the Gelrahtem were right not to fight. The Humans would have destroyed them. It was sad, but at least they were alive." Verina nodded sadly. Jestartam added, "But now, seeing what we've seen, and hearing the stories that we've…I was wrong. The Gelrahtem should have fought back. Maybe if they did, the Humans wouldn't be here, now."

"Or they'd be extinct."

"Maybe. I don't think so. I don't think things would be much different than they are now. I do know that I have no intention of being a slave."

Li walked up, enduring the dampness with less aplomb than the pair of Ligrosians. "We just heard from Thothwai, if anyone's interested."

Verina motioned Li to sit. He knelt down instead, in a close approximation of the Ligrosian posture. "Eir survey of the cells in the western hemisphere through the Divergent Zone indicates about a hundred squads of an average of twenty-two or so members. Most have at least irritated the ground forces, but less than half have actually engaged in fighting."

Verina's fingers on eir left hand danced from forepalm to back-palm as ey considered this. "We need to harden them. Tonight, after you two rest—and I'm serious about you getting rest—we'll set up a series of raids designed to give those squads experience. Before too many lives depend on them, we need to weed out the ones who shouldn't be in the fight."

"Weed out?" Li asked.

"Find out where best to use the ones that survive. Not everyone can become a soldier."

Li scowled and nodded. It turned his stomach how casual these

Serees were about death. *"The ones that survive"* is what Verina said. That was damn cold-blooded, in his opinion. The trouble was, he didn't have a better idea. They didn't have the option of setting up large camps to train the rebels. Earth Fleet would easily wipe them out.

General Chavez stared at the missing tip of his left ring finger. He was sixteen and in initiate training. The defective round exploded in his hand while he loaded his sidearm. It taught him early to always expect outside forces to exert their will. The comm announced, "Colonel Smythe to see you."

"Enter."

Smythe strode into the command room, looking more tan in person than Chavez remembered. The colonel stopped and stood at attention. "As you were, Enrique," Chavez said.

"Thank you, sir. It's nice to be back in space, General."

"That's where we old horses really belong, isn't it?"

"Yes sir."

"Sit." Chavez waited for Smythe to situate himself. "Don't get too used to it, Colonel, you'll be back planetside soon enough. I figured you could use a little R&R before starting the next stage of your assignment."

"Post-bellum operations?"

"Yes, but there are a few things I want you to do first. As a result of the events over the past hundred or so days, there are elements of infrastructure that need attention. High on my list is that dam in the So-so Canyon—the one we damaged trying to force out the terrorists? Intelligence reports indicate that it's significantly weakened and threatens some ten thousand lives downstream."

"Yes sir. But, pardon me for asking, does it really matter?

Shouldn't we be redirecting our—"

"Have you ever seen a catastrophic flood firsthand, Colonel?

"No sir."

"I have," Chavez said, staring at the wedding ring his injury forced him to wear on his middle finger. "So has my family. It's a maelstrom of tragedy and disease I don't even wish on those aliens down there. We're going to make sure that the dam's repaired or they are relocated. Understood?"

"Yes sir. Merely playing devil's advocate, General."

"There are more projects like this. Coordinate with Bhoutto about the eastern and southern regions. I want you to look after the north and west."

"Yes sir. And Colonel Bryce, sir?"

"I have her involved in enough at the present time. Don't hesitate to ask for her help but understand that her priorities rank higher with me at the moment."

"Yes sir."

Chavez stood up, necessitating Smythe to do likewise. The general said, "Go over to your ship for a day or two. Decompress a little. Until we have that Sereesian tech in our hands, we've got some long days ahead of us."

"Yes sir. Thank you, sir."

"Dismissed."

Smythe left the office smartly. Chavez turned his attention back to his missing fingertip. *Many long days…* he thought.

Gahleh's return was a bigger relief to Verina than ey expected. Though eir friend bore the terrible effects of fighting the Humans, ey was one of only a handful of Ligrosians Verina trusted to tell em when ey was wrong. Despite the amputations, Gahleh was imposing. The effort to rendezvous with Verina gave em time to overcome the effects from so much bed rest. Now, ey was simply happy to be back at eir duties. Staring at reports with eir lone eye, Gahleh said, "This isn't good."

"The eastern hemisphere?" Verina asked, already knowing the answer.

"Public opinion is working against us. I don't know how it's happening. It doesn't look any different from what the Humans have been doing since they landed, but they've somehow figured out a way to make the eastern cities think that—"

"We're the enemy?"

"No. Not exactly. More like dangerous; not just to the Humans but to everyone in general."

Verina walked out from behind the massive paper-and-map-strewn mosaic of tables. Standing next to Gahleh, ey read the same information. Verina said, "It looks like my little surprise left us worse off than before."

Gahleh stayed quiet. Ey wasn't long enough out of the infirmary to read Verina's new subtleties. Verina said, "Go on. You're one of the people I depend on to tell me what's on your mind, and I know you want to say something."

The soft hum that accompanied the statement confirmed for Gahleh that this was, indeed, what was expected. "I think that morning surprise was more of a failure than not—certainly in the cities who didn't see it first-hand. I'm not sure we can recover from it before the Humans gain more in opinion than we can overcome."

"What if we talk to the people directly?"

"I don't...how?"

"We pick a city, say, Maya-tan since it's closest, we sneak in and join a communal service. We know the Humans don't guard the interiors during the meeting. Once there, we let the people know some of what we know."

"And when you say, 'We...?'"

"Me and one or two others. You'd be great. I mean, with my back and your..." Verina mimed the amputation line of Gahleh's head.

"And we get captured by the Humans. Then, for the short remainder of our lives, we get to enjoy the simple pleasures of torture."

Verina turn eir attention back to the reports. Gahleh tried to do the same but couldn't let eir leader's suggestion go. Verina said, "You know I'm right."

"No offense, but you being right is why we're in this mess."

Three days later, six Ligrosians sat at the outskirts of Maya-tan as dusk fell. When it was dark, two of the group disappeared into the now-glowing city. Two more soon moved off to parallel the city limits, inside the security perimeter. The last two, Verina and Gahleh, entered the city as nondescript textors—teachers of the sacred books. They wore robes with their hoods drawn up, ostensibly as protection against the just-beginning rain. While no one, Human or Ligrosian, gave them a second glance, the rebels were extra vigilant. One mistake could result in being captured or killed. "This was a bad idea," Verina whispered.

"I told you that three days ago," Gahleh replied.

Verina's anxiety reached a point where ey needed a distraction from the negative scenarios ey was imagining. Ey noticed the city. Verina had never visited here before the war and had to admit that Maya-tan was beautiful. The slanted lines of its architecture and design elements were augmented by light pipes powered by photonic solitons fueled by captured sunlight. The color of every line had been considered during construction, the effect making the city seem alive. Not all of the buildings could be done to this high level of artistry. The residences, in particular, bore simple lines and basic lighting. "It's beautiful."

Gahleh was astonished by the comment. Their lives were in danger and Verina was sightseeing. Ey pulled on the leader's robe, "This way."

The pair turned down a side street. Ahead of them was a very well executed building. The lighting, more impressive as the ambient darkness deepened, created the illusion of the structure growing before their eyes. Six armored Humans stood at the building's perimeter but otherwise seemed oblivious to the scores of Ligrosians who gathered inside—which now included two of the most wanted rebels on the planet.

The communal building's interior shone with an abundance of ambient light. Chairs were grouped in triplets around the floor space. They all faced toward the lectern/altar at the far end of the open hall. Half the Ligrosians were already seated, while most of the rest stood and visited, creating a cacophony of voices and tones. Colorful pieces of three-dimensional artwork were scattered throughout the hall. For the first time since breaking Li out of security, Verina felt like ey was home—like ey was safe. This place was very similar to the communal building ey visited once or twice a week in Czep-tan for local meetings as well as spiritual services. Verina felt that the spirits were with em, even if their unseen presence didn't help calm eir nervousness.

The two doors at the end of the building, on either side of the hall, were closed and locked. As far as the Humans were concerned, this was a church—their own law forbade desecration of such a place. At the alter, an older Ligrosian rose. What was obviously once a magnificently fit and muscled body now stood withered with age, but eir presence of character shown nearly as brightly as the room itself. "I call to order," the Ligrosian said quietly, though it seemed much louder. Most of the standing attendees found seats. A few, Verina and Gahleh among them, remained standing, though careful not to block anyone's view. The old-one continued, "Please take this beginning time for quiet contemplation of life as well as that which is beyond our life."

Though ey wanted things to move faster, Verina didn't want to unnecessarily disturb these people who ey needed to think well of em and eir cause. Ey quietly sank to eir knees and sat. From several meters behind em, someone started humming a tune that seemed familiar. Verina found it distracting as it wasn't loud enough for em to hear more than half of it. Soon, other nearby voices joined in the tune, adding resonant sounds in complicated structures. Within minutes, the entire hall had joined in a massive impromptu choir voicing a melody taught to children around the world—a song of loss and of hope. It echoed the reality that even a rich life knows both triumph and tragedy. When the last note was sung—a single lingering note hanging in the air from one lone voice—the hall broke into cheers and applause. As order was restored, the old-one said with a smile, "Well, I was hoping for something a little quieter than that."

The people in the hall laughed, catching Verina off-guard. Ey couldn't remember the last time ey'd heard this large a group of people enjoying themselves. The old-one continued, "But I can't think of a better way to start tonight's meeting." After waiting for the hall to fully settle, the old-one said, "Navegil?"

Replacing the old-one on the altar was an amazingly tall Ligrosian. Standing two-and-a-half meters, Navegil was one of the tallest living Ligrosians. With spidery arms as long as poles and knobby hands that could easily enfold two heads, this was one Ligrosian who would never find it easy to hide in a crowd. "Thank you, Hai-Popituv."

Verina fought to keep from audibly gasping. The old-one was Popituv? Fifty-four years ago, Popituv had stepped away from being maetor after serving for twenty-six years. It was all but unprecedented. For at least six Baileriat, no popular and healthy maetor had ever relinquished the obligation of leadership. It made eir legend grow beyond the popularity ey earned from eir wise stewardship. Verina never thought ey'd meet someone so great.

While Verina's eyes remained on the former leader, eir attention shifted to the blue-green tree of a Ligrosian standing on the low stage. Navegil said, "We still have no reports of any major attacks since the last meeting. While we doubt that the madness has ended, Hai-Popituv and I agree that we all should do what we can to assure the Earthers that we are no threat."

As if by reflex, Verina stood suddenly, catching the attention of the half of the hall who could see em. Navegil directed eir attention to the still-hooded member. "Yes? Do you have something to say?"

Verina replied, "May I say it there?" motioning toward the area where Navegil stood.

"Of course."

As Verina and Gahleh moved through the crowd to the stage, a buzz rose in the hall. The hooded voice wasn't recognized, and no one had seen eir face. This was different and unexpected, neither of which were appreciated in these dangerous times. When the two rebels stepped on the stage, Navegil moved off to the side a few paces. Verina said, "Placating the Humans is only going to make your lives harder in the long run. We have but to look at the tragedy of Lrat to know that. They will take our freedom to choose for ourselves as a people. If you are willing to trade that freedom for the illusion of peace, then maybe you don't deserve either."

A rumbling rolled through the crowd. These were dangerous words. Navegil said, "And who are you to lecture us?"

Verina pushed back eir hood. The Humans had long made em into their prime enemy, a fact made very public. Ey knew eir face would be recognized instantly. The crowd didn't bother to stifle its collective gasp. "That's right. I'm Verina. And at the risk of sounding immodest, I'm the one who has been leading the fight to win our planet back for you."

An anonymous voice in the crowd shouted, "Butcher!" Both Navegil and Popituv immediately motioned for silence. Popituv walked slowly to the rebel pair with more command than Verina had ever seen. "Tell me, young Verina, how have you helped?"

Truth be told, especially recently, ey hadn't been helping the cause at all, but at least ey was trying. "You aren't slaves…yet. The Humans are so distracted with me that they haven't been able to focus on you. Do you really want that to stop?"

"I see. So, the attacks at Brisma-tan and Zhawi-tan…they were to distract the Humans?"

"That wasn't us!" Gahleh said.

Verina quickly added, "We don't kill Serees—either Ligrosian or Haipuxan. The Humans can't say the same."

Popituv said, "Whether that is true or not, your actions are making us all pay a price."

A general murmur of agreement rose in the crowd. Popituv continued, "We are led to understand that you are well fed, have medicine, have access to communications, and many of the other things your actions are forcing the Earthers to take away from us in order to fight you. I'm thinking you are in it for your own glory and comfort, and you don't want that to end."

Another unknown voice yelled, "What price are *you* paying?"

After Popituv motioned the assembly to calm down again, Verina smiled. "What price have I paid?"

Finally, something Verina had prepared for. With practiced ease, ey unfastened and dropped eir cloak. As ey turned eir back to the crowd, ey lowered eir jacket. Eir dark-blue, red-mazed remnant of skin told of never-ending pain and of the battle that must have caused it. The massive wound elicited the appropriate amount of shocked disgust from the crowd. This was easily eclipsed when Gahleh dropped eir own cloak. The partial head and missing arm were hard-to-ignore injuries.

With Gahleh's help, Verina carefully slipped eir jacket back on and replaced the robe on eir shoulders. Ey then said, "I think we pay. And, as you can imagine, there is some need for things like medicine and other 'luxuries'."

Popituv couldn't help a grudging admiration for the person standing in front of em, misguided though ey might be. It had been quite some time since the former maetor felt out-maneuvered. Ey heard that this Verina was the youngest First Negotiator in quite some time. Apparently the position was deserved. Popituv lowered eir voice so only Verina could hear and said, "Can you win?"

Verina stared back at eyes that looked like they had the wisdom of a planet behind them. "That is a question."

The ex-maetor was well-versed in interpreting the meaning of non-answers. So everyone could hear, Popituv said, "Why are you here?"

"I'm not here to find recruits. I'm not here to ask for your aid. I'm not even here to ask you to agree with the fight. All I'm asking is that you don't work against us. You don't want to antagonize the Humans? Fine. Just don't go out of your way to help them."

"And if we do this, you won't bring trouble to Maya-tan," Popituv said, more command than question.

"I can't promise that."

Another round of mumbling rose in the crowd, and this time Popituv didn't raise a hand to stop it. Verina conceded that Popituv was likely a better negotiator than ey was. The rebel leader never saw the trap. Under eir breath, ey asked, "Will you allow me to exit the city peacefully?"

The former leader said, "That is a question."

Verina pushed up the sleeve of eir robe and pressed two buttons on a wrist device. Popituv asked, "What did you do?"

"You gave me no choice. I had to have the Humans guarding this place killed. I'm sorry to say that trouble is now at your door."

Hand weapons drawn, Verina and Gahleh, both again cloaked and hooded, rushed to the back of the building before the stunned crowd could react. One member did break away from the rest and stood in the path of the escaping pair. "Verina, let me join you."

Verina stopped to take a close look at this volunteer before lowering eir weapon. "Nancimare?"

The former intelligence officer simply smiled. The door beside em burst open and two well-armed Ligrosians stepped inside. Verina said, "Stay close and do whatever we say."

Nancimare nodded. Without another word, the band disappeared into the city night.

10

Ten Thousand Plus Fifteen Hundred

Escaping Maya-tan became more difficult with Nancimare now in tow. With the dead Human soldiers at the communal building, plus the likelihood some Ligrosian at the meeting would sound an alarm, there was little doubt that armed troops would soon be on their trail. The plan was for their exit to be smooth, fast, and…"Wait," Verina said, stopping in eir tracks.

Everyone stopped. Gahleh and the two attending rebels looked around, trying to see the trouble Verina saw. "What?" Gahleh said.

"We have to get a push-plate."

Following Verina's eyes, Gahleh looked at the newcomer, and realized the problem. Ey said to Nancimare, "Where's the closest place that would have large push-plates? A store, or—?"

"There's a market one street over and halfway down the block, that way," Nancimare replied, pointing back in the direction they'd just come.

Verina said, "Gahleh, you and Tamira take Nancimare to the rendezvous. I'll go with Chelexen. Two minutes."

"Come on," Gahleh said, taking Nancimare by the arm as

Verina turned and went back towards downtown.

Abandoning the pretense of inconspicuousness, Verina and Chelexen ran to the market. With a well-practiced hand, Verina severed the door locks with the small, improvised, triple-beam laser that had become an increasingly useful tool among the rebels. The moment the door opened, the alarm sounded. To open the storage room, Verina needed to cut through a Terran-made lock— something that was happening with more frequency. "Here," the leader said, guiding a plate to eir wingman, "We're riding out of here."

The rebels quickly removed and deactivated the Earth-made tracking devices on the push-plate controls, something the resistance was also increasingly seeing. Inserting their standard-issue crystals to override the plates' programming, the looters hopped onto their makeshift transports and sped toward their rendezvous —Verina taking point . Human troops ran up the street behind the Ligrosians just as Verina and Chelexen started their getaway—the swarm of tiny projectiles whizzing by underscored how narrow their margin of escape had been.

Their circuitous escape through the city ate up some time, but the speed of the push-plates more than compensated. Verina's two-man squad arrived at the meeting point only moments after the others who had remained on foot. The rebel leader hopped off eir push-plate and said, "Someone double-check that this plate is secure and then slave it to mine."

Verina slipped off eir robe and walked over to Nancimare. The two brought their foreheads close without touching, in a greeting typical of a casual friendship. Verina said, "You're a surprise."

"Me?"

"Yes, you. I thought you disappeared like almost everyone else connected with the maetor's office."

Nancimare smirked and looked down. "That's a long story."

"I'm sure. You can tell me later. We need to get out of here."

Verina turned to see the progress of eir previous order. Nancimare said, "Verina, I just want to—" just then, to get eir attention, ey tapped Verina's back.

Letting out a momentary ultrasonic squeal, Verina went down on one knee with a stab of electrifying pain. Nancimare found three lasers and two Earth projectile weapons pointed straight at em. Gahleh said a short phrase to Verina that Nancimare couldn't translate which meant, "Are you OK?"

Verina slowly regained eir feet; the patches around eir eyes now showing bright red. "I'll live," Verina said in the same undecipherable language. Switching back to Limto, ey said, "Stand down."

As the squad lowered their weapons, Verina turned to Nancimare, who looked more than a little nervous. The rebel leader said, "For obvious reasons, you shouldn't touch me."

"I…I get that."

Gahleh strode up, very serious. "Verina, you'll go with two of the squad on our planned route. I'll take this one," indicating the new recruit, "and the others on a new course."

"That's not what—"

"Security."

It was one of those moments where Verina realized that if ey was to have trusted advisors, ey would have to trust their advice. Turning to Nancimare, ey said, "We'll talk in a few days." Then to Gahleh, "Keep em out of trouble."

"I'll do my best."

The sound of Humans approaching increased everyone's alertness. The Ligrosians mounted their personnel-plates just as projectiles, plasmas, and unseen beams caused havoc with the surroundings—slightly wounding two of the squad. The rebels broke away in a rehearsed scramble designed by Verina's advisors to increase their leader's chances of escape in these situations. They recognized, even if ey did not, eir importance to the fight.

Bryce's teams hounded Verina's squad for two days. While Earth's forces never got a clear offensive opportunity against these three rebels, their constant pursuit exhausted the trio, who couldn't afford the luxury of rest. On the third day it became increasingly clear that the Humans finally conceded Verina's escape. Deciding it better to push on to base instead of staying out in the open, the Ligrosians traveled well into the night. Bailera's rising ushered their return to safety but at a different refuge than originally planned. Instead of meeting up with Gahleh, Verina stopped at Thothwai and Li's new locale.

The exhausted leader went straight to the quarters that were usually reserved for em at large bases. The simple mattress in a cramped room was more than sufficient for eir current needs. No bed had ever felt as soft as this one did to the road-weary commander when ey finally collapsed onto it after three stressful, sleep-deprived days.

The lights turned on scant moments after Verina fell asleep. Li rushed in through the planning room to Verina's alcove. The spent leader was not happy. Li said, loudly, "What the hell did you do on your trip?"

Thothwai appeared, a few seconds behind Li. "Hai-Verina, I'm sorry for this—"

"Shoot him," Verina said before rolling over.

An awkward silence grew as Li and Thothwai looked at each other. Thothwai finally said, "You might not want to make a joke like that around most of the other fighters."

Verina forced emself back to facing them. "You're right." Then, with both fatigue and anger coloring eir tones, ey said, "Is this anything that can't wait, or that specifically needs me?"

Thothwai looked sharply at Li, and said, "No. Of course not.

We'll be ready to brief you when you've rested."

"Good," the leader said as ey again turned eir back to eir advisors and fell into a sound sleep.

Thothwai continued staring sharply at Li as the duo backed away from Verina's nook. They quietly exited the conference room, remembering to turn off the lights before closing the heavy door.

Verina became alert. Alert and so tired ey didn't want to move from the mattress. It was like ey had never gone to sleep. From the timesync at the head of the bed, ey knew ey had slept nearly six hours—three-fourths of a day(!)—but every fiber of eir being told em it was time to go to back to bed. As ey worked up the energy to stir, Verina noticed a trickle of water flowing down the wall. It was raining again outside. It was amazing that no matter how strong a thing was, water would always win in the end. It seemed like it had to mean something, Verina thought, but ey was simply too tired to try and work it out. With reluctant effort, ey got out of bed and prepared emself to meet eir duties.

Three seconds. From the time ey opened the door to the conference room, just a crack, until staffers entered wanting attention—three seconds. Thothwai got Verina's eye before Li managed to enter the room. Ey said, "We have a serious morale problem, Hai-Verina. Former maetor Hai-Popituv has started sending public messages. I think the Humans are either helping em, or casting a blind eye. Ey's saying that patriots will insist on diplomacy."

"Yavaktu-prithal-esto!" / "Savio'ktuwe sthfreh!" Verina spat with two very clear voices, shocking some within earshot who weren't in the inner circle. "I knew ey was going to try something like this," ey said to no one in particular. "I could see it in eir eyes. Ey thinks the Humans are like the Quinkst, or the Ju-a-e'I, or any of the rest. Ey thinks that if we play nice long enough, they'll leave. *And* ey's going to do everything ey can to turn public opinion against us."

Li said, "Ey's doing a pretty good job of it."

Verina sneered. Turning to Thothwai, ey said, "What do you think?"

"Honestly, if I didn't know what I know from being here and serving with you, I'd follow em. Ey's too respected not to."

Nodding, Verina said, "I know. Me, too."

Thothwai asked, "Couldn't we ask for help from the…" Ey couldn't finish that sentence. Not with Li in the room.

Verina stopped eir simultaneous Quinkst translation for Li at "from". Not being of Serees, he was forbidden to know of this. Verina switched to the interspecies language, Haia. This tongue was generally used only when Ligrosians spoke to Haipuxans—as a consequence, there was no automated translation matrix. Ey did not translate for Li. "We've tried, but they don't want to contact us. They're still helping some fishers bring in seafood, but that's all. They've all but disappeared since Gopro."

"What about the fishers?"

"I personally know one, but ey'd never trust any of us except me. And even then, there's always the chance ey might side with Hai-Popituv." Switching back to Limto and Quinkst, Verina continued, "And that's the last we should talk about that."

"Of course," Thothwai agreed.

"Where are we on the mission?" Verina asked.

Thothwai led Verina, with Li in tow, to a collection of papers and tactical maps on the large table. "Li and I have set up several small mobile training groups around the band. As part of their training, squads go out and make sure the Humans never get comfortable. We're particularly thin between twenty-four and thirty-six secir and in the agricultural plane, but because of the terrain, I don't think that's much of a problem."

"Estimates?"

"We have maybe four thousand training survivors who are loyal. Of those, maybe twenty-seven hundred I'd call ready for battle."

Li did some quick math in his head…a little over two thousand, and just under one-thousand-five-hundred. That matched his estimates. Verina asked, "How many days since the invasion?"

Thothwai consulted eir Infolux. "One hundred seventy."

Verina's fingers started forepalming and backpalming as ey thought. "It would take, what, twenty-four or so days for the farthest to trek to outside Czep-tan?"

Thothwai shuffled through some maps and then did some quick calculations on eir Infolux. "Minimum. That's assuming clear passage on the transways."

After some more thinking, Verina said, "This is what I'd like to do: a few days from now, I want to start building-up forces in that area a few secir to the east of Halvek-aziq. Movements will be cautious, and only with battle-ready fighters. Those that are left behind will continue their raids." Verina glanced at Thothwai and saw eir furiously inputing the scenario on the Infolux. "Can we get everything in place by day two-forty?"

Li asked, "Why two-forty?"

"Why not? It's a little after the half-year mark of the invasion, which is actually only about fourteen days away. I figure the Humans will expect us to do something on that date. If nothing out of the ordinary happens then, and for a while after, they'll relax their alert status. It might give us a small advantage. We might have to wait a little longer, but with most of our forces all in one place, I don't want to risk waiting too long."

"What do you need me to do?" Li asked.

"I need you to come up with a way to get as many Earth Forces into the kill zone as possible. It has to be enticing enough that they'll come even if they suspect an ambush."

"That shouldn't be too hard."

Verina straightened up. "OK. I really want your opinions. Can this work, and what do we need to have in place for it to work? We only have fifty days."

If Colonel Bryce could avoid her weekly visits to Communications Research, she would. Most of the effort to decipher the mysteries of the Seetun technologies were located in the lowest four levels of the third-tallest building in "Minneapolis", as the Humans had re-labeled Czep-tan. Non-military research specialists worked in every room. Because the exotic energies in use could be contamin-ated by a number of external sources, only the ambient light emit-ted from the equipment was permitted. This was more than suffi-cient to read by, but it made these labs seem like the dungeon-lairs of mad scientists. "What progress, Ng?" Bryce asked the lead researcher.

"Same as always. As I've said before, I don't think there is any way to break or reverse-engineer this technology. We have to find documentation."

"We gave you documentation."

"Yes. In a language no one understands. The fragments of illus-trations make no sense. We need a Rosetta Stone."

"Ng, I appreciate your position, but the general isn't going to wait forever. Neither is the Presidium. I'm going to authorize you for moderated request authorization. If you need specialty items or tasks to be done, send it through my office. As long as it isn't too outlandish, I'll authorize it. If you need translators, more cryptolo-gists, archaeologists, whatever…get them. I need you to get this done."

"I understand, Colonel. I'll do my best."

Bryce squeezed Ng's shoulder in solidarity. They both understood that their jobs required results, and time was running out. "Dinner for you and ten of your team at my mess tomorrow. And rec time. Let's see if we can't civilize these conditions for your crew a little."

"Yes, Colonel. Thank you."

The dark cloud Bryce had when she entered had dissipated. Sometimes the best way to get a machine moving was to stop pushing so hard. The question was: would it work? Maybe the nature of the problem was too big to solve, or the technology too alien. She believed her teams could accomplish anything given enough time, resources, and will. Unfortunately, Chavez didn't share that belief. He demanded results now, with low cost, and just because he said so. As much as Bryce hated visiting the communications dungeon, she hated having to report "no progress" even more.

Verina stared at the timesync as it changed from 7:77:77 to 0:00:00. Today marked two-hundred-forty days from the start of Earth's invasion. Around Serees, it wasn't a day any more notable that the one before or the one to come. Here, Verina planned to change the course of the war. The Humans needed to have their noses bloodied. The rebellion required Earth Fleet to take it seriously. More than that, the Ligrosians needed to believe Verina not only fought for them, but that ey was fighting a war ey could win.

Emerging from eir field shelter made of interlocking, EM-absorbing plates, Verina savored the cool, humid, midnight air. Bailera would be rising in the east, but the Ligrosian's view was blocked by the thick woods. Thothwai joined the rebel commander. "Should we start final positioning?"

Verina stared at the ground. It was one thing to engage in a series of opportunistic hit-and-runs with small squads. Ey had never committed an army to battle before. What if ey was wrong? What if this was a mistake? Looking up, ey thought, *What choice do we have?* Without facing Thothwai, Verina said, "Start it. Make sure that everything's in place by this time tomorrow. I want our people to get some rest before they have to fight."

Thothwai nodded then left to issue the necessary directives. Li walked up to Verina. "Are you going to give a rousing speech to the troops before sending them off?"

"Why? They know what's at stake. If they need me to motivate them, then we deserve to lose our planet to yours."

Li still thought it was a cold way of looking at things, but he conceded to himself that he was hardly an expert on Serees psychology. "OK. Then, is there anything you want *me* to do?"

Verina looked closely at this alien face. What, really, was there for him to do? The rebels wouldn't accept him as a commander if ey was gone, and he still knew much too much to be left to his own devices. Now that most of his practical armament and tactical expertise had been mined, what *could* he do? "One thing would be of great comfort to me."

"Please," Li prompted.

"If I'm not fated to see this to the end, all I ask is that you don't let me die alone. Now, I'm not saying that I'm eager for the last thing I see to be a Human face, and it doesn't have to be you. You can send someone. It's just—"

Li interrupted, "I'll do it. But you're not going to die. You're like a cat."

Verina's face screwed up in a non-Human way that Li had come to recognize as confusion. He said, "It's an animal on my planet that...oh, never mind. It doesn't make any sense anyway. I'm just saying that I don't think I'll have to make good on your request, but I promise that I will."

Moments passed before the proverbial lightbulb come on over

Li's head. "Wait a minute. How am I going to know—?"

Verina smirked. "You're coming."

Li stared back, surprised. Except for impromptu battles when Verina changed bases, Li never participated in engagements. After all this time, Verina was trusting him to go out in the field with em. Li's smile waned and his jaw slackened. Going out in the field meant his life was now on the line. Li stammered, "Th-thanks."

Verina's eyes twinkled. "Yup. That's the look that's been missing."

Verina's attention stayed focused on the details without a break. Moving so many people and supplies in so short a time was a logistical headache. Eir only hope was that the Humans would take the bait.

Halvek-aziq suffered from a chronic inferiority complex. Being the sibling to the capital city of Czep-tan meant it was frequently overshadowed, if not completely ignored. Being an inland city also meant more difficult access to fresh seafood staples. In the aftermath of the Human occupation, the general situation grew worse. Half of Czep-tan's population were forcibly relocated here. This put considerable strain on the carefully-planned infrastructure. Overcrowding, and a very conspicuous Human presence, tested the legendary patience of the residents.

Nancimare walked uneasily down the crowded streets in the middle of the day. Having spent so many years in intelligence, ey knew that eyes were on em. While that was the intent of eir trip, it didn't ease eir mind. Ey entered a large open-air food court. Humans and Ligrosians co-existed here with a mixture of familiarity and unease. The crowd thinned as lunchtime waned. Nancimare purchased a seafood variety platter then sat at an open table. While enjoying eir first taste of vahr since joining up with Verina, a very corpulent man pulled up a Human chair and sat across the table from em. "I should have you shot right here," the intruder said via a hand held translator.

Nancimare's eyes quickly scanned the area for sharpshooters. Eir awareness of nearby sounds increased. "Now, now. There's no reason for that, Ben."

Ben Ziffle picked a piece of grilled vahr from the Ligrosian's plate. Though dressed in the lightest-weight clothing available, Ziffle's physique rebelled against the equatorial climate with a never-ending river of sweat. "You've been off the screens for something like forty-five days. You don't think that merits some worry?"

"Not from me. And trust me, you'll be happy I did. Chavez will probably give you your own air-cooled office for this."

Ziffle leaned back in his chair. "You have my attention. This better be good, or you're not leaving this table."

Nancimare turned left at the intersection on Library Corner with less anxiety than before eir meeting. Every facet of eir mission had gone smoothly. The wild card was whether or not Ziffle would sit and listen. It was nice to know that Verina would—

The next moments blurred as the confident Ligrosian found emself spun and thrown into a recessed doorway. A burning talon ripped into eir throat, strangling eir ability to cry out. Clutching eir neck to staunch the bleeding, Nancimare didn't look up to see eir assailant. "I never thought you were sincere," Gahleh said. "Thank you for proving me right."

Nancimare managed to issue some muted clicks in protest. Gahleh continued, "We were listening. You leaked the information just fine, but then you had to try to slip in more. You're the one who sealed your fate."

Using eir Earth sidearm, Gahleh shot Nancimare three times in eir lower abdomen. The two other rebels used lasers aimed at the same area to ensure lethality. When it was over, Gahleh said loudly enough for the others to hear, "At least this will make the Humans think."

"Aren't you full?" Lieutenant Potaryanii said to Ben Ziffle as the large man snuffled down the last of his first slab of barbecue ribs. "You were at that restaurant for quite a while."

While wiping away only some of the excess sauce from his mouth with a napkin, Ben scoffed, "What they have here isn't food. It's just as bad as that sushi crap."

"Fine. Whatever. Did you get the information I needed?"

While exchanging his bone-covered plate with one containing a fresh blanket of ribs, Ziffle nodded and said, "The names and contact information of two nearby rebel factions willing to do some freelance missions. The agent said that it would be a one-shot deal, and that they wouldn't do anything against their own cause; but, if we needed special help, they'd be willing to trade for it."

Potaryanii smiled to herself. The groundwork she'd lain was finally starting to pay off. Before long, she'd entice enough Ligrosians to fight with her against the colonel's forces. Then the command chair in Bryce's office would have a new owner— someone the fleet marshal trusted and owed.

General Chavez knelt low during afternoon prayer. As was his custom, he asked for forgiveness of the mistakes he made and wisdom to act wisely in the future. Mostly, he thought about both his current and historical families. He wished prosperity on everyone still living who had touched his heart, and peace to those who had passed. His holy reverie broke when the urgent-message alarm sounded. Trying to maintain the calm that came from prayer, Chavez said, "Computer, put the message through to the command room."

Chavez walked out from the Ready Room and saw the head of Colonel Smythe filling half the wall. "Computer, reduce subscreen."

With Smythe's image now less frighteningly large, Chavez moved into the sensor's field of view. Smythe said, "My apologies for disturbing you, General, but I didn't feel this could wait."

It damn well better not be something that could wait, Chavez thought. "Go ahead, Colonel."

"Sir, we've received credible information that the terrorist leadership is near St. Paul," he said, referring to the Human re-designation of Halvek-aziq. "I've sent special force recons who have confirmed enough of the information to make me think that terrorists have gathered to attack our bases at either or both of St. Paul or Minneapolis."

"Why are you calling me? You should be able to handle it. I've given you enough troops."

"Sir, we have every indication that this isn't just about a gathering of a few rebels. They've massed at least five hundred blueskins, maybe more. I think they mean not just to attack but to take our base and possibly the city."

Chavez had to admit that this prize was too tempting to leave for a colonel to handle alone. "Save me some time, Enrique, how many forces do we have in the area?"

"Two brigades of mobile ground and one multi-terrain wing—in addition to support and logistics."

Chavez quickly worked out several scenarios in his head in less than a minute. The general said, "Colonel, I want you to send the whole of your fighting forces to deal with these terrorists. Temporarily reassign your city support units to field duty. While you deal with the details of your attack, I'll arrange for a battalion from Minneapolis to be on alert to defend your city…which won't be necessary, will it, Colonel?"

"With a twenty-to-one advantage and the element of surprise on our hands? I don't think so."

"Take care of it, Colonel. Computer, close message."

For the first time in months, Chavez felt a change in the wind. Getting rid of this band of misguided fanatics would go a long way toward getting focused on the primary mission objective: that damn Seetun technology.

A large flight of aircraft rocketed to the expanse one hundred kilometers to the east southeast of Halvek-aziq. Three trios of air fighters broke away in series, white contrails following them in the otherwise blue sky. Each group of three fighters settled into their glide slopes targeting the rebel base below. They didn't know this base, populated the day before with half the rebel force, had been abandoned an hour before the attack. Upon reaching optimum range and altitude, the fighters launched their complements of bombiles. These intelligent munitions, once launched, were completely autonomous and completely deadly. Explosions destroyed the base as well as the half-dozen rebels left behind as decoys to sweeten the target.

Ten surface-to-air missiles streaked up from nearby positions toward the aircraft.

"Five of the eleven are hit," reported Gahleh, in command of the southern half of the rebel forces.

Verina clicked acknowledgment, focusing eir attention more on theater-wide troop readiness. None of pieces on this battlefield could start their parts of the operation prematurely. The margin of victory was slim enough without mistakes so early in the confrontation. Errors could come—likely would come—once the battle was fully engaged.

More flights of fighters split off from the closing airborne armada to attack the positions of the just-launched missiles. The automatic launchers had already done their job; to Verina, their loss was of no consequence. Again, as Earth forces launched their attack, more guided explosives rose up and destroyed a portion of the fighters.

Once more, several flights attacked the missile launch areas. This time there was no retaliation. As the fighters pulled away, they reported seeing movement consistent with an emergency evacuation.

At the command hub, Li said to Verina, "You can see the LZ-creation bombers over there," Li pointed high at three large dark-blue dots. "They just turned."

Verina said to Gahleh, "Tell Thothwai to alert eir troops, 'Standby.'"

The bombers grew imposingly large in the sky. Ignoring the token small-arms resistance from the ground, the elephantine jets dropped their anti-personnel and ground-clearing ordinance on four expanses of mostly-wooded territory. What had taken nature decades to grow was downed and compressed in moments into cleared areas large enough to fit a small town. The smoke, dust, and debris took several minutes to settle.

The first group of troop-landers hit the ground and disgorged their companies of soldiers. As the second wave flew in, the airspace haze cleared enough for more rebel missiles to lock on the approaching targets. Two troop carriers were destroyed before landing, eliciting a furious response by another flight of fighters which obliterated the launch sites. Opposition to the troop landings halted. Plane after plane arrived, dropped off their armed passengers, and rose to make room for the next wave. The last six craft were destroyed by the last of the rebel missiles.

Aircraft circled beyond hearing range, and the area grew eerily quiet. Neither Human or Ligrosian troops made much more noise than walking.

Then all hell broke loose.

Remote mines, still in place under the landing zones and active despite the ground clearing, were detonated by hidden Ligrosian operatives. Platoons of Humans splintered as the high-explosives went off to maximum effect. The rebels took quick advantage of the confusion. Emerging from underground blinds and from the woods, the freedom fighters attacked swiftly and without remorse. Their initial weapon of choice was the laser, with which they were the most practiced. The incidental dust and the smoke grenades set off by the Humans soon rendered these silent and accurate weapons useless. Both sides now fought with the same weapons. The Humans held greater numbers; the Ligrosian had more ammunition.

The metallic aroma of blood vapor—combined with the dusty, coppery taste of explosives—confirmed to everyone on the expanding battlefield that war was on. Verina didn't bother watching the engagements that were now shrouded in smoke and dust. "How many?" ey asked.

Gahleh, juggling several items on eir Infolux, said, "Approximately twenty-three thousand Humans against our twenty-seven hundred."

Li said, "Less than ten-to-one."

"Ten? How do you…? Oh. Do the conversion. It's a little more than six-to-one."

Again, the number system tripped up Li. After so many months, he thought he had a handle on everything being in octal.

He immediately set to double-checking his parts of the battle plan. At least there the numbers came out correctly.

The communications tech reported, "Hai-Verina, we've lost contact with the other command."

Verina quickly moved to the side of the young rebel. "Destroyed?"

The young fighter's hands danced on the controls, finally reporting, "I don't think so. I have fractions of a second that have information. There isn't enough to process, but it's definitely more than just the sub-carrier."

Verina looked around hoping someone would offer a suggestion. The eyes looking back at em seemed even more lost. "Keep trying," ey said, "and let me know if there's a change."

"Yes, Hai-Verina."

The Ligrosian leader went back to the tactical maps that were constantly updated by four experienced rebels. From the relative strength projections they posted, it looked like Thothwai's command was in trouble. Ey and eir staff were probably fine, but if they lost comm, or if the leadership was hurt, it would explain this weakening front. Verina couldn't afford the chance that Thothwai was no longer in command. "Gahleh, Li, I'm going with a squad to the other front."

Li said, "No."

At the same time, Gahleh said, "No, I'll go."

Verina replied, "There's no time for argument. I might be worrying too much, but there's too much at stake to take that risk. I'm going. I'll take Dilopto and Baresle with me and a backup comm unit." Ey motioned to the two chosen members of eir small squad "Go, get the plates ready."

Turning to eir two senior staffers, Verina said, "You both know the plan. Keep it working, even when it looks like we might lose. Have faith that we will succeed in the end. I'll stop en route for updates. Don't worry."

Verina clapped Li's shoulder's. Ey then turned to Gahleh and lightly touched foreheads. "I'll check in when we start crossing." The rebel leader turned to join eir new squad.

Fleet Marshal Chavez scowled at what the tactical display showed him. The landing zones turned into killing fields almost as soon as the troops hit the ground. Though inflicting damage, Earth's forces were taking serious losses. This was one bloody fight. The worst part was that even after three hours of battle, Earth time, he couldn't tell if the terrorists would come out weakened, even with the losses they were taking. It was turning into a nightmare scenario. Anything less than a clear Human victory could incite the locals to join this Verina character. If that happened, then all bets were off.

He thought back to when he was a major, preparing for his Practical Degree in Foreign Invasions. His instructor posed a theoretical scenario inspired by medical science. It suggested that battles were similar to how some infectious diseases attacked an otherwise healthy body. In the current, real world situation, Chavez wasn't sure he had the authority to use the solution his younger self had suggested. The lack of communication from Earth could probably be used as justification. Plus, there was always the rule that it is easier to ask forgiveness than to ask for permission. With little doubt that the tactic itself would work, Chavez swallowed down his misgivings and said, "Computer, overlay Snowball Hex Tactic over tactical battle map."

Overlaying the on-screen battle area, there appeared seven dots: six formed the points of an equilateral hexagram with the seventh dot positioned in the center. Using his finger, Chavez realigned three of the dots over nearby hot spots. "Computer, add targets here, and here."

Dots appeared over the two battle zones Chavez touched with his finger on either side of the hexagram. The general paused to say a quick prayer of forgiveness. He then commanded, "Computer, using this configuration, execute the program."

On the opposite side of the planet from Chavez's ship, the three Earth destroyers most directly above and to the west of the battle-field disgorged three tactical weapons each. All nine non-nuclear devices together yielded in the hundred-kiloton range of destruct-ive energy, but with refined blast shapes for "situational lethality". Their entry into the atmosphere was synchronized. They would all be at their optimum placement so their simultaneous detonations would have maximum effectiveness.

Many people in the nearby cities to the west likely saw contrails of the weapons' approach or heard the hypersonic booms as the bombs traveled to their targets. In contrast, neither Human or Ligrosian troops witnessed the explosions whose combined concussive blast shattered machines, splintered bone, rendered flesh, and liquefied organs.

In an instant, the battle was done. Both sides had been annihil-ated.

Chavez retreated to his ready room. He needed to reflect on the costs of fighting for what was right. He sat heavily in his chair, staring at the polo ball he kept on his desk—a gift from his father when little William was six. The urgent-message alert sounded, followed by the computer saying, "Colonel Bryce has sent an urgent alert."

Sighing, Chavez said, "Put her on."

The projected display from his Infolux showed an obviously displeased Bryce, sporting flecks of broken glass on her uniform. Before she could say anything, Chavez said, "I've taken care of your terrorist problem, Colonel, since you couldn't do it on your own."

"General," she said with measured control, "I can read a battle-field map just as well as you can."

"Are we going to have a problem, Colonel?"

"You do realize there will be repercussions. The Presidium will certainly start an inquiry into the obliteration of not only the enemy, but your own—"

"That's not what will happen, Colonel," Chavez interrupted.

"General, I watched the—"

"Colonel, perhaps if you had looked at the same details of the battle that I did, you would have seen that the terrorists were positioning some of our own high-impact bombs—heaven knows where they stole them from—at locations designed to massacre our troops. They clearly exploded prematurely when we provided some precision space-support. Of course, if intelligence had told us about the blue-skins having those weapons in the first place, we would have targeted better, but we simply had no way of knowing."

Bryce simply stared back. She couldn't believe that Chavez seriously thought he could get away with such a large and transparent lie. And what, exactly, could she do about it? He controlled the lines of communication to Earth. He rewarded his friends and depended on their loyalty. She wasn't his friend. Given what she knew of what he was obviously capable of, the colonel definitely didn't want to be his enemy at this moment. "So," she said, "you'll want me to—"

Chavez smiled inwardly. High-and-mighty Rachael Bryce was going to play along. "Clearly, we're going to need to ask a great deal of your forces. You should immediately send your stand-by force to St. Paul for support…as we discussed earlier."

"Already on their way. We can't risk civil unrest."

"Exactly, Colonel. Exactly. You will need to send at least half of your remaining personnel to sequester our surviving forces for debriefing. I don't want your troops to *do* the debriefing, just sequester. Also, this force is to look for any surviving terrorists. You've shown that you've learned how to deal with them."

"So…security work."

"Of course, Colonel. We aren't a conquering force. We are just here to ensure that Earth's concerns are dealt with in a necessarily prescribed manner. Now that the insurrection is effectively dealt with, I hope we can finally get on with the business of making certain the Sereesians become good and trusted allies."

As practiced as she was masking her emotions, Colonel Bryce had trouble completely hiding her disgust for this serpent. "Of course, sir. I'll send troops to their stations within the hour."

"Very good, Colonel. I'll be dispatching teams from throughout the fleet with specific assignments. Please give them every courtesy."

"Yes sir, General."

"Dismissed. Computer, end communication."

Bryce's image disappeared. The fleet marshal smiled broadly. The colonel didn't even argue. Chavez reflected on something he was told when he first started studying the blessed texts: When you are in the right, your foes will have no tongue to speak against you.

11

Hurt and Alone

Desolation. Yesterday, this land boasted thick woods, copious wildlife, and open areas perfect for activities ranging from picnicking to ballooning. Now, it was lifeless. Trees were splinters. Open areas were now fields of debris. Even the hills had flattened some. Nothing moved.

Dust and smoke formed a thick haze that floated above the shattered remains. Maygola's dimmed light was colored with an emotionless brown cast. Nothing complex lived. Nothing larger than a fist remained intact. Creatures who dwelt easily just below the surface were crushed just as decisively as everything above.

Outside the island-sized, lethal blast area, the damage quickly became less apparent. The thick woods eventually withstood the power of the shaped concussion waves. The still-standing trees closest to the blast would soon die from their catastrophic injuries, but those farther back faired better. The transition from devastation to survivable spanned little more than fifty meters. From the aerial vantage point of the flock of morops now flying over, the transition seemed abrupt.

Within this demarcation, closer to the twin cities than to the fighting, three Ligrosian bodies, covered with forest detritus and other debris, lay motionless on the ground. Above them, a perilously hanging branch submitted to gravity and landed hard on the arm of one of the bodies. The resulting snapping sound clearly came not from broken wood but from an arm bone. The recipient of the new break shot upright and three-voiced in pain.

Eye patches glowing as red as biologically possible, eir skin covered with an oily sheen, Verina's only sense was pain. The minutes it took to remove eir jacket were worth the draining effort —the shards that tore through the fabric into eir back pulled off with the garment. The pain didn't so much lessen as dull. Verina stared out at the devastation, not comprehending it. Ey cradled eir injured arm. Blood leaked from the compound fracture but wasn't too serious. Slowly, due to half a year of built-up tolerance, Verina's body became more accustomed to the pain. Ey noticed eir increasing nausea and the loud buzzing in eir auditory canals. Every move ey made only added to eir disorientation, which then added to eir feeling of nausea. The battered Ligrosian gave in, voiding eir stomach's contents.

Verina looked around and noticed the two bodies near em. The injured rebel couldn't focus on who they were or why they were there. Ey couldn't tell if they were alive, for sure. The only thought ey could form was, *I have to find help*. Like a mantra, this echoed in eir mind, driving em to complete that mission. Verina's damaged body, however, was reluctant to cooperate. Standing took several minutes and the help of a stout branch. More minutes passed as ey rested against a helpful tree remnant. When it became clear that resting wasn't helping, the bloodied Ligrosian used the branch as a support. Ey moved one foot, then the next, in a very slow walk from eir survival site.

The lengthy exercise did nothing to sharpen Verina's ability to focus. Once, during one of eir frequent rests, the rebel shook eir hips in an effort to clear the cobwebs. The resulting ache told em not to do that again. As confused as ey was, ey knew that eir brain wasn't going to tolerate much more jostling like that.

As the Ligrosian approached the crest of a very tall hill, a large number of aircraft coursed overhead. Ey saw them travel toward the big cleared-away area. Verina considered trying to get their attention, but they never seemed close enough. Besides, there were enough trees around that they probably wouldn't have seen em in any case. Why waste the energy? Ey pressed on to the top of the hill.

Reaching the summit, the battered fighter saw the familiar skyline of Czep-tan in the foggy distance. Though the city was distant, the survivor's eyes could see only that—even though Halvek-aziq was also in sight, and closer, to the west. The capital city tugged at em. Czep-tan was comfort. Czep-tan was safety. Czep-tan was love. Czep-tan was home. Fighting for every step, the traveler pressed on to the only place ey wanted to be.

Two days following the great battle, just after dawn, the fugitive walked into eir home city. Ey came in via a back way—through the woods that ey'd plied since childhood. The city was unnaturally still, but that was only a vague distraction to Verina. Two days of walking without food, water, and with untreated injuries, left few reserves for anything other than the one driving purpose: *Get help. Find home.*

With the way now paved, Verina abandoned the walking branch. It no longer helped, and the survivor much preferred the opportunity to hold eir broken arm—relieving it from the stress of gravity and movement. In truth, ey had long passed the point where pain registered as anything noteworthy. Eir route through the city came from rote memory. Years spent walking these paths didn't require eir attention. Eir pulse quickened when ey arrived at the zone trisection. Home was close. From behind em and to the right, a voice quietly shouted, "Verina!"

The warrior stopped but couldn't respond. Fortunately, stopping was enough. It allowed Elekin to approach quickly and quietly. "Oh, Bailera," ey exclaimed in hushed tones. "Verina. Look at me. Look at me. It's Elekin."

Verina turned and looked at the face, but eir eyes remained blank and unfocused. Elekin said, "It doesn't matter. What matters is that I'm your friend, and we need to get you off the street."

"Friend?" escaped from Verina's lips.

"That's right. I'm a very good friend. Come. Come with me. We have to get you out of sight."

Without much effort, but considerably slower than was prudent, Elekin guided Verina into the not-yet-open-for-business food market where ey worked. Once inside, Elekin locked the door and coaxed Verina to sit out of sight behind the counter farthest back from the entrance.

The fisher walked off for a moment, returning with a bottle of transparent, grayish-yellow, syrupy liquid. "Here. Here's some gadoj."

When Verina didn't acknowledge the offered drink, eir friend opened the bottle and gently poured a small amount into Verina's chapped middle mouth. Following the reflexive swallow, some life filtered back into Verina's eyes. Elekin poured a little more of the liquid into Verina's mouth. This time Verina eagerly accepted the sugary, nutrient-rich drink. Elekin put the bottle in Verina's hand and guided it back up to the broken leader's lips. Verina took control, drinking on eir own. Ey still didn't seem to know who eir benefactor was, but it was a start.

While Verina drank, Elekin took a closer look at eir friend. Eir wrap was barely attached, fastened not much better than young children managed. Blood clotted around the obviously broken arm, but there was still some oozing. Scars dotted Verina's face and body, and some fragments of metal, ceramic, and wood were embedded. But nothing was as obvious or shocking as the never-going-to-heal scarring that covered the back of Verina's body. And so much of eir fringe was gone. Many Ligrosians, Elekin included, envied Verina's fringe. Ey was always considered empirically attractive, but eir fringe made em stand out. Ey could have gone into entertainment with assets like that. Elekin looked on with great admiration and sorrow for eir friend. Before the Humans came, Verina was happy and enjoyed life more than most... usually. Now, ey was badly hurt, unaware of who ey was, and the most hunted person on the planet.

Or was ey?

If the rumors could be believed, a great battle was fought not too far away from Czep-tan. Supposedly, everyone on both sides died. The Humans probably thought Verina was dead.

Elekin knew ey needed to find some place to keep Verina safe. Elekin also knew ey needed help. Maybe the Haipuxans. They knew the fight Verina had been waging. Surely they would be more than willing to help. It was probably too late to do anything about it now, but it would be hard to keep eir battered friend out of harm's way for a full day. Ey needed to get a message to eir Haipuxan friend right away. "Stay here, Verina. Do you hear me? I need you to stay here for a few minutes."

The addled leader showed no intention of answering—or that ey comprehended. Verina also didn't look to be in any kind of shape to go anywhere. Elekin got up and disappeared into the back room.

Verina's attention focused on eir drink. It was gone. Ey had finished it. That task was done. This place where ey was now was not where ey wanted to be. Muttering to emself, "Have to get help. Have to get home," Verina muscled emself back to eir feet and shuffled to the exit. It was locked. Seeing the security panel next to the threshold, ey released the locking bolts and pushed open the door without thinking to turn off the alarm.

A thick-waisted Ligrosian rushed out from the back room, stopped at the counter, and saw the disheveled Verina walking outside. Ey yelled, "Hey! What do you think you…?"

The words faded as the knife-holding shop owner slowly realized who the vagabond was. Ey had once been a customer. Now the Earthers wanted em. *Verina.* That was eir name. By the time the shop owner processed this, Verina disappeared from the windows' view. The heavy Ligrosian made for the door just as Elekin exited the back room saying, "Vintiny, what are you—"

Vintiny stammered, "Ey was here. That one the Earthers are looking for. There's a price on eir head."

The shop owner rushed out of the market, knife still in hand. Elekin dashed to where ey had left Verina. Ey picked up the empty gadoj bottle and threw it in a receptacle. Grabbing some cleaning cloths from under the counter, ey wiped away the smudges of blood Verina left behind. With a sad smirk, Elekin said to emself, "You're a fool."

On the street, Verina never noticed Vintiny pursuing em—the marketer mistakenly choose a different route than Verina's. The bloody Ligrosian's only goal was going home. Eir body guided em without conscious volition. Ironically, following the battle, Colonel Bryce issued restrictions on movement within the city during non-business hours. Few Ligrosians ventured outside during the curfew period. For this reason alone, Verina wended eir way through the residential section of the city without being seen on the street by others who knew em. There was only one close call, but Verina's honed survival instinct let em find the temporary cover needed to avoid discovery.

The days-long journey neared its end as Ceyelna's apartment

building came into view. Seeing Ligrosians waiting in the lobby for the curfew to expire, Verina chose to enter from the rear of the building. The service lift was surprisingly unguarded.

Reaching the apartment door, the exhausted warrior realized ey didn't have eir personal access crystal. There was a pass-code option, but ey couldn't remember was it was. Frustrated by eir inability to fix eir thoughts on something so simple, Verina resorted to the only option that ey could think of—ey activated the system and said, "Pame, it's me."

The door opened. Verina would have jumped back, startled, had ey the energy. Gathering eir reserves, ey stepped inside, closing the door behind em. Ey made it. Ey was home. But why was ey here? Help. That's right. Ey had to get help. But why? As Verina pondered that, habit drew em to the couch, where ey found immediate comfort in the soft padding. Gently, protecting eir arm as much as possible, ey lay down on eir side and slowly rolled to a semi-prone position. Though eir body intensely ached, ey couldn't remember feeling something this good. Ey slept.

Verina's sleep shattered when Xadow bounded onto eir broken arm and rested on eir back. The Ligrosian was only aware of sharp, electrifying pain so severe ey couldn't even cry out. The haiwa immediately jumped from its owner and made the whimper that begged for forgiveness. A familiar voice called, "Xadow! Xadow, get back in…who's there?"

Something tugged at Verina. The words and sounds filtered through the hurt. Ey pushed up from the couch. "Verina?" exclaimed eir astonished sibling.

Akehru rushed to eir little sib, wanting to hug em right away, but stopped short. The cuts, scars, dirt, debris, and the ugly arm break were terrible to see but not the worst Akehru saw. Verina's eyes, red-patched and creased with pain, looked out with the glaze of a severe concussion. Verina's expression upon recognizing eir older sibling tore at Akehru's soul. Verina choked out a relieved, "Aki," before wrapping eir good arm around Akehru's neck and drawing eir sibling close to touch foreheads very tightly.

The pair released their embrace after several minutes but never stopped the back-and-forth sonaring that was an instinctual homing signal for the very young. "You're hurt," Akehru said.

"Li'l bit."

"Relax here. I'll get the med-kit. Come on, Xadow."

The haiwa had settled down immediately upon realizing his favorite Ligrosian was badly hurt. Since the first exuberant jump, he stood watch at Verina's feet. "No," Verina said, the fear of separation creeping into eir voice. *He's not bothering me*, she thought but couldn't say.

Seeing eir sib's desperation, Akehru said softly, "Whatever you want, Verni," while second-voicing, "Stay, Xadow."

Akehru left, adding a comforting coo to their sibling sonar, reinforcing Verina's growing feeling of safety. As ey lay back down on eir side, Xadow moved closer. Verina absently stroked eir long-time pal, and once again fell asleep.

Even without the concussion, it would have been difficult to fathom the flashes of activity, given that Verina was tranqed before ey'd even woken up. A burning sensation spread from eir chest where the drug entered. Xadow made a protective ruckus. So many voices; only one recognizably Ligrosian. That voice soon went missing. Armored Humans sprung up like trees. Verina didn't fear them, the tranq being already well-established. Those Humans, whoever they were, paid no attention to eir condition. The powerful sedative and neural blocks didn't significantly alleviate eir anguish—at first—but that soon changed.

Verina noticed ey was not unconscious. Though ey saw nothing but darkness, ey was aware that the dark ey saw wasn't a mental aberration. A quick series of low- and high-clicks showed em that ey was in a very plain room. Something filled the space in front of em, but sonar didn't give em the resolution to make it out. The darkness slowly eased. The area around Verina, still very dim, was noticeably lightening. The Ligrosian saw that ey was restrained on a padded, inclined platform. Medical tubing fed into eir broken arm, which didn't hurt, as well as to other places on eir body below where eir restrained head could see. "Don't worry," a definitely Human voice said via a translator, "we aren't doing any experiments on you, if that's what you're concerned about."

Colonel Bryce emerged from the shadows. To Verina's eyes, still unaccustomed to the variety of Human forms, the differences between Li and the person in front of em were interesting. This alien was from the other of the two Human genders. Though ey had seen females before, it was always in the course of a mission. This was the first opportunity ey could remember where Verina could take a focused look at the distaff part of humankind. Even with all of the clothing the colonel wore, it was clear the two genders were physically distinct; something that wasn't so obvious when they were clad in their fighting armor.

"In fact," Bryce continued, "we've spent the last week trying to get you into some sort of reasonable condition."

"Why? You're just going to kill me."

Colonel Bryce pulled up a chair suitable for Humans. She sat closer to the prisoner, in Verina's eye line. "Let's not get ahead of ourselves, here. Yes, it's a foregone conclusion that you are going to be tried and executed. After that little stunt with putting all of those bodies in the streets, you pretty much guaranteed your fate."

"Your people killed more than that…on both sides."

"Yes. But, you see, we won. You lost."

"So why keep me alive?"

Bryce leaned back comfortably in her chair. "Actually, we thought you were dead. When we stopped your little insurgency, we assumed that you had been blown apart like everyone else. That was a problem. A martyred Verina might inspire her…him…? I'm sorry, which do you prefer?"

"Your species has tended to settle on 'her' in formal negotiations," Verina said with self-surprising disdain.

"Okay. Her. A martyred Verina might inspire her people to take up the cause and continue fighting. And frankly, even though you were never going to come close to winning, your constant stream of terrorism was annoying. Actually, I should thank you."

"Thank me?"

"If not for your incredibly stupid all-or-nothing battle, I might be out of a job. Now, with you being captured and all, I will in all likelihood get a promotion."

"Glad I could help."

Bryce moaned slightly. "Oh. I've been sitting all day. Do you mind?" Bryce stood and slowly paced around. "I should also say that your Little Big Horn probably saved you a great deal of discomfort. Or, rather," Bryce glanced as if peeking at Verina's back, "additional discomfort. Yeow, that must hurt." When Verina didn't respond, the colonel continued, "But, with you in custody and almost all of your followers dead, there isn't much reason to exercise a lot of duress. For the benefit of the public, you'll stay in custody until general interest in you goes away; afterwards, you'll just disappear. Oh sure, there will be occasional questions, but nothing that will be a problem. As far as your people will know, you will still be alive. We'll then be able to guide your world so that it becomes a reasonable member in the family of planets."

"Puppet of Earth."

"To-may-to, to-mah-to. I'm not here to debate policy with you. I'm just a soldier following orders. You *were* the enemy, the one giving orders. Now, you're an instrument of propaganda. Your people will see how well we've treated you—saving you from the brink of death and all—despite all of the destruction you caused. The Ministry will ratchet up the press on how well the person who turned you in is doing, and trumpeting how being a good citizen is rewarded."

Shocked, Verina said, "I was turned in?"

Bryce smiled. "What? You thought we tracked you? No, my dear, you were turned in. By someone you know very well, in fact."

"Who?"

Bryce's smile widened. "That I won't say. Not that I care if you manage to revenge yourself on them or not, but because it's more fun if you never know who among your friends, family, co-workers, neighbors, or 'whatever' you can trust. Who is more loyal to *my* people than they are to you? And let me tell you, the reward was…well, it was pretty darned nice."

Emotions stoked with the fuel of betrayal, Verina struggled to remain calm and reasonable. "What happens next?"

"The doctors tell me that you're well enough to be moved out of the medical bay. So, we'll be transferring you to a private room of your own."

"With guards outside ensuring that I'm not unnecessarily disturbed."

"Exactly," Bryce said.

The colonel returned the chair to its original spot and walked away. Verina tried lifting eir arm to beckon her back but was stopped by the restraint. "Before you go…?"

"Yes?"

"In the battle…how many of my people survived?"

"Including you, eleven survived the initial blast that we know about. All of them were at the fringe of the blast area, as you apparently were."

"How many of…wait, you said, 'Survived the initial blast.'"

"That's right. You're the only one still alive."

Still the strategist, Verina again interrupted Bryce's exit, "Excuse me. How many of your people?"

"Forty-seven in the field. Now if you will excuse me, I have pressing business I must attend to."

"Wait," Verina called. "Wait." When it was obvious that Bryce wasn't returning, Verina finished to emself, "Which number system?"

12

Dropping the Shoe

Verina's cell wasn't unpleasant, but it was hardly a place where ey wanted to spend the rest of eir life. The four-meter by three-meter by three-meter room was lined with one seamless piece of gel. Surfaces were generally firm but never hard. The ambient lighting sourced through the walls could be varied by voice control—something Verina discovered late on eir first day of captivity. Ey couldn't make the room blindingly bright nor completely dark, but the range between the two extremes was sufficient to satisfy both eir needs and Earth security's. After what ey guessed was three days, Verina discovered the color of the entire room could also be changed by voice command. To do this, ey had to ask the room if it might like to adopt a new color—a ploy, Verina surmised, to teach the prisoner that rewards came with submissiveness.

Molded into the long side of the room, starting at the corner to the left of the entrance, was a chaise longue. At the far corner of the opposite wall stood an all-in-one *lavette* that provided sanitary functions as well as fresh water for cleaning and drinking. The room held nothing else, not even clothes or a blanket for warmth.

Time was Verina's currency. How ey spent it defined eir life. Ey mourned the people ey knew whom ey would never see again. The recent loss of people like Gahleh, Thothwai, and ever Li, who had fought with em for so long, needed to be respected and honored. While there were moving laments in the scriptures, Verina constructed eir own. The lyric poetry with the two-language rhyming followed traditional lines, with overlapping verses complementing a third-voice melody in the emotive musical language of Hafel. "My. Forever. Trusted. Honored. Join. Dance. Loving. Touched," sounded eir first voice in counterpoint rhythm to eir second's , "Friends. Free. Life. Death. Bailera. Free. Breaths. Me."

Verina had come to enjoy eir life, even though filled with pain and the crushing responsibility of leadership. It wasn't in em to mourn the life that ey wouldn't get to live. Book fourteen of *Hasek Vartu Shibi-ieth* taught that while individual life was temporary and the transition to death wasn't to be feared, life itself was persistent. Wherever there was life, there would again be life. It might transform, but life endured. It felt like that now. So much had been destroyed and yet Verina endured. Ey wasn't dead; not yet. The struggle was not over. You had to fight for your home, otherwise you ceased to be who you were.

Verina's confinement, whether laying on the chaise, pacing, or exercising, often focused on a ten-centimeter by six-centimeter area of floor at the far left corner of the room near the lavette. Sometimes this small piece of floor quickly and quietly deformed upwards before the gel on top peeled away to merge back with the floor. This left a bowl-like depression filled with a slimy gravy. Verina hoped it was nutritious. At least it quelled eir hunger. This was the twelfth "meal" since ey'd been placed in this room. There didn't seem to be a pattern for how often this meal appeared. Judging by eir hunger, Verina estimated the bowl appeared more than once a day. With the third meal, Verina made a discovery: if ey went down on arms and knees and ate face-down like a haiwa, then the food was available long enough to finish; if ey used eir hands to scoop up the contents, then the food melted back into the floor before half was eaten. The Ligrosian supposed it was another trick to break eir spirit. The Humans probably laughed about it in the surveillance room, which was fine with em. At this point, ey really didn't care what the Humans thought.

Lying on the chaise, thinking it was about time for eir twentieth meal, Verina felt the couch beneath em turn watery. Ey quickly sank a few centimeters before the watery gel around em became rigid as stone, immobilizing em. In eir peripheral vision, Verina saw the gel at the entrance site, near eir head, peel away, revealing a doorway. An armored soldier entered, followed by a smallish Human male with skin almost as white as chalk. The doorway disappeared in a gel-fall. In one hand, the small man held out Ligrosian clothes. The jacket was blue with turquoise trim, and the folded wrap was pink with purple swirls. "What's going on?" Verina asked in a heavily-accented version of the Human language Li had been teaching em.

From no specific direction, but definitely not from the soldier or the man, Verina heard, in eir own tongue, "You are not allowed to communicate from this point until you are given permission. Do you understand?"

Verina almost answered the question but realized that it might be best to be literal. Ey didn't given any hint of a response. The voice said, "Very good. You will put on these clothes and follow the person who brought them to you. The soldier will follow."

The rigid gel once again softened, returning to the cushiony state it had always been before. Verina took the offered clothes.

The pareu went on quickly. Without an analgesic to spray on eir back first, Verina donned the jacket gingerly. The small man, barely coming to the level of Verina's chest, turned his back to the prisoner. Verina took eir place between him and the soldier. A doorway appeared from behind melting gel. The trio walked out.

The graduated color scheme, from a deep sea blue at floor level to a nearly-white ceiling, was familiar. After turning right at the first intersection from eir cell, the Ligrosian knew that ey was in the Adjunct Advisory Building that many government officials once considered their home base. Most of the lower-ranking Advisors had offices and libraries here. A number of regional Responsiblars, the middle-managers directly responsible for ensuring the duties of government got done, also had their offices in this building.

They walked down the central third-floor hallway. In a niche near the main hall junction, Verina saw a purple double helix glittering with Fa'run-enhanced base-pairs the Humans were unable to see. The sculpture was one of the three best-known pieces of interior art in Czep-tan. The legendary artist, Fideesu, created it over a millennium ago in recognition of the anniversary of the Ligrosian discovery of the genetic structure.

The trio entered an office once assigned to the researchers for the Responsiblar of Parks. Now it was a deserted, dull-yellow room with a satin-finished synthetic-composite table and two chairs—one each for Human and Ligrosian—on opposite sides of the table. The small man said, in a voice inappropriately deep, even to Verina's ears, "You may talk only with your lawyer. Sit."

Despite the intense, though infrequent, lessons with Li, Verina's command of this Human tongue fell short of fluency. "Lawyer" was a new word, but given the context of eir situation, ey thought ey understood.

A Human female, looking very underfed, entered through the

door at the far end of the long room. Verina noticed she was dressed similarly to the one Verina saw after eir capture—but this one wore fewer decorations. She sat opposite the rebel and activated the Infolux she'd brought with her for translation and reference. "Hello. My name is Captain Marley Mei-Pei. You will address me as 'Captain Marley,' or 'Ma'am.'"

Both the Human's voice and the Infolux translation were thin and high-pitched. After spending so much time listening to translations from Li's Infolux, Verina didn't expect to hear one that matched its owner and carried no hint of a cybernetic accent. Verina asked, "You are my…lawyer?" using the Human word, which was translated back to em.

"Essentially, yes. I will represent you when we appear before the court."

"That's what I thought. The female who talked to me earlier, she said that I was…tried and executed…that I was going to be tried and executed."

"That was Colonel Bryce. The fact of the matter is that yes, the outcome of this trial is pretty much a foregone conclusion."

"Yes. She said the same thing. Then why—?"

"The trial? We aren't savages, Miss…ah, Verina. There are forms that must be followed. The rule of law must be adhered to."

Verina sat back defiantly. "I don't recognize your law."

Not even looking up from her notes, Captain Marley said, "Tough. Um, here we are. You are charged with one thousand eight hundred ninety-four counts of aggravated blah, blah, blah…eleven thousand six hundred seventy-eight counts of blah, blah, blah… my, you have been busy…yeah…yeah…heh, littering and jaywalking."

Looking Verina in the eyes, Marley continued, "Miss Verina, I think it's fair to say that reading the charges is going to take longer than the trial itself. If we stipulate to them and plead guilty, saving the court a lot of time, we might just get you a swift and relatively pain-free execution."

Verina stood, immediately prompting the soldier guarding the door to aim his weapon. Captain Marley said, "Sit down, Miss Verina."

Verina instead leaned on the table. "I'm sorry. Maybe I'm not understanding the terms correctly. Aren't you supposed to be my advocate?"

"Please! Miss Verina. Sit down!"

With a glance over to the living suit of armor to one side of the door, Verina lowered emself down to sit on eir heels. Once ey did so, the Captain said, "That's what I'm doing. The only thing I can do in your best interest is to try and get you one of the better forms of execution."

"What happens if I don't want to make it easy?"

"You mean, plead not guilty?"

Verina did a fair imitation of a Human shrug. Frustrated, Marley sat back in her chair. "Then we have a trial. Beginning with opening statements, the prosecution will paint you as the worst terrorist humanity has ever seen. They'll bring in wounded. They'll show the dead. They'll—"

"Wait," Verina interrupted, "there is an opening statement?"

"Yes. Both sides get to say how they intend to prove their cases."

Verina leaned forward slightly, "Then I will plead this 'not guilty'. I want to make my statement."

"You do realize that because of this situation, and since this is a military court, your opening statement must be prepared for and approved by the court? If you deviate from it…well, just don't."

Verina was too enthusiastic about this strategy, which raised the Captain's suspicions. The Ligrosian said, "That won't be a problem…Ma'am. Just tell me how long I have to prepare and when I will be able to put my statement in a form the court will accept."

The Captain fidgeted slightly in her seat. "Uh, actually, the trial is scheduled to begin in about ten minutes."

Verina nodded and said with sarcastic certitude, "Of course." Quickly assessing all of eir options, Verina said, "I'll make it brief, then. If I could quote some passages from one of the books of my faith and make some relatively non-inflammatory comments, would that be acceptable?"

The emaciated face of the young Captain showed uncertainty. "That would probably be acceptable."

"Good. Then I'd like to begin."

Captain Marley requested that the small man, whom she called "Jai", bring another Infolux. When it arrived, Verina quickly assembled eir statement. The device was forwarded to the court.

Fifteen minutes later, Verina stood in the defendant's pit in the building's Courtroom Three. The walls of the chamber were covered in a yellow, acoustically absorbent, fabric. The visitor's gallery, to Verina's right, was empty. Captain Marley sat at the desk attached to Verina's raised defendant pit. On the opposite side of the room, one Human officer, a large and creased male, stared intently at one of his three Infoluxes.

Everyone stood when, at the head of the room, three Human officers filed in and took their seats at the bench, which was about a head higher than the defendant's and witnesses' pits. General Chavez took the center of the five seats. Colonel Bryce sat to his left, and to his right sat General Bhoutto. All three wore their standard military dress uniforms. As the tribunal sat, the people in the rest of the chamber resumed their places. General Chavez introduced himself and his fellow judges, and said through a bland and generic translation matrix, "It is my understanding that the defendant would like to make a brief statement. Although it is not in strict accordance with the rules of the court, we are allowing it in the spirit of mutual cooperation."

The Infolux screen built into the defendant's pit came to life. Verina's prepared text, in its entirety, displayed clearly. The Ligrosian nodded to the bench and received a nod in reply from General Chavez. Verina positioned emself so ey could look straight into the defendant's camera. "My name is Verina Tan-quan-es Hai-tan-tal Sum-Ceyetua-izhd-Lasertono. Prior to the arrival of the people from Earth, I was a First Negotiator. Since then, as you can plainly see, events have left their marks on me. I am accused of a great many things. I don't intend to present an argument to them. Instead, I would like to read some passages from the *Haiserees ya Ligro, Book Twelve* that meant a lot to me growing up. First— chapter seven, line three-five-one. 'Yagavey left the safety of eir camp and saw the sky for the first time. At noon of that day, a bright star danced on the horizon for a few moments before once again hiding.'

"Now, chapter fourteen, line twenty-two, 'With the curiosity of youth, Irestol and Xarnom abandoned their chore and left the woods. With Maygola at its highest point in the sky, they looked to where sky and land met. Half a circle appeared, much larger than a star. It did not tickle the land but rose to above the height of the trees.'

"And finally, chapter twenty-six, line six. 'Ligrat stood in front of the town and told them that the God would not destroy them. Seeing that the people did not take Em for granted, Ey was now going back to Eir home in the sky.'

"Bailera is large in our sky today. Soon ey will wane from our view. To the ancients, Bailera was once thought fearful. Now we greet every appearance with joy and celebration. All it required was time and perspective. Thank you. That's all I have to say."

General Chavez sat up. "It's my understanding that the defendant will waive the right to the reading of the charges and allow them to be entered into the record at this point."

Marley stood. "Yes sir."

"Then it is so ordered. Counsel, how does your client plead to these charges?"

With some trembling in her voice, the Captain said, "Sir, my client has instructed me to inform the court that she does not recognize the court's authority on matters concerning this planet, and refuses to submit a plea."

Chavez sucked on the inside of his lower lip. He hadn't expected this. It had been understood that the prisoner would plead. Colonel Bryce seemed equally annoyed, while General Bhoutto barely hid a small smile. Chavez said, "Since the defendant refuses to claim innocence in the charges before this court, we have no choice but to summarily enter the plea of guilty unless the other two judges disagree." Both Bryce and Bhoutto shook their heads. Chavez banged the spent casing that acted as his gavel, "So ordered. We will recess for one hour to allow both counsels to submit their sentencing recommendations. The prisoner will be returned to her cell."

The triumvirate exited the court room. As Verina once again placed emself in step between Jai and eir armored guard, Captain Marley sent along her already prepared recommendation for a quick and painless execution.

Verina sat in eir cell—eir jacket and wrap reclaimed by the Humans. Ey hated not knowing if eir attempt to subvert the trial succeeded. So much had to go right. Even if it did, there likely wasn't enough time. Eir chances of surviving much longer than the sentencing recess were impossibly bad. Ey was going to die. Probably. Verina's hopes depended on the passages the Humans allowed em to read in eir statement. These aliens made it so easy. There was nothing more ey could do except wait.

And wait.

With no source of reference other than the rhythm of eir own fore-and-back-palming, Verina knew that much more than a Human hour had passed since eir court appearance. Ey knew how much General Chavez wanted em dead. Any delay gave the Ligrosian reason to hope eir message *had* been received.

The code ey devised had been difficult to commit to memory. In eir statement, ey confined all the quotes to book twelve—indicating commands from the leaders of the resistance, and was a modifier for the three following commands. The seven in "chapter seven" ordered an immediate reforming of rebel cells and pods, with three-five-one indicating the coordinates—in this case, outside Reyva-tan, where the bulk of Verina's remaining fighters stayed in reserve. Fourteen specified a military objective, with twenty-two targeting an armory that was one of the Humans' largest munitions dumps on the planet. The final order, twenty-six, requested immediate assistance, with six giving the location as a government building. The two lines ey read decoded as the second-ranking government building, though it did not specify in which city.

Verina hoped the Humans would pay more attention to the words and not the reference numbers. No matter what happened to em, the troops needed to continue with the fight. If an attack was indeed occurring at Reyva-tan, then those judges—from eir intelligence reports, the three highest-ranking Humans in the occupying force—were likely preoccupied with the renewed insurgency. For now, it was all out of eir control.

"Some people can sleep through anything."

Verina's eyes popped open. It took a moment to find the source of the voice. "Aki? What are you doing here?"

Standing over eir reclining sib, Akehru said, "'Immediate

assistance.' Ring any bells?"

"But you're not—"

"Do you really want to talk about this now?"

Verina wasted no more time in getting to eir feet. Akehru said, "Wait. Put this on."

Akehru held out a hooded red jumpsuit. "What's this?" Verina asked.

"It will block any tracking device the Humans put in you." Holding eir tongues on questions that could wait, Verina put on the body suit. "Follow me," Akehru said.

The corridors of the familiar building were filled with a dense, foggy haze. *Laser weapons are useless*, Verina thought out of habit. Ey knew the Humans would fight to hold on to their prize guest, yet the halls were strangely quiet. "Get in this," Akehru whispered.

Effectively blinded by the fog, Verina sonared a box about the size of a large computer case. Not knowing the plan details, the escapee followed orders and stepped into the one-meter-cubed box. Akehru whispered, "Find all the straps and hold onto them. This is probably going to be unpleasant."

The lid closed. As the box was being sealed from the outside, ey hurried to find the restraints. Verina secured emself with straps for eir waist, both feet, and a pair for each arm. Ey then braced emself for…what? Ey felt movement, but didn't find it uncomfortable.

An unexpected, bone-jarring jolt clearly communicated that the word "unpleasant" wouldn't come close to describing this experience. Verina's body was battered by large and sudden gee-forces as eir padded crate accelerated, decelerated, and abruptly changed direction countless times. Ey suspected ey may have briefly lost consciousness once or twice. At some point during this unrestrained tumbling, Verina lost eir stomach contents. With the abuse ey was experiencing, ey wasn't surprised that ey didn't notice eir own act of vomiting—but the warm splashes and the increasingly abhorrent smell gave effective confirmation. The container finally settled. Verina focused on settling eir breathing and fighting some lingering vertigo.

Though the box ceased being an uncontrolled amusement park ride, it stayed in motion. The movement was smooth, suggesting ey was now on a push-plate or maybe a cart. *Plink!* Verina startled at the muffled sound of projectile fire. *Plink! Plink!* Verina felt the dent next to eir fingers caused by one of these hits. As much as ey'd grown accustomed to being in the thick of the action, at the moment ey was happy enough to be in this bullet-proof cocoon. The sounds of fighting grew fainter.

After another brief spasm of tumbling, all sense of motion stopped. No sound leaked in from outside. Did the escape fail? If no one was around to let em out, could ey do it emself? Lacking any information, Verina's heart slowly increased and eir breaths shortened. The continuing silent darkness would have definitely been more bearable without the vomit smell. With no other sensory distractions, the stench only seemed to intensify.

New, faint sounds filtered in. It could be voices, but they were too muffled to be anything other than a frustration. If the horrendous trip was finally over, in whose company was ey? Verina braced emself for anything as ey heard the sounds of the box being unsecured.

13

Journey

Verina's dented box sat in a cleared area within a large, low-ceilinged storage room filled with containers nearly identical to the one holding the rebel leader. The seal of the box was released and the lid raised. "There ey is, our...oh! That's awful! Verni, take that suit off and close the lid. Ugh!"

Akehru fled from eir sib, joining two others in an alcove a dozen steps away from the box. Verina was happy to breathe fresh air again. Ey sloughed the odorous one-piece, threw it into the box, and slammed the lid shut. As Verina turned to eir rescuers, a damp towel hit em in the face. The naked Ligrosian wasted no time in cleaning off the last of eir revisited meal. Looking up, ey saw three very happy, if tired, faces: Akehru, Elekin, and Li Rinaldi. Frozen between joy and surprised shock, Verina simply stared. "Welcome to freedom," Elekin said.

Akehru stepped forward, afraid to touch eir very-damaged sibling. Seeing eir sib's smiles, Verina emerged from eir stupor, smiled, sonared back, and pressed eir forehead tightly to Akehru's. The patches around both their eyes shown red—but a different shade than when Verina suffered, Li noted to himself. When they separated, Verina stared at Akehru's face. Eir middle mouth's lips parted slightly, but a smile formed instead of words.

Verina glanced over to the other familiar Ligrosian. Elekin stepped up and touched foreheads with eir friend less cautiously than Akehru had done. As with eir sibling, Verina lingered…clinging to the long-absent connection with people who cared about em as a person, not as a leader.

Completing the set, Verina offered Li eir hand in the Human custom. He surprised em by pulling em close and wrapping his arms around his friend. Verina braced for a wave of mind-numbing pain that didn't come. Li knew those small patches where he could awkwardly hug his friend without putting pressure on eir most sensitive areas. Realizing his consideration and ignoring how it looked to the other Ligrosians, Verina echoed the embrace with bone-crushing enthusiasm. Ey had missed this presumed-dead Human—a fact no less surprising to em than to the other Ligrosians. When they separated, Li said, "See? I told you that you were like a cat."

Verina still wasn't sure what that meant, but smiled anyway. "Apparently you were right. But what about you?"

Verina resumed eir habit of synchronous translating for the different species as Li said, "You'd left the command post. Since neither side was obviously winning, I figured we'd be there for a while. I went to the supply dump for drinks and food. Earth forces made a push that forced me to take a route outside the heavy fighting. On my way back, I saw the last few seconds of the bombs coming in, so I took cover behind a retaining wall and prayed like I never prayed before."

There was more to be said, but Li wasn't offering. Verina prompted, "Did anyone else…?"

Li shook his head. "No. No, not that I know of. Not until you—

I can't tell you how surprised we were, back at one of the reserve camps, when news of your capture leaked out." Li stopped to consider how best to put it. "Hope returned."

Elekin and Akehru waited patiently as the two warriors caught-up. Verina turned to the pair and said, "And you two. How did you get tied up in this?"

Seeing Akehru's hesitation, Elekin said, "You did, when you wandered back into Czep-tan. How could we not help?"

Verina retorted, "That was more than just help."

Li said, "The details can probably wait a while. Suffice it to say, Elekin had already met with Akehru. I was sent by the reserve cell who took me in because I was the only one who had enough personal information about you to even try finding you in the city. After I found Akehru and talked with em, things fell into place quickly. You still have friends in strategic places—friends with a surprising amount of access. But we'll talk about that later, too. In the end, you're the one who made it easy. When you issued your order at the trial, all we had to do was put into action the plan we'd already worked out."

"But now, Verni," Akehru said, "we have to get you to the medical bay."

"To scan you for tracking devices," Li added.

Verina nodded in agreement, then said, "Medical bay? Where are we?"

Elekin answered, "The main cargo hold of the lead ship from the Quinkst Diplomatic Legation."

"The what? When?"

Li said, "I told you, you still have friends in high places."

Accepting that, for now, Verina motioned for Li to lead the way. Verina didn't immediately follow, pausing first to again touch foreheads with eir sibling before moving into the bowels of the ship.

The Quinkst vessel suited their builders, Verina noted to emself. Though impeccably modern and clean, the interior immediately brought to mind the maze of tunnels many lower-level social lifeforms constructed: the worm-like jibkik on eir own world; the almost microscopic v'vriv on Ig's moon, Ju-a-e; or even the ants on Earth. It made perfect sense—what else would giant slugs prefer? No Quinkst were in sight, of course. Though an amiable race, unafraid to deal with other species, their peculiar xenophobia made for an interesting contradiction. In deference to their own sensibilities, the Quinkst made certain that the trek from the cargo hold to the medical bay was short and quick.

Verina carefully lay on the central examining table. An articulated bar gyrated efficiently around em. A Quinkst-wide track separated the table from the equipment and lockers ringing the crystal-and-white oval room. Verina watched the bar as it scanned em thoroughly. The Human and the Ligrosians stood away from the table near a bank of displays. The bar finally stopped and retracted from view. Li studied the data now filling the screens and said, "That's what I was afraid of."

"What?" Verina asked.

"If you were any more wired, you'd be glowing. Look here."

Verina hopped off the table and joined the others around the display, examining the diagnostics list. Li continued, "I used to give this sort of stuff away for free. Here. They did a good job repairing your broken bone, but the synthetic they used to fill the gap is one powerful transmitter. Your body is crawling with replicating nano-transmitters, and your fluids are doped with just about every tracking substance we have. One thing's for certain: if you got away, they were determined to find you."

Interrupting Verina before ey could comment, Akehru said, "The suit we made you wear should have blocked everything, or at least most of it, and severely weakened the rest. And that's why we put you in a shielded box, too. Now, it doesn't matter. Quinkst ships are fully shielded."

Li said, "More than that, they're sovereign territory. Even if you were tracked here, there's nothing Earth can do about it."

"So, how do we disinfect me?"

"That will take some time," Li said. "The doping can be filtered. The nano-trans need to be deactivated and attacked with hunter-nans. The nasty bit is that bone replacement. That's probably going to need to be removed."

"So, what's the problem?" Verina asked.

"The way this was installed…almost all of your upper arm bone needs to be replaced with a clean synthetic."

"Will it hurt any more than losing half my skin?"

Li shook his head. "Well, no…"

"Then what's the problem? Let's clean me out."

Akehru and Elekin swallowed their shock with this exchange. Clean em out? Replace an arm bone? It seemed the stuff of nightmares. It forced them to look at the naked warrior more critically. From the front, Verina still had much of eir innate good looks—the scars, many from jujibtanibarre, didn't change that. But eir back…

Though the darkness of the new blue skin had lightened since the first regrowth, its current shade of cobalt blue wasn't likely to get much lighter. The pair had been taught in school that with so much skin torn off, Verina's nerves were all but fully exposed to the environment—protected only by a few layers of cells. Fifteen percent skin loss caused so much pain most victims were sent to neuro-psych clinics. Verina had lost more than that. The lost fringe was even more painful, and Verina had lost most of that as well. Yet ey behaved as if ey felt nothing. No wonder the prospect of replacing eir upper arm didn't affect em much.

Elekin finally asked, "Does it hurt?"

Confused at first but then seeing where Elekin's eyes kept darting to, and to where Akehru's eyes remained fixed, Verina said, "You have no idea. But it's what life has given me." With both eir sib and eir friend's expressions looking so pitiable, Verina added, "I have a job to do. I can't worry about myself until the Humans —" Verina bowed eir head slightly toward Li, "the uninvited Humans—are off our world. Then I'll be so happy I won't care." Seeing the attempted reassurance wasn't helping, ey said, "Please. Don't worry about me. I'm OK. I don't even take meds for it anymore," turning to Li, "do I?"

"I can vouch for that. Ey hasn't taken any pain meds for eir back in several months. Just an occasional anesthetic spray when ey needs to wear a jacket."

Verina paused in eir translation in order to do the math to convert "months" into "days," for clarity. The two other Ligrosians looked like they accepted the situation, though the patches around their eyes still held some pinkness.

A pause hung in the air. An unanswered question. Taking the bait, Verina said, "When do we start?"

Li looked around to see if Verina had spoken to someone else. "Don't look at me. The Quinkst medical staff will tend to it. I've already uploaded your scan to them."

A bit of disappointment with the delay darkened Verina's mood. "Fine." A thought crossed eir mind, and ey turned to Akehru. "Do you know anything about Pame?"

Akehru lowered eir head. "I don't."

"Aki?" Getting no response, Verina used eir command tone, "Aki!" Akehru looked back up. "What happened?"

Verina's sibling slumped slightly. "The night you took him," pointing at Li, "I got a message from Pame to go to eir apartment and take some bags ey left there and drop them off in the woods outside the city. I did that. When I got home…after I got home, the security force came—looking for you. They said you'd kidnapped someone Earth wanted and that you'd lost your position."

Verina realized, "The apartment," referring to the most visible perk of eir job.

"They let me pack some things, and then they locked me out. Then the attack started. I didn't know where else to go, so I went back home. Xadow was there, but Pame was gone. There have been some rumors, but I didn't know what to believe."

Elekin said, "They say that ey was with the maetor throughout the attack. Later, well after the invasion, I heard ey was a prisoner. The only ones who got released were the ones agreeing to be puppets. The rumor is that they don't keep their other prisoners alive for long."

All eyes turned to Li. Defensively, he said, "I don't know. Thothwai and I tried to find some news for Verina, but we couldn't break through the security. The official procedures about prisoner treatment are closely held by the military—and they don't share."

"Not even to a member of the diplomatic corps?" Akehru asked with some disdain.

"Especially no. What if we let something slip? I was instructed only on those things I needed to know, and generally a little less than I *really* needed to know."

Verina clicked and replied, "I know what you mean. Maybe it's true, the one constant in the universe is—"

Interrupting, a synthesized voice coming from the ceiling said, "Pardon the interruption. We request that Akehru Engineer-in-structor of Serees, Elekin Fisher-merchant of Serees, and Li Milit-ary-merchant of Earth return to their quarters or to their designated common room. Verina First Negotiator of Serees must be tended to."

Akehru said, "Time to get you patched up, Verni."

They touched foreheads. Akehru then stepped back and loitered by the door. Elekin reached out and intertwined the fingers of one hand with Verina's in a forward-and-back sort of arrangement that made Li think of his grandmother's macramé plant holders. After they parted, Li simply put his hand on his commander's shoulder and said, "See you soon."

He joined the other two. As they left, Verina said, "Thanks, you three. For everything."

Verina sat on the edge of the examining table, nervously fore-and-back palming eir fingers. The Ligrosian was soon in the company of three matted-hair-covered, two-and-a-half-meter-long tubes of flesh. What surprised Verina wasn't that the three individuals squeezed into the room, but that ey was in the presence of three Quinkst. No aliens ever saw more than one Quinkst at a time.

The aroma of the three large aliens in such a small space was… profound. There was little to visually differentiate the Quinkst from each other. Verina's focus on telling the aliens apart helped distract em from the smell. The one with the brightest orange hair had a streak on the top pincer of one of its claws. The hair on another was—it was hard to describe—it had seen more use. The third Quinkst was the most distinct. The used-hair member spoke, with a raspy, heavily accented voice, "I am Lekrurstha Gevathorweykh, holder of the glowing orb, seated with Jeg. With your permission, my team and I will do what we can to cleanse your body of the foreign tracking devices and substances."

Verina said, in eir very best Quinkst, since the doctor had been considerate enough to speak Haipo, the very formal Ligrosian language, "It is an honor to be seen by someone so highly esteemed by his people. Without reservation, I grant my body totally to your healing skills."

Verina's words weren't born of diplomatic nicety. Before eir last negotiation, ey learned everything ey could about Quinkst society and their rather complicated hierarchy. A holder of the glowing orb was a healer of very high esteem. That he was "seated with Jeg" meant that this doctor was qualified to practice on the top echelon of Quinkst and also on several other species. Given the apparent high-priority his government placed on this mission, it shouldn't have been a surprise to see this expert here. Verina doubted that ey would ever be treated by anyone more qualified, even among eir own people. "Please lie back on the table," Lekrurstha said in Haipo.

Verina lay down. Despite eir pain and nervousness, ey relaxed. Lekrurstha said, "You will be anesthetized throughout the procedure. You will wake in your quarters."

A comfortable, sedate darkness filled Verina's mind.

The sound of surf rolling on a beach, and the gentle rising of the ambient illumination, eased Verina back to reality. Waking up here felt like waking up on the shore near a holaxex in the middle of a holiday. No rush. No demands. No pressure. No stress. On the whole, a very pleasant way to greet the day. Memories reasserted themselves: fighting; capture; escape. Something was missing...

Ey couldn't remember the last time ey felt this good, with or without meds. Whatever the Quinkst used for an analgesic was amazing. Ey sat up in bed. An obviously synthetic voice said, "Good day, Verina of Serees. A message has been sent to the medical staff that you have awakened. With your permission, your caregiver of record, Lekrurstha, would like to visit you."

"Yes. Yes, of course," Verina said.

"Please stand by."

Verina looked around eir room. Although the ceiling of the round, blood-red room arched lower than ey preferred, the Spartan decor was more than adequate. It was certainly better than at most of the bases ey journeyed through during the war. The bed felt like gel. A chair carved from a single piece of some light-yellow wood sat in the corner—but it was of the design Li's people preferred which, while usable by Ligrosians, wasn't very comfortable. A small table, carved from the same type of wood as the chair and adorned with a small bas relief that at first glance looked like inlaid bands, stood next to the bed. On it were four different devices, including a timesync. With no idea of how long eir incarceration had been before eir liberation, the display of this clock didn't tell Verina anything useful.

A chime sounded, followed by the synthetic voice saying, "Lekrurstha asks if he may enter."

"Granted."

The door slid into the curved wall. The Quinkst doctor glided inside, the door closing behind him. "Greetings, Verina First Negotiator. I hope that you are feeling well?"

"Very well, thank you. Whatever meds you have me on are wonderful."

"You are not on any medications."

"But…my back."

"Yes. I realize that you did not specifically mention those injuries. Since your medical disciplines can't deal with such extensive dermal pathologies, it is not surprising."

"But how—?"

"We have developed an *in situ* cellular cloning method that can effect limited tissue regrowth. Your species' immune system. with its genetic defenses, makes these treatments less effective than with many others. While there was little we could do to repair the extensive damage to your skin, or lessen the over-stimulated neural signals you are interpreting as pain, our methods were able to repair much of the unresolved trauma from the loss of your vibrissae…I believe you call it 'fringe.' Our desire was to lessen your chronic discomfort."

"Less discom—? Lekrurstha, from the difference between

when I put myself in your care, until now, I must fully agree that your honors are entirely deserved. Since I cannot be in your debt, due to your calling, please let me say that I am available to you whenever, or if-ever, you should have need."

While the distinction was a fine one, it was very Quinkst in flavor. Lekrurstha accepted. "I might say that your rank is equally deserved. You understand our sensibilities well."

Verina respectfully bowed, a fairly common gesture that was generally recognized by all articulated species. The Quinkst continued, "While I was also able to repair the extensive damage to your ora, the damage to your internal reproductive organs is beyond our ability to heal. I cannot say that you are sterile, for your organs still have some function, but breeding, either as sire or parent, will be, at best, problematic."

In all of these days, though it had been briefly mentioned when ey was recovering in that first refugee mine, eir ability to breed wasn't something Verina gave a thought about. There were always more immediate concerns.

Lekrurstha continued without pause, "All of the tracing elements have been removed, save for one: an interesting retro-virus that had infected about three-fourths of your cells. We have quantum-repairers in your system now correcting the infestation. Currently, the infection is down to less than half. My estimate is that it will take another three days for you to be rid of all tracking devices…at least those we know how to detect.

"You will want to know about your arm. We replaced your entire humerus with a regrowth lattice which will supply all normal strength and structure while your body regrows its own tissue to replace it."

Verina twisted a little to see the result of the procedure. A thread-thin blue scar paralleled the thicker one left by the Humans, crossed by the dark-blue scar tissue from where the bone had pierced eir skin. "My thanks, Lekrurstha, holder of the glowing orb, seated with Jeg, of the Quinkst."

Lekrurstha's normally cylindrical body flattened and held for a moment. Verina never saw this before, but suspected that it might be the Quinkst version of a bow. As the door opened, the doctor said, "It was my honor to help a person of destiny. The thanks are mine."

The hairy sea cucumber glided out of the room as silently as he entered. Verina reached around and felt eir back. It remained terrifyingly sensitive and painful. But on the lines where fringe were lost, there was only the slightest of tingles. The lessening of eir overall pain was such a difference, Verina almost felt normal. Ey then moved eir hands nervously to the three-centimeter-long ora on either side of eir lower back, just behind and above eir cranial box. The contorted scarring was gone; they felt normal. Unnoticed, smiles appeared on Verina's mouths as ey continued contemplating eir new lease on life.

Earth's military governor on Serees, Fleet Marshal Chavez, rebuffed every attempt made by the diplomatic mission to broker an amicable withdrawal. The alien delegation argued that Earth's point had been made and it wasn't civilized if its only means of diplomacy was invasion. Chavez retorted that what Earth had done was for the benefit of all. Without offering proof, he reiterated the public pronouncements coming from Earth's government that the Sereesians had been spying on all of their civilizations for almost as long as the Seetun devices had been distributed. The general maintained that the rebellion forced his fleet to remain; they were needed to ensure peace and to help in reconstruction. When offers of aid for the reconstruction were also rebuffed, the diplomatic fleet left.

Three days after leaving Serees, having been politically insulted, the members of the legation were not reticent to meet with the rescued leader of the rebellion against Earth's occupation. They sat in a large, oval conference room. Polished latticed stone papered the maple-colored curved walls. Each of the four-person delegations, save for the sole Quinkst representative, had species-specific chairs placed evenly about a round table that looked like a single polished slice of a very large tree trunk.

The representatives spoke for most of the civilizations local to Serees. These worlds maintained excellent relations with Serees extending back for longer than Earth had been space-faring. Sitting nearest to the three Ligrosians, on their right, were the Antyerians, with whom only the Ligrosians could communicate directly in their musical language. Their relatively good relations with Earth made them a top choice for this diplomatic congregation. Ironically, it was this same good relationship that indirectly placed two members of their race on Li's ship days before it crashed on Serees.

Trying to forestall any interest from Earth invading *them*, the Ju-a-e'I volunteered to join the legation—the opportunity to gain some direct intelligence outweighed their fear of attracting Earth's attention. Ssurnai, the sixth moon of Ig in the Takat system, provided a frigid and resource-rich environment for technologies the Ju-a-e'I were more than happy to keep private. Technologies that Earth would dearly covet if they knew of them. But the Ju-a-e'I were skilled at maintaining their privacy. No one had ever seen a Ju-a-e. Their environment, hovering around sixty degrees Kelvin, forced an improbable evolution of beings with small tolerance for "high" temperatures. Even the waste heat from an alien spacesuit could kill them in minutes. As a result, whether at home or off-world, the Ju-a-e'I always wore their own fully-enclosed egg-shaped environment suits when with aliens.

The Tariri, from Krantozenia in the Y system, joined the legation more to protect their Seetun licenses than to broker peace. They expected a return of Serees rule would ensure uninterrupted communication lines. As the Tariri relied on visual communication, only Seetun devices provided the bandwidth this colonizing society required. Looking much like trees composed of densely-wadded, clear fishing line, the Tariri were considered among the most aesthetic of beings. Their style of communication resulted in a beautiful light show ranging from small sparkling dots appearing seemingly randomly on their limbs, to a neon-like glow of their entire body. They shone in a wide spectrum ranging from high-frequency infrared to a medium-energy ultraviolet. When necessary, they could make sounds by vibrating some of their filaments, but it was taxing and always sounded synthetic.

Lastly, across the table from Verina sat eir biggest surprise: Thignis kra-Ra'Yijas, the exiled Planetary Minister from Lrat. The chlorophyll-tinted Gelraht elder, like the rest of the Gelrahtem, might be easily mistaken for a plant on most worlds. Standing about two meters tall, with three levels having a number of multi-brachiated limbs, the Humans disparagingly referred to them as walking Christmas trees.

Once the Quinkst at Verina's left made the introductions, Verina broke with standard protocol and said, "Minister Ra'Yijas, it is an honor. I'm curious—"

"Why someone almost as wanted by the Humans as you would volunteer to come to a Human-occupied world?" the exiled leader said, though no one could tell where her mouth was.

"I was going to put it a little differently, but yes."

"My purpose here was purely out of curiosity. I knew I couldn't leave the ship, and I was relatively certain that this mission would fail. But I had to take a chance that I might get to meet you."

"Me? I'm not…why?"

"Because, as a negotiator, you are known to several species and are well-respected…and because you know how powerful Earth is. You know what they have done, and are still doing, to my planet. And still you fought them. You fought them well. Don't give me that look. News of your fight has leaked from your planet, despite the Earther's efforts. Surely, you knew you were going to lose. So, why did you fight?"

All eyes turned to the exiled rebel. A fire burned in Verina's heart. "They threatened, attacked, and invaded my world…not because we were a threat to them, but because they are spoiled children who lash out when they don't get their way. They were not invited to stay, and I want them off my planet. That's why I fought them. That is why I'll continue to fight them. They took my home…and my life…and I want it back!"

After a pause for that to sink in, Thignis asked, "How?"

The Quinkst said, "That is a purpose of why are here, now. Unfortunately, I am being called away. I think Verina of Serees will be interested in my replacement."

The Quinkst glided out of the room without so much as a by-your-leave. Moments later, he was replaced by a familiar body. "Javrurhal!" Verina said enthusiastically.

Many in the room, including all of Verina's companions, were surprised that ey recognized the new attendee on sight. Almost all aliens had trouble distinguishing one Quinkst from another. "Verina," he said informally, "it is happiness unfolded that I've gotten to see you again."

"Can we visit, later?"

"Of course." Javrurhal situated himself in the spot to Verina's left that was reserved for the Quinkst. "We must first define exactly why we are here. Verina…because of our planet's long and fruitful history with Serees, and due to our very comfortable rela-tionship with the honor you always show us, the Quinkst would like to help you in your cause. The reason we convened a formal meeting was to encourage all of your other neighbors to join with us in giving you support.

"It's true that most of us have treaties and alliances with Earth —and that will no doubt complicate our discussions—but I think the true question before us is: if we don't help you, which of our worlds will be the next to fall? How long before there aren't enough left to fight back? We were wrong in trying to appease the Humans with Lrat. History will judge all of our worlds harshly for it. Our only choice is to help the Serees now."

Various sounds and lights emerged among and between the various alien groups, much of it filled with worry and doubt. Still, no one disputed Javrurhal's statement. Looking over to the familiar Quinkst, Verina felt certain he enjoyed this moment of solidarity.

14

New Serees

Popituv entered Yavent with no fanfare. From eir two-vehicle convoy, eir examined the thoroughfares of the once awe-inspiring repository of so much of the planet's art and history. The ruins of the city—the first and hardest hit by the Invasion Wave—had long been cleared away. Under the "protection" of Human troops, Ligrosians worked to rebuild some of what had been lost.

General Chavez and General Bhoutto watched the former leader's entrance from a balcony high up one of the three tall buildings that survived the destruction. Chavez said, "Are you certain you can control her? You saw what happened with the other one."

Bhoutto remained focused on the vehicles and said, "It won't be a problem. Corroborated reports say she argued with that other one in public about what was best for their planet." Turning to the general, he continued, "We don't have to condition her. She's already on board of her own free will."

"Just make sure. I don't need any more dead soldiers."

"The Presidium?"

"No, the administration. Seems somebody…spoke out of turn. I've managed to cover the records trail, but they keep asking questions."

"If I can be of service in any way, General."

"I know, Mearann. I count on that. That's why I'm putting you in charge of her." Chavez looked at his watch and headed for the door. Before exiting, he added, "Make this work."

"Yes sir. I already have plans in motion. These Sereesians will be allied with us in short order."

Down on the street, the tiny parade continued its slow tour.

General Chavez strode into an equipment-filled communications room. "Well? Where is it?"

A nervous lab technician stood and pointed to a door at the end of a short hall.

When the general walked into this room, he was startled to see Minister Naveen's head showing ominously large from a display. Naveen said, "General, it's nice to finally be able to speak to you in real-time."

Fleet Marshal Chavez sat down at a utilitarian ceramic table. He said, "Thank you, sir. We were fortunate to discover this feed while clearing away debris. Now Bryce's team can monopolize the other link without affecting necessary communications."

"How's Bryce's research coming, General?"

"I'm assured that we are only one or two crypto-breaks away from freeing up the network. I'd be happy if they'd PAN us with this feed, but they say it's impossible. For now, we have to be planet-side to use either line."

Naveen nodded. "Before the rest of the administration muscles in on this link… Between you and me, any immediate problems that need tending to?"

"Yes sir. Overall, things are progressing well, but I think that I have an upper-level leak going to someone on the administrative staff. I don't have any evidence, but I've received inquiries about items that should have been compartmentalized locally."

The Minister's brows creased downward ever so slightly, reinforcing his official scowl. "That's worrying, General. Are you certain that it's an internal matter?"

"I believe so. All communications off-world have to go through my command. Only someone with high clearance can get information out. All those sources are trusted and closely monitored."

"What about that terrorist that escaped? Couldn't she be spilling everything to those sympathizers who helped her get off-world?"

"I don't think the information would be sent directly to our government, sir. I haven't seen intelligence about these leaks traveling to other worlds, but my resources aren't as extensive as those available to your office. Also, some of the inquired subjects seem to be outside of anything she could possibly have learned, in any case."

"Understood. I'll start looking into it at this end."

"That's much appreciated, sir."

"Anything else? Any more major terrorist activity?"

"Nothing beyond simple vandalism since the prison break. They may have used the last of their resources to free their leader. I don't think they have the fight, or the weapons, to be a lingering threat. I'm not letting our guard down, of course, but I think that stage of this mission has closed."

"That's indeed hopeful news, General. Just keep an eye on your flanks. It wouldn't do to have those giant slugs mount an attack out of sympathy."

"No sir. I extended and modified our outer system patrols for just that sort of problem as soon as the Quinkst ship left the gravity well."

"I'd expect no less. I knew you'd be the right person to replace General Pervikh, peace be unto him. Crack this communications problem, get to the business of reinvigorating the planet's industry, and you'll be relaxing on your own conservancy out in the country soon enough."

"Yes sir. Thank you, sir."

"My time is up. I'll be in touch with you soon."

A bland graphic popped up on screen with the words, "Please Stand By." While waiting for the next Minister in line to talk to him "live" and confidentially, the general's mind focused on the leak. The weak link was Bryce. Or was. Since the battle that crushed the rebellion, she'd come around to accepting the way he was running this war. He'd continue to keep his eye on the Ice Colonel, but his gut told him it wasn't her. But if it wasn't her, he could think of no other suspect.

The graphic disappeared, replaced by the face of Extra-solar Affairs Minister Chopratama. Chavez allowed himself a mental sigh in preparation of being annoyed. "Good morning, Minister. I'm happy to once again have the opportunity to speak to you face-to-face."

The Minister bore an expression that implied she was allowing herself her own mental sigh.

Verina stood in the Quinkst ship's common room. Except for a a long, multi-sectioned couch instead of a conference table, and some changes in wall decoration, this was a twin of the conference room ey'd been meeting in. Ey stared out the large window into interstellar space. A long day talking to various alien delegations accomplished little except to darken eir mood. None of them would accept the risk of antagonizing Earth, but all were more than willing to let *em* wage war so long as nothing could be traced back to them in any way. Letting others fight the battles, it seemed, was a key component to multilateral diplomacy. Verina wouldn't accept this. If they were to be allies, they would have to commit to getting their proverbial hands and feet dirty. The Quinkst stood alone in their willingness to accept that responsibility, but even they hesitated about being a majority partner. With eir frustration building, Verina had excused emself from the proceedings.

Verina's mood wasn't helped by what the Earth woman said: that someone ey knew was a betrayer. It gnawed at em. The three with em on this ship all had opportunity to turn Verina in to the Humans. Earth offered tempting rewards, including amnesty. Or, it could have been someone else entirely. But everyone else ey knew was dead or missing. Would the traitor have helped em to escape? If so, why?

No.

Verina resolved long ago that ey wasn't going to play that game. Ey had to trust those around em. The Faith demanded that leaders trust those they led in a righteous cause. It was the highest and riskiest burden of leadership. Verina often fought with emself not to succumb to suspicion and paranoia. And yet... The biggest risk was Li. He was one of *them*. He shouldn't have been able to escape Earth's battlefield sterilization. Still, since ey rescued him —so long ago, it seemed—Li had been as loyal and helpful as anyone ey had ever known. He had earned the trust due to him.

Verina startled out of eir deep contemplation when something rammed into eir leg hard enough to make em stumble. The Ligrosian became hyper-alert and focused solely on survival. The source of the assault wasn't difficult to locate, though it's unexpected nature took a moment to recognize. "Xadow!"

With childish happiness replacing battlefield wariness, Verina scooped up eir all-too-happy-to-see-em haiwa and smothered him with a very loving and firm embrace.

"I thought you'd like something from home," Akehru said as ey entered the room. Ey multi-grinned with seeing eir sib so happy and surprised. Verina said two overlapping forms of thank you while punctuating it with a simultaneous whistling purr used by siblings reveling in the safety and comfort of their shared company. Akehru added, "I couldn't leave him alone on Serees. But I didn't realize so many species don't like living animals as pets. Since it was you, and it was their ship, the Quinkst were willing to let me bring him."

Verina showered attention on the haiwa for a number of minutes before the lure of a new place to explore lured Xadow from his owner's arms. Verina turned to eir sibling, saying, "I'm guessing nothing much changed after I left?"

"No. Worse. After a while, they started going on about these trade agreements that really had nothing at all to do with us. The Quinkst agreed it was too far off-point. That's when the meeting broke up."

Elekin entered, followed by Li. Eir face showed concern as ey said, "We've just intercepted a message that Hai-Popituv has been reinstated as maetor."

"No," Akehru said with some surprise.

"And with Earth's blessing," Elekin added.

Looking at Verina, Li said, "It's not like we weren't expecting it."

Akehru and Elekin turned to Verina, who explained, "I had a small run-in with Hai-Popituv a little while before the big battle. Ey wasn't exactly on my side."

"I think you made an enemy," Li added.

Verina shifted into eir leadership mindset. "That's really not the point. Ey's letting emself be used. Ey thinks that if ey's a symbol, then things will return close to normal—that Earth will be nothing except a distraction now that I'm out of the way. I know ey believes it.

"One thing's certain: we can't sit back and let a figurehead turn Serees into Lrat. I've got to go back."

Akehru protested, "No! You can't."

"Verina," Li said, pausing to give the moment more weight, "you have to stay here and forge alliances." He lifted a finger, preventing the rebel leader's impending interruption. "The secondary network is in place. You just need to tell them what to do."

Verina hated it when this particular Human was calm and reasonable. "You're right. I can't go right now." The Ligrosian looked at eir rescuers. "You three are going."

Words eluded Elekin, but Akehru said, "What?!"

"You three are going back to Serees to make sure the people don't forget that we want our planet back."

Akehru protested, "I'm not a terrorist!" Then, seeing Verina's eyes, ey amended, "Or a rebel, or freedom fighter, or whatever in Gav-tewes Zher you call yourself."

Verina calmly faced the two Ligrosians, not noticing the haiwa heeling just behind em. "Yes, you are. The minute you two decided to free me from the Humans you joined up. You're fugitives, now. You might as well do some good with it."

Akehru looked confused and scared as ey slowly sank to eir knees and sat on eir heels. Eir only thought had been to free eir little sib. Ey knew consequences were likely, but until this moment it all seemed like a kind of adventure. A never-to-be-repeated adventure. Now it hit em. Eir life was gone. Eir job. Eir home. Gone. Ey looked at Verina's scarred head and remembered eir scarred body. What had ey done?

Verina said to Elekin, "You're taking this well."

"There's nothing to take. If I'd known how to do it, I'd have joined up on the first day. I'll do whatever you want…Hai-Verina."

"Now don't *you* start," chided the rebel. "You're my friend." Verina touched eir forehead to Elekin's and softly added, "Don't you ever forget it."

"OK…Verni."

"That's better."

Li fidgeted while waiting for the the public display to finish. Didn't these people know there was a war on? With a resigned tone, Akehru said, "What do you want me to do?"

Verina broke the touch with Elekin, subtly motioning for eir to join em as Verina sat on eir heels to face eir older sibling. Verina also gestured for Li to complete the group. While petting Xadow, Verina said, "Nothing big. I've still got a small army that knows how to fight. I just can't communicate with them at the moment. You three have to be my eyes and ears and mouths. They know Li —but since he's Human, he can't lead. It needs a Ligrosian…or two." Verina then said something to Elekin which ey didn't translate and which didn't sound to Li like the language he was starting to become familiar with. When Verina resumed translating, ey said, "Now you two, I don't want you out in the fight when you don't have to, except to save your lives. I can't afford to lose anyone else."

Following Verina, everyone rose, Akehru looked as if ey had been hit with a barrel-full of bricks. Verina said, "We're going to need some comm equipment and a transport."

Li said with a smile, "Transportation won't be a problem."

Five minutes later, the group of four stood in a spacious cargo bay. Parked there, fully repaired and showroom shiny was Li's ship, the *Mir 4 Arms*. Li said, "I found her when we were scouting escape routes. It took some finagling, but I had a team swap her with a derelict before we destroyed the hanger. Earth Fleet will think she was destroyed in the blast…which actually solves a problem I had before I crashed." Seeing the curious looks he was getting, Li added, "And that's not important right now."

Verina asked while unconsciously rubbing eir arm, "Tracking inserts?"

"She's clean," Li said. "Aren't you, Ship?"

"Very much so," the techno-sentient machine replied in Limto, since Li was hearing his language via the comm implant in his ear, as he'd arranged with Ship beforehand.

The main hatch on the side opened in the same manner Verina remembered. As they entered, both Akehru and Verina thought that the vessel was much less forbidding this time. "Welcome back on board," Ship said.

It took a moment for Verina to realize it was em and Akehru being addressed. "Thank you. You were very helpful."

"Thank you," Ship replied.

With a twinkle in his eye, Li said, "Ship, the Serees you just spoke to, named Verina, is to be given the same security and operational access as my own. I trust eir no less than I do you. I hope you two will one day be friends."

Stunned, Verina said, "Li...I—"

Ship responded, "Clearances amended."

Li had actually entered all the codes and commands necessary for this request when the others were meeting with the diplomats, but he thought the show was important. "There," he said to Verina. "Now, if something happens to me, Ship will still be an asset to you."

The Ligrosians had some trouble coming to terms with this. While a very few of their species had gone off-world for specific business reasons—or in Verina's current case, survival—manned space travel was not something that had been part of their culture for over a millennium. The idea of being given free access to a space vehicle bordered on the fantastic. But if their recent experiences taught them anything, it was to swim with the current.

Five days later, trapped in another interminable meeting with the alien representatives, Verina regretted encouraging *all* of eir friends to go. Verina opted to stay quiet in all of these sessions to see what sort of alliances this unlikely collection could form on its own. Hour after mind-numbing hour passed filled with petty squabbles about import/export agreements, trade routes, mutual protection policies, and self-promoting puffery about how each and every one of them was taking a risk by simply sitting at this table.

As the third, and last, session of the fifth day drew close to its scheduled adjournment, Verina slapped eir hands on the table and stood.

Silence.

The Ligrosian said, "Javrurhal of the Quinkst, may I say something?"

"You may, Verina of Serees," Javrurhal replied with obvious relief.

"Thank you. I have sat here listening to all of you for days. I've listened because at no point during any of these sessions has one of you bothered to ask what *I* want or what my planet needs. Before making any official offers, you have all been trying to ensure you can make maximum profit with minimum risk.

"You all know my previous profession, if not firsthand, then by reputation. You know that I understand diplomacy and government bureaucracy all too well. I'm telling you now, my world is not some business deal, and I won't let you treat it that way."

No one spoke in reply, but there was some rustling that spoke of agreement, discomfort, and a little shame. Verina continued, "Here is what's going to happen: I'm going to tell you what I require. I'm going to say which of you will provide what…though I am willing to negotiate some of that if better arrangements can be made. The amount of help I get will dictate how favorable future contract negotiations will be with my planet's government when it's re-established. If you have a problem with that, feel free to leave this table." Noticing the stunned silence, Verina added, "And I do mean right now."

The members nervously looked at the others. Minister Ra'Yijas of Lrat stood up, making Verina's internals go all queasy. She then started rustling some of her brachia, which Verina chose to interpret as some symbolic form of support. "You are well suited to be a leader. We didn't have that." The minister became quiet, and Verina thought, reflective. "Perhaps we could have driven the Humans off my world long ago. Perhaps we'd be free."

The Minister sat down. With no other displays imminent, Verina said, "Minister, if not for the harm done to your planet, I don't know if I'd be inspired to stand here now. Thank you." The Lrat minister shimmered. Verina stared at the other participants around the table. "If you are all ready to get serious, let's set things in motion before we break for the night."

Verina returned to eir chair, feeling rather pleased with emself. Ey might get some genuine assistance out of this group.

Popituv walked into the spacious office with the dignity that followed em wherever ey went. Ey had once been maetor. Now, ey was maetor again. Ey once had sole authority over the visible planet. Others had power this time, and those others were not only of another species but of another planet. It was hard not to doubt emself.

The office evoked the crystalline salt forest in the southern ocean of Silvehi. No one knew the forest's current condition, but it was likely destroyed. Several branches, clear with colorful veins of minerals, accented the room. The dark mauve inlays of weeya'atim wood in the desk, shelves, and other accouterments balanced the theme of "trees of the sea" with "trees of the land".

Popituv's first impression of eir new working space was definitely favorable. A glance to eir aide, the arboresque Navegil, showed that ey, too, approved. General Bhoutto entered. "How do you like your new office?" he asked via the small translator affixed to his jacket.

"It's not the traditional maetor design. I suppose it will do, depending on what will be expected of me."

"All we ask is that you be a moderating influence on your people…the voice of reason. There have been reports of a new wave of terrorism. Nothing big, but enough to be annoying. It's important that you don't let those misguided people of yours ruin everyone else's safe-and-ordered life."

Popituv walked to eir place behind the desk and remained standing. "I was maetor for a long time. I know that even if you filter information of the events, it still seeps into the populace. It can't be stopped; at least, I didn't know a way."

"You don't have to stop it," the general said reassuringly. "We've had centuries to learn how to handle these situations. All you have to do is tell your people they are being attacked, and then denounce the citizens who don't back the government…who don't back *you*…for their lack of patriotism and exposing everyone else to danger. It always works. This way, the more the terrorists try to ruin the peace, the more the people will trust in your leadership."

That sounds like a typical Earth thing to say, Popituv thought. "I might have to modify the wording some so that I'm comfortable with it."

"You can try. I think you'll see that it's the simplest way to maintain the peace. I do suggest that if you make significant modifications that you run it by me or my office manager first. Like I said, we're pretty experienced in these things."

"Of course."

Popituv turned to look out the wall-sized window onto eir new capital. Yavent had always been eir favorite city to visit. The sky-reaching buildings that looked like solid pieces of carved crystal were breathtaking. Below them, augmenting the aesthetic value of the mineral-like facade, were buildings and gardens thoughtfully designed to make the entire city a work of art. Though the large buildings could never be changed much, all of the enhancing elements below them were in a constant state of creative flux. If you visited Yavent at the start of the year and again a quarter of a year later, it would look similar in form but very different in its details. The loss of that beautiful city saddened Popituv more than ey could express.

Yavent was the heart of Serees. It was the *first* city. Yavent was Yavent, and needed neither the "-tan" or "-aziq" suffixes used by every other city. When the seat of government moved to the newer cities, Yavent changed to be a vanguard of scholarship, history, and art. Only the best works found homes here, though not exclusively. No city was left wanting for the gifts Yavent had in surfeit, but the most treasured gravitated here. The destruction of the seaside towers went beyond tragic. The buildings themselves could be rebuilt, but the original artworks and texts had been lost. Fortunately, they were too precious to exist only as originals. Copies of all of these works were reproduced and stored throughout Serees. But while the knowledge remained intact, some of the flavor was now gone. Of all the losses Serees experienced, Popituv felt this one the most.

The construction teams on the street scurried about rebuilding. More than twenty meters of a new tower had been erected, as well as fifteen of another. It would take many years to restore the city to anything near its former glory, but the first steps were underway. "Your people are diligent workers," Bhoutto said, now standing beside Popituv.

"Rebuilding would go much faster if the security checks were more efficient."

"May I tell you something?" Popituv turned to Bhoutto, who said, "I'm not a fan of all of the security. Personally, I believe those notes left by the terrorists: that they targeted only my people. It's also obvious that someone, somewhere, made some mistakes. In any case, just as you aren't being given free reign to rule your subjects, I have my own restrictions. If I lessen security and anything...*anything*...happens, you will lose your most supportive ally—namely me when I get reassigned—and your people will see stricter measures. That's not a threat; it's just how things are."

Candor was something the restored leader wasn't expecting. Though ey couldn't yet read the Humans' subtleties of expression, eir alien handler's words seemed sincere. Popituv said, "I understand your people are starting to call this city, 'New Serees.'"

"It's better than what many were calling it, though the literary reference would be lost on you. Your people are, of course, free to continue to call it however you see fit."

With an undertone of two dissonant notes denoting disapproving sarcasm, which Bhoutto couldn't quite hear due to some low-frequency deafness, Popituv said, "That's very generous of you, General."

Bhoutto's wristcomm beeped for attention. "Excuse me," he said as he stepped back and activated the device. "Bhoutto."

"General, we've just gotten word about London Bridge."

"Where?"

"Manchester."

The general touched a stand-by button on the wristcomm and turned back to Popituv. "If you will excuse me, I seem to have an appointment I must tend to."

Popituv merely nodded assent, and the general quickly left the office. Navegil followed him to the door, making certain it was locked from the inside. With em and the leader now alone, ey said, "Are you certain this is the place for us?"

Popituv said, "I hope so. Maybe we can work with this Bhoutto. I sense that he does want to do the right thing, but he is caught in a system preventing him from doing it."

"And if he's better at deception than you're giving him credit for?"

"He may well be. 'Tell the people that they are unpatriotic', indeed. Still, at least we have more freedom to reach our people than we did before. Hopefully, that will allow us to negotiate a livable peace."

After several minutes of unanswered requests, Javrurhal called security to unsecure the door to Verina's quarters. The Quinkst shivered with fear with the horror inside. The small, furry animal Verina kept was now scattered across the blood-spattered room— torn into several bloody fur-covered pieces of flesh. And Verina was gone.

15

Plowshares and Swords

Verina floated. Though ey'd never experienced weightlessness before, the change from planetary gravity to micro-gravity was unmistakable. Being a member of an ocean-going species helped make zero-gee something familiar and almost comforting. However, the darkness and confinement in what was some sort of flexible bag more than offset any feeling of comfort. Verina knew of individual survival bags only from books. Ey had never actually seen one, but it was the only thing that made sense. Trying not to panic, the Ligrosian began a careful study of eir current home.

The bag's fabric felt roughly woven but was flexible and partially deflated, despite the breathable air pressure within. The fabric resisted being pulled taught to lessen the risks of punctures. The Ligrosian found the somewhat flaccid material combined with the size of the bag, being large enough to fit two massive Ligrosians easily, made exploring the interior cumbersome. Twice, Verina's movements accidentally set emself and the bag tumbling. Eir desire to avoid getting sick motivated em to quickly counteract the momentum. An unexpected bonus to this effort was the discovery of a box at one end of eir life raft. The gentle flow of air from one of its vents, as well as an equally soft flow of air into the device, suggested it was the life support unit.

Continuing eir exploration within the frustrating shelter, Verina accidentally located a lumistick—one of the most foolproof inventions ever and almost as ubiquitous as the Infolux. When activated, its core glowed from pressure, warmth, or motion. The very act of touching an "on" lumistick created the power necessary to make it light. As a result, emergency sticks in survival bags were left inactive until life support started, staying in a stand-by state until enough external stimulus caused it to light—which is how Verina accidentally found this one.

Now able to see, Verina quickly found labels printed on the light-gray bag interior. They contained instructions in a variety of languages but none of the languages used on Serees were included. Predictably, Quinkst was the first of the several choices. Using these instructions, Verina quickly found the stores of supplies in compartments on the life support unit as well as tucked among the folds of the fabric. The inventory included enough foodstuffs for no less than seven days survival. Factoring in additional ingredients, such as various carbohydrate solutions for those species who didn't consume solid food, Verina figured ey had sixteen day's worth of calories available if ey didn't scrimp. The stored water plus the recycling function of the life-support unit meant ey didn't have to worry about rationing. The meager contents met the design goals of this under-inflated balloon: emergency survival until rescue.

Verina slipped the lumistick back into its holder and let the glow die out. Ey didn't need light to survive. Ligrosians still retained a vestigial trait where extended sensory deprivation slowed their metabolism so they needed less food and water. Verina didn't know if anyone was looking for eir minuscule bag in the vastness of space. Ey needed to manage the available resources so they'd last as long as possible.

The rebel leader was comforted that eir companions were back on Serees. Before eir "bagging", ey received a report of a raid on the industrial city of Miklao-tan that yielded necessary supplies and weapons. More importantly, it raised the morale among the faithful, who now knew their leader was off-world and alive. It also stemmed a burgeoning new resistance infrastructure begging to emerge in Verina's absence. While proud that the fight no longer depended solely on em, it was troublesome that new cells could form so quickly. There could only be one leader at a time, and ey wasn't done yet. There were bound to be repercussions. With Li to plan, and Elekin and Akehru to issue directives, perhaps the movement would retain its singular focus and avoid fracturing from internal politics.

Verina gave Li standing orders to continue the harassment of Earth Fleet for as long as it took for em to open another front with the help of their alien allies. Because security concerns meant updates were infrequent, it could be quite some time before eir friends knew ey was missing—assuming ey actually *was* missing and not just floating around a cargo bay with the gravity turned off.

The bag suddenly inflated, prompting Verina to scream in surprise. The Ligrosian saw that eir shelter's skin was now a taut egg shape. Before ey could speculate on what had changed, ey slammed into the fabric and felt emself pressed uncomfortably tighter against the firm, but not rigid, shell. Moments later, the force lessened and Verina slid down the fabric. When ey settled, ey felt something solid outside eir cocoon. Gravity weighed on the Ligrosian, making em feel weak, but the force was also comforting after the days of being adrift.

The survival bag suddenly opened and collapsed. The flood of light momentarily blinded the disoriented Serees. As eir vision cleared, Verina trumpeted, "You?"

Standing over the Ligrosian in a cramped loading bay was an oversized walking blood blister of an alien who musically polyphoned, "You recognize me?"

Verina chorused back, "You're the second-lowest ranking member of the Antyerian delegation."

"How? Most species have trouble recognizing individuals."

"You have a very distinctive Fa'run shimmer on your right side."

"Interesting. I've never been told that before."

"It's like a crescent," Verina melodied while also tracing the shape in the air with a finger.

The motion startled the fragile alien, prompting her to take a step backward. She orchestrated, "I'm returning you to the Humans. I only came down to confirm that you were uninjured."

"You took quite a risk."

"No. We left you floating in space for five days to incapacitate you when you were back in gravity. It was enough of a limitation that I could risk this visit." As the alien backed toward the hatch, she added, "There is food and drink in those containers. More than enough for the trip. Feel free to indulge yourself. You will not be visited again until the exchange takes place."

"Excuse me, before you go…"

The sentient red bag stood at the opening, ready to close it with less than a moment's warning. "Yes?"

"Why?"

"To continue our good relations with Earth. And for the reward."

"Is the ambassador in on this?"

The Antyerian backed up one step and sealed the hatch.

This is getting ridiculous, Verina thought. "I've got to get some personal guards," ey mumbled to emself.

With some exercise and stretching, it only took fifteen minutes for Verina to get eir gravity legs back. Feeling normal again, Verina took advantage of the provided food and grabbed a couple of pieces of preserved ha'poehn to munch on while ey examined eir new cell.

The loading bay was small; the conference room on the Quinkst ship had been much larger. An outward-dropping hatch consumed most of the narrow far wall, with the door the Antyerian used to exit located on the wall to Verina's left. Two crates with a variety of Ligrosian food and drinks sat lonely in the middle of the floor near the collapsed survival bag whose life support device would apparently have to continue its work as a waste reprocessor. Except for some pipes and conduits crisscrossing the ceiling two-and-a-half meters above Verina's head, the room was empty.

The rebel examined every nook and cranny of the bay looking for any exploitable weakness: access covers, ventilation, a misplaced tool. Ey found nothing. Verina climbed onto eir stacked food crates. Moving hand-over-hand, ey traversed every pipe and examined the light panels. Everything was solid and seamlessly closed. Ey had to admit, the Antyerians built well.

Verina turned to the supplies in the two crates. Dried and preserved fruits, a variety of gel-packed seafood, broth mixes, pickled vegetables, and some nuts. *Wait a minute*. The Ligrosian backtracked and grabbed a couple of the broth mixes. A small smile grew as ey saw something that might help: the broth mix packages were also heating packs.

When the rebellion started, before they had acquired a significant armory, they experimented with everything they could scavenge that could conceivably be used as a weapon. At one point, they made some improvised mines out of heating packs. While that bit of creative munition was great to have, the details of its construction weren't what Verina was focused on at the time. Ey had read the reports, of course, but hadn't really paid close attention to the mechanics. Something about super-heating a reactant and then…something…causing a small, but useful, explosion. What was it?

Verina tried reconstructing those early reports in eir mind, but the solution stayed out of reach. The information simply wasn't there to be recalled. Annoyed with emself, ey took a mental step back to think it through. Ey had dealt with explosives for a while now; maybe that knowledge would be enough to improvise something on eir own.

The heat packs would obviously be the ignition source. Ey needed fuel. Verina stared at eir available supplies. Nothing stood out as useful. Eir mind wandered and latched onto the phrase: quick energy. Over and over it turned in eir mind until ey remembered a slogan that promoted gadoj as a source of quick energy after strenuous exercise. Ey gathered some of the glucose from the survival bag and spread a large, thin layer on the deck. Once it dried, ey hoped to have sugar crystals to use as fuel. Taking an empty pickled-vegetable container, ey filled it with excess hydrogen drawn from the life support device's waste by-product tank.

Disassembly of the heat packs went very slowly. Verina did remember that oxygen contamination had been the single worst failure point. Ey didn't have enough materials on hand to be wasteful.

More than a day's worth of work went into the construction of eir hydroxy-glucose bomb. It wouldn't be powerful, but if positioned well it might create enough noise to draw some attention.

Verina placed the makeshift device, about the size of eir two hands, on the hatch leading to the ship's interior. A full food crate pressed it to the door and would help shape the blast. Verina donned a breathing mask from the survival bag and wrapped its rugged fabric around em for protection.

Ey waited for the heat packs to first warm and pressurize the hydrogen and oxygen, and then to melt the two collections of sugar acting as fuses. One melted blob needed to fall and short-circuit the heat packs; the other would time the release of oxygen and hydrogen into a combustion chamber filled with sugar and salvaged food starch. Verina hoped the result would be a bang loud enough to get someone to open the hatch—but everything would have to work close to perfectly. More likely, there'd just be a little bit of smoke and maybe a brief *fsssszzz*ing noise.

The Ligrosian waited.

Scores of days and countless missions in the field taught Verina the most difficult lesson about improvised explosives: don't lose faith when nothing happens as expected. Invariably, someone would go to check on the malfunction only to be sent to an aid station when the gadget, as Li called them, went off.

Verina itched to find out why the bomb hadn't detonated yet. It had been much too long. Even though the smell of burning sugar found a way through the mask, that didn't mean the—

BANG!

Food and debris shrapnelled through the bay. Thick smoke moved quickly from the inner hatch to become a uniform fog. Though protected from the projectiles, Verina hadn't planned on protecting emself from the blast waves that were confined to such a small area. It took several seconds to regain enough focus for em to realize where ey was and what had just happened. *Wow.* The blast far exceeded Verina's expectations, though ey was at a loss for a reason. Ey didn't have the expertise to know that the material of the combustion chamber had acted as a catalyst increasing the efficiency of this particular kind of explosive. Recovered from the brief stunning, Verina moved the ripped-open crate away from the hatch. Ey then lay against the far bulkhead, scattered some debris on emself, and played dead.

The hatch opened sooner than expected. The Antyerian led with what was apparently a weapon. A cacophony of musical epithets filled the air before the alien spotted Verina. From all appearances, the Ligrosian had been injured by the explosion…or worse. If the rebel was dead, there would be less money. On the other hand, if the rebel was still alive, the Antyerian could be injured…or worse.

Verina sensed the alien's unease. Ey moved slightly, as if coming to. The Antyerian stepped back immediately. In the middle of eir move, Verina stopped, clutched emself, and issued a two-voiced scream with a third moaning tone that combined to give the unmistakable impression of severe pain—even to an alien. With a kind of whimper, Verina relaxed into faux unconsciousness. Ey had improved eir position. Ey could now make a dash to the hatch when it was time.

The Antyerian threw solid food remnants at Verina with some force. Nothing. A ceramic fragment followed, hitting Verina on the head. Again, no apparent reaction. Tightening her grip on the weapon, the Antyerian nervously stepped closer to Verina, and slipped just enough on a vegetable piece that her weapon no longer pointed directly at the Ligrosian. Verina reacted immediately. With practiced speed, and a healthy dose of fear, ey sprang from eir race-ready position and charged the Antyerian. A hard leg-sweep buckled two of the alien's legs. Verina wrested the weapon from the hobbled profiteer. "Hold it!" ey commanded.

Holding the completely unfamiliar weapon in a similar manner as the alien, Verina hoped the upper hand was eirs. The Antyerian said, "You don't know how our weapons work."

Mustering eir bravado, Verina said, "I've been fighting a war using whatever came my way. I know a lot of weapons from a lot of species, including yours."

Laughing, the red alien said, "You're holding it backwards."

"No, I'm not; but nice try," Verina said, hoping to call the bluff…if it was a bluff.

For moments, neither combatant moved. The Antyerian then slowly knelt, saying, "Please kill me quickly."

It worked.

Verina grabbed the survival bag and dragged it with em as ey exited the cargo bay and sealed the hatch, locking the still cowering Antyerian inside. Quickly and cautiously, the Ligrosian moved up the passageway. Verina assumed the ship must be on alert following the explosion. Ey needed to find cover quickly—it was not safe to stay in the open. Having no informed options, the hatch at the end of the passageway didn't look any more dangerous than any other destination.

Inside, the engine room glowed at the upper limit of Verina's vision. Swirls of Fa'run materials and energies inside a screen-covered cylinder one meter high and half as wide were the apparent source. The engine was large for a ship about the size of an envoy-transport. That meant it was built for speed—which suggested a variety of uses outside the diplomatic realm.

Ignoring the warmth emanating from the propulsion source, the Ligrosian maneuvered around to the main console. Li had once mentioned to em that engineering sections generally had the second best computer access to their ship. "Computer," ey said in the Antyerian tongue.

A display immediately came to life. The musical language filled the room, saying, "Enter your query."

Verina always found it ironic that a language sounding so beautiful could, in reality, be so pedestrian. "Number and location of all personnel on the ship."

"Three beings detected. Captain [untranslated musical passage] is in the cargo bay. Sub-captain [untranslated musical passage] is in corridor B moving fore. An unknown Sereesian is in the engineering room."

"Extrapolate and speculate destination for the sub-captain."

"Probability thirty-two percent, the waste room. Probability thirty-one percent, the galley. Probability twenty-eight percent, the flight deck. Probability six per—"

"Enough. Show me a map of the ship. Highlight the position of all personnel, the flight deck, engineering, and where the majority of the weapons are stored."

The rebel had been correct, this was a small ship with only two decks. The lower deck, where Verina was, contained little of interest except the cargo bay and the engine room. The upper level had two parallel passageways, each leading to the flight deck. The passageway with the free Antyerian hosted the galley. The other passageway had the weapons locker.

Verina quietly made eir way to the upper deck and raided the unlocked armory. Most of the weapons were as distinctly unfathomable as the one ey'd taken from the captain, but two of the hand weapons were of an Earth design. They would be loud but effective. More importantly, the Ligrosian knew how they worked.

Ready to counter any resistance, Verina invaded the vacant flight deck. The plain green room contained two simple consoles with chair pads meant for the quadruped crew. The cabin was eerily quiet with the ship functioning on automatics instead of being crewed. Apparently the other alien was still taking time to savor his or her meal. Verina exited to corridor-B. Ey had taken only a couple of steps when the Antyerian walked out of the galley. Verina aimed eir weapons and melodied, "I can kill you right now, or you can join your friend in the cargo bay."

The red ottoman knelt down on its front legs and said, "I surrender."

After spending so long battling an enemy more than willing to fight to the end, it was oddly disappointing to find this second alien as compliant as the first. Subconsciously, Verina hoped for a fight—it had become part of eir nature. Ey escorted the sub-captain to the cargo bay and locked the alien in with the other Antyerian without incident or conversation.

Back on the flight deck, without remorse or sadness, Verina commanded, "Computer, release safeties and open the loading hatch to the cargo bay."

After a couple of minutes, Verina said, "Computer, number and location of all personnel on the ship."

"One being detected. An unknown Sereesian is on the flight deck."

"Computer, close and seal the loading hatch to the cargo bay and re-pressurize the cargo bay to standard ship's atmosphere."

The computer soon responded, "Cargo bay hatch closed and sealed. Safeties are in place." Followed not long after with, "Cargo bay pressurized."

A day-and-a-half later, the envoy-transport rendezvoused with the Quinkst diplomatic ship. Both traveled well off their previously planned routes. By using unrestricted thrust, they reduced the time to reunite by days.

Verina exited the small Antyerian ship in front of the full legation, minus one Antyerian. Javrurhal was closest and the first to approach Verina. "Verina of Serees, I am more happy than I can say to see you back safe."

"Thank you, Javrurhal of Quinkst, I—"

The Antyerian ambassador stepped forward and said, "May I see the ship's crew?"

Verina turned to the ambassador, saying, "I spaced them."

"You barbarian!" opera'd the ambassador, who immediately and uncharacteristically charged the Ligrosian.

The attack stopped quickly and profoundly as Verina drew eir Earth-designed sidearm and aimed it directly at the Antyerian's brain case. "I've had enough of this. I don't like being kidnapped, and I've had too many very-long days. Give me an excuse."

Javrurhal said with diplomatic calm, "Verina of Serees… please. Your actions are insulting."

Verina held eir stance. In seconds, the Antyerian went down on his front legs. With rage still flowing through em, Verina once again felt disappointed by this species' easy compliance. *No wonder the Humans like them so much*, ey thought.

With the threat now over, Verina lowered eir weapon, turned to eir Quinkst host, and placed the weapon on the deck in front of him. While still in the subordinate position, Verina said, "My fullest apologies to you, Javrurhal of the Quinkst. You have shown me nothing but kindness, and I have violated your hospitality. I am more sorry than I can say for the insult to you, specifically, Javrurhal of the Quinkst. I can only offer the explanation that I've become a warrior, and I honestly didn't realize I was armed when I left the Antyerian ship."

In a quiet voice so only Verina could hear, Javrurhal said, "Stand up, my friend. We don't have a problem." In an official tone loud enough for all to hear, the Quinkst said, "We will have to strongly consider your actions here, Verina of Serees. Threatening use of a weapon on our ship is very serious; threatening another sentient being with that weapon, even more so. While you will remain free to move about as before, I am ordering non-stop surveillance as long as you are our guest. No offense is intended, but it is for the peace of mind of all."

Verina admired the agile mind of eir alien friend. Under the guise of protecting the others, he had actually arranged to protect em. As evidence of this skillful diplomacy, the rest of the aliens noticeably relaxed, include the Antyerians.

In meetings later that day, a tacit agreement to renew resistance aid planning was reached. After they adjourned, Verina returned to eir room, which had been well cleaned since eir abduction. Ey sat on the edge of the bed—eir eyes fixed on a tiny speck on the far wall. Though it was less than a millimeter across, to Verina it was as large as a hand. The specific ultraviolet signature ey saw labeled it as Xadow's blood. Days before, as ey was blacking out, ey saw eir long-time pet being torn apart—not because he was a threat, but because it would hurt Verina. And it did hurt. Not the emptiness, which was considerable, but because it was a mirror into how ey had changed.

Red flowered around the warrior's eyes. The events that happened in this room were not far removed from what ey emself was capable of. Ey had killed so many Humans. Two Antyerians were now on that list…and one more almost joined them. What was happening to em? Was this sort of casual violence something always in em? The righteous nobility of it all—the forced necessity—had disappeared somewhere along the way. Now killing was simply something ey did.

Verina rationalized that it was all for the purpose of saving Serees. Some would pay dearly for it and carry scars for the rest of their lives, however long or short that might be. Bailera-only-knew Verina bore enough of those already. Though the Quinkst had lessened eir physical pain, they could do nothing about the images that persisted whether or not ey closed eir eyes, and whether or not ey slept or woke. It was difficult for the warrior to find any comfort. In order to fight monsters, ey had become one emself. Ey was no longer a government employee enjoying life. Even if Serees magically became what it had been before the invasion, that version of emself was gone forever. As much as ey would miss eir haiwa, that drop of blood reminded em of eir more profound sadness.

The memory of the kidnapping gave the assembled delegates a greater urgency. It made very real the sort of danger Serees was enduring. Verina used this to press for overt military support. The Antyerians, now in a more conciliatory frame of mind, offered twelve warships, two of which would be of their most modern design. With that on the table, the alliance turned to the resources of the Ju-a-e'I and the Tariri. The Ju-a-e'I offered every warship they had available, excluding those required for necessary lunar security. The Tariri had little choice but to follow with a promise of no less than a twenty-ship task force. Combined with the Quinkst's open-ended support, Verina tallied an armada of at least sixty-two warships. It was an impressive fleet for em to wield against the force parked around eir planet.

Agreeing to supply the ships was easy, but negotiating the command structure and protocols brought the talks to a standstill. Verina stipulated up-front to eir ignorance about space-based war. Ey encouraged the rest to settle on an experienced commander for the battle fleet. Unsurprisingly, no one was willing to relinquish control of their warships to a rival species. What was to prevent the Tariri, say, from sending in the Ju-a-e fleet first, as sacrificial decoys, and then turning their resources not on Earth's fleet, but on the Ju-a-e home moon of Ssurnai? The same argument held with the Quinkst and Tariri, and every other possible combination. It seemed hopeless.

"I'll command the fleet," Verina said with resigned sadness. The room went quiet. Verina continued, "Serees does not have a military to threaten any of your worlds. It never has. My only agenda is to rescue my planet. I'll listen to all of the recommendations of your commanders, but I'll make the final decisions." Ey looked around the table and added, "If anyone has a better solution, believe me, I'll be the first to sign on."

The quiet held for over a minute. It occasionally seemed that one of the diplomats would say something, but nothing new was offered. Finally, Javrurhal said, "It appears that we all agree. Verina of Serees will command our fleet against Earth's invasion force."

The only dissenting voice was the one inside Verina's mind.

16

The Business of Earth

Popituv watched the enthusiastic crowd file into the Jaris-laq concourse. The building was opening its doors to the public for the first time since the Day of the Waves, as the first day of Earth's invasion was locally known. With Navegil acting as a buffer, the maetor joined with the swarm of Ligrosians in revisiting some of the beauty of their planet.

Though tall and stately, Jaris-laq was long considered the lesser sibling to the monuments Unir-laq, Pwis-laq, and Zhai-laq. These three pillars withstood nature for centuries. Their oceanfront location served as a perfect bridge to the two environments the Ligrosians called home. Unir-laq housed the artistic antiquities whose brilliance survived faddish conceit. Pwis-laq preserved many of the most cherished historical artifacts from all disciplines—more of a school than a museum. Zhai-laq shone in its celebration of the new. Breakthrough inventions shared space equally with artwork from young Ligrosians in their first year of school.

The restoration and repair of Jaris-laq was the first of Yavent's rebuilding projects. This largest surviving repository, and the last of the famed repositories, focused civic pain into something useful. It was the sort of building even the Humans could appreciate—although they thought it wasn't much more than a storeroom of the past, much like their own museums.

Popituv noted that being among the public was different than when ey first led as maetor. Back then, Ligrosians would approach em freely and warmly. Now, few residents tried meeting the legendary leader. Popituv knew that eir relationship with the Humans would be problematic, but ey couldn't see another way to keep eir people safe. That emotion-fired pest, Verina, had accomplished nothing more than angering the already irritating invaders —which got so many well-meaning, if misguided, Ligrosians killed. While appreciating a paneled mural, Popituv admitted to emself that had ey been more vocal earlier, then maybe there would have been less death and destruction. The Humans were right—Verina needed to be caught and contained before things got worse. "Maetor Hai-Popituv, excuse me," said a young Ligrosian.

Popituv turned eir attention to the unexpected, though welcome, interruption. The bold youth, about a year from being an adult, stood half-a-head taller than the aged leader. Ey wore an intricately decorated jacket and pareu, which indicated some unexpected status. "Good morning," the maetor said in eir best greet-the-public tone. "Is there something I can do for you?"

With one voice, the Ligrosian introduced emself as Stramist and prattled on about how wonderful it was that the new building had opened, followed by a seemingly non-stop stream of unctuous comments about the exhibits. With eir second voice, quieter than the first, Stramist praised the cooperative nature of the Humans— how everyone ey knew appreciated the safety in the streets, and other such flattery. Eir third voice modified the second, often indicating that the spoken phrase should be negated. Taken all together it formed a gibberish that the Earth translation matrices couldn't accurately decipher. It proved to be the most illuminating five minutes of Popituv's time in the city so far.

When Navegil and Popituv returned to the maetor's office, they used a more sophisticated, multi-language version of the technique Stramist employed. "Do you really think there is that much unrest, Hai-Popituv?" Navegil asked.

"Not really. When I was maetor, and a popular one at that, there was constant grumbling in the streets. Under stressful circumstances like these, that could easily be misconstrued as unrest."

"But the rumors, which happen to be true, about the terrorism —"

"Actually, that makes me happy." Off Navegil's shocked expression, Popituv continued, "Really. It means that, somehow, the Humans' efforts to isolate every city isn't as leak-proof as they seem to think. Though, I imagine, the layers of protection they install slows down the speed the information spreads by quite a lot. What that teen…Stramist…said happened more than a dozen days ago, and even at that ey didn't have any details. If the Humans continue their campaign of half-truths, then the rumors won't foment. For all of their weaknesses, the Humans are good at that."

"And what about that, Hai-Popituv? Aren't you afraid that the Humans are simply using you as another one of their half-truths: you're in charge, but you aren't?"

"Every hour of every day. Despite how history might paint me following this dark period, I'm not stupid. I know I'm being used. I'm hopeful that I'm also using in kind. Every Jaris-laq that I can keep getting built preserves who we are. We can't defeat this Human infection with threats or violence. I think that's been made very clear. We can defeat Earth by not becoming another Lrat. It's like the message in *Gavet Issta Geyvai*: 'Knowing the storms would come, Geyvan used uvaket for the foundation instead of the more plentiful ibvaret. Ey had learned that to endure, the remliv'ze must bow to nature, else it would shatter.' If we are to endure, we must do the same."

With the curfew in place, the streets of nighttime St. Paul echoed Potaryanii's every footstep. It reminded her of growing up in old Delhi in that it was exactly the opposite. *This* city could deal with a few hundred thousand bodies bustling throughout the night. She startled when a voice with a heavy Sereesian accent said, "Lieutenant?"

"Is it done?"

"Our agent couldn't get close enough to talk privately with the maetor at Jaris-laq. We will have to wait for another opportunity."

The small, weathered woman's emotions compelled her to pace, but prudence defeated that impulse—she didn't need surplus footstep echoes attracting attention. Now was not the time to let a small setback derail the larger goals. "I can't say that I'm not a little disappointed, my friend."

"As I said, we'll keep trying."

Potaryanii looked at the shadow-cloaked form. What would it do if it knew where its real place was in the lieutenant's world? She said, "The new in-drop is at location twenty-four. The out-drop at nine."

With that, the Ligrosian blended silently into the city. The Human turned on her heel and wandered back to her quarters, no longer worrying about her footsteps. So far as any of the sentries would now know, she was simply out for a quiet nighttime stroll.

"We've got a problem," Li said via a translator. He, Elekin and Akehru crowded under a semi-flexible lean-to that served as their small field shelter. "Patrols around three more cities have increased. Out to another fifteen kilometers, at least."

"How far?" Elekin asked.

"About twelve thousand dis," Akehru converted.

"Thanks. Which cities?"

Li brought out a map with the locations already circled. All were in the same general area along the equator—about a third of the way between Fan-tan and Czep-tan. The three enlarged patrol circles now created a large triangle of Earth-controlled zone. Elekin said, "I agree. This can't be good. They're up to something."

Li pointed to the center of the triangle. "Is there anything interesting in this area?"

The two Ligrosians looked at each other before Elekin said, "Not that I know of. But I was never really that good in geography."

"Akehru?" Li asked.

Akehru simply shook eir head. The freedom-fighter life, especially of command, wasn't sitting well with em. Ey was an engineer, not a soldier.

The Human stared at the map for a few moments more and said, "Elekin, you're going to have to take a scouting party and get as much information as possible about what Earth is doing."

"Me?"

"It's not wise for us all to go. Akehru and I have to stay here to coordinate the plans already in motion. Don't worry. You'll do fine."

Images of Verina's scarred body flashed through Elekin's mind. Going out on missions with Li in charge—though the rest thought it was the Ligrosians leading the way—was scary and exhilarating, but ey didn't have to make the decisions. This was different. This was no longer "fun". Li touched eir arm. "Really. You'll do fine."

Despite Li's assurance, joining the fight didn't seem like such a good idea anymore.

"And lastly," General Bhoutto said, sitting across the desk from Maetor Popituv, "I, and the rest of the command staff, want to commend you and the citizens of New Serees on the reopening of Jarislack."

"Jaris-laq," Navegil corrected.

"Jaris laCK," Bhoutto echoed. "Everyone on the staff wants to pay a visit and appreciate your culture whenever they get leave."

"Thank you, General," Popituv accepted. "It would be an honor to receive them."

"Thank you." In a quieter and less officious voice, the general continued, "In my reports, I've often remarked on how industrious the people of New Serees are. Not only have you opened Jarislack, but you have many other construction and reconstruction projects proceeding as well."

"Yes. The residents of Yavent have always taken great pride in their city. They understand and appreciate the importance of this place, and want to be good stewards of it for the future."

The general sighed. "I wish everyone felt that way." He leaned forward. "I hate saying this—but frankly, several cities that were early targets of the terrorists are still in need of repair. Your people haven't taken the initiative, and we can't spare the manpower. Even if I could authorize reconstruction, to be honest, nothing we could do would come close to complementing Sereesian sensibilities. I mean, looking out at those buildings…your people have an artistic bent my corps of engineers aren't trained to match."

"What, exactly, are you asking, General?"

"I'm not exactly sure. Because of the on-going terror situation, General Chavez and many of the leaders back home are very suspicious of your people. As a result, I'm ordered to manage things very tightly. Not helping matters is the fact that I've also been ordered to not let the planet fall into ruin. So, this is what I'm thinking: I'm thinking that you could ask the residents of two or three test cities if they would be willing to rebuild in the name of mutual peace. Not just the cities but also the infrastructure that's been ravaged throughout the interior. If they agree, then I can't see how my superiors could object. In fact, it's very likely that they will let your people living in those cities have the sorts of opportunities as the ones here."

"Which cities?"

"I'd have to go back and look up the names, but remember they are between here and Minni…er, Cheptan to our west. They were hit pretty hard, but since that the small insurgency has retreated to the other side of the planet, I think now would be a good time to move back to productivity. I'm hoping that you agree."

Popituv leaned back on eir heels. Ey was more certain than not that the general was playing em; ey just couldn't quite figure out how. What he said was true—the cities had been targets, and they did need to get organized to repair the damage. If, indeed, it was going to be like Yavent, as this Human said, then it would be a very good thing for calming down the situation and maybe returning to some sort of normalcy. "General, I'm certain that you are painting a better picture than reality would describe. For now, I'm willing to encourage the people of those cities to come together in the spirit of cooperation. I'd like to see the ruined parts of some of our jewels being restored."

General Bhoutto stood, which prompted the maetor to follow in kind, and said, "Thank you. I think this is going to be a good thing."

"I hope so, General. Much depends on it." *Like my future cooperation*, ey thought.

Even with the personnel-plates, which Elekin thought were a very clever idea, it took twelve days to move from the small rebel base in the subduction zone over to the target area. Though some veterans on eir team had been to this region on missions before Verina's capture, the countryside was all new to Elekin, who had never before been this far away from home. Even during the two pre-maturing years ey spent at bartidol, working with other young Ligrosians and Haipuxans, ey hadn't been as far from Czep-tan.

Once the Human airborne patrols became visible on the horizon, the reconnaissance team became more focused and their movements more circumspect. The goal was to do a full intelligence reconnoiter of three cities: Saemu-aziq, Gacer-aziq, and Taef-aziq; as well as the large triangular area they vertexed. It all had to be done on foot, using only forty agents to accomplish it in a limited time. Elekin split eir teams into four groups. Ten agents each would speed to the farther two cities, Gacer-aziq and Taef-aziq, to gather what information they could. A large group of fourteen would monitor, in detail, the activities happening in Saemu-aziq. The remaining four, led by Elekin, would venture into the heart of the beast to find out what was so special about the land in the middle of the guarded triangle.

The interior patrol, code named Tk-green for the hard-to-catch forest worm, soon discovered that the "increased patrols" they'd been briefed about actually meant incessant surveillance. Autonomous airships, ground patrolling Humans and robots, a variety of visual and audio sensors, and more than a few traps created a frustrating mix for the quartet. Good progress was advancing two meters before having to stop, effect concealment, and scan for inanimates. The only positive was that the woods provided a lot of cover opportunities. They mapped every found sensor and trap in the hope that the squad's exit would be faster than the journey in.

At the end of the sixth day, the woods came to a sudden end, prompting Elekin to examine eir map. This was wrong. There was supposed to be nothing but woods. Instead, a roughly triangular area, easily fifteen kilometers on a side, had been cleared of every natural thing. Several layers of various security barriers ringed the perimeter. Ranging from five-to-ten meters high, they created a three hundred meter deep detect-and-subdue zone between the woods and the mysterious interior. Towers lined the inside of the security area one hundred meters apart in most places, though there were larger gaps scattered around.

Using every observation and recording device in their small inventory, Elekin's team tried penetrating the thicket of counter-measures in the security zone without success. Interference beams, diffraction aerosols, random dissonant sounds, and other methods thwarted every attempt to see, hear, sense or otherwise discover the secrets of this barren land.

Maygola set soon after the team's arrival, but it didn't get very dark. The local sky glowed from the waste light of the mystery activity inside the fence. Combining the effect of this pollution with the brightness of Bailera, there might as well have been no stars at all. The large amount of spilled light did, however, make avoiding obstacles easier as the team evaded the never-ending patrols. During one of the surveillance lulls, Ititchu sidled up to Elekin and whispered, "I think I know how to get our informa-tion."

Quietly, and with four changes of location to avoid the Humans, Ititchu outlined eir plan. The idea came from Bailera and all of the light the sibling planet reflected from the sun. Why couldn't they use something else to reflect back to the team what was happening in the unexplained area? Maybe the autonomous airborne patrol vehicles? These drones were all festooned with clear but very reflective windows on small portions of their under-bellies, presumably for visual sensors. Why couldn't the team focus their own cameras on that small area, use it as a mirror, and piece together the images later, when they got back to camp?

Elekin wasn't sure. Ey hadn't been the best general science student; the required physics course was a memory ey was happy to forget. Optics and parallax reconstruction were far beyond eir knowledge. Ey knew it would require a lot of pictures and a bit of luck, but without a better idea on the table, the decision to proceed was easy. For the rest of that night and all of the next, every team member shot as many sharp pictures of the reflection from as many angles around the area as possible. During the day, they rested when they could while also trying to find other sources of intelligence.

Both night missions went off without any problems. A sampling of test images gave Elekin more confidence that the plan might actually work. In contrast, the day proved to be a prolonged period of frustration. There was no way to circumvent the region's security from the ground.

Having used the last of their surveillance time with the second night mission, Tk-green retreated from their positions and retraced their route through the woods. As hoped, the detailed maps made on the way in made the egress much easier. One missed explosive trap went off at midday of the third and last scheduled day of their mission, but the quickly responding Human patrol didn't find any hint that Ligrosians were near. Elekin's squad rendezvoused with the other three teams only an hour later than originally planned.

Although the return of the intelligence was high-priority, Elekin decided that continuing to push eir team was asking for mistakes. The extended period of high stress and little rest had taxed all the members, but most especially those of Tk-green. Now that eir pod was out of the extended patrol zone, Elekin directed them to a small, undiscovered, rebel shelter. During the height of the homeland fight, Verina ordered that small bases be set up all around the planet. They would hold emergency supplies for those who knew how to find these caches—robust camouflage making them difficult to accidentally stumble across. The shelter Elekin's platoon found was indistinguishable from wooded ground clutter. Though built to hold just twenty-four, all forty members squeezed in. Being able to relax their constant state of alertness was more restful than the few hours of sleep only half the warriors achieved.

Elekin opted to base here for an extra day so that small groups of the RECON team could stretch out comfortably and really rest before the long trek back to the main camp. Talking was minimal. The past days pushed everyone into a state of silence-awareness.

Twelve days later, Elekin and eir team returned to their base in the subduction zone. Road-weary team members reunited with old friends. Elekin and Ititchu guided a push-plate covered with cameras to Li and Akehru, and explained the improvised espionage tactic. Li said to Akehru, "I think this falls into your area of expertise. Can you do it?"

"I'm almost positive. That was clever."

"How soon?" Li asked.

"I don't know. I have to see the pictures, but it'll probably take a while. I'll have to adjust for position, focus, refraction, curvature, parallax—"

Li interrupted. "Just do what you can. Recruit anyone you need."

Akehru nodded, but eir focus had already shifted to the problem at hand. Ey had no stomach for leadership or fighting, but a tedious problem in optics…? Ey couldn't remember the last time ey felt so useful—or happy. Akehru disappeared to do eir magic.

Li said to Elekin, "We were starting to get a little worried."

"I know. The security around those cities is incredibly tight. That's not just me saying that, that's from some of your experienced fighters."

"What do you think it will take to break through?"

"The cities? Several days of surveillance and a lot of luck. As for that area in the middle? I don't think you have any chance without approaching from the air or space. And given what was on the ground, I think they're prepared for that."

"Lost cause?"

"With what we have? Right now? Yeah. Maybe when Verina arrives with a bunch of high-powered spaceships we'll have a chance, but I think that's going to be the only way."

"You know," Li said, wearily running his fingers through his slowly thinning hair, "I was worried before you went, but now I'm getting a knot in my stomach. What's going on that needs that sort of protection?"

Akehru finally felt in eir element. From the moment ey entered the modest computer center dug into the side of a hill, ey was useful in a way ey couldn't be with Elekin and Li. Using eir position as Verina's sibling, ey commandeered ten of the fourteen available computers. Ey would have taken all of them, but the overhead required to maintain fighting forces around a planet required those remaining four stay dedicated to logistics.

Using one computer as a workstation and arbitrator, and the other seven as clustered processors, Akehru knitted together the small reflected images contained in the hundreds of pictures taken. The processing itself didn't take much time with the computers working in concert. What consumed Akehru's time was correctly positioning the camera and the small reflection in a virtual three-dimensional world. Every picture had to be placed, by hand, one at a time.

Two days of non-stop work from Akehru, working alone, resulted in as complete a photo-mosaic as was possible. Ey brought the two-meter by one-and-a-half meter full-resolution printout, as well as several reduced copies, to Li and Elekin to evaluate. "You look tired," Elekin said.

"Yeah," was all the exhausted Akehru could muster.

The leadership trio headed for a holaxex they'd chosen for a temporary command center. The inland retreat bore no resemblance to those near the Czep-tan coast. The one-story abode melded into the woods so completely it was difficult to notice it was not a natural part of the land. Li likened it to a log cabin, due to its rustic exterior of fallen timber. The interior was finished and automated, much like the places Verina and Akehru grew up in.

After dismissing a handful of rebels from the large main room, Li spread the reconstruction across the dining room table. While he and Elekin studied the image carefully, annoyed at the many blank areas, Akehru contented emself with leaning against a decorative pillar in the middle of the room.

"That looks like a launch facility," Li said. "See? Over here are the storage tanks and over here is a half-finished landing field."

"But that doesn't make any sense," Elekin countered. "Look here. These have got to be tunnel openings. And here are buildings. It looks like one of them is already finished."

"You're right. That doesn't make any sense. No one would build…wait."

Li closed his eyes. "What are you—?" Elekin started to say.

"Wait…" Li interrupted.

The Human kept his eyes closed for over a minute. The Ligrosians couldn't tell if he was figuring something out, or if he was trying to remember something—but whatever it was, it required all of his attention. He opened his eyes, took a breath, and matter-offactly said, "It's a mining port."

"A what?"

"It took me a while to remember. Whatever we did—Earth did —during the early occupation of Lrat is classified higher than I have clearance for. But I remember, back in one of my history classes, that there was a discussion about some of Earth's early colonization efforts. At first, they were set up like on Earth: the mine was where the minerals were, of course, and then the product was hauled to a transportation hub for distribution off-world.

"Here's the trick. Once engine design got safer and less dependent on dangerous fuels, the accounting managers decided to put space ports next to mining operations; that way, the time and expense of the intermediate transport would be gone."

"That makes sense," Elekin agreed.

"What confused me was all of this here. The buildings, and what looks like...well, I don't know what it looks like, I know it isn't storage. Then it hit me. The difference is the TVerse engine. It isn't particularly hazardous to be around during operations. It's almost like ancient times when jet aircraft dominated the skies. Anyway, with the TVerse engine you can house and possibly feed —if these are farms—all of your workers without having to worry about that profit-draining transport."

"It's a slave camp," Elekin said with disgust.

"What?" Akehru said, suddenly alert.

"It's a slave camp," Elekin repeated. "They are going to do to us what they did to Lrat."

Akehru looked to Li for a denial. The Human just stared at the images, ashamed to be linked in any way to the species that kept committing these sorts of atrocities. "Well," Akehru said, "say something."

With great moral effort, Li said, "Ey's right. It's a slave mining camp. Oh, the generals and politicals will call it something like,

'An employment opportunity zone,' or 'An economic rebuilding district,' or something perfectly bland like that; but the reality is that it's a forced labor camp."

"We have to do something!" Akehru demanded. "We have to attack them and—"

"We can't," Elekin three-voiced, quieting the other Ligrosian. "We don't have the strength to do anything about that place without getting ourselves killed or captured. Not until Verina returns."

"We can't just sit here," Akehru protested.

"We won't," Li said. "We can't do anything about this particular camp. It's foolish to even speculate on it. But we can still do something. This is only the beginning of what Earth's forces will want to do. Now we have intelligence telling us what to look for. What we *can* do is prevent another camp from being built. This place didn't happen overnight."

Elekin, visibly agreeing, said, "Hit them hard at the first sign of preparations."

"Every time," Li added.

"How long can we do that?" Akehru asked.

Elekin said, "As long as we have to."

Li smiled, "That's a good attitude, but it's a great question. Frankly, I don't know how long we can keep it up. We aren't nearly as strong as we were before, and now there is so much more to do."

"But when Verni comes…" Akehru offered.

"That's the big question mark. We need Verina, and we need that fleet," Li said.

"What should we do in the meantime?" Elekin asked.

"Spread the word?" Akehru mused.

"How?" Elekin replied. "The maetor is broadcasting eir 'All is well' talk every day—saying how *we* are the danger to peace, and how the Humans only want to help us rebuild what they've destroyed. Who's going to listen to us?"

"But if we show them these," Akehru said, pointed to the images.

Li said, "Earth will simply spin it as your people agreeing to build a necessary space port. They'll see staged pictures of happy Serees faces. All we have is a cobbled-together piece of confusion. It's hard to even tell there are any Serees here. Those figures could just as easily be Humans."

"But they're not!" Akehru argued.

"I know that!" Li countered.

After several tense moments of silence, Akehru said, "So we fight."

"Yep," Li answered.

"And hope Verina comes soon," Elekin said.

"Yep," Li agreed.

"WHAT!?!" Colonel Bryce whined, less than an hour after she'd gone to bed.

"Colonel, the R.I.G. supervisor requests your immediate presence in the communications lab," a young male voice said via the comm system.

"Are we under attack?" Bryce asked, her tongue thick with sleep.

"Not that I'm aware of, Colonel."

Bryce growled quietly to herself. Twice. "Colonel...?" the voice prompted.

"I'll be there shortly."

The colonel donned her uniform and tried storming over to Communications Research but lingering sleepiness prevented building up the necessary attitude. "This better be good, Ng," she said the moment she crossed the room's threshold, "or I'm throwing you in the brig."

"Yes, Colonel," the researcher said casually. He pointed to two tables covered nearly a half meter deep with various non-Human documents. "We found the mother lode."

"Of…?" Bryce yawned.

"Seetun."

Bryce's eyes cleared; Lieutenant Potaryanii entered the lab. Ng continued, "We discovered this in a hidden vault. Really hidden. I can't say that I've been able to understand more than twenty percent of what's in here, but I'm confident that we can restore our high-speed communications ability immediately. I just have to enter a couple of command seq—"

Bryce spoke into her wrist-comm, "I want a full guard detail, level one, around the communications lab, now. Also, a Stage Two alert for the complex."

"Immediately, Colonel," came the unlistened reply.

"Lieutenant, send a Priority 2A alert signal to General Chavez."

"Right away, Colonel," Potaryanii replied, quickly usurping the position of the on-duty communications officer.

Seconds later, the face of a miffed Chavez appeared on the main display. Before he uttered a single epithet, Bryce said, "General, the Seetun has been cracked. Full communications can be restored on your order."

General Chavez stared out from the screen, his expression frozen in mid-gape. He said, "Colonel, I don't want you do to a damn thing except lock down that facility."

"Already done, General."

"I'm coming down."

The screen blanked. Bryce turned to Ng and said, "I figure you have about thirty minutes to prepare your briefing for the general's arrival. Where's the coffee?"

Ng pointed to a door leading to a side room, his smug facade weakened with the anxiety of reporting to Chavez. He had to supply the right answers and, more importantly, have everything work as just announced, or…well, he knew the general's reputation.

The researcher needn't have worried about the thirty-minute time limit. Because the increased security slowed everything down, thirty-three minutes passed before the general arrived. After the perfunctory greetings, Bryce ushered Chavez to Ng. "This is Jacques Ng, our primary researcher."

"Mr. Ng. I hear you've broken the Seetun mystery."

Ng wasn't prepared for the intense, piercing gaze of the general in person. "M-More like cracked, in-instead of broken, General. I couldn't tell you how to build one. Yet. Not yet. But I can restore communications. I'll just need a minute or so."

"Who knows about this?" Chavez asked.

"Just the people now in the room, General, unless you mentioned it to someone," Ng replied.

Though unhappy with the insolence, the compartmentalization pleased Chavez. "Do it."

Ng walked over to the console next to the one where Potaryanii stood. He entered a variety of keystrokes with her looking over his shoulder. In short order, the researcher walked back to the general and Colonel. "Done."

Chavez half-smiled at Bryce. "I almost thought it was going to make me feel different…taller maybe."

You could stand with being taller, Bryce thought, but held her tongue. "How do you know it worked?" she asked.

"Out test box confirms the connection. And it appears the entire network is available."

"Test box?" Chavez prompted.

"Yes sir. We had to have one of our standard Seetun devices

available so we could test our hypotheses."

"So," Chavez mused, "we can do an actual test, now, without using a direct link?"

"Yes sir," Ng said.

"Get me Minister of Military Affairs Naveen."

17

Late For the Party

Two more days. Battle would be joined in two more days.

As central commander of the modest multi-world armada, those two days seemed both eternal and momentary to Verina. Success wasn't dependent on totally surprising the Humans, but the Ligrosian's fragile alliance would have to out-plan and out-maneuver the smaller, but more experienced and better-armed, Earth Fleet. A protracted battle would almost certainly guarantee defeat for em and eir allies. The big uncertainty was how far would General Chavez go to win when he, himself, was at risk in space? He seemed more than willing to use annihilation weapons from a distance. Intelligence confirmed his ordering the planet shakers and the massacre that ultimately led to Verina's capture. What if that was no longer his easiest option?

The management of this unlikely force never stopped being problematic. While, in concept, the vastness of interstellar space was more than sufficient to hide a small fleet of ships, the reality of TVerse engine design meant that any culture capable of detecting small-scale gravity disturbances, which Earth was, could sense the approach of any significant number of ships—sometimes even just a single ship, if it was large enough. Most thought surprise attacks with ships running in Fa'run space were impossible.

A flurry of messages Earth could intercept were dispatched between the Antyerians and the Tariri. Though fraudulent, the exchanges implied a flare-up of a longstanding trade dispute which had deteriorated to where negotiations weren't an option. A flight of warships from each planet were dispatched, their expected conflict point about four light years from Serees. Since Earth seemed to like this sort of "diplomacy", Verina hoped the spectacle would draw some of their attention. When this faux-battle appeared imminent, there would be a swift attack at the flanks of Earth's force around Serees. The rest of the fleet, including the flights from Antyera and Krantozenia, would attack Earth's forces in three waves of intense fire, hopefully knocking out the majority of the most-powerful warships.

Verina sent a coded message to eir friends on Serees indicating the time of attack. Ey requested ground actions to add to the general confusion. Now, with everything set in motion, all that remained was the start of battle.

Two-and-a-half hours before the first wave of fast-but-small interceptors was due to attack the underbelly of Earth's forces, Verina was awakened by a message from eir Quinkst hosts: "Verina of Serees, please come to the command center."

Taking time only to dress, Verina rushed up two decks to the hastily-assembled command and communications center. Three rows of six input/display combinations filled the central portion of the darkened room whose walls were covered with deactivated display grids. Javrurhal, and only Javrurhal, was present to meet em. The empty room confused Verina. "Javrurhal?"

"It's over. Earth intercepted the Ssurnai wing and destroyed seventy-six percent of their force with no losses of their own ships. The remaining Ssurnai vessels retreated. Both the Antyerians and Tariri then abandoned the plan—presumably to return to their homes. Without support from the alliance, the Quinkst will not commit our ships against a much stronger force. We will send ships to help guard the Ju-a-e'I, however, so that our other 'allies' won't take advantage of their momentary weakness. It's over."

Verina sunk down to eir knees and sat. "How? How could they have found out?"

"I don't know that we'll ever discover that. Too many players knew about the plan: my people, your people, the others. I wouldn't be surprised if the Antyerians are holding a bit of a grudge against you."

Staring blankly, Verina said, "So, it's over. We're alone."

Javrurhal, looked about as compassionate as a giant, hairy sea cucumber could. He said, "I am so sorry. I thought we could all come together in this."

"I know. You've been a good friend."

"Past tense?"

"I'm going back. I'm going to have to lead this fight and try to get more of my people to join with me. Even if we lose, maybe I can at least deny Earth its slaves."

The Quinkst stared at the valiant, but disheartened, Ligrosian. "You may have whatever we can spare. You'll need a transport, of course. And supplies. We have a variety in the cargo bay from all of our supposed allies in this venture."

"I'll need a good diversion or camouflage. The Humans can't know I've returned. Not right away."

The Quinkst clicked his claws. "We might have something…"

———— ⊖–⊙ ————

"Well done, Colonel!" General Chavez said to Colonel Smythe as the colonel entered Chavez's command room.

Smythe returned his superior's smile. "I'd have loved to have seen their faces when *zoom*, our ships bounce on them and kick the…stuffing out of them."

"It constantly amazes me that these other races think we are idiots. Misinformation messaging, fleets engaging without any buildup…that's so antiquated that it's almost laughable."

"I loved it when the Antyerians and the Krantozenians turned-tail and ran."

"We'll deal with them in short order," Chavez said. "Now that the counter-offensive has been turned back, we can fully exploit our new bandwidth."

"I don't know. With all due respect to the secretary general and the Presidium, I've rather enjoyed not having the administration on our backs."

General Chavez started unbuttoning his jacket. "I couldn't agree with you more, Enrique. If the civilian authority simply told us the mission, the mission goal, and the timetable to completion, we'd be so much more efficient. But if they don't get to pretend they're soldiers, they feel weak and impotent. They need to let the military actually run these campaigns and not worry so much about the politics. All of that mush-mouth garbage gets forgotten soon enough anyway. You put the military in charge and you'll win. You'll win decisively. *That's* what gets remembered in the history books."

At Chavez's invitation to sit, Smythe relaxed in a chair at the table. "If I haven't said it before, General, I'm happy you were placed in charge of this fleet. While there is no doubt that General Pervikh—"

"Peace Be Unto Him."

"Peace Be Unto Him—was a great leader, his heart didn't seem like it was in it anymore."

"Your promotion papers are already in the system, Colonel," Chavez said with a smile, "there's no need to flatter me."

Smythe echoed the general's good humor. "Then I should stop the commission on the statue we're putting up in the middle of New Serees?"

"I know you're kidding, Enrique, but yeah. For the moment, it might be considered to be in bad—"

The lights reddened and the wall display subscreened several sensor images. The computer said, "Unknown ship approaching at very high velocity."

A quick examination of the displays focused both officers' attention on the gravity-effects scan. Something needing a large TVerse-class engine was on an intercept course. Given current projections, it could seriously damage Chavez's flagship. Smythe said, "Computer, launch protocol four at incoming ship, immediately."

"Launching protocol four," the computer replied.

Two missiles, traveling so closely together that most of the subscreens showed them as one object, headed out to intercept the incoming contact. Their speed combined with the high velocity of the mystery ship made the distance close quickly. An almost unnoticeable glitch blinked the displays at the instant of impact. Various subscreens now showed only an expanding debris field accented by secondary explosions. Orbital projections showed that much of the debris would soon burn up in Serees' atmosphere; the rest would be a temporary menace to the fleet. A number of small objects that survived the impact floated in all directions, exploding at random. Smythe looked to General Chavez with the happy relief of the successful intercept. Chavez's good mood had disappeared. "Clean up that mess, Colonel. I don't want it interfering with operations."

"Yes, sir."

Chavez headed toward his ready room, but then turned back to Smythe. "Try for a little more containment if another Kamikaze comes this way. And make sure *that* doesn't happen."

"Yes, sir."

I have to be out of my mind, Verina thought as the second stage of eir journey began—not that ey thought ey was remarkably sane for the first stage of the mission, either. Javrurhal assured em that acting as eir own decoy, or rather, having the decoy wrapped around eir transport and supplies, would not only work, but would be safer than any other method. As with many things surrounding this conflict, Verina learned that the plan was much easier to swallow than the experience. The only variables the Quinkst couldn't guarantee were: exactly when Earth would try to destroy the mystery ship, and what weapons they'd employ. Too far away from Serees and the cargo might be lost in space. Too powerful a weapon and the cargo would *be* spaced. To the Quinkst, the most important factor was that this method risked only the contents of the ship: the contraband supplies as well as one slightly-damaged Ligrosian.

In all fairness, Verina admitted to emself, the scheme worked at designed. Ey entered Serees space, the Humans destroyed the outer decoy ship, and the confusion caused by the pyrotechnic-enhanced debris masked the re-entry of eir small craft and eir supplies. Ey also had to give credit to the Quinkst for designing an ingenious insertion into the atmosphere. Instead of plummeting like a meteor or bleeding off speed in a fiery-hot blanket of plasma, eir one-person glider entered the planet's gas shell at a speed relative to the atmosphere of about two hundred kilometers per hour. The slow, controlled descent would take hours. Verina's only protection would be the stealthy features of the glider.

The Ligrosian and the Quinkst debated how best to direct the trajectory of the supplies. The containers could be guided before atmospheric insertion, but after that point, the four pods of equipment would be ballistic meteors until a few hundred meters off the ground when they would soft-land at a relatively gentle three gravities. The Quinkst favored one of the two oceans. Knowing the problems ey would have with the Haipuxans, Verina vetoed the idea without comment. The supplies would have to settle on land —ideally near a rebel area but not close enough to one for the Humans to discover the hideout and target eir troops. At least Verina had the in-flight option of landing near the supplies or gliding to the primary camp.

It really wasn't a decision. Following eir uneventful descent, Verina touched down less than two hundred meters from one of the supply pods. When ey reached it, close examination revealed only cosmetic heat damage to the skin. The three other pods were all within a hundred-meter arc from this first one, but were entangled in grass and deadfall. The pod's active camouflage, the same sort that covered the skin of eir glider, worked as advertised. Though not impossible, it was extremely difficult to detect these containers without an accurately tuned transceiver. Verina used a custom tracking device to find them all.

The pod Verina landed closest to was a problem. It stood out in the grass, plainly visible. The rebel made one attempt to push the container toward a pair of trees for cover. Even with its low-friction skin, the pod was simply too heavy. Since the Quinkst had nothing similar to push-plates, they couldn't supply Verina with a way to move the massive contents of these containers. Each six-meter by two-meter lozenge massed from a low of seven-hundred kilograms, to more than double that. Ey needed help. A lot of help. Turning to the east, the rebel leader hiked to where ey knew ey'd find some.

Though ey never admitted it to anyone outside eir inner circle, Verina overshot the hidden camp. Ey had stayed briefly only once before in this area and wasn't as familiar with it as ey thought ey was. Backtracking, Verina knew ey was in the right place when a Ligrosian appeared from nowhere and pointed an Earth rifle at em. "Tamora," the guard said.

Verina rummaged through eir memorized challenges and found a dozen coded replies. Security was incredibly important, but at this moment ey almost felt trapped by how complex the challenge-response system ey set up had become. This challenge was the name of the speaker from Book Two of the *Hasek Vartu Shibi-ieth*. The reply was…was…the speaker from the same chapter of one of the complementary works, in this case it was the story of *Ip Et-ris*, though it could easily come from any of a dozen other books from the *Ig'itwa-toh* Library. "Thuv-set," ey said upper-voiced while echoing, "Tamora," with eir middle mouth.

The guard immediately lowered eir weapon. "Welcome. Your identity, please."

Verina smiled to emself. It had been a while since ey wasn't recognized on sight. "Verina."

The guard maintained eir air of detached interest until ey noticed the tell-tale scarring. Eir expression changed to surprise. "H-Hai-Verina. Welcome. P-please…enter."

The stunned sentry began escorting Verina when the leader said, "May I ask your name?"

"My…? Pauless."

"Pauless," Verina repeated. "I think I remember the way. Maybe you should stay here, on post?"

Embarrassment colored Pauless' eye area a deeper blue. Ey feared this would be a black mark in the eyes of eir superiors. How could it not? Verina was highest ranked. "Yes, Hai-Verina. Of course."

"Don't worry about it. I think I caught you by surprise."

Verina worked eir way from the shaken guard toward the main shelter. The landmarks became more familiar the closer ey got. Several freedom fighters stood in formation awaiting Verina's appearance. Apparently, Pauless messaged ahead. The pod commander walked up to the new arrival, issued a continuous respect-tone, and said, "Hai-Verina. It's an honor."

"Thank you. Wait…I know you. Tamira?"

Trying not to smile like a hero-worshiping recruit, the Ligrosian nodded, saying, "I'm the local commander."

"I'll want to visit later. But right now, I need to know if you are currently in an operation?"

"No. Not for another day."

"Good. I'm going to need to borrow ten of your strongest troops as well as twenty or so push-plates. Is that going to be a problem?"

"No. No, of course not. When will you need them?"

Verina's expression said "Now" without a tone passing through eir lips. Tamira immediately turned to fill the request.

Back at the landing zone, an unpleasant surprise greeted Verina's retrieval squad: a Human patrol closing in on the pods' location. Since ey always expected being cut off whenever ey traveled from base, Verina insisted the team be more equipped than Tamira originally ordered. The wisdom of Verina's experience with unexpected bad luck proved the difference. Ey split eir squad into two. A three-person team occupied a five-person Human scouting party while the remaining five Ligrosians attacked the primary sixteen-member search team with swift, powerful, accurate firepower. With that larger squad eliminated, the full force of Verina's unit quickly overwhelmed the small remaining pocket of aliens.

After averting the disaster of incriminating supplies falling into the wrong hands, Verina had to admit to emself that ey had missed the fighting. It stretched reason to say ey enjoyed it, but the discomfort and stress of battle had become a familiar ally. Being in command, ey realized, made it too easy to forget the personal nature of combat. It wasn't symbols on a tactical chart. Here, not only did your colleagues depend on you, you depended on them in kind. Unfortunately, survival sometimes clashed with the "larger strategic goals," which is why you needed good commanders who maintained focus. But in this case, Verina was ashamed to realize, seeing those dead Human soldiers was satisfying.

The team loaded each of the four pods onto four push-plates. The heaviest pod exceeded the combined load capacity of its four disks, so two Ligrosians had to carry some of the weight as well. Despite the burden, returning to base went smoothly and without delay.

Upon the squad's return, Verina sought out Tamira. "We need to move to other camps right away," the leader said. "We attacked a Human squad. They'll likely seek retribution."

Though a commander, Tamira's field experience with the responsibility carried by that rank was limited to a few "nuisance" incursions on Human positions. The concept of immediate command decision followed by immediate action induced in em an unexpected confusion. Verina had seen this before. Ey looked eir officer in the eyes and said, "Tamira, look at me. At this particular moment, I'm the one in charge. Understand?"

"Yes, Hai-Verina."

"That means that I'll worry about what to do. All you need to do right now is follow my orders. Don't worry if you don't fully grasp things right now. Just trust me that I do know what I'm doing. Okay?"

"Okay. I mean, yes, Hai-Verina."

"Good. Now, have everybody prepare to move out. We aren't taking everything; just enough to make it to our destination and fight if necessary." Verina put a hand on Tamira's shoulder. "Try to embrace the fact that this isn't a big deal. I was probably going to have us move anyway."

"I understand," Tamira said, unsteadiness still accenting eir voice.

"Good. Now go. Let's be ready to leave in under an hour."

Tamira nodded and tended to eir duties with renewed confidence. Verina never doubted it. Not long after starting the campaign against Earth, the Ligrosian began reading whatever materials on Human war history ey could find. Though the intent was to better anticipate the Humans' deployments and strategies, ey also learned about the common psychology of war. Commanders in every species, it seemed, when having to direct a mission they personally weren't prepared for—whether due to inexperience or unexpected events—had a random tendency to become useless for a brief period of time. It always passed and rarely lasted more than an hour or two. The danger was the tendency for those hours to be decisive. In eir own experience, Verina found it almost never happened more than once to a commander. As long as every fighting unit was peppered with personnel able to backup a paralyzed leader, then the problems could always be managed…ey hoped.

When Verina was inventorying and distributing the supplies provided by the Quinkst, a young Ligrosian, barely an adult, approached. "Excuse me, Hai-Verina?"

Verina turned, smiling at the anxiety in the young one's face. "May I help you?"

"I…I was wondering if I could ask you a question?"

"Of course."

Taking a calming breath, the rebel asked, "I was wondering if you were at Foer-tan when the storage facility blew up?"

A moment of worry crossed Verina's mind, as well as a self-admonition that ey'd promised emself that ey was going to get some guards. "Yes, I was."

Nodding, the youth said, "Do you know who helped a young Ligrosian injured by the blast?"

Verina smiled slightly. "I helped a young one. I did some first-aid, then sent em on a push-plate to where I hoped ey'd get better care."

The rebel smiled, and eir eye-patches shaded orange. "Hai-Verina, thank you. That was my sibling. If you hadn't helped em—"

Verina fought to keep eir own patches from changing. "How is ey?"

"Ey's fine, now. In fact, ey wanted to join the fight but our parent and sire wouldn't hear of it."

"So you joined."

"They weren't happy about that, either, but we all knew it was right. I'm happy I did."

"What is your sibling's name?"

"Bodouthen. I'm Articca."

"Thank you, Articca. Knowing that I helped…I can't tell you what that means. But, we both have duties and not a lot of time. Would you mind if we talk again?"

A shocked smile preceded, "No, Hai-Verina. I wouldn't mind. I'd be honored. Thank you."

Verina returned the smile. "Would you track down Tamira; tell em that I'd like to see em?"

"Of course."

Articca left, the weight of gratitude lifted from eir shoulders. Verina, too, felt lighter. The difficult times seemed only to grow worse. Though the injuries to Bodouthen were due to actions ey commanded, Verina felt like ey'd done something of worth. Ey had helped, and it mattered.

18

Flush

Fleet Marshal General William Chavez hated the re-establishment of communications. Once the flood gates opened, the general fielded calls from every member of the Presidium. Only the secretary general gave him peace. Minister Naveen was the worst of the lot, seemingly unable to go twenty minutes without needed something. "General, we need to be able to copy those boxes," Naveen said again, as he had every day since the Seetun device was unlocked.

"Minister, I assure you that just as soon as that problem is solved, you'll be the first to be informed."

"Bill, I don't want to sound ungrateful. You wouldn't believe what a change there's been, now, with the spigot open. We can't have a recurrence of that attempted power-play by those damn blues."

Now it was time to reveal his little bone and throw it to the dogs. "I can't see that happening, Minister. I've been informed that we now have the capability of tapping into alien lines as well… without detection."

Naveen smirked. "I wondered what you were holding back."

"It wasn't held back, sir. It's just not at a hundred percent, yet. We—"

"Never mind. It'll be enough to placate the S.G. Things would go a lot smoother if you'd send us your materials."

"As we've discussed, Minister, there is no way to keep them as secure as they are here. I have complete manned and electronic surveillance of our six researchers and a total lock-down of the complex. Even though there is a lot to understand with everything we have, we *do* control it."

"You need to break the logjam soon, General." Naveen glanced off to the side. "I'm being called for a vote. I'll talk to you later today."

Naveen's subscreen disappeared, only to be replaced by a new incoming-call announcement. Chavez got up to pour himself a scotch. The call could wait.

The heavy downpour that started in the morning showed no signs of letting up in the afternoon. Even as a descendant of an ocean-born species, Verina grew increasingly annoyed with the unrelenting deluge. The fifty other Ligrosians traveling with em grew so tired of complaining about the abysmal weather they'd stopped talking completely. An "improved" mixture of brown-face makeup —often used on missions so the turquoise-colored Ligrosians could blend in with the surroundings—was abandoned when the reality sunk in that that "water-resistant" didn't mean "waterproof". So, they improvised. Each rebel wore two pareu, one in the usual skirt-like fashion, the second wrapped around the neck like a poncho. When not marching, this second wrap was pushed up over the face, leaving only the eyes visible under the brimmed caps they all wore.

As they approached the landquake-laden western edge of the Divergent Zone, a thousand kilometers southeast of Esri-tan, Verina grew excited with the familiar territory and took the lead. Even without breaking into a run, ey quickly outdistanced eir new guards and the rest of the column. When the rebels lost sight of Verina after ey crested a hill, they grew anxious. Tamira joined the guards as they all sped up to keep their leader in sight. Reaching the top of the hill, they saw Verina about thirty meters away, standing in front of an armed Ligrosian. That Ligrosian lowered eir weapon and touched foreheads with the rain-soaked leader. Tamira looked at the fighters at eir side and said, "I guess we're here."

When eir guards finally caught up, Verina continued on with them in tow. Ey rushed into the familiar base and headed straight for the command room, ignoring all of the surprised faces recognizing em as ey passed by. The open central hub contained five people, three of whom Verina recognized immediately. In a custom very Human, but very apt, ey put er arms around the shoulders of two very surprised Ligrosians. "I'm back."

Turning into the embrace, Akehru and Elekin faced the returned leader and pressed their foreheads strongly against Verina's. After about a minute that seemed like much, much more, Akehru said, "Verni, you know I love you, but you're getting me all wet."

The embrace broke and unselfconscious laughter pierced the air. Ey *was* home. Finally. Out of the corner of eir eye, ey saw, "Li! Get over here!"

Li rounded the table and was about to stand at a respectful distance when Verina surprised the Human and embraced him as well. "I even missed you," ey said.

With a quick platonic hug back, careful not to hurt the Ligrosian, Li took a small step away and said, "Not nearly as much as you were. Look."

Ligrosian warriors, including a few remnants of the pods Verina held in reserve from the massacre, didn't try hiding their happiness. The patches around their eyes and their melodic tones of relief filled the scene, catching many of the fighters by surprise. Verina savored it for a few moments, but the mantle of leadership settled back upon em quickly. Responsibility replaced joy. Responsibility to eir fighters. Responsibility to eir planet. "I can't tell you all how much I'm looking forward to spending some time with each of you—and I will—but as you know, we all have serious times ahead of us. The sooner we tackle the problems at hand, the sooner we'll be free. Let's not lose our focus. So, tell me 'Welcome back' and let's move on."

Most everyone smiled with approval at the command and said their welcomes before quickly clearing out. Before long, the room held only the command group, necessary staff, and Verina's guards outside the entrance. The leader said, "I can't wait to show you what I've brought. I think it will—"

"Earth is communicating with Seetun again, without restriction," Li interrupted.

Slightly confused, Verina said, "What? When?"

Akehru said, "We're not really sure. We think that maybe it was a little before you—"

"The attack. Of course," Verina interrupted. "That's how they…wait a minute. That means they can tap into non-Earth comm, too."

"At least partially. Yeah," Li confirmed.

"Far-naganu" / "Slip-et'a thegkt!" Verina two-voiced.

Elekin looked away, and Akehru's eye patches darkened. The other two Ligrosians in the room tried disappearing into the background, pretending they didn't hear. Nobody, but *NOBODY*, swore like that without being cited and eventually ending up in court. Akehru didn't even know eir sibling knew an epithet that…that…

well, ey just never even imagined.

Verina regained eir composure and saw the expressions around em. "Sorry," ey said curtly. After a few laps of pacing, Verina said, "We're going to have to destroy the relay."

Akehru said, much too calmly, "You can't."

"Ohhhh you just watch me."

"I'm not saying that you shouldn't. I'm saying that you can't." Now Verina was listening. "Never mind that it would cut off all the other races as well, but the fact of the matter is the system is designed so that it can't be destroyed. I don't know exactly how the…" Akehru paused, realizing Li was in the room, and said, "designers made it so fail-safe, but the fact of the matter is that even if you blew up the planet, Seetun would still operate."

Verina sat. Stunned. "That's it then. They are going to turn us into Lrat…except with Seetun instead of engines."

Elekin clicked to get Verina's attention. When ey had it, ey said, "You asked me to look into something?"

It took a moment, but Verina's funk suddenly lifted. "And?"

"I think we need to take a little trip…without the escort."

For the briefest of moments, Verina's mind flashed to the possibility that Elekin was the one who turned em in and was now going to do the job properly—paranoia being tough to keep in check when you're on the losing team in a war. Fortunately, the flash was transitory and didn't linger. Ey trusted Elekin with eir life. If ey was wrong…well, ey could only die once. "Let's not waste any time, then," Verina said.

The deluge gave way to drizzle and broken clouds. The reflected light from Bailera shown through clearly where the breaks were nearly overhead. Verina barely noticed it was night, having spent so much time in the dark going to, or returning from, any one of scores of missions. Riding on their personnel-plates, Verina and Elekin made good time on the meandering course which

Verina thought was taking them toward the Czep-tan coast. The journey continued two more days when, just before dawn on the third day, Elekin stopped. "We need to get off the plates and strip."

It had been a long three days. Elekin was adamant about not even asking questions about the trip; it didn't markedly reduce the conversion, which was mostly about their days before the war, but it did strain Verina's trust. However, since trust was both binary and reciprocal, Verina continued to do whatever eir friend said. Which, at this point, was, "Now, we walk."

After a half-hour, Elekin said, "I didn't want to risk us being bugged, either from the personnel-plates or from anything we had on us. It's too important."

"Okay. So, where are we going?" Verina asked, though ey thought ey knew.

"Do you remember that day, last year, when I showed you the shmuptl?"

It seemed like a lifetime ago…and just yesterday. "Yeah."

"Only Haipuxans farm it. I've been able to keep sporadic contact with my source, though it's been tough."

"So, when I…"

"When you asked me, on the Quinkst ship, to try to find out if they planned to help us, I swam out and got a message to my friend."

"So? What are their plans?"

"I don't know." Cued off of Verina's look, Elekin smiled and said, "Because they'll tell you when they see you."

"We're going to see them?"

Elekin nodded. "I didn't want to risk exposing them in any way; that's why I was so evasive. I don't know how trusted anyone can be, except you. And of course, I can't say anything with Li around. He doesn't…?"

"No! Of course not. First law."

"My friend, Grahless, seems to think his people might help us in some way, though he didn't exactly say that. You know the Haipuxans."

"Yup. 'Never expose yourself to danger when danger can in any way be avoided.'"

Elekin took a path that Verina was certain paralleled the coast. The rebel leader said, "Flow hole?"

"Yeah. The Humans finally figured out that we come from the sea, not the trees like they do, so they've been putting more and more sensors and traps on the shore. I don't know how far from the cities they go, but I do know they installed a lot around Czeptan. Why risk it?"

Verina couldn't help but be impressed by how well eir friend was adapting to eir new situation. "Where were you when I was getting my fringe blown off?"

"Waiting 'til the time was right, I guess. Bailera's rule."

The pair entered a brush-hidden low cave not dissimilar to the one Verina escaped to when ey rescued Li. Like that one, this passage led to a pool feeding directly to the ocean. Since they'd brought nothing with them except themselves, the Ligrosians had to echolocate their way through the profoundly dark tunnels. Even so, the going was cautious: their sounding organs were designed for the viscosity of water, not air—it didn't give as detailed a picture. When they found the pool, they slipped right in.

Verina had almost forgotten the ocean's comfort: the cool pressure of water, the total immersion of sounds, the welcome taste of salt. But it was also different. Her dorsal skin ached from the constant touch of the water but was also soothed by its softness. It hurt, more than being naked in air, but not as much as ey thought it might. As ey followed Elekin, Verina tried remembering the longest time ey had ever gone between visits to the sea. Maybe a handful of months. Certainly not for over a year. Like all Ligrosians, ey loved the mother sea too much to voluntarily stay away for long.

"Elli," Verina whistled, "how are people getting to the ocean with the occupation?"

"A lot don't. They improvise by going to sport-pools every once in a while, but the Humans are careful about letting too many of us be in one place at one time. I was lucky. Since I got fish for the market, I always had access. Same for the head fishers at other markets. The Humans want us fed."

Added to the information Elekin discovered about the mining port, this worried Verina. Why did the Humans want eir people fed? Certainly not because they cared. Was it simply for laborers?

The temperature of the water suddenly dropped as the pair swam past the continental shelf. Just as suddenly, Verina became anxious. Beyond the shelf was Haipuxan territory. Except for emergencies, Ligrosians were not permitted in the deep ocean. The water tasted different; the salinity was "cleaner" somehow. Elekin whistled and clicked, "How are you with deep diving?"

"Not since I was a kid," Verina replied.

"Hold your canals, then. We're going down."

With a kick and a flurry of cavitation bubbles, Elekin zoomed down into the darkening depths. Verina followed as fast as ey could. Eir muscles, though steel-strong by Human standards, were soft when it came to sustained swimming, especially at speed. Ey didn't know why, but ey also had trouble maintaining eir orientation. It was a frustrating mystery at first, but ey soon realized that eir missing fringe decreased eir stability.

Elekin slowed now and again for Verina to catch up and get eir breath. Oxygen processed less efficiently after your membranes got too accustomed to the easy exchange available in the air. It might take hours or days, but eir body would remember and adapt. Verina was relieved when Elekin guided them to a slanted hollow in the underwater cliff, one of countless deep diagonal scars in the escarpment—a result of the eons-long movement of the continental band moving around the planet from the Divergent Zone to the Subduction Zone.

They waited. A few passing silvery-purple chapitch were snatched and eagerly consumed. Eating seafood on land, even freshly caught seafood, lacked a certain primordial "something" when compared with eating it as nature intended. "That was good," Verina complemented.

"How long has it been?"

"For chapitch, or anything wild?"

"Anything."

"Two…three years?"

"Why didn't you say something? When you're close with a fish marketer, you should take advantage of it."

"Hey, you offered me two shmuptl at below market value."

"And I still couldn't get you to buy them. It was almost insulting."

"Sorry."

"Don't worry about it. It's your nature. Ooh look over there… chekcheks. I'll be right back."

Elekin darted into the inky sea after prey Verina never saw. Moments later, ey returned with four eel-like fishes ten centimeters long with toothed beaks. Each was held by two fingers on either side of both hands. Carefully, not allowing them to slip away, Verina took possession of two of the new menu items. Elekin said, "Put one all in your mouth and bite down slowly."

Verina suctioned in one of the morsels and slowly bit. At first there was a saltiness due to the blood vessels breaking. Then something burst open. A sweetness ey had never known filled Verina's mouth. Ey didn't want to swallow, it was so good, but it was getting difficult to contain all the food in eir closed jaws. Ey swallowed. Warmth followed the food down eir throat and slowly ebbed into the rest of eir body. Elekin said, "The Haipuxans call them 'candy of the sea'."

"They aren't wrong," Verina agreed as ey savored eir second chekchek. After the delightful warmth began to fade, Verina said, "Have you given any thought about what you want to do if we manage to survive this war?"

"All the time."

When Elekin didn't flesh out the comment, Verina prompted, "And…?"

"Shhh."

The water was now almost black; only the fractured reflections of what was probably Bailera filtered down and broke the uniformity of visual emptiness. Acoustically, it just seemed like the ocean. Wait. Something. "I think I see bio-lum approaching," Verina said, adding a musical measure pinpointing distance and bearing.

"That should be them," Elekin agreed. "I think our hosts have arrived."

Three Haipuxans rosed from the depths, their bodies outlined with hundreds, if not thousands, of small blue-gray bio-luminescent dots. Descended from the ancient jellyfish, these creatures retained the bell-shaped body of their ancestors. Their membrane had long since evolved from a gelatin to a flexible, almost leathery skin. Topping the bell were three long tentacles, equally spaced apart; various sensory organs ringed the top like a crown. These three-meter tall, two-meter wide creatures wouldn't look particularly noteworthy to most species had they known of their existence. The Haipuxans lived their own lives, hidden from the universe—arguably the most intelligent species of the worlds known to have sentient beings. To maintain their reclusion, they were content to let their most recent symbiont, the Ligrosians, be the sole representatives of Serees.

The lead Haipuxan stopped a few meters away from Verina and Elekin. The other two Haipuxans floated in, almost close enough to touch. "Hold out your arms," the leader said in a near-subsonic rumble that set Verina's mouths on edge and reminded em why ey hated talking to Haipuxans under water.

Both Ligrosians reached out. Their arms were engulfed up to the elbow by strong tentacles. "Relax and enjoy the ride," rumbled the leader before turning back in the direction he came.

Held firmly but away from the pulsating bells of their "rides," both Verina and Elekin savored the amazing speed the Haipuxans attained. No Ligrosian could ever hope to move this fast unaided. It was a heck of a ride. The only thing that would have improved it was being able to see something other than the glowing outlines of the Haipuxans.

The Ligrosian pair noticed the pressure on their bodies increasing and that breathing was more difficult—though less from the pressure and more a result of the lower amounts of dissolved oxygen at depth. Their speed quickly dropped. Not far away, lit only in ultraviolet, was a tunnel opening. "Go inside," the lead Haipuxan rumbled. "The path to take is clearly marked."

Verina clicked a thank you and swam inside with Elekin following at eir side. Arrows on the floor of the passage, personalized with their names, guided them through a short maze of tunnels. The trail ended in a room brightly lit as if by sunlight. The water felt slightly warmer and more oxygenated, though the pressure was still on the high side. The room itself, more like a cavern, was roughly spherical with a diameter of fifty meters. Plants lined the walls, top to bottom, on the far hemisphere. An artificial light source floated in the middle of the space. A large reflector concentrated most of the raw light on the far wall. The opaque reflector shielded the nearer half of the room, but more than enough light bounced back to give a feeling of daylight. Seven cup-like stalks stood at the demarcation of the plant area and the smoothly polished coral-like walls. A Haipuxan sat in each of the three central cup stalks, filling the bowls with their bells. "Welcome," the Haipuxan on the far left said in a sonic range much more compatible with Ligrosian physiology. "My name is Lovrem. I am the Primary Adjunct for Thought. The Responder to my immediate left is Limilel. The Assistant to his left is Wemaiyal."

Verina whistled and clicked tones honoring the Haipuxans while saying, "We embrace your welcome, Ta-Lovrem. I am—"

"There is no need to introduce yourself, Verina," Lovrem interrupted. "Or should I say, 'Hai-Verina?' What you have tried to do, and what you have accomplished so far, is worthy of respect. Even with us, you have your honorific. It has been earned."

Verina's eye patches turned a slightly darker shade of blue. For once, at least in recent memory, ey was genuinely speechless. Ey simply bowed eir head in reply. Lovrem continued, "Since the killing day, when the Humans arrived, we hoped for a Ligrosian to take the fight to them. Despite the annihilation of one-fourth of our kind in those first hours, we knew that our place was where it has always been. With the help of Elekin and others, we have kept some lines of communication available for the day when we could directly aid in our common cause."

Verina tried getting past the news that one-fourth of the Haipuxans died when those massive bombs first shook their planet. If ever there was a moment for em to be a commander with focus, this was it. "And now is that time, Ta-Lovrem?" ey asked.

Limilel answered, "As you know, we invented the Seetun technology that your race builds and shares with others—the focus of the Humans' avarice. We made it very durable and very secure. Until now, there was no way to violate the technology."

" 'Until now,' Ta-Limilel?" Verina asked.

Limilel waved a tentacle at Wemaiyal, who left his cup, swam over to Elekin, and handed em a box forty centimeters square and half as tall. Limilel said, "We have designed a terrible weapon. Its use will change the perceptions of power in our part of the galaxy."

Lovrem said, "We gave lengthy consideration about the morality of this device. We also considered that it will mean that Serees is no longer as safe as it was. We made the unfortunate conclusion that our safety was compromised, regardless, and the only moral thing to do was freeing our people. There is also the possibility of even greater freedoms, but that is not our motivation.

"In the first directive we've given your race since the middle of our current Baileriat, we are commanding you, Hai-Verina, to take these plans to your people, build this weapon, and use it against the Humans if the threat of this device alone isn't enough to force their surrender. You are also directed to continue the fight until our planet is rid of these invaders. Until this business is settled…in our eyes, you are maetor."

Verina once again wanted to go speechless, but ey was hardly in a position to give in to eir petty little insecurities. "I will do my duty to our peoples, Ta-Lovrem, just as I have since this abomination started. You have my word. You have my life."

"Then go and do what you must do, Maetor Hai-Verina. We will not keep you from your duties."

Both Verina and Elekin bowed their heads as if touching foreheads with an invisible someone in front of them. Taking their leave of these Haipuxans, they retraced their path from the room to the open ocean. Outside the entrance, the three guides once again took them in their tentacles, along with the box, and returned the pair to the scar on the shelf. The sea above showed the increasing light of dawn. Verina said, "Thank you," and the Haipuxans disappeared back to the depths.

"Wow," Elekin gasped. "Maetor."

"Shut up," Verina said, hoping the leadership title might go away. "We need to get back and tend to this new task." Then, smiling, "Besides, I'm getting hungry."

"In that case, here, hold this."

Elekin handed the box to Verina and darted out from the shelf. A minute later ey returned with four more chekcheks. "For the swim."

Verina touched foreheads, and meant it, before accepting eir share of the seafood delicacy. With the warm glow of the meal lingering within them, the two Ligrosians began their lengthy return trip back to the war.

19

Kidnapped

"That's unacceptable, Colonel!" General Chavez yelled from behind Colonel Bryce's desk.

Even though it was physically impossible, the colonel could swear her commander's eyes glowed red. She said, "I've run out of things to try, General. Potaryanii surely told you that."

Chavez glared. "Apparently that isn't the case, now, is it? We'd have answers. You never wanted this post, Rachael, and I think you aren't giving this your full effort."

"You can have my resi—"

"Don't you dare try that resignation crap. You're stuck here, Colonel, until I say different. Or until you are dead."

As much as she wanted out, Bryce wasn't yet ready to be at the wrong end of Chavez's wrath, or at the end of her own noose. She wanted to see Kala and Kar again—she'd pulled too many strings to have children to abandon them, now. She'd make it home so they could enjoy their lives in spite of this schmuck general with a Napoleon complex. Bryce dutifully played his game of physically and mentally torturing the locals. If her own well-being wasn't at stake, she never would have done it. "Then I'm open to suggestions, General. I simply can't get any information about those plans. Clearly they are about Seetun, but we have no frame of reference to use for translation."

"That's impossible. The blue-skin researchers in holding obviously know it."

"Yes sir, but I've had four die rather than tell me anything."

"Then, Colonel, you need to lighten up on the persuasion techniques a little."

"General, they died before we could impose duress. I don't know how, but whatever the secret is, every Sereesian we've questioned seems conditioned to die rather than give it up."

"Then keep them alive."

"Don't you think we tried that?" On Chavez's glare, Bryce added, "Sir? This is all very deep conditioning; I'm not even sure they are in control of it."

Chavez had no more arguments. The fact remained that, despite their differences, Bryce was a patriotic and by-the-book officer. This wasn't politics she was playing. He knew screaming and threatening her more wasn't going to do any good. Chavez got up from Bryce's chair, picked up his hat, and walked to the door. "General," Bryce called, "what are your orders?"

Without slowing his exit, Chavez said, "Succeed, Colonel. Do your job."

The stunning view of the ocean contrasted sharply with General Bhoutto's dark mood. His intelligence operatives had intercepted a crystal intended for Maetor Popituv. It contained numerous stills of the mine port. Though heavily processed and of poor quality, there was little doubt about their authenticity. Despite all of the security, the terrorists had managed to find out about the camp much sooner than expected. Information Minister Psiharis telling him to with-hold information on the breach from the rest of the leadership wasn't helping his disposition. "Minister, I'm not sure I can do that."

The female image on the display said, "I think it's in the best interest of everyone concerned. Minister Chopratama and I are in full agreement about this."

"I have to tell you, it seems pretty chancy…and I'm the one putting his head on the chopping block."

"Don't be so dramatic, General. You don't actually have to *do* anything. Just omit the fact that you have knowledge of what's likely to happen. Maybe you'll get a tongue-lashing, but nothing more."

"It just seems to me that there has got to be a better way."

"We're running out of time, General. The time for non-action is now. We'll just let events play out from there."

"You owe me a big one, Minister."

"That was never an issue, General. Signing off."

The display went dark.

Well, that settled that. Reports of this crystal would be withheld from the briefing to General Chavez. While risky, it could be blamed on some bureaucratic SNAFU; heaven knew those were becoming more of a headache. Psiharis was right, letting the Sereesians run the course of events was probably the surest and safest way to go. The alien leadership was intelligent and, as these pictures demonstrated, resourceful. There was little doubt that they, too, understood time was running out for them.

Bhoutto walked straight to Popituv's office for their scheduled meeting. He had no intention of discussing this latest development with the Sereesian leader. If she was going to find out about the mine port, it would have to be without his help. Even so, he still had staffing quotas to con out of her in order to meet the requirements for both the mine port that was on-line as well as the one starting construction in two weeks. Without pausing to be announced, the general walked into the maetor's office. "Excuse me if I'm interrupting but there is…a…matter…"

Six armed Ligrosians trained their weapons on the unsuspecting Human officer while another held Bhoutto's hands open to prevent any covert communications. Since resistance wasn't a viable option, Bhoutto surrendered and was quickly bound. A fist-sized device that Akehru had designed was slowly waved across each of the general's palms, disabling the subcutaneous controls. From the far side of the room, Elekin said, "That was easy. Take him away. I'll be with you in a moment."

Without any fuss, five Ligrosians led Bhoutto from Popituv's office, leaving Elekin and eir guard, Popituv, and the bound-and-gagged Navegil. Elekin turned to Popituv and said, "Since we got what we came for, we'll leave peacefully. Hai-Popituv, it's been a great honor. However, I think it's important for you to realize that while the Humans installed you as maetor, the *legal* maetor is now Hai-Verina. Stay here, try to make your diplomatic deals, but know that by command directive you are not, in fact, in charge."

Popituv tried looking like a powerful person for a few moments before relief and reality caused em to lower eir eyes and say, "I know. My respects to Hai-Verina."

Without further word or acknowledgment, Elekin and eir guard left.

"Computer, run 'Devil's Due'," Potaryanii said after watching on her display the sextet of Ligrosians leaving the residence complex with their spoils. The computer acknowledged the command.

The lieutenant turned her attention to her Infolux. As far as anyone else would know, the security information detailing the kidnapping had been either deleted or altered…for some unknown reason. Potaryanii smiled as she thought about the irony of the night's events. While Verina had ruined her original plans to gain power, that very same alien had executed a covert operation that effectively put Potaryanii where she wanted to be. There was little doubt that Chavez would finally reward the lieutenant for her years of loyal service. Even better, the Sereesians were unwitting accomplices to Potaryanii's upcoming reassignment. The days ahead were certain to be good ones.

The last thing Colonel Bryce remembered was going to bed. Now…now she didn't know quite where she was. One thing was clear: she wasn't waking up, but coming to. Restraints held her to some sort of table or bed in a darkened room. Though she couldn't see anything thing else nearby, the colonel had the feeling she was being watched. "Don't worry," a Sereesian voice said, in the dark, "we haven't done any experiments on you. Not yet."

Coming from the dark into the brighter area where Bryce lay, was a familiar face. "Verina," Bryce said, resigned to her imminent death.

"You remember me. Good. We can skip the preliminaries, then."

"What's the point? I'm going to be tried and executed, right?"

"Hardly. Yes, you've done us a great deal of injury, but I have no great desire to kill you. I will, if it comes to that. If you believe nothing else that I say, believe that. But I just want you gone— back to the planet that spawned you. Until then, maybe you can be useful."

Swallowing down her relief, the colonel put on her soldier's face and said, "I'm not going to collaborate with you. And forget about getting any information."

"You don't have to do any of that. I just need to make your commander think you are. We've been watching his reactions. He tends to lose focus when faced with adversity. Yes, my people pay the price for his rashness. For now, it's more important to keep him off balance. Your capture is one part of doing that. And you don't have to do a thing."

"You're assuming that he's gong to try to get me back?"

"No. No, I expect that he's going to try to kill you to keep you from talking."

Bryce had to admit to herself that was very likely what Chavez would do. Verina continued, "Based on everything we've learned, I imagine that he's going to massively bomb every place he thinks we're keeping you. Not all at once, of course. He has to bomb and then investigate. It won't be quick. Also, he can't bomb in a pattern where we'd be able to anticipate the next likely targets, otherwise we'd simply move. So it's going to be random, and it's going to be harsh. And it's also going to present us with some opportunities to further distract him as we randomly attack his bomb site investigators. How am I doing?"

No wonder she's so annoying, Bryce thought, *she does her homework*. Donning a sarcastic demeanor, Bryce said, "That's it exactly. General Chavez will do everything you say. He won't bother torturing the citizenry or destroy a city or two to make a point. You're overmatched in this, you know. He's a career soldier. You're just a bureaucrat."

"Your leader loses too much political capital if he does either of those things. He lusts for the feeling of power and control. I'm taking away the control, so he can't afford to lose his power by being replaced. Now, with communications restored, he can't do anything obvious or big. He has no choice but to chase me."

Damn. "Think what you want. We always win."

Verina smiled and walked away, leaving Colonel Bryce with

the unsettling feeling that the terrorist had some surprise up her proverbial sleeve.

Elekin met Verina outside Bryce's cell. "You had fun. I can see it on your lips."

Verina suddenly felt guilty. Ey *did* have fun. Ey finally had the opportunity to directly confront one of the people who had changed her world…who had changed *em*.

General Chavez emerged from his personal transport in a foul mood. He didn't much care for planetside…any planetside. He'd joined Earth Fleet after his required service when he was a teen. It took him off that Earth rock and gave him a home in space. He belonged in space. The chaotic randomness of gravity-bound nature made his skin crawl. So, the less time he had to stay on *this* world, the better. "Welcome, General," Potaryanii said, snapping a crisp salute, "I trust your flight was uneventful?"

Not breaking stride, Chavez replied, "At ease, Lieutenant; walk with me."

The junior officer fell into step to the side and ever-so-slightly behind the general as the guard detail maintained a discrete interval. "It's a terrible thing," General Chavez said, "this kidnapping business. Two regional commanders in one night."

"Yes, sir."

"I'm assigning Major Bagheri TAD to cover Bhoutto's region. As for here, I thought your service to me merited a face-to-face."

Forcing down an insistent smile, Potaryanii said, "Yes, sir."

Chavez stopped and faced his junior officer. "I'll be taking over this command until Earth can supply me with another colonel." Potaryanii's face betrayed no expression—a feat worthy of Colonel Bryce, herself. The general continued, "Regs mandate the rank of colonel and allow for a major only in critical circumstances. Much as I'd like to…with your record, I can't give you a two-step promotion."

"I…I understand, General. I *will* be staying on as your assistant?"

"Of course. Report in thirty minutes to brief me."

With a slightly-too-long pause, the lieutenant snapped a salute. "Aye, sir. Thank you, sir."

Chavez casually returned the salute, turned on his heels, and continued on to his new office. Potaryanii stared at the general's back, fighting with herself to decide if she was more disappointed or more angry. All of that work…

As she set course for her own office, the lieutenant thought back to her years of service under the general. She'd destroyed her career while currying his favor. The frame jobs, the altered books, the covering for his indiscretions, the…well, the list was too long. Had she played by the rules, been a stick-up-her-ass officer like Bryce, then *she'd* be a colonel taking over a command. Even factoring some of the perks she received that were over her rank, the ledger didn't balance.

She was a prostitute! The realization constricted her chest. She'd sold herself to Chavez in exchange for momentary gain. Now, when she most deserved her reward, it was gone. At least there was one glimmer of joy: helping those blue-skins, even though it didn't advance her career, at least screwed Chavez. He hated planetside. Besides, her sources still might be useful.

Verina and Elekin marched upstairs to one of the holaxex's bedrooms. Leaving their beefy guards outside, the pair entered the starkly unfinished room. General Bhoutto sat on the floor, still gagged and fully restrained. Verina walked to the Human; Elekin hung back, weapon in hand, with another holstered in reserve. The rebel leader said, "It's my understanding that your position required you to be primarily involved with communication and propaganda. Is that accurate enough?"

Bhoutto nodded.

"You are also one of the command staff."

Bhoutto nodded.

"And you aren't going to tell me anything about your leadership."

Bhoutto nodded emphatically, which caught Verina a little off-guard. "Let us be clear," ey said. "Are you willing to discuss areas of interest about your leadership with me?"

Bhoutto nodded.

Verina glanced back at Elekin, who casually double-checked that the safety on eir weapon was disengaged. Verina reached over to Bhoutto's gag and entered the code required to unlock it. The general quickly stretched his mouth once it was freed of that insidious contraption. The Ligrosian said, "To save some time, I'll tell you that since you are a highly-ranked and trained officer, I'm not likely to believe anything you say to me."

"You'd be a fool if you did."

"Why are you willing to volunteer information?"

"I'm not a traitor," Bhoutto protested, causing some noticeable alertness from Elekin. Calmer, he continued, "We answer to many voices. Military personnel obviously answer to our superiors in the chain of command, including government leaders. However, we also have strong ties to our faiths, which require us to make moral choices even though we wear a uniform."

"As do we."

"Of course. I respect that, you see. How much do you know of our faith structure?"

The Ligrosian understood this tactic. The Human thought if he could engage em, he'd gain some advantage. Intrigued by this strategy, ey decided to play along for now. "Some. Three equal religious traditions co-exist after thousands of years of various degrees of violence based on the proposition that only one faith could be right. Now, your government has faith-based representatives at every significant meeting to ensure that the laws of your faiths are met."

"In theory. In practice, personal corruption tends to skew things in favor of those in power, often in opposition to the words of the Supreme."

"I thought as much."

"The basic problem is that two of our three faiths still believe that Humans are specially chosen, with dominion over all other creations. As a result, anything done to other species…well, that's simply the will of the creator. Morality doesn't really enter into it on any significant scale."

Verina quickly lost interest. This wasn't helping. "General, as much as I would love to stay here and discuss comparative theology with you, the fact of this matter is you aren't my only concern at the moment, and you aren't giving me anything to compel me to stay."

Bhoutto nodded. "I said all that to let you know that so long as I don't violate my duties as an officer and my loyalty to Earth, my faith requires me to do the moral thing and help you regain your world. I'm not the only one willing to do so, either, but I won't tell you who they are."

Verina picked up the gag; Bhoutto accepted it without complaint. As ey locked it in place, Verina said, "I'll consider what you've offered."

Back in the hall, rejoined by the guards Verina insisted upon, Elekin said, "You're not thinking about believing him?"

"Not really. Here's the thing: if he tells nothing but the truth, then there's no harm to us. If he tells nothing but lies, it will be

easy to simply ignore him. However, since he is trained in the way
Earth uses communication, he will tell us truths or half-truths in
order to make the lies seem real. I'll listen to him so we can find
out some of the truths he has to tell us."

Elekin touched Verina to get em to stop. "Verni, this is a little
scary. Where did you learn to think like that?"

"What?" Verina then clicked some amusement. "Oh, this isn't a
'war has changed me' moment. This was part of negotiator training. We had to learn to understand the meanings behind the words.
I admit that I wasn't specifically trained to deal with Humans, but
I've been studying."

Elekin and Verina continued walking downstairs to the
command center. "Do you know how Aki is doing with the
device?" Verina asked.

"I haven't heard a word for days. Ey locked emself in the lab.
Except for a couple of supply requests I handled, I don't really
know what's going on."

With a smile, Verina said, "That's my big sib. Ey's always been
like that. I guess you need to get us another guard and some
weapons."

"Uh…of course. Why?"

"This isn't some academic research project. I have to know
what's going on. So, we're taking a little trip."

After increasing their protection, Verina and Elexin traveled
four kilometers to the well-hidden lab near the shore. The distance
from the camp protected it from being an obvious target as well as
providing security of its own. The lab was placed in a cave leading
to a flow hole. It provided two small rooms for quarters and
supplies, and a low-ceilinged four-by-five meter space for the lab
itself. Because of the open pool, the lab rats could flee to the ocean
with critical plans and components if necessary. These treasures
were always positioned for easy access in the event of a hurried

escape.

The smell of humidity, ozone, and a nondescript spicy odor permeated the cave. Heat wafted from a far wall where a small sonic/photonic kiln was anchored. Though well-insulated, the kiln's heat had to be bled off periodically, which was happening now. Three rows of long, triple-decked work tables filled most of the space from floor to ceiling. Boxes with ominous warning symbols were stacked on the tables. One label indicated Fa'run materials, another identified nano-scale dusts, and one was so spattered with its own box-melt that it was impossible to decipher. Ceramic parts—as well as some rare metal ones—littered every available centimeter of counter space, but it in no way looked haphazard. The scattered madness of parts were where they needed to be in anticipation of their future assembly.

"Where did ey manage to get all of this?" Verina asked Elekin.

"Ey's the sib to the maetor. Eir assistants sent messages to every cell we know of. The supplies have been coming ever since."

"They've been…"

"…careful to make sure nothing intercepted can be traced back or reverse-engineered," Elekin finished. "I know some items are being fabricated at other sites simply because we don't have enough room or power to do everything here."

A frustrated klaxon-scream burst from behind a partition, start-ling Verina and Elekin, but none of the three lab assistants seemed to notice. From behind the movable wall, Akehru popped in, out, in, as ey paced to rid emself of some anger. On eir third pass, ey noticed the new arrivals and beckoned them over. When they got close enough for Akehru not to have to raise eir voice ey said, "I swear, if I ever get my hands on any member of that Haipuxan design committee…I'm going to make them wish they were still jelly enough to slip through my fingers!"

"Problems?" Verina asked with feigned innocence.

"Come here," Akehru snapped as ey led Verina around the partition. "There's the non-functional prototype. I thought I should build a practice one before risking our Fa'run materials; all I've got is in that box, and I'm not likely to be seeing any more."

Verina looked at the device. It seemed so innocuous. It was all a charcoal gray-black, owing to the particular ceramic materials used. A circular base, sixteen centimeters in diameter and tapered along its six centimeter height to a diameter of eleven centimeters, seamlessly joined with a cylinder eleven centimeters in diameter and sixteen centimeters high. On the top were three concentric disks, each two millimeters thick; the largest was three-fourths the diameter of the top cylinder, and the other disks were each three-fourths the diameter of the one they were stacked upon. In simple terms, it looked like a thick black candle sitting in a basic no-tip black base. "Aki," eir maetor sibling said, "I'm sorry, but I just don't see the problem."

With obvious emotional restraint, Akehru reached past Verina and picked up a small vial that emitted a very quiet tinkling sound. "See these two parts?" Akehru asked as ey thrust the finger-sized glass tube at Verina.

Verina lifted the vial to a nearby light. Ey saw inside a small silvery triangle, one millimeter on a side, and a small pink hemisphere less than half-a-millimeter in diameter. "Yeah."

"They are supposed to go in that, but I can't figure out how. There's no room."

"You're kidding."

"Assembly instructions would have been nice. I'm wasting almost all of my time trying to figure out some sort of puzzle."

Astonished, Verina handed the vial back to eir sibling. "That can't be right. Surely there must be—"

"Verni, have you ever seen the Seetun plans?"

"No."

"It's just like the plans for this. All the parts. All the science. Nothing about how to actually put it all together. It took seven years of work before we figured it out. Apparently it was supposed to be 'obvious' from the plans we were given. I swear, Verni, if I had the courage to utter that phrase you did, I would."

"Hey, I'm maetor. I won't tell if you don't."

Akehru let a momentary series of chuckle-clicks escape eir bad mood. "No. That's okay. It's a lot like the Seetun instructions. I'm almost there. Just those two pieces. I'll get it. Hey, Elli," ey said, finally acknowledging eir friend.

"Hi," Elekin said with obvious humor. "How's it going?"

Before Akehru could respond, one of Verina's guards rushed in and handed the leader a message before returning to eir post. Verina read the note, put it into one of eir jacket pockets, and turned to Elekin, "We need to get back to our jobs." Ey said to Akehru, "You'll let me know when you've solved the puzzle?"

"First one."

Verina pulled eir sibling closer. As they touched foreheads, ey said, "Be safe, Aki."

"You, too."

Outside the cave Verina had the guards move out of earshot. Ey spoke quietly with Elekin. "That Chavez is bombing us again."

"Where?"

"That's the thing. Nowhere important. The outskirts of one of our old bases took some damage, but we haven't used it since before the big battle. It doesn't make any sense."

Elekin thought out loud, "Maybe a Human perspective?"

Taking eir friend's cue, Verina and eir entourage returned to their base. Once there, the maetor received news of two more bombed sites which, again, were of no tactical significance that ey could see. Ey sent Elekin to the nearby base where Li worked on the weapons and supplies Verina brought back from the Quinkst ship. Worried that General Chavez might have a surprise in store for eir diminished collection of fighters, ey wanted to have a surprise or two of eir own…just in case.

The leader returned to Bhoutto's cell, pleased to see the reques- ted table and chairs already in place. With help from a guard, Verina guided the gray-haired general onto the Human-specific chair on one side of the heavy table. Once he was secured and comfortable, Verina unlocked and removed Bhoutto's gag then went to sit opposite him on the other side of the table. "Mister Bhoutto, you mentioned before that you wanted to be of some assistance to our homestand fight."

"As long as I don't commit treason, yes."

"Were you aware of planned bombings at various locations on my planet? They started today and are on-going."

Having spent so much time with Li, the Human's reaction was easily read. It was settling to note that it matched his words. "No. This is the first I've heard of it."

"So, since you have no knowledge of this action, anything you say will be purely speculative based on your experience. You won't be committing treason."

Bhoutto considered this quickly but carefully. "I think that is correct."

Satisfied, Verina took from eir pocket the half-size Infolux that had been doing eir translating, placed it on the table, and slid out and unfurled the included presentation screen that allowed for a display twice as large as on a standard-sized 'lux. It showed a map of the planet with bomb targets plotted. Bhoutto stared at it for a Serees minute before saying, "Could you overlay the orbital tracks of the non-stationary Earth craft and also plot their positions at the time of the bombings?"

A score of sinuous lines streaked the display; the positions requested flashed in various colors. Bhoutto chuckled to himself.

"What?" Verina asked.

"You said before that you wanted to rattle General Chavez. I'd say that you've done that. Except for this one target," he pointed to the abandoned base, "it appears that he's ordered all of the low-orbiting ships to release ordinance whenever they cross the land band. He's trying to confuse you with a more-or-less random bombing pattern. That one target suggests, and I may be wrong, that he also has specific objectives in mind."

"He's hoping to get lucky."

"More-or-less, yeah. You should be able to anticipate when and where each bomb run will take place within a modest footprint."

"Is he likely to change the pattern?"

"I'd say most certainly. Ships have to enter and leave various orbits to re-supply, after all. It's naive to think he won't employ any of the larger ships stationed outside the immediate gravity well. There will definitely be more randomness than this simple tactic suggests."

"Is there anything I can do about it?"

"Not really. We've been using this tactic since not too long after we first learned how to fly. Random, high-intensity bombing is pretty darned effective."

Verina thought about this. If there was one thing ey learned since this struggle began, it was that every tactic had weaknesses. "Do you think he'll bomb the cities? After all, most of your ground forces are there."

"Probably not, but then I didn't think he'd kill ten thousand of our own troops just to try and get rid of you, either. I will say this: areas that he's not intentionally bombing I'd stay away from. He wants you to see the pattern and go there." Bhoutto paused for a moment, a sparkle of inspiration enlivening his eyes. "Maybe the best bet is to do exactly the opposite and move to places that have already been bombed."

"That's an interesting possibility," Verina said with perfect negotiator non-emotion. "I'll have to think about that."

In truth, the prospect of outwitting Chavez at his own game held a certain appeal to the Ligrosian leader. Stress had been growing within the unit as they tried to guess when and where the next Human offensive would come. Moving eir command to a previous target might give the force enough peace to prepare for the final stand. Earth was entrenching itself more and more on the planet with each passing day. Time was running out to free eir world.

20

Freedom fighting platoons created mischief around Serees. Though the missions remained serious and dangerous, Verina's plans now focused more on distracting the enemy instead of direct confrontation. It might make Chavez think eir forces were larger than they were. The reality was that even if ey used eir entire force, they'd likely end up dead without Chavez having to massacre his own troops again. Force was no longer a rational option to compel the Humans to leave.

Twenty-two days had passed since the command staff, the rebel technical team, their two prisoners, and a handful of guards returned to the disused base near the lakeside shores of Ter-ip, one of the first targets to endure the new round of bombing. The over-all damage was actually rather slight and would have added an almost romantic air to the proverbial "last stand" were it not so close to the truth of the situation.

Seventeen days ago, Akehru succeeded in figuring out the assembly puzzle of the Haipuxan device. Now the push was toward completion of what promised to be a weapon whose power would profoundly alter the relationship of Serees to every other known civilization. For Verina, the one person with final responsibility to order the use of the device, the implications were terrible and daunting.

That is, if it worked. All Akehru had done was get all of the parts of a model put together. Once. After scavenging components from some of the most advanced weapons Verina brought back with em from the Quinkst, the rebels had scraped together enough hard-to-find elements to create one device. No mistakes could be made at any stage; none of the material could be wasted.

With little to do until the weapon was finished, Verina took advantage of the respite. Ey sat alone on the top of a mound that hundreds of millions of years before had been a small mountain. As the highest point available, it provided a view of the lush agricultural flats to the northeast and the rippling waters of Ter-ip to the west. It felt good to take off eir jacket and let the sun warm eir back. "Am I disturbing you?" Li asked as he approached from behind.

"Not really."

Li sat down near Verina and looked out at the cratered, but resilient, landscape. "I wish I could have seen your planet before."

Verina thought about all the different ways ey could answer. Ey never felt so much a part of Serees' life as ey did now, and, at the same time, so detached. That the Haipuxans would put the fate of their shared world on eir actions and judgments was surreal. "It will grow back. Maybe not exactly the same, but it will be vibrant again."

The two sat without saying a word for a handful of minutes before Elekin came up the same way as Li had and sat on the other side of Verina, sandwiching the leader between eir two advisors. Another handful of minutes passed before Elekin said, "They hit the base we stopped at twenty days ago. Same as this one:

damaged, but not destroyed.

"Did you check with Aki?" Verina asked.

"Ey's still working. Frankly, I was afraid to disturb em, Ey's so focused."

"I know."

"Like Edison inventing the light bulb," Li added, his Earth-specific analogy sounding oddly dissonant.

The awkward silence broke when Li got up, too casually, and said, "I'm going to get something to eat."

The two Ligrosians were alone, enjoying the beauty of their world. Verina said, "I think all the time about what happens if this doesn't work. What will it be like to be a slave?"

"It will never happen. They'll kill you, first."

"True."

"If it comes to it, I think that we should have one more big battle."

"What's that that Li says—'Go down fighting'?"

"Exactly."

"Do you realize how many thousands have died because they followed me?" Verina said with a tiredness in eir voice.

Elekin didn't press the issue. Time enough for that decision, later. Instead, ey said, "What if we win? You're maetor, after all."

"I think that worries me more than losing. I'm not qualified. I'm just available and…and momentarily necessary."

"That might have been true at the very beginning, but if…*when* we win, you will be worthier than anyone else. You'll have saved us, 'From those who take what they covet.' You'll be the nexus that kept us from Lrat's fate."

"I've been thinking about that, too. If this works, maybe we can help out the Gelrahtem."

"Verni, let's worry about us first, okay?"

With the wind momentarily calm, Bailera reflected on Ter-ip's glassy surface. Elekin said, "One hundred days before the dance."

If everything worked out right, then maybe Verina's world would be free when Serees and Bailera's shifting orbits were briefly equidistant from the system's star, Maygola. It was always a special holiday, happening only once every three-hundred-and-one years. With victory, it would be a powerful symbol. Verina filed away that possibility in the back of eir mind. Ey didn't have much control of the timing of events. Or their outcomes. Better to let things take care of themselves. Well, most things. "Elli, can I ask you something?"

"Of course."

"You know that I went through rothshah without a union. I was wondering, if we do win, if you'd be willing to—"

"Yes," Elekin interrupted.

The sudden answer caught Verina off-guard. "What?"

"Yes. I've wanted to be with you for a long time," Elekin said with a serious voice colored by an accompaniment of excited tones.

"You do realize that I'm not talking about short-term. I want to —"

"I want that too, Verni. Very much."

Elekin reached over, bringing Verina's head closer to touch foreheads. Soon, both Ligrosians sounded tones of contentment and bonding that quickly started evolving into the first stage of their own unique "song". Whether this shared composition was cultural or instinctual was still a matter of some debate since the Haipuxans refused to give any information on these sorts of issues. They said it added to the necessary mysteries of life.

Once the initial rush of joy and satisfaction reached its peak, Verina and Elekin settled back to watch Bailera-set. "I wish the Humans hadn't started this," Verina said.

"I think everyone wishes that, Verni."

Verina looked Elekin in the eyes and said, "That's not what I mean."

Elekin knew what ey meant. Verina's eyes spoke of sadness and a sort of fatigue only the most severely tested ever earn. Now the survival of their way of life depended on the decisions the once-negotiator had to make alone. Though ey saw Verina almost every day, it was unimaginable what that kind of responsibility did to a person's soul. "Just remember," the master fisher quipped, "I said, 'Yes.' I'm not going anywhere."

For a moment, the smiles on Verina's face held the easy joy from before the invasion…but just for a moment. The tired sadness crept back into eir eyes much too quickly. Even so, it touched Elekin. Despite all of the scars, the never-ending pain, and all of the responsibilities, there was still a spark of the old Verina ey could reach.

Verina fidgeted, in the throws of another night of eir usual restless sleep. Earlier, ey directed a few minor incursions into the second slave camp the Humans were building. The stress of that campaign finally caught up to em once all the rebels returned safely. Ey was exhausted.

When light streamed in through the door, Verina knew that whatever sleep ey had gotten was nowhere near enough. Ey instinctively sonar-blasted to get a rough idea of eir surroundings —someone was here. Ey worked to clear eir eyes and tried to focus on the Ligrosian standing in the doorway. Akehru said, "I finished."

Verina's vision cleared. Ey saw eir sib, standing in the middle of the threshold, holding up that black candle of a device. "You look tired," the roused leader said.

"Yeah."

Verina got up from eir narrow sleeping shelf that didn't deserve the title of "bed." "Lie down," ey said. "We don't have to do anything tonight."

Somewhere in the back of eir mind, Akehru wanted to make an argument about…something. But the lure of rest was too compelling. Ey didn't notice when eir sibling took the precious device from eir hand. The engineer lay down and closed eir eyes; sleep consuming em immediately and completely. Verina bent down and touched eir forehead to eir sib's, softly saying, "Thank you."

Verina walked to the entrance and told one of her guards, "Call for a second unit to join you tonight."

"Yes, Hai-Verina."

Holding, almost cradling, the weapon, Verina moved to the desk that nearly overwhelmed the space. From a semi-hidden holster attached to one side of the heavy office furniture, ey removed a sidearm and turned off the safety. Ey sat down in the room's dark far corner, placing the device beside em. Verina fell asleep almost as quickly as Akehru.

Thirty-one Ligrosians and one Human filled the lower level of the two-story tall, large conference room that echoed the local aesthetic for simple shapes and clean lines. Extending out from three adjoining walls, the wide, second-floor walkway remained empty. Verina and eir command staff stood at the far wall, under the tip of the left arm of the upper deck. The modest black device upon which all their hopes of freedom rested sat on the table placed between eir group and the crowd. The atmosphere was electric. Conversations employing many voices at once made it much louder than a gathering of an equivalent number of Humans. With the din being an adequate acoustic shield for the leaders to speak privately, Li asked Akehru, "You're sure it's going to work?"

"All of the subsystems work. All the interconnects and instructions work. Power flows. Everything has been checked five times against the plans. Assuming the…planners didn't make a mistake, then yeah, it should work." At Li's raised eyebrow, Akehru added, "It's not like I could actually do a full-up test. Either it works or it doesn't. But it should."

If the Ligrosians were better at reading Human expressions, they would have noted Li's fake optimistic agreement. He'd been around too many military development projects to trust in the success of the first full-up test. They never worked.

Verina raised eir hand and within seconds the room stood quiet as a grave. Ey didn't like making speeches, feeling them superfluous, but this time ey relented to the insistent opinions of eir advisors. "It's come down to this. All of the fighting and all of the sacrifices have brought us to…well, I don't need to tell any of you about that.

"We have built a weapon that will terrify every species that has developed technology sophisticated enough to reach beyond their atmosphere. It will make us a target. But, if we don't use it, we will be slaves. History might condemn me for this. The fact is, I'm more concerned with our freedom, now. If we don't have that, what difference will our high-minded ideals make?

"So, it's important you understand that using the…" Verina turned to Akehru and whispered, "What are we calling this?"

"I call it the dzad."

"Seriously?"

Akehru nodded assent while Verina's face still bore the lines of incredulity. The leader asked, "Why 'dzad'?"

"That's more-or-less the sound it makes when it's powered up," eir sibling shrugged.

Verina's incredulous stare stayed on eir sibling for a few more moments. Ey turned back to the crowd. "Sorry. I was saying that it's important that you understand that we are not using the dzad out of anger, or revenge, or malice. We've run out of options. It's either this or live under the thumbs of Earth. As maetor, it's my decision alone. I hope that the next time Bailera returns to fill the sky this choice will be considered to have been a wise one."

Verina nodded to the guards standing next to the entrances on the upper tier. All eyes turned when the doors opened. A gasping cacophony of surprise rose when two bound and gagged Humans, Colonel Bryce and General Bhoutto, were led out to witness the proceedings. Verina said, "What we do here affects our guests, so it is only right that they understand what is going on."

The crowd quieted down and once again faced their maetor. Elekin walked to the table and picked up the dzad. Ey said to Verina, "Akehru said to wait for the sensor to pop up. We'll then be tapped into the grid and have a private line. Less than a minute."

Verina smiled and nodded acknowledgment. All eyes followed Elekin as ey took the dzad to a console on the side of the room near Akehru, who was busy with several Infoluxes.

The lights dimmed theatrically except for a diffuse spotlight on Verina. A ten-centimeter sphere rose from a pocket in the table and settled at Verina's eye level, two meters away from the Ligrosian. Elekin clicked a cue for Verina to begin. The maetor said via a translator, "Good day, leaders of Earth. Please forgive our temporary intrusion on your private government channel. To those who don't know, I am Verina. I have led the battle to rid my world, Serees, of your invasion forces since the day you arrived. Those of you who aren't busy trying to trace this broadcast may be wondering if I'm about to announce my surrender. The answer is an emphatic, NO. I initiated this communication to demand *your* surrender. You will leave my planet and abide by any restrictions we deem necessary to prevent a future incursion onto our soil.

"I can issue this demand because you have forced us to build a weapon so powerful that it will disrupt your lives to an even greater extent than you have ours. We will demonstrate this weapon now and return to broadcast in one thousand tics, standard…which, from what I understand, is just over one of your minutes."

"Off-line," Elekin said.

"Activate it," Verina commanded. "Twenty-three seconds."

Akehru pushed the button on top of the cylinder. The device produced a noise that did, indeed, sound like *DZZAAAD*. "Powered," Akehru said before pressing three buttons on the console. "Activated and functioning."

Twenty-three expectant seconds later, Akehru said, "Power off."

Verina asked, "Did it work?"

"It seems so," Akehru replied.

The tension that had built up throughout the room now retreated a bit. Verina also appeared less stressed when Elekin clicked to em that they were back on the air. Verina said, "I'm sure that our little test got your attention. Around Serees, for an area surrounding about sixteen thousand lyd, standard—roughly five of your light years—we cut off all of your communications including all Seetun connections wherever they were. That was only a taste. Our system has much greater range, is adaptive, and very broad— encompassing bandwidth possibilities your race hasn't yet theorized about.

"I want you to fully appreciate what that means. Your navigation systems will be, at best, unreliable. Your ships will be stranded in space with limited ability to call for help. You will have moved from Seetun technology back to simple radio and light waves. Your civilization will be effectively silent and alone. You will be completely defenseless to any space-faring culture that seeks to do your planet harm. We can and will tune our weapon to affect only Human and Earth communications, so our friends and law-abiding contract holders need have no concerns that this device will be a threat to them.

"I know that bureaucracies take time to work. You have to have a chance to absorb and believe the dire threat you are under if you don't leave my world. I will guarantee you ten Serees days—twelve decimal five kex, standard—to consider your position and transmit your capitulation on an uncoded channel. After those ten days, the weapon may be activated at any time. If that happens, I can guarantee you that it will not be turned off after only one thousand tics.

"Take your days and consider them carefully. Leave my world, accept your just punishment, and your civilization will survive. If not...well, the decision is up to you."

"Off-line."

A great cheer rose up in the conference room. They had a working weapon to use against Earth. Either Earth left, or their fleet would lose the ability to communicate, leaving every soldier and ship vulnerable to even a rag-tag rebellion. Victory was only days away.

Verina didn't share that optimism. While ey accepted many congratulations, and deflected many more for the still busy Akehru, the leader worried. Ten days was a long time to wait for things to go wrong.

21

Sucker Punch

"You aren't listening to what I'm saying," Akehru protested. "If the dzad is to be fully effective, we have to put it in the middle of Human-controlled space. It's primary range is only 150- to 200-thousand lyd, standard."

"But it worked in the test," Elekin countered.

"They weren't ready for it so it tunneled through their systems just like its designed to. Within that sixteen lyd radius, the effect is so powerful that they can't do anything to overcome it. Beyond that, if we relying only on its ability to tunnel through the communication streams, it's possible that they'll eventually find a way to defeat it. How long, I can't say, but they have proven to be good code breakers."

"Why can't we move it after it's on? They won't be able to stop us."

"But then they could track the effect and find where it was placed. If they can find it, they can destroy it."

Verina had enough listening to this back-and-forth. Ey sat up straighter and said, "We don't have an option. For this to be effective we have to place the dzad somewhere in the Sol system or perhaps the Centauri system."

"Can we send a message to the Quinkst?" Elekin asked. "They seem willing to help. If it gets Earth off their backs, too, maybe they'll be willing to risk a few ships."

"No," Verina said. "*We* have to do this. We rely on ourselves so that we know the job is…" Verina cocked eir head to the side. "Listen."

The sound of distant thunder quickly grew louder and obviously artificial. "Attack!" Verina yelled.

Akehru said, "The dzad!" before running out of the room.

Elekin started after Akehru, but hesitated. Ey looked at Verina who was being surrounded by guards and ushered away. Verina called back, "Go! I'll be fine."

Elekin rushed down the hall leading to the lab. With every step, the rolling thunder of bombs closed in. An explosive maelstrom of debris shot from the ceiling and walls. The ground shook from a quick succession of concussions.

In less than a minute, the rebel base's pre-invasion airport architecture had been transformed into broken buildings and debris-lined craters. Building dust, combined with smoke from burning furniture and supplies, created a dense fog that muted all but close-range echolocation. Cries for help littered the air but replies were slow to arrive.

Pushing pieces of wall off emself, Verina dimly recalled having been through this before. Fire coursed through eir body as the cuts and scrapes to eir exposed skin fired up eir over-excitable nerves. All ey wanted to do was lay still and let the pain subside—but ey couldn't. Ey had to lead.

Fractured pieces of the building surrounded the maetor-rebel. The exposed edge of a nearby crater spoke to how close the bomb came to landing directly on em. Eir phalanx of guards all lay dead, pools of blood growing around their broken and maimed bodies. Because they had been between Verina and the explosion, their lightly armored bodies absorbed and deflected enough of the blast to keep their leader alive. They did what duty required: they died so that the maetor could live. Verina's thoughts weren't so high-minded at the moment—but they weren't on the fallen guards, either. Ey had seen enough death that a few more random bodies barely registered. What filled Verina's mind was concern about the safety of both eir sibling and eir fianceir.

About half of the base was spared direct hits. However, the shockwaves from the blasts caused at least two-thirds of the structure to crumble. It was nearly impossible to move from room-to-room. Ligrosian klaxon calls alerted anyone nearby of survivors trapped in the ruins. The amount of heavy rubble meant there would be few exits without help from heavy-duty tools and machines.

Verina stumbled from the debris, physically unable to straighten. Eir ribs hurt, but ey knew more was definitely wrong. Ignoring it for the moment, ey easily pushed down a door to an office, its inner wall crumbling into the adjacent corridor leading to the atrium. From here, Verina saw a breach at the far outer hallway that clearly led to outside the building.

Hearing calls from within, Verina returned to the first office. The last hints of daylight flowed in from the open doorway—enough for the injured leader to find the adjoining storage room. Here the voices of the trapped were definitely louder. As quickly as ey could, ey cleared out the office supplies lining the small room's walls. As ey did, ey called out, "There's a way out! Break through the wall!"

The muffled voices on the other side grew silent. Verina triple-voiced, "There's a way out! You need to break through this wall!"

Moments later, the wall shook as it was struck from the opposite side. Verina couldn't do any more—it was hard staying awake. A hole burst through the wall as a ragged boulder made a hole in the barrier, about chest-high. Verina said, "Keep coming. You can get out this way."

A spasm of coughing doubled Verina over as the dust coming from the effort to enlarge the hole enveloped em. Coughing was too painful. From the other side ey heard, "You go first. If you can make it through, we all can."

One of the logistics grunts, a burly Ligrosian whose name Verina couldn't recall—Fisth-something—struggled through the cramped opening, widening it slight with eir own passage. Ey fell against the opposite wall as ey cleared the hole. Verina, still bowed over, said, "Welcome to freedom."

"Thanks," the large Ligrosian said, unaware of who eir savior was in the dense cloud of dust.

Another rebel, this one hurt, passed through the opening with another close behind, lending support. One by one, the dozens of trapped rebels gathered in that one small office. When all were accounted for, Verina led them back out through the atrium and showed them the opening to the outside. As they passed, Verina spotted one of Akehru's assistants. "Where's Aki?" the leader asked.

"I don't know."

"What about Elekin? Have you seen em?"

"I don't know. I think they were running to the lab when the explosions were…when the bombs were exploding."

"Thanks," Verina said as ey turned and stumbled toward a possible path to the building's interior.

Another Ligrosian grabbed Verina's arm, saying, "Wait. That isn't the way to…" Realizing who ey just grabbed, ey let go of Verina's arm like it was covered in acid. "My pardon, Hai-Verina."

Verina looked carefully at the unintentional assaulter. "Articca, right?"

"Yes, Hai-Verina; thank you. Forgive me for saying so, but it's not safe for you to go that way."

Verina managed a smile before turning to resume eir search. Articca said, "Where are your guards?"

"Dead."

Verina felt her arm being taken again—not restrained as before, but in support. "Then with your permission, Maetor, I go where you go."

Verina nodded, unexpectedly relieved. Ey led the way over a mound of building detritus that had been the hall where ey made the broadcast to Earth. It had been bull's-eyed. The section to the right where, on the upper level, the prisoners had been held was largely destroyed. Nearby, pillars of still-intact corners, now missing the walls which spanned between them, spoke to the hit the storage area and armory sustained. Verina thought that the precision of the strike had to be dumb luck. Chavez didn't have the time, much less the technology, to trace the signal they had sent to Earth.

As Verina and Articca approached a still-standing section of corridor that had connected the lab with the storage area, the leader two-voiced, with an added siren call, "Elli! Akehru!"

Silence. No nearby replies. Verina coughed again, forcing em to bend over in pain. When ey did, ey felt a laser in a pocket of eir pareu. Ey'd gotten so used to carrying it that ey'd forgotten about it. Turning it on a wide and unfocused beam, ey scanned the area. Then it went dark. "Sprag! Doesn't anything work around here? How about your—"

Verina stopped emself upon finally noticing, even in this poor light, that eir guard was all skin and no pockets. Articca said, "Sorry, Hai-Verina, I was on sleep rotation."

Despite the dark, Verina pressed on toward the lab. Only a

mound of fallen ceiling slowed em. "Elli! Akehru!"

From several meters behind them, someone moaned. Back-tracking, Verina and eir guard found a just-rousing Ligrosian amid a small mound of debris. Verina cleared away a piece that laid on the victim's arm. Ey said, "It's going to be alright. You probably aren't—"

"Verni?"

Verina felt a rush of relief. "Elli? Bailera's soul, Elli, are you okay?"

"Give me a sec." Elekin shuffled about in the darkness, testing eir parts. "Yeah. I think so. I think I got hit in the abs."

"Do you have a concussion?"

"Maybe. Not too bad, though. I'll live."

Verina let slip some bonding tones. Being strong was import-ant, but ey was only Ligrosian, after all. Ey said, "Did you see Aki?"

"Barely. Ey was way ahead of me. Ey's got to be in the lab."

Articca helped Elekin to eir feet. Verina touched foreheads with em. The leader flinched when eir fianceir accidentally brushed eir back. Elekin said, "Verni, what's wrong?"

"Nothing. Just a little banged up."

Elekin took the small laser out of eir jacket pocket, set its beam to wide and diffuse, and looked at the maetor's back. "This is going to hurt."

Before Verina could brace, Elekin removed a finger-long ceramic splinter from the middle of Verina's back, about three centimeters from eir spine. In moments, the rebel leader said, "That's better. Thanks."

"Wait, I need to check you over."

"Later. I'm fine. We need to find Aki."

With Elekin's laser lighting the way, the trio detoured around the mound of fallen ceiling, through a sizable hole in the corridor wall, and found their way into the lab. It was surprisingly intact, with only a lower portion of the far wall having collapsed. Verina could have simply walked around the outside of the building to get here. Off to the side, by a heavy workbench, Elekin's laser light fell on Akehru. "Aki!" Verina called.

As the group approached Akehru, ey said, "It's gone."

Verina stopped. "What?"

"It's gone!" Akehru snapped back, looking at eir sib with sad and angry eyes. "The dzad. It's gone. Someone took it!"

Verina retreated within emself. It couldn't be far away. They had to find it. "Elli, get seven of our most discrete fighters; tell them what we're looking for. I want the ten of you to find whoever has it, kill them, and bring back the dzad. You have two hours. If it takes longer, then come back. Articca, show em the way out then return."

Accepting the instructions as they were intended—from the maetor of Serees—Elekin and Articca rushed out of the lab. Verina turned Akehru around and touched foreheads. The engineer said, "I'm sorry."

"None of this was your fault; don't you try making it your fault. We'll get past this."

"I don't want to do this anymore."

"What?" Verina said, concerned.

"This. The fighting. The being attacked. The scriptures say, 'When in the heat of battle, Shavtipwa realized...'"

"'...realized that faith was stronger than anger, and in that moment knew that...'"

"'...knew that ey was free'," Akehru finished. Looking at eir scarred sibling, ey said, "I'm older than you. And I'm trying to be strong for you—*I am*—but I can't, Verni. I just can't."

Verina cooed to comfort eir sibling and said, "You don't have anything to prove to me, Aki. But I *am* so proud of you. I knew you hated being a part of this fight, and you've stayed with me." Verina gently touched foreheads with eir sibling. "Thank you. What ever happens from now on doesn't matter. You're my sibling; I love you."

Akehru toned a reply that could be variously translated as: "I love you"; and "You are a part of myself"; and any of a dozen other variants.

Verina soon straightened and said, "Unfortunately, we still have a crisis to deal with. I need you to come and help me figure out how badly we've been hit. Do you have a laser?"

"Huh? Yeah, there are a few on that table over there."

Verina grabbed two lasers each for em and eir sibling, and led a reluctant, but complaint, Akehru through the lab. Noting that no one else was in here, and there was little material damage, they exited through the breach in the far wall and walked around to the storage room.

Struck by three near-hits, the storage area suffered a great deal of damage. Of more concern was the danger the fires posed to the arms caches. One had already been compromised, incinerating one-fourth of the area. Tens of rebels hurriedly moved the rest of the arms to other areas while also recovering bodies. Safety was the least of their concerns. Against eir better judgment, Akehru joined in the frantic rescue work but two rebels physically restrained Verina—eir well-being was more important than a few grenades. Accepting that eir desires needed to take a step back, Verina agreed not to interfere, which freed the two protectors to get back to the necessary business at hand.

Having little else to do, Verina started taking census of the casualties being moved behind an aqueduct shield a safe distance from the growing inferno. As ey walked through the rows of burned and broken survivors and dead, something caught eir eye: a misplaced color—a Human color. Verina rushed over, disappointed that it belonged to Colonel Bryce. A raspy breathing sound came from the woman. The colonel's eyes were open but glazed over. Her breathing grew increasingly labored. The large damp spot on her uniform dripped blood to the ground from an obviously fatal injury. Apparently unaware of her condition, the colonel said, "Kala, you can't go out. You have to watch Kar. Your brother needs you. When I get home, I'll read you…I'll…" Bryce looked at Verina, "It's funny. You never suspected how we knew where…"

As if suddenly turned off, Colonel Rachael Bryce died. Verina got up and stared at the body. The Ligrosian didn't think; ey just stared. Then ey kicked Bryce in the ribs, once, as hard as ey could.

When a second arms cache exploded, Verina ordered the area evacuated. The survivors and wounded were set up in a temporary camp on the far side of the building, where further explosions wouldn't be a threat. A preliminary accounting of their situation was grim: almost one-fourth of the local force were confirmed dead. Over a third more were missing and presumed lost. Li couldn't be found. Verina was a little surprised that it mattered. Ey'd grown accustomed to having him nearby.

"How does it work?" General Chavez said, as he stared at the stocky black device five days after it had disappeared from the rebel base.

"That I don't know. I couldn't even tell you how to activate it."

"Then what's the point of bringing it to me? That terrorist is simply going to activate it remotely."

"It has to be on before it will work, and it's definitely not on."

"How can you tell?"

"It makes a fairly distinctive noise. But that doesn't matter. We don't have to know how it works. As long as *we* don't turn it on, then it can't be used against Earth. I don't think that we have to make the problem any more complicated than the fact that the Sereesians don't have their master weapon…and we do."

Chavez smiled as he looked more avariciously at the device. "It's good to see your time with the blues didn't dull your thinking. You're right, of course. If they can't use this, then we win."

In the middle of the woods, Verina, Akehru, and Elekin huddled quietly under their isolated lean-to. A meager campfire in front provided little warmth or light. The rest of their depleted rebel force bivouacked a short distance away—close enough for observation but far enough distant that the trio could speak in normal tones. Verina said, "Aki, do you remember that trip to Yavent when I was five?"

"Yeah. Of course I do. I'm surprised that you do."

"That was the last time we were a family, You, me, Pame, and Mape. Mape was carrying."

Akehru's mood darkened. "Can we not talk about em?"

"Sorry. I just wanted to say…thinking back…you and I were really close then. Why haven't we had that?"

"You're kidding," Akehru said.

"No, I'm not. Look, I know that we're hardly on a family holiday—and this certainly isn't a holaxex—but I can't remember a time since then when we've spent so much time together and not fought about everything."

Filling in Akehru's too-lengthy pause, Elekin offered, "Shared adversity?"

Verina said, "That's a scary thought. Millions had to die just so my sib and I could get along?"

"That's a little too philosophical for me," Elekin said. "I'm just saying that both of you are…you both need to be…" As ey struggled for the words, Verina and Akehru stared intently at Elekin, with amused expressions on their faces. When Elekin noticed, ey continued, "No. You're right. Millions had to die just so that you two could get along."

Footsteps approached, muffled by the composting under-growth. One of Verina's new guards came into view and said, "Excuse me, Hai-Verina. A message just arrived."

The guard handed a small crystal to eir leader and returned to eir post. Verina popped the crystal into eir portable Infolux, worked through the six layers of security, and quickly read the short communication. "Popituv is sending eir aide, Navegil, to a town about five hours from the base we're heading to. Ey wants us to meet with em."

"How did ey know where we were?" Akehru said with a nervous sub-harmonic.

"Ey's not stupid," Verina said. "Ey was maetor for a long time."

"But how did ey get the message to us?" Akehru said, still concerned.

"There are always people who try to play both sides, or all sides. After a while, you know who most of them are. They become convenient intermediaries. How do you think we've managed to sneak into cities for so long?"

"Are you going to meet with em?" Akehru asked.

"Might as well. It's not like much else can go wrong," eir sibling answered.

"You could get captured again," Elekin said, with the same concerned sub-harmonic that colored Akehru's voices.

"Then we'll *all* get captured. I never said I was going alone." Verina scooted back into the lean-to. "I don't know about you two, but I'm going to get some sleep."

Both Elekin and Akehru looked at each other. Neither one was going to think about sleep any time soon.

The abandoned town of Jazper-aziq had never been much more than a way station to those on the road from Zhawi-tan, on the north coast, to the calm beauty of Palis-ip, on the equator. The rest stop boasted only two restaurants, a small compound for short-term lodging, and a modest general store. Since the invasion, Jazper-aziq had been abandoned. Even Verina's forces had never visited during the nearly year-and-a-half of insurrection. As a result, though the town was disheveled and the woods were creeping in, the way station was ready to provide much needed supplies to the war-weary rebels. Whether or not Navegil showed up, visiting this town would be a major boon to the disheartened force still following Verina.

An hour after the maetor's pod arrived and took cover, Navegil walked into town. Ey was led and followed by two squads of rebels. Verina spotted a familiar and welcome face in the trailing pack. Ignoring all pretense of protocol, Verina walked by the lanky tree of Navegil and reunited with eir commander of the third region. "Tamira!"

Though no less happy to see Verina, the new arrival was very aware of the difference in their ranks and stations. "Hai-Verina. I'm happy to find you well."

As they matched steps, side-by-side, Verina said, "I hope this wasn't too big of an inconvenience."

"Of course not, Hai-Verina," Tamira said with some incredulity.

"Why don't you and your people join up with mine? Usual protocols. I have some business to conduct."

"Yes, Hai-Verina."

With the swift response that only pure respect of a leader can motivate, Tamira and eir troops disappeared into the surrounding wilderness. Now Verina, Navegil, and four conspicuous guards were the only Ligrosians on public display, and even the guards were out of conversational earshot. Navegil bent down respect-fully, but still remained slightly taller than the rebel leader. Ey wore a richly textured jacket and a subtly textured pareu that was clean to an extent Verina thought no longer possible. "Maetor Hai-Verina, thank you for seeing me."

"Navegil, despite what you might think, I still have a great deal of respect for Popituv. I understand why ey took the path ey did. I hope you and ey appreciate why I went a different way."

"That is why I'm here, Hai-Verina. Hai-Popituv asked me to convey to you eir willingness to help you in any way. Especially now."

"Why especially now?"

"Forgive me, Hai-Verina. We have heard that the Humans are in possession of the weapon you planned to deploy to free our people."

Verina knew immediately that ey had paused too long to answer, thus fully confirmed Navegil's rumor. Or was it fact? "What do you know?"

"There was an internal broadcast showing the device and General Chavez gloating about his victory. It was meant for his general staff, but our office also has access to these local feeds. Upon seeing this, Hai-Popituv sent me to tell you that ey will supply you with as much material as ey can smuggle from construction projects so that you can continue your fight. Ey acknowledges your rightful position, and pledges eir full loyalty to you."

"A little late, but welcome just the same. Let me ask you this: what about access to Fa'run materials?"

Navegil's tendrilly arms folded as the aide considered the prob-lem. Verina tried being patient, but having been so long in battle, ey grew increasingly anxious about being out in the open. Navegil said, "I don't think it will be impossible. Difficult. Very difficult. But it could be done."

"Navegil, you have made me happy."

"Thank you, Hai-Verina."

"But before I get too excited about this, how are you going to get back? Won't the Humans be suspicious that you've fallen outside their surveillance?"

Navegil smiled. "One of the things you learn about these Humans when you are around them for a while is that they require clearances for almost everything. This flood of data creates so many delays in analysis that it's not difficult to slip away unnoticed for a day, sometimes more. My staff and I have figured out how to alter some of the databases using only an Infolux and a data path. While I can't stay here long, I'm not going to be missed."

"Will that also work to get some of my fighters into, and out of, certain controlled areas when it's necessary?"

"That depends on the circumstances. Without knowing details, all I can give is a guarded 'yes.'"

"Navegil, you have made me *very* happy. Let's get something to eat and we'll talk more."

Verina pressed a control on eir jacket, and the whole of her local fighting force emerged from the woods. The size of the well-armed and tempered militia surprised the executive aide. Verina noted Navegil's expression and said, "Just in case you were followed."

Verina, Elekin, Akehru, and Tamira sat alone in the communica-tions room at their new base not far from Jazper-aziq. They all stared at the time displayed on the fold-out presentation screen of an Infolux. Akehru said, "I don't know why we keep staring at it. It's already more than two hours past the deadline."

"Just basking in the fantasy of what might have been," Verina replied.

"Are you sure you want to do this?" Verina asked Elekin as the fisher outfitted emself with the special-operations tools of survival.

"It's like you said, the war doesn't end just because a battle was lost."

"That was, what, twenty days ago? I was drunk on that jzesta you found when we met with Navegil. More importantly, I didn't know *you* were going to lead the team."

"Someone has to. You know what that Human said: with the new replacements coming in from Earth, now is the time to strike. It can't always be Tamira."

"I'm not joining with Tamira."

"You'd better not! Besides, you can't be Verni, now. You're Maetor."

"I know. I am. It's just that this is the first time I—"

Akehru burst into the room, short of breath. "Verni, you have to come."

All semblance of being anything but a leader immediately disappeared from Verina's countenance. Messages like the one Akehru gave were never without consequences or the need for immediate decisions. Akehru, Verina, and Elekin shortcut through a conference room filled with rebels receiving mission instructions. When they reached their communications room destination, most of the screens were blank. Verina looked, not registering anything amiss, and said, "What?"

"The screens are dark."

"And?"

"We've been intercepting and monitoring the Human communications local to Serees."

"I know tha…"

22

The Exercise of Power

Realization dawned on Verina. There were no Human communications. None.

Ey moved to one of the control consoles and punched up a variety of monitoring diagnostics. The equipment here was functioning. Signals from every civilization were detectable, which hadn't been the case yesterday. Clearly, the local communications block was off. Every race could now be heard…except the Humans. Verina wanted to shout with excitement, but this was too new and too unexpected.

"Hai-Verina," a communications specialist said, "we are receiving a directed message addressed to you."

"From who?"

"It…it doesn't give that information. The signal is coming from about seven lyd away, in the direction of Earth. It's heavily encrypted."

"Well," Verina said, looking at Akehru and Elekin, "the worst that happens is that we have to change bases again." To the specialist ey said, "Put it on."

One of the blank displays came to life; the screen filling with the smiling face of Li Rinaldi. "Like my surprise?"

Three very stunned Ligrosian faces stared back at the screen, unable to bring themselves to do anything more. Li grinned broadly, "I guess you liked it."

Verina said, "Where are you?"

"On my way from Earth. I had to pick up a little something. Come over here, Suxinha." An eight-year-old, honey-skinned, curly-haired blonde girl walked into frame and stood beside Li, who said, "I'd like you to meet my daughter, Susan."

Verina's emotions were very confused. Ey wanted to kill Li but also understood his motivation. The result created an almost grotesque smirk on the Ligrosian's face. Li continued, "I couldn't risk not seeing my little girl again, and I knew you weren't going to risk Serees for just one or two lives. You're too focused for that. I've seen it. So, when the opportunity presented itself during the attack, I decided to kill two birds with one stone. You needed the dzad somewhere in Earth-controlled space, and I needed to get back to Earth to pick up Susan.

"So, Verina. Hai-Verina. Maetor. Since I can't return to Earth, and since I was instrumental in making your planned attack successful, I'm officially asking for asylum for Susan and myself on Serees."

Verina closed eir eyes and focused on controlling eir emotions. Li was very fortunate to be so far away. In a tone of voice even Li could tell was deliberately measured, the Ligrosian said, "I'm not going to pretend that I'm not angry with you. You put us all at great risk. I don't guarantee that there aren't going to be consequences for that…when you arrive." Then, more conversationally, though still not particularly casual, ey said, "Of course you will always have a home here. You've earned that. And I can promise that I won't separate your family. There's been enough of that, too. As for anything else…I'm going to have to think about what will be fair."

"That sounds pretty fair to me, thank you." Turning to Susan, "What do you think? Serees is really a pretty place when it isn't being all invaded."

Shyly, Susan said, "Okay."

"Okay," Li echoed back as he kissed Susan's forehead. Turning back to the screen, he said, "We'll be there in about twenty days."

"I'll look forward to it. Call me when you reach the system."

"Will do. Signing off."

"Wait! Li… Thank you."

Li respectfully tilted is head and then switched off the transmission.

Akehru and Elekin looked ready to explode with a rush of victory when Verina saw their expressions. The maetor said, "Before you get too excited, let's make sure, first."

Though the chide wasn't enough to bring them completely down to Serees, the mood immediately got more serious. Verina turned to the communications specialist, saying "Not a word of this is to be made public, hinted at, or rumored. Do you understand?"

"Y-yes, Maetor."

Verina hadn't meant to scare the young fighter quite so much, but now wasn't the time to snatch defeat from the jaws of unexpected victory. Turning back to Elekin and Akehru, ey said, "Elli, you're going to have to put your mission on hold. Call it a communications problem that we're working to resolve."

"You're sounding like a Human," Akehru quipped.

"Now, now…there's no need to be nasty," Verina good-naturedly replied.

"Are you gong to talk to Earth's leader?" Elekin asked.

Verina considered the question. "No. Not until tomorrow. I

want to monitor the situation for a while. Is their general still on the planet?"

"As of the latest report, yes," Elekin answered.

"Good. Then he can't order another bombing. We need to make sure he can't take a shuttle back to his fleet, either. Nothing is more important. After that, let's activate some of the urban cells to test the communications the Humans have left. They aren't Seetun, but they should be down, too. This is the first time the dzad has been used for real. We can't take too many risks until we *know* it's working as promised."

"How much damage?" Elekin asked.

"Not much. Not too much killing, either. We just want to scare them a little. Don't have our people take any significant risks other than to ensure the general stays on the ground. I mostly want the Humans to worry about our next move. It's about time that we become the fishers."

Elekin left the room to carry out the maetor's orders.

Akehru said, "Don't you want to celebrate at all? Not even a little?"

"More than you know. But it can wait until tomorrow—after I've talked to Earth. Business first, that's our way. Besides, once the party starts, it's going to go on for a long time and there'll be nothing I can do to stop it."

If eir other arguments weren't persuasive enough, the last was so obviously true that it sealed the plan. Akehru asked, "Shouldn't we at least pray? If not in thanks, then in hope?"

Verina wasn't sure how she felt about Akehru embracing the scriptures. Like all Ligrosians, they'd studied the texts, but this was the first time Akehru had ever seemed to take them to heart as something more than words to be memorized. Still, it was nice seeing Aki grow from an anxious rebel into a calm student. Verina smiled at eir sibling, "I think that would be very appropriate."

Verina and Elekin walked through the rough-hewn base a day after the news from Li. The maetor asked, "So they were totally isolated?"

"Definitely. They tried communicating with the local commanders but all of the signals were silent—even when they used Ligrosian equipment. I don't know what the Haipuxans did to achieve that, but whatever it is, it's very effective."

"And the target?"

"In our possession."

"That settles it. Time to talk to Earth."

The makeshift conference room differed greatly from the one used during the dzad announcement. One wall had been finished less than an hour before to give an air of civilized government. One chair was positioned behind a comm table near the wall. Off to the side, Akehru sat at a portable control console. Unlike the previous broadcast, the only ones in the room were Verina, Elekin, Akehru, Tamira, and three guards. When the space was being secured, Verina changed eir days-worn jacket to one borrowed from the disguise cache. The higher quality of the cloth and tailoring was obvious for all to see, and it provided a cosmetic legitimacy to Verina's rank.

Akehru said, "I've received the phase adjustments for the conference. We can start at your word."

Verina sat behind the table and clicked to begin. A sphere popped up from the receptacle in the table top and settled at Verina's eye level. Two signals were being sent: one was unidirectional, meant for viewing-only by the ministers in the Earth Presidium, the other was a near-real-time two-way link directly with the secretary general, who was the only person Verina allowed for negotiations. Akehru signaled eir sib that the broadcast was live.

"It's been a long fight for me," Verina began, speaking in Quinkst so ey could be unambiguous and free of any translator inaccuracies. "I can't begin to describe the pain and suffering you have visited upon us simply because you decided that abiding to the terms of our signed, mutual agreement were inconvenient. The question for me is: how harshly do I punish you for what you have done to us?

"This isn't something that I take lightly. Though I have a right to seek a high cost, that does not reflect well upon my people. Plus, it leaves you open for immediate invasion. As tempting as that is, it would be bad for business.

"Your culture is one of war, Secretary General. Pretending that it isn't doesn't make it so. When it is in your best interest, you get along well enough with your neighbors. It's possible that in the future, whether it be tomorrow or several hundred years from now, your neighbor civilizations will need your particular expertise to aid in some common cause. Where would we be if I let my own personal enmity for your culture take away that option?

"This is what is going to happen. Serees will open a managed number of one-way, unencrypted lines of communication so that you can coordinate the carrying out of the agreement we will reach here. Your first order will be to command the local fleet and all personnel to stand down and relinquish all control to Serees personnel or any alien helpers we may designate. Your people will give my government a full—and I do mean *full*—account of every single one of my people who passed through your care. Once that is done, you will take every unwanted Human being off of my world and never return to our space without an invitation.

"You will also cede control of Lrat back to its indigenous race and to its legal government. Because of your protracted control of that planet, you are to stay and guide the liberation back to a state that the Gelrahtem desire.

"When all of this is done, I will order the loosening of restrictions on your communications. In time, depending on your behavior, we will further increase your bandwidth, encryption abilities, and other items that are generally contracted out. As an expression of goodwill, once your ships leave Serees space, I will open up communications within the local Earth system so that you may provide for your own defense and domestic commerce. We will be monitoring.

"Make no mistake…if at any point we feel you are threatening us, or one of our allies, we will once again silence you.

"Lastly, on a personal note, I am going to detain certain local earth commanders and have them face our justice. You shouldn't expect to see them again. So, Secretary General of Earth, I yield the floor…for comments."

Douglas Mitchell was not a happy man. Though he looked defeated, the loss was so new that he still managed to hold himself up with an air of defiance. "What is the timetable you expect for this?" he asked, obviously via a translator.

"No timetables. This is goal-oriented. You achieve something, you get something in return. However, sooner is considerably better than later. If you become more troublesome than your potential future value is worth, we'll silence you just as completely as you were ten minutes ago."

"So, we are to live with your sword hanging over our heads."

"As every other civilization has lived under yours since your avarice prompted you to conquer Lrat. You've brought this on yourself, Secretary General. Your empire just happened to run into a world willing to fight back. We didn't ask for it, and, frankly, the consequences of this sicken me. That doesn't mean that we are unwilling to let you regain your legitimacy. You simply have to learn how to play well with others."

Mitchell scowled. "So, in reality, this is, to me, less of a negotiation than it is an unconditional surrender."

"As there are clearly conditions attached, let's just say that you have no provision to modify the contract. At this point, my world has won. The only question that remains is: how badly is yours going to lose?"

The secretary general of Earth stared back through the display. Subtle variations of expression crossed his face, but they were unreadable by the Ligrosians. Finally, he said, "Agreed."

"We will finalize the details through lower levels. I do expect you to send the message for the fleet to stand down within the next few minutes, however. We are now sending you the channel specifications. Thank you, Secretary General."

Akehru shut off the broadcast. Verina said, "After we monitor the stand-down command and see it being obeyed, I'll tell the world."

Privately, in this room, Verina finally relaxed for the first time since before ey had heard about any problems with Earth from Javrurhal. It felt like a lifetime ago. For now, it didn't matter. Ey had somehow managed to bring it all together. Serees was free at last.

Verina walked into the windowless room that housed the bound, gagged, and naked William Chavez laying on the floor. His breathing quickened upon seeing Verina walk closer, a laser in eir hand. Ey said, in the Human tongue, "Just so you know, we also have your other commanders in custody. They are being dealt with. Thank you, by the way, for stationing your command planetside, it made these captures much easier.

"We found the dzad prototype in your office. You came so close. If your source, I'm guessing it was Mister Bhoutto, had picked up the right device…well, there's no changing a stream once it has passed. Just to be clear, you aren't going to trial. There's really no point. So, this is my last act as a freedom fighter."

A beam of coherent light burned a hole into Chavez's skull. The practiced pivoting dance of the beam, which Verina learned from the necessity Chavez forced on em long ago, quickly made the general's brain non-functional.

Dropping the weapon, Verina said, "War over."

23

Serees Sundown

Bailera hung large in the sky as Maygola continued its path toward noon. From eir unobstructed view from eir mountain residence east of Czep-tan, Verina saw the distant contrail of the last Earth ship leaving the surface of Serees—taking with it the last of the Human occupation force…but not the last of the Humans.

Li Rinaldi casually joined Verina on the spacious wood deck overlooking the impressive expanse of countryside. "You did it," he said. "You saved your world."

Sighing, Verina said, in Li's language, "It shouldn't have needed saving at all."

Li wasn't going to argue the point; he agreed with it. "How long, do you think, will it take for life to get back to normal?"

Verina looked at the alien, sadness permanently etched on eir face, "It's never going to be like it was. Now *we* are the most dangerous civilization. Every other race knows that. We can isolate any or all of them simply by throwing a switch. Nobody should have dominion over others like that. Now that we have it, we can never give it up. My people have a terrible power and yet we are less safe than ever. Your kind has ruined us."

A Human girl came running out onto the patio being chased by a small two-legged red-furred haiwa. With her eyes glued to the small animal, Susan ran into Li's legs, nearly bowling him over. "Whoa!" he said. "You need to look where you're going."

"Sorry, Dad. I was just playing with Fireball."

Li kissed his daughter on the forehead. Verina said, "How do you like my world?"

Less shyly than usual, Susan replied, "It's nice. Does everyone have a home like this?"

Verina smiled. "No. You have to do really good things for a long time to get a home like this."

Susan's new pet nudged her legs for attention. From inside the house, Akehru shouted in Limto, "Food's ready!"

Li's ears picked up and he said, "Dinner's ready, Suxinha. Why don't you go inside and wash up?"

Susan turned and ran back inside, her eager haiwa pup fast on her heels. Verina told Li, "You go. I'll be in in a minute."

Taking the request for the command it was, Li quietly followed Susan's route into the house. As Verina watched him go, ey saw, through the wall-sized window, Akehru and Elekin doubled-over in laughter at the dining table. Maybe it wouldn't take so long after all for life to get back to normal. At least, not for most lives.

Ey turned eir eyes back to the dance of Bailera just above the stands of slispitren and craftentz in the distance. Verina understood eir life had set below some other horizon a long time ago. The person ey had been was gone. Ey'd never be em again—ey carried too many scars. Though the war was over, it felt like the fight would never end. Not for em.

Looking back through the window, Verina saw two Humans and two Ligrosians flinging toasted gapi at each other, all laughing in their own way. Elekin saw the voyeur through the glass and beckoned eir soon-to-be-mate to join them. Verina waved eir hand in compliance and headed for the entrance, taking just one more look back at the sibling planet, and one-time god, who had watched over them for yet another day.

Afterword

When I started writing this version of *Que Sera Serees* (QSS) —which is actually a page-one rewrite of an earlier attempt—one of my intents was to have a single-gendered species. You don't see them around much, not even in science fiction. It wasn't my intention to develop a new pronoun category, regardless of how generally useful I now believe it to be (more on that, later). The rough draft started with the Ligrosians being referred to consistently by pronouns of one of the conventional genders. About 60,000 words in, I knew that this gave a gender-specific slant that wasn't the intent of the story—not that I'd have a problem with that, it simply wasn't the story I wanted to tell and was a potential distraction.

I did what any author would do when faced with a crisis of alien gender pronouns: I searched the Internet. I found some interesting material on efforts to create a neuter single-person pronoun for English. In the end, I didn't find any of the ones I came across to be what I was looking for. Often, they seemed to carry with them some very subtle bias. The few that escaped that weakness had rules that seemed to make novel-length implementation more work for the writer and reader than I thought was necessary. In the end, I decided to go my own way. I felt it needed to be simple, as I was going to be writing a book using these and I didn't want to be stumbling over a pesky little neologism every other sentence.

Ey, em, eir was simply a modification of a modern misappropriation of pronouns to deal with exactly this issue of gender neutrality. In some circles, instead of saying something like: "He/she ran after the ball," the neutral form would be: "They ran after the ball." True, this is gender neutral, but there's a big problem with the hard-to-ignore fact that "they" is a plural pronoun, not singular. So, I killed two birds with one stone by making the plural into a single. What I did was slice off the "th" from the beginnings of they, them, their, etc. Not only did this make sense—the singular form being shorter than the plural form—but I also had new words that weren't commonly used in English. It also made it much easier to write than using some alien words. "They ran after the ball," could now easily be changed to: "Ey ran after the ball."

Following the completion of the first draft of QSS, I've been advocating to anyone who will listen that we adopt ey, em, eir as a new set of English pronouns. It's an easy addition. If nothing else, I'd love for us to give it an honest try. You have a book here that shows you how it would work. It avoids needless juggling of various pronouns in order to be "politically correct". If nothing else, legal papers become more accurate. Just think: not having to write he/she, or s/he, or juggle between feminine and masculine pronouns (sometimes, confusingly, in the same paragraph). It's easy and makes sense. I encourage all of you to not only give it a try but to spread the word about it.

There was one other language quirk I consistently put into the text. Generally speaking, non-English words containing the letter "X" consider the "X" to be sounded as "sh"—similar to how it's used in Portuguese as well as Chinese and other languages. Thus,

"Xadow" is pronounced as "Shadow". Oh, Li's last name, "Rinaldi", is meant to be pronounced with a Brazilian sensibility —Hi-nal-dzhee—but most of the characters actually pronounce it as spelled.

I didn't worry about Ligrosians giving numbers in octal, or that they used both local and "standard" measurement systems while the Humans used metric. In most cases, it was the sense of the number that was important, not the exact conversion. Where it was important, I usually gave you the conversion in Human terms.

QSS was founded on the premise that invading another land is problematic at best. History has shown that while annexing a neighbor is difficult, invading a distant territory with the intent of holding onto it is all but impossible without genocide. Time and time again, empire builders and meddlers find themselves caught in unpopular and expensive positions that they cannot sustain indefinitely for one simple reason: the land belongs to the people already there. They will fight for their homes with more determination and patience than any invading force can maintain for long.

As my basic model, I often took cues from the campaigns of Washington army and the British army and navy in the war the saw the United States declare and win its independence. But I didn't draw inspiration from only this conflict. Carthage versus Rome. Athens/Sparta versus Persia. Bolivar versus Spain. Anyone versus Afghanistan. The Huns. The Gauls. Genghis Khan. Over and over again you have conflicts where people fight desperate battles against outsiders. In the end, one fact becomes clear: empires don't last forever.

Lastly, this is a book that is meant to be sympathetic to the troops that fight the wars. From the time they join the fight, they change. Along with the physical casualties, this is the terrible cost of war. The warrior-survivors on all sides pay a heavy price for the hubris of those "at the top". Too often, once they are off the front lines, they are forgotten. It's important that we don't forget. It's also important that we work harder to keep from having to put more people into this situation.

And above and beyond all of that, I hope you enjoyed this adventure. Regardless of the grammar stuff or the history, it's still just a story…though it's probably not all of the story.

— CJ Carter, March 2006